HOLD ME UNDER

By Riley Nash

Copyright © 2022 by Riley Nash

All rights reserved.

The characters and events portrayed in this book, as well as the involvement of any existing institutions, agencies, publications, or public figures, are entirely fictitious and have no basis in reality. Any similarity to real persons, living or dead, is coincidental and not intended by the author.

No portion of this book may be reproduced in any form without written permission from the publisher or author, except as permitted by U.S. copyright law.

ISBN-13 (e-book): 9781736082621
ISBN-13 (paperback) : 9781736082638
ISBN-13 (special edition paperback): 9781736082683

Cover illustration by Seaj Art
Cover design by Cormar Covers

*To anyone who has been hurt or caged by love,
may you find freedom*

And to Dev, for being my Ethan

TRIGGER WARNING

This book contains dark themes and potentially triggering content, though every effort has been made to portray these thoughtfully and sensitively. Specific trigger warnings for this book are listed below.

Be aware that they may contain spoilers.
Stay safe and take care of yourselves!

Triggers: Sexual abuse (off the page), suicidal ideation, drug abuse, disordered eating, trauma, death, mental illness, homophobic language

Contents

Chapter 1	3
Chapter 2	8
Chapter 3	14
Chapter 4	18
Chapter 5	24
Chapter 6	28
Chapter 7	37
Chapter 8	44
Chapter 9	54
Chapter 10	62
Chapter 11	70
Chapter 12	76
Chapter 13	81
Chapter 14	92
Chapter 15	98
Chapter 16	106
Chapter 17	113

Chapter 18	118
Chapter 19	124
Chapter 20	133
Chapter 21	141
Chapter 22	149
Chapter 23	156
Chapter 24	162
Chapter 25	168
Chapter 26	173
Chapter 27	178
Chapter 28	185
Chapter 29	194
Chapter 30	203
Chapter 31	209
Chapter 32	214
Chapter 33	222
Chapter 34	230
Chapter 35	238
Chapter 36	244
Chapter 37	250
Chapter 38	255
Chapter 39	259

Chapter 40	266
Chapter 41	275
Chapter 42	281
Chapter 43	287
Chapter 44	294
Chapter 45	300
Chapter 46	304
About the Author	311

you're all the worst days of my life

I'm drowning, but I feel ok about it.

Some people are fated to drown, just like some people are fated to get struck by lightning or fall into the Grand Canyon. I like the idea of fate, a world with rules where everything happens just the way it's supposed to. Even if it means I'm on the losing end.

If I open my eyes, I can see the hard-on straining against my grass-stained cargo pants. Hopefully erections go away after you die, or fishing my body out of this pool is going to get really awkward. I should have Googled that question drunk at 3am instead of 'do gay penguins know they're gay'. (Answer: inconclusive.)

My life can't flash before my eyes because I'm busy picturing a team of coroners standing around my bloated body, speculating whether I was a deviant who jacked off at the bottom of celebrities' swimming pools. I'll end up in one of those warning pamphlets about autoerotic asphyxiation they hand out at high school PTA meetings.

The black-tiled floor of the pool presses into my hip. I close my eyes again, pretending I'm a teenager at Lake Chelan with my cousin Danny. A deep lake surrounded by dry hills where we played Marco Polo and shook off water like puppies in the last carefree day I ever had in my life.

I want to breathe now. It's going to hurt so bad. And suddenly, I'm scared.

Chapter 1

ETHAN

Three hours earlier

Never gonna give you up, never gonna—

I punch my alarm so hard my phone flies into the crack behind my nightstand, where all the spiders live. Peyton must have guessed my passcode again when she brought over a load of clean laundry yesterday. My groan sounds more like a sob as I rub my aching eyes into my pillow. It's just as dark now as it was two hours ago, when I got home from my night shift at the Qwik N' Go.

Grabbing a sponge, I stumble into the shower and alternate rinsing myself off with scrubbing hair and hard water stains off the plastic walls.

I polish the mirror as I brush my teeth, struggling to keep my eyes open. I don't look at myself in the clean mirror, because no one wants to see that shit.

My Emerald Lawncare polo doesn't stink too much, so I pull it on and hide my messy hair with a ball cap. I unhook the rod that opens and closes my curtains and use it to fish my phone out of spider land before heading to the kitchen.

Listening to the gurgle of the coffee pot, I crack eggs into an Olympic National Park mug with the handle missing and stick them in the microwave. "Good morning," I mumble at Petunia as her fat tortoiseshell body weaves between my legs. Her purr vibrates against my calf like she's trying to give me a deep tissue massage. "Thanks, girl." When my eggs are done, I drop a bit on the floor, just to watch her foggy old eyes light up.

The wireless pager clipped to my belt loop beeps, so I pad toward Mom's room as I shovel down eggs too hot to taste. My heart sinks when I get to the door. Mom has an open box on the floor, an album sitting in her lap, pictures scattered across the bed. I need to move this stuff to my room so she stops finding it. "Who is this?" She holds up the album.

"Morning, beautiful." I kneel down by the bed and open her medications one by one, dumping them into my palm. Fetching her a glass of water, I sit next to her and rub her back gently while she takes the pills, watching to make sure she doesn't miss any. Then I start gathering up handfuls of pictures and throwing them back in the box, careful not to look at them.

"Wait," she protests, her brown eyes full of anxiety. "What are you doing?"

"Tidying up so you can get dressed. It's all good." I keep my voice upbeat. When I try to take the album, she tightens her grip on it. "Who *is* this?"

My head throbs when I see the little boy she's pointing at. It's always him. Some part of her remembers that he's important. "That's Danny. He's your sister's son." I'm very careful never to say *was*.

"He must be big now," she muses. "Can we have them over?"

Back when she was diagnosed with early-onset dementia, the hospital made me go to some class full of shit I didn't understand and referrals to grief counselors I couldn't afford. They said a dementia patient's world has its own rules and reasons and structures, a *sacred piece of their personhood*, and the worst fucking thing you could do is twist reality or hide the truth.

I lie to her every day.

The truth is too brutal to repeat, and if we're both broken, then I can't take care of her.

"He got a job in London, and Aunt Cath is too busy. It's ok. They know you care about them." Finally, I nudge the album out of her hands and throw it in the box, slamming the lid. I'm tempted to take the thing out back and burn it.

I pull her into a tight hug. Her hair smells of lemon and baby powder as I drop a kiss on it. It has barely started graying at the roots, but her life's practically over. Maybe if I had taken her hiking every weekend, or to the symphony instead of buying records from the thrift store, maybe the enrichment—another dementia buzzword—would have helped. If every day was different, maybe she'd forget fewer of them.

"Check this out." I swallow past the lump in my throat and pull open her dresser drawers, pointing to the piles of clothes my best friend Peyton helped me coordinate. "Each of these is an outfit, remember? Created by your personal stylists."

Her face brightens as she studies the row of tops. "Did you fold these?"

"If they're good, yes. If they're bad, then it's Peyton's fault."

"They're perfect. Did I teach you that?" When I smile in spite of myself, she puts her arm around my waist and points to a blue cardigan. I hand her the tidy stack of clothes. "Get ready and I'll make your cereal."

Her favorite bowl goes on the table. Box of Cheerios on the right, spoon and oat milk on the left. I don't know if the routines are for her or me anymore. Collapsing in a chair, I check the time on my phone, wondering why the nurse is late.

"Where are your scrubs?" Her voice cuts through the headache banging against the backs of my eyes. I blink at her as she sits and pours her cereal, before glancing down at my shirt.

"They're in my locker at the clinic. I'll change when I get there." *Liar, liar.*

"Don't let your boss see you all dirty like that."

"It's ok, Mom. I won't." I stare at my feet, twisting them around until I can fit all my toes in one of the squares patterning the faded linoleum. The summer before I was supposed to start studying biology at Washington State, I had a great internship at a local veterinary clinic. They said I could work for them every summer and break until I finished vet school. Mom ironed my navy-blue scrubs about fifty times, and we went out for steaks and ice cream after my first day.

At the end of July, *it* happened. She was a completely healthy woman, until she wasn't. And because of the way it all went down, what happened to Danny, not a single member of my extended family offered to help a scared eighteen-year-old take care of his mom.

I never went to college, let alone vet school. But of course, that first day is one of the things she can't seem to forget. So now I work at a nameless vet clinic, day in, day out, forever. Because if I tell her the truth, all the things that are her *fault* even though she can't be blamed…there's just no fucking point.

The doorbell finally rings. I shove on my boots and hold the door open. "Morning, Ana."

"How are we today, June?" The petite Hispanic woman ignores my grimace as she waves at Mom. I've made it clear just what I think of all the cheery voices, the *we* this and *we* that, the memory games and activities. Like Mom's a preschooler. But Ana wins because she makes my mother happy and bills my insurance the lowest rate she can.

"You girls have fun," I call, blowing Mom a kiss before running for my truck. It always takes a few tries to get the thing started, and I can't afford to be late.

As soon as I open the front door of Emerald Lawncare's shitty office, my boss Roy shoves a work order into my hands and points to the company truck, already loaded up with tools. "Medina client; I want it done before noon. Make us look good." Some of the richest people in the world live in Medina, on the shores of Lake Washington.

The other guys are watching cat videos and eating breakfast burritos. Scooter gets up and hands me one as an excuse to read over my shoulder. "Holy shit. Why does Ethan get all the celebrities?"

I push his arm off my neck. "Because you stole a squeaky dog toy from Bill Gates' yard and tried to sell it on eBay."

"Uh-oh, guys." He minces back across the room. "Daddy Ethan's mad at us again."

I open my mouth to bitch about why doing my *job* makes me a downer with a stick up my ass, but the name written on the work order makes everything else disappear.

Victor Lang.

It can't be. He's more elusive than Bigfoot, more controversial than Tonya Harding. The sheet of paper in my hand is the only evidence I've seen that he's even alive.

I re-read the name, like I might be mixing it up with some other Victor who isn't the gay swimming prodigy that captured the imagination of the entire world. As teenagers, my cousin Danny and I watched every one of his competitions and interviews, wondering how someone our age could be so fucking cool when we were busy dealing with acne and braces. My closeted ass idolized his effortless confidence about his sexuality. And the way his lips twitched into a smile when an interviewer cracked a joke did something indescribable to my stomach. Hell, I had a life-sized poster of him on my bedroom wall.

On his eighteenth birthday, the day his plane was scheduled to take off for the Rio Olympics, he failed his dope test—not just a little, but catastrophically. He earned a three-year ban from the sport, went on a cocaine-fueled bender, and disappeared off the face of the earth.

I guess even Bigfoot needs his hedges trimmed.

Chapter 2

ETHAN

Anyone would miss the mansion at the end of the cul-de-sac if they weren't looking for it. The glass and concrete box, set far back from the front gate, fades into the perma-gray sky. My gate code works, so I pull my trailer up the long drive. There's an imposing Bentley parked to one side with the engine still warm. According to my instructions, I'm supposed to hit the backyard, re-shape the hedges, clean up the edges of the lawn, and leave again.

The salty air feels tight and breathless, like something important is about to happen. Like it matters that I'm here. I chug the butt end of whatever energy drink Scooter left in the cupholder and drag my wagon full of tools around the house.

Even though it's wrong, I stop and look through the windows at the cold, slightly threatening mid-century modern furniture and abstract paintings. I can't help it. There's no way the universe would bring me here, like this, and not give me at least a glimpse of the man whose poster I used to lean against and talk to about my problems. Sure, I ripped up the poster after he got ejected and stuffed it into the trash, under the dog turds and moldy leftovers, but part of me has always believed that he'd redeem himself and come back better than ever.

This is my chance to find out.

The backyard slopes toward a boat house on the lake, framing the brooding Seattle skyline on the far side. He hasn't given up swimming, because there's a black-tiled pool behind the house, surrounded by cedar-colored composite decking. Keeping far away from the water, I tackle the untidy topiaries under the back windows.

But my eyes don't stay on my work, and the first window I look into isn't an office or a kitchen. It's a massive wet room of veined, off-white marble, divided in half by a clear pane of suspended glass. Victor Lang stands wrapped in a spray of shower water, back arched and hands deep in his messy, blond hair. His toned ass sports a blatant speedo tan, like that's all he wears. I don't even know how you get a tan like that in the Pacific Northwest.

I must be gaping like an idiot when he turns around. My eyes don't travel any lower than the toothbrush hanging out of his mouth before I scramble backward like a dog with its head stuck in a paper bag.

The pool makes a terrific splash when I hit. To most people it would be just a mishap, a few strokes to the ladder, climb out, apologize. But I haven't been in the water since the day at Chelan with my mom and Danny and the end of the world, and my whole body just shuts off and becomes a block of concrete that unfortunately has my soul tied to it.

I'm coming, Danny.

When a muted shockwave hits the water, my first feeling is disappointment. I'd rather the world didn't know that I got hard for my landscaping client's showering ass. Then a hand grips the back of my t-shirt and yanks upward.

Air rips my lungs apart like glass. I snort water and cough until I'm dizzy and my sinuses are burning. The lip of the pool appears in front of me and I cling to the concrete, wheezing and trying not to throw up.

My apathetic dream state burns away in the sun and all I can see is Peyton sobbing as they ask her to identify my body with its pathetic rigor-mortis hard-on, and worse, the way she would have to tell my mom the news again and again until the pain is too much and they let me become a picture in her album that she points to and asks "Who's he?". I start shaking uncontrollably.

Big, long-fingered hands grip the wall on either side of me. One of the middle fingers has a signet ring I recognize—the dragon-bird hybrid from the Lang family crest. ESPN did a segment on it between commercials during one of the world championships. I can feel a breath on the back of my neck, the churn of water around my legs as he keeps himself afloat. I wanted to see him, and here I am. This is the part where I pray he won't get me fired.

When I turn around, Victor lets go of the wall and floats low in the water, staring at me as tiny waves lap at his lower lip and his arms make lazy circles. People claimed that his *GQ* cover was photoshopped, that no one has such pale eyes, but I can see clearly that they're wrong. He has chameleon eyes, colorless until they take on the hue of whatever's nearby. Right now, it's a bruised purple, like the dark circles beneath them.

His face is all angles and warm skin, flecked with spots of sunlight reflecting off the surface. He has thick brows and a mess of half-curly hair that looks well past the point of needing a trim. Water trickles down the sides of his lean nose and gathers in the corners of his mouth, which turn up slightly when he catches me looking.

"Who are you?" It's the exact mesmerizing, slightly bored voice I heard so often on my TV, but it sounds ragged around the edges. He takes a mouthful of water and spits it out again, waiting.

"Thank you." I'm still struggling to breathe. "I'm so sorry about this. It was an accident."

He cocks his head like a puzzled animal. "You're a pervert, aren't you?"

"I'm your landscaper," I protest, trying to keep my hold on the wall.

His smile is wrong, disconnected from the rest of his face, not the dazzling, camera-ready grin I remember. "Uh-huh. Tell that to your cock."

One of his hands slips suddenly under the water and cups the bulge in my pants, fingers wrapped up under my balls, hefting me as I make a strangled sound. My knee jerks up reflexively and he catches it with his other hand, huffing a soft laugh.

"I really need to cover the pool. I hate cleaning out trash."

Then he's gone, lifting himself out of the water in a long, easy motion that rains droplets across the deck. He must have come straight from the shower, because he's completely naked. I fix my stinging eyes on the wall in front of me and wish I could get the fuck out of here. But he crouches down until I look at him.

"What's your name?" He rocks back and forth slowly on his toes.

"Ethan Lowe."

"Why are you in my pool, Ethan Lowe?"

"I was cutting the hedge and I tripped."

He scrunches up his face, glancing across the garden toward the lake. Then he starts prying my fingers off the wall.

I slap his hand away, heart still going a million miles an hour. "Stop it."

"Stop lying."

"I saw you through the window."

"Good." His tongue tastes the water at the corner of his mouth. "What did you think? Did you want to come in and try me on?"

I open my mouth to say something professional. All that comes out is, "What's the matter with you?"

Then he grins for real, flashing his expensive teeth, grabs my wrists, and shoves me off the wall. He hops up and trots toward the large French doors that he must have thrown open on his way to rescue me.

Since my body has decided it doesn't want to die, it lashes out and finds the side of the pool, scraping my palms and knees. I prop my elbows securely on the decking and watch my childhood hero grab a pair of red boating shorts from a basket by the door and pull them on. He picks up a towel draped over the door handle and ruffles it in his hair.

My muscles are shaking so badly it takes me three tries to get out of the pool. I limp to my wagon and grab my wallet; maybe my business card will prove that I'm not some kind of sex offender.

"Excuse me, sir?"

Leaving the towel draped over his head, he studies me up and down. "Jesus." He reaches out and swipes a thumb across my knee, coming away bloody. I look down. It's barely a scratch, but the water is carrying rivulets of red down my calf, staining my sock. He sticks his thumb in his mouth and straightens up, nose wrinkling slightly. I'm surprised to see that he's shorter than me.

"On behalf of Emerald Lawncare, I want to formally apologize and assure you that you won't be charged for this visit."

He sighs and drops his towel on my feet, retreating into the tiled hallway leading to the rest of his mansion.

I make a terrible mistake. Maybe everything is inevitable after all. Maybe none of us have any choice. But by any measure, if I had a choice, the one I make now is the wrong one. "Wait."

He stops with his back to me. He still has a swimmer's profile, wide shoulders above a narrow waist, but it's obvious that whatever steroids gave him such a jaw-dropping body in his prime haven't been in his system for a long time.

"This is a ridiculous thing to ask, but I have a cousin. We were huge fans. I promised him I'd get this signed someday, somehow." I pull a pristine, foil sports trading card out of my wallet. Part of me wants to explain that I'd never ask this if my promise to Danny hadn't become the last one I ever made him.

He turns around, frowning, and squints at the card in my hand. It was a lucky find from a *Rio Olympics Young Champions* set printed months before the fateful drug tests. A younger-looking Victor beams at the camera, goggles dangling from one finger and a thumb looped in the waistband of his high-tech swimming trunks. Danny memorized the stats on the back, promising he would beat them someday.

Abruptly, Victor laughs. He pulls the card away and studies it incredulously. "Young Olympians? This is fucking hilarious. Where did you get this?"

"I—" I want him to give it back. I want him to get out a pen and say nice things about Danny while he writes his name. Because that's the guy I worshiped.

"How much do you want for it? I'll beat whatever you were going to get on eBay, signed. I need one of these."

"It's not for sale."

He holds the card up between two fingers, eyes dangerous, and for a second, I'm certain he's going to tear it in half. "You have some fucking balls to show me this." His other hand cups, like he's still holding mine.

And without another word, he walks into the house.

Chapter 3

VICTOR

Three hours earlier

Every morning I wake up too early, sick to my stomach. I curl into a ball under the covers and scroll through my phone for an undetermined amount of time—celebrity gossip, people from *The Bachelorette* and *Love Island* that I know better than my own family. Then it's straight to the pool. No piss, no breakfast; I don't even bother to open my eyes properly until I've coasted along the bottom from one end to the other and back without taking a breath. Because the ache in my lungs, pretending I might not choose to surface this time, is the only thing that gets my heart pumping anymore.

But today, I stop dead in the doorway of the dining room I never use. I close my eyes and open them again, hoping it will make everything disappear. It doesn't. There's food all over my table—croissants, Danishes, crullers. A pitcher of orange juice. A *vase* of yellow flowers.

Whatever employee of my family delivered this shit must have let themselves right in when I didn't answer. I wish I could nail boards over the door.

I dump one tray in the garbage before the doorbell rings. I wish I lived in a normal neighborhood so that maybe I would see a gang of kids running away, leaving a flaming bag of shit on the step.

Instead, it's my father. I haven't seen him in five years and eight months.

We stare at each other. He's big and square in a big, square suit. My pajama shirt is a baggy tee with a ripped neck that says *Salty Bitch* over a picture of that Morton salt umbrella girl. He probably gets a good look at the ass of my neon yellow briefs as I turn around and walk away.

He bangs the front door shut as I strip my clothes and take a running jump into the pool. Hope he enjoys the fucking crullers. Hope he chokes on one.

The man is alive and well when I come back inside with a towel around my waist. He's buttering a croissant and reading a newspaper he carries around in his suit pocket to remind people he's a traditional, salt of the earth fellow who couldn't speak English until he was fifteen but still came to America and made billions.

I sit down at the far end of the table and rest my chin on my arms, watching him, waiting. A clock ticks in the next room. I forgot I had a clock. Time doesn't pass in this house.

"Are you or are you not going to accept my job offer?" I guess he means the one from six years ago for me to become some boot-licking manager in his tech empire. I was a little distracted at the time, what with the doping scandal of the decade and all. He pushes an empty espresso cup at me and I stand up automatically, turning on the dusty machine. I've had his obscenely complicated drink order memorized since I was twelve.

All the food is making me hungry. I dig a pack of gum out of the credenza drawer and chew on it as I wait for the coffee to brew. "Absolutely not."

"You understand that if you never learn to run your family's company, I won't pass it down to you. I'd rather leave it to my dog."

"Mhmm." Hiking my hip up onto the table, I pick up pastries one at a time and lob them at the trash. I'm no good at any sport besides swimming, so most of them hit the floor in a mess of crumbs and powdered sugar.

"This is your final offer."

A cinnamon roll bounces off the can so hard it tips over. I raise my eyebrows at him.

"Very well." Instead of leaving, he reaches into his briefcase and pulls out a folder, setting it on the table. I hold my breath. Nothing good comes out of that case. "I'm buying an Italian dating app."

"I don't think Mom uses those. You should have just kept her phone number."

"You're going to be the face of their new ad campaign."

Finally, I look into his watery, slate eyes. "What?"

"You heard me. It's time for you to bring something to this family."

"No." I stand up. I pour his espresso into the flower box by the window, probably killing whatever plant the decorator put there. "No. No, no, no."

That's all the power I have, all the power I've ever had, to repeat that two-letter word again and again. And just like every other time, no one listens. He taps the folder. "You signed your right of publicity over to me the day I gave you this house."

It rained that day. I hadn't eaten or even taken the blanket off my head in six days. I chewed my lips bloody so that I couldn't cry as the Olympic opening ceremonies played on the TV in my dad's penthouse flat. I was disgusting.

"We're going to put this aside," he said. "All of it." He handed me the key to a safe place and told me I never had to come out again. But first he slid some documents across the coffee table, offering me a pen as I sat up, shivering. "These will allow me to manage your affairs, so you don't have to worry about anything else."

I thought I'd be dead in a month anyway, so it didn't matter what they said.

"What can you do," I ask, very slowly, my voice hoarse, "if I refuse?"

"You know the answer to that, son."

I do. He owns my pathetic life, all the wretched secrets, and there's nowhere safe in this world but the cage he built me.

"We're having a press conference later this week to announce the sale and launch the campaign. Gray will help you prepare. Don't worry about the rest of the details. You wouldn't understand them anyway."

I don't have any pride left. I'd fall on my knees in front of him, if I thought it would change his mind. I'd beg. I'd lick the bottom of his shoes. Some people like to see me do that.

My breath starts hitching uncontrollably, so I slide off the table and leave the room. I set the downstairs shower as hot as it will go and try to warm up my insides as I scrub chlorine out of my hair.

Every inch of my skin knows the feeling of being watched. I turn around in time to see the splash outside. Still toying with my tasteless gum, I switch off the water and walk naked out of the bathroom, down the hall, and onto the deck.

The piece of trash has thick, dark hair and dirty clothes and a broad, blue-collar body. He's sitting at the bottom, not moving, staring at nothing. Stretching my leg out, I hook his hat off the surface with my toes and examine it. *Emerald Landscaping.* I look around the garden, seeing for the first time all the plants I don't recognize and didn't choose. Anything that isn't between me and the lake has never captured my attention. I wonder who hires these people.

The thought of having to shower again makes me tired, but I like to keep a tidy pool. Protecting my junk with one hand, I step off the edge and drop straight down into the beautiful rushing sound of water wrapping around my head.

Chapter 4

ETHAN

Terra cotta tiles covered in months of dirty footprints lead me deep into the Lang mansion. Because one of my shoes came off in the pool, my feet make two different sounds—the *creak* of a boot and the *slap* of a wet sock—like a cartoon.

The back of the house doesn't match what I saw through the front windows at all. I pass empty rooms and furniture draped with sheets, crusty yellow squares on the walls where pictures used to hang. A half-eaten box of Oreos sits on an antique table that looks like it could pay my mortgage for a year. I almost trip over a scrap of black fabric I'm pretty sure is a G-string, and I imagine Scooter's face if I gave him that to auction on eBay.

Everything about this situation is so *off* from my mental image of a billionaire celebrity athlete that I start opening drawers and sticking my head into rooms as I pass by, looking for anything that makes sense. I stop in the doorway of a cramped bathroom with no windows, barely big enough to turn around in. A worn-out dog bed occupies the floor, edges crammed in around the toilet and cabinets, along with a messy duvet and a load of pillows. It smells, not a stink but musty, like nothing has been washed in a while. As a hopeless animal lover, I wonder what kind of dog he has and feel sorry that I didn't get to meet it.

There's a TV balanced on the sink, cord plugged into the outlet meant for shavers and toothbrushes. As I turn around, I notice two deadbolts nailed to the door. Something feels off about them, but the sound of voices down the hall distracts me.

The house starts to look brighter and more habitable as I get closer to the voices, until I stumble into a dining room that seems ready for a magazine shoot, with pastries and orange juice and vases of snapdragons arranged on the big table.

Victor is standing across the table from an old man in a suit, a man whose face I recognize from the covers of countless business magazines and websites: Werner Lang, the German-immigrant-turned-tech-mogul who broke every record for fastest self-made billionaire and who happens to be Victor's father.

I'm trespassing, dripping wet, missing my shoe, in front of a man who has the power to not only get me fired but probably buy the entire city of Kirkland and turn it into a shopping mall. Father and son are both staring at me, so I focus on the less scary one. "If you're not going to sign it, give it back." I hold out my hand, which is still trembling with adrenaline. When he narrows his eyes at me, I stare back, refusing to blink.

"Why?"

That's not the question I expected, and the audacity of it irritates me. I take a step toward him. "It belongs to my cousin, and it's important to him."

"You were big fans. Of me." Victor speaks hesitatingly, eyes tracing down to my feet and back to my face, like he's struggling to remember what I said just a few minutes ago.

"Yeah, of course." Flattery seems like a good option. "We dreamed of meeting you."

He splays a hand flat across his bare chest, runs it slowly down his ribs as if daring me to count them. It's barely a shadow of the body that carried him to fame. "Happy? Is this what you wanted?"

Werner sits back in his chair. He doesn't seem surprised at his son's behavior or interested in helping me out.

Victor smiles tightly. "Did your little cousin cry when they banned me?"

My vision flashes white. I grab his wrist, squeezing it when he tries to pull away as I pry his fingers off my card. Like kids on a fucking playground. When I cradle it in my hand, I see that one corner has bent and an unfamiliar urge to kill someone rises in my stomach.

Victor backs away. His chin is tipped up like he wants to fight, but his eyes look wary. "Congratulations. Now stop fucking dripping on my floors. Unless you want to pay to have them refinished."

The hardwood looks like shit: patchy black water stains, dirt ground in between the boards. I snort in disgust and walk away. He had everything I ever wanted, and he's wasted it all.

As I storm down the hall, trying to smooth the card flat between my palms, I finally realize what was bothering me about those deadbolts on the bathroom: they're on the wrong side, the inside. I guess if I was his dog I'd want to lock him out too.

My shoe is still at the bottom of the pool, and I don't see any kind of pole or net to fish it out. I'll have to skip some meals to afford another pair, especially since I'm *not* getting paid for this job. I slam my tools into the wagon and drag it around to the front. I'm about to spit on the driveway when I realize Werner Lang is standing next to the Bentley, arms crossed.

He has a commanding presence, like I should be bowing as I apologize. "I'm really sorry about this, sir. Please don't sue my company. We seek to provide only—"

He scoffs impatiently and holds out a slip of paper. It flutters in the muggy breeze off the lake. I've never seen a check for twenty thousand dollars, but if I had, I think it would look an awful lot like this.

When I don't touch it, he sets it on the wheel well of my truck, weighing it down with a very expensive-looking pen. "My son needs a boyfriend."

I sag against the truck, exhausted. "Excuse me?"

"Victor has decided to return to the public eye as the face of my newest advertising campaign."

I can see him as a model, the high cheekbones and the permanent smirk on his pouty lips. Maybe looking pretty is all he's good for, now that he blew up his career. Plenty of more problematic celebrities have managed to make a comeback in a different line of work.

"Have you heard of the dating app comeVa?"

I nod mutely, like I'm a kid trying to please his teacher. ComeVa connected me with my only relationship: a nice few months with a nice guy that ended nicely when I realized none of it—the fuzzy feelings, the physical connection, sharing activities that I could just as well have enjoyed alone—did anything for me. Not good, not bad, just nothing. This morning was the first boner I've popped in I don't know how long, and that was just a fluke.

"I'm holding a press event to announce my company's procurement of the app and my son's role as the face of the brand." He waves his hand like he's trying to turn the cogs of my brain himself. "The press will go wild when they catch sight of him, and I want his story to be as compelling as possible—something like 'I was lost until I met my partner through this app; he gave me the strength to go on.' Yes?" He pauses like he expects me to agree.

When I just stare at him like he's speaking a foreign language, he continues. "It's simple: one night, twenty thousand dollars. Complete an NDA, smile and nod as you stand next to him, and make sure he doesn't go off the rails—" he points at the check "—and I'll sign that for you. Everyone hired to work on this property has already had a background check run on them, so we can skip that step."

After a long silence, I laugh weakly and slide down the truck until I'm sitting on the concrete with my head in my hands. My brain is too short-circuited from almost drowning to have a filter. "Why the hell wouldn't you just hire an actor or a model or some kind of escort?"

"If I chose someone who had a social media presence, the lie wouldn't last an hour."

"So the next logical choice is a random guy off the street whose name you don't even know? God*damn*."

"Do you believe in fate?"

"Huh?" I blink. That word came to me out of nowhere when I was in the pool, three heartbeats from inhaling water. It felt important, like I had just discovered the key to a mystery I've been trying to solve my whole life. Now that I'm not high on death, I don't know. But hearing it a second time in less than thirty minutes shakes me up a little. "Not really," I lie.

When Werner doesn't answer, I look up. He's studying me appraisingly, lips pressed together. "My advisor and legal counsel, Gray Freeman, has been responsible for keeping an eye on Victor since the scandal. Besides Gray and a stream of anonymous male escorts with cocaine crusted around their nostrils, my son has refused to see or speak to anyone in six years. Until today."

I run a hand through my hair, staring up at him. "He didn't have any problem talking to me."

Oh.

He looks at the trading card in my hand. "Victor has always done exactly as he pleases, and no one on this earth can tell him otherwise. Except you, apparently."

"I took this by force."

His lips twitch. "If he had wanted to keep it from you, you wouldn't have it right now." After letting that sink in, he continues. "Given his appearance, the state of this house, he's incapable of managing his own life. Marketing optics aside, this weekend is going to be his first public outing in half a decade, and it will go better for everyone if he has someone who can...stabilize him."

It feels wrong for a dad to talk that way about his son. But I've never had a son—or a dad. Maybe this is how it works. Getting to my feet, I study the front of the mansion, all the big windows blanked out with some kind of protective coating, reflecting the slate-colored clouds. "I don't care who he talks to or doesn't, with all due respect. He's never going to listen to me."

"I just think it's interesting that you showed up here this morning, of all places on all days." He shrugs. "Take your time."

"I don't—"

He shuts me up with an impatient shake of his head. "Sleep on it. And if you decide no, shred the check and we'll find another way to control him. By the way, I'm sure you know how painful it would be for you if you tell anyone about what you've heard from me."

The Bentley's paint gleams as he climbs in and drives away. As I fold the check into my wallet and drop the pen in the truck cup holder, I imagine paying off the last of Mom's medical debts and saving up for the around-the-world vacation I promised we'd take before she's too far gone to remember it.

I feel eyes on my back, but when I turn around there's just the mansion, the lake, the empty yard. He's in there, somewhere in the grime and the silence, watching like a ghost in a haunted house.

Chapter 5

VICTOR

Dad sends Gray over to make sure I don't kill myself before he can make money off my face.

I crack the front door. "No."

Before I can close it, he holds up a plastic bag. I can see peppers, tortillas, raw steak. He has an apron in his other hand, rolled around a bundle of chef's knives. When I open the door further, he raises his eyebrows at my oversized Vampire Weekend t-shirt and wet hair held back with a leopard print headband. This from a man who shows up to cook fajitas in a Versace suit.

He follows me into the kitchen and I slide up onto the counter, holding out my hands for the plastic bag. Everything inside is still in sealed packaging, even the veggies. I concentrate on opening everything and lining it up while Gray takes off his jacket and hangs the apron around his neck. He turns his back to me so I can tie the strings. "Too muscle-bound to reach your own ass?" I ask, and his lips twitch, which is as close as he gets to smiling.

He's a good-looking guy, if you want someone who can take you to court and suplex you in the same day. The way he pushes his glasses up when he's concentrating is sex on a stick. He's also a fag, like me, much to Dad's chagrin. I'd let him fuck me if he wanted to, I guess, but he's never asked and that's one reason he's the only person in this world I trust even a little.

He lines a pan with strips of steak and cuts up one of each color of bell pepper. The smell of charring makes me hungry and nauseous at the same time, so I tip my head back against the cabinets and try not to breathe. Every time he does something to the food, he moves slowly, so I can watch. That's another reason I trust him.

I pull one knee up, rest my chin on it, and run my finger along the hot edge of the pan he's using. He glances up at me while his hands continue flipping the bits of meat.

"You knew, didn't you?" My voice comes out hoarse. "He couldn't have drafted that right of publicity thing without you. You knew what he was trying to do."

His hand goes still, and he stares at the stovetop as his jaw works. Finally, he points at the cupboard behind me and I take out two plates, handing them to him. He spoons the fillings into the tortillas with silent precision. The third reason I trust him is because he lets things be quiet when he doesn't have a good answer.

"I didn't know what else to do," he says finally. "It was chaos after your test results hit the news. I wanted your father to give you the house and leave you in peace." He closes his eyes for a second, then shakes his head and carries on. "Signing away your commercial rights was the only way he was going to let that happen. I hoped that circumstances would change and he wouldn't use it against you."

"Ha," I scoff. He wraps one of the plates in cling film, holds it up for me to inspect, and puts it in the fridge. I pad after him on bare feet as he carries his plate out the back door, to the patio furniture I let rust in the rain because I couldn't be arsed to cover it. He knows I like it out here, where I can smell the water. "So you're going to show me how sorry you are by getting me out of this, right?"

It's almost too dark to see his expression, but I know it's not good. "My contracts don't have loopholes."

"I know." I bury my head in my arms and listen to frogs calling in the distant dusk.

"You're not going to like what I have to say."

"Then don't."

"If you agreed to take a role in the company, even a small one, he'd drop this whole thing." He holds up his hand when I open my mouth. "It's your family's legacy. And it would give you a purpose you desperately need."

When he goes to spear a piece of steak, I snag the edge of his plate and pull it out of reach. "There is *nothing* that man can do to me that's worse than spending the rest of my life working for him. If that means doing this commercial or whatever, so be it."

Gray pushes up his glasses and studies me. I always say he sold his feelings to the devil in exchange for his brain, but right now he looks sad. "Victor, this is going to be brutal for you. It's more than just a commercial. You can't magically switch yourself back on after this long. Fuck, you barely remember how to be human." He cuts himself off, rubbing a hand over his mouth. "Sorry."

I sink back in my chair, blinking at the Seattle skyline lit up across the water and smiling. My smile has been broken down, rinsed out, used up, and torn apart over the past ten years, but the one thing a good celebrity always knows how to do is smile, no matter what. "It's ok."

After an awkwardly long silence, he wipes his hands on his napkin and stands up with one of those groans that makes me tease him about being a decrepit thirty-five-year-old. "Excuse me."

My back stiffens. I tip my chair on two legs as far as it will go, watching him walk down the hall. "Hey. Use the toilet in my room."

He pauses. "What did you do to the downstairs one?"

"You really want to hear about my shits?"

He squints at me, then rolls his eyes and climbs the stairs. I lower my chair, blowing out a slow breath. While I wait, I stare at my hands. I squeeze the fingers of my left hand around my right wrist like Ethan Lowe did this morning, and hold it that way, watching white marks appear on my skin.

My safe world blew apart today, and I can't help but feel like it's all his fault.

When Gray comes back downstairs, I'm standing in the hall with his jacket and apron full of knives. He takes them hesitantly. "I don't have anywhere to be. We could watch a movie or something."

"Why?"

For once, he looks nonplussed. "I don't know." He takes his things and opens the front door. Then he pulls in a deep breath, like he's going to blow my house down. "No one deserves to live like this, Victor. Not even you. I don't give a fuck what you find to live for, but I need you to promise me that you won't give up."

"You're letting in the damp."

He slams the door unnecessarily hard. I stand still, shivering, rubbing one foot against my bare calf. After I hear his engine start, I put on headphones and sit cross-legged on the kitchen floor, unwrapping my cold dinner. When I'm finished licking the last bits of juice off my fingers, I slide down onto my back on the tile and close my eyes.

Chapter 6

ETHAN

I'm standing at the edge of the road in an orange vest, turning that little *Slow - Stop* sign around and around and waiting for Roy to call and tell me I'm fired. Last night, when I finally fell into bed, I dreamed about water up my nose and the way that man caught his lip in his teeth when he stared at me. Then dream-Victor grabbed my head and forced it under the hazy, ash-flecked water of Lake Chelan, holding it there as I struggled. I woke up, coughing and gasping, to find Petunia draped across my face.

My phone rings, and I feel dizzy. Why did Roy wait so long? But when I pick up, I hear Peyton's dry, effortlessly cool voice. She plays competitive soccer and first chair violin and gets approximately fifteen phone numbers every time we go to a bar. I have no idea why she still hangs out with me.

"My guy. When is June's appointment?"

I adjust my sunglasses, staring down the dude in the lead car who is getting more and more pissed off that I haven't given him the signal to go. "One o'clock. Why?"

"My lunch break starts at twelve-thirty. I'll meet you there." As if she couldn't get any more accomplished, she's also an emergency room nurse.

"It's just routine," I lie. Mom's getting worse—crying uncontrollably for no reason, waking up in the night to take apart the puzzles she works on during the day. I want to break down and tell someone, anyone, if there's a chance they can help me. But I'm too scared that they'll take her away. It feels like ninety percent of the words that come out of my mouth now are lies.

"See you there."

I flip my sign and offer a wave as the angry driver roars off with his middle finger in the air. "Thank you."

Peyton and I met when we brought Mom to Peyton's ER after Danny's accident. They took her away for a scan and I sat shivering and alone in the waiting room in dirty clothes, still traumatized from nearly drowning myself. Something warm tapped my arm and I looked up to see a dark-haired nurse with green eyes holding out a cup of coffee. The edges of our broken parts just happened to fit together, slide into place in a way we both needed, and she became part of my family.

Getting to UW's Memory and Brain Clinic should take twenty minutes, but as usual in Seattle, traffic and a squall make it fifty. Rain soaks my clothes as I run between the parking garage and the front doors. In the hushed waiting room, full of people double my mom's age, Peyton waves me over. "They just took her back. Ana's with her."

This is the first time I've missed hugging Mom before one of her appointments, from her first diagnosis until today. "Fucking traffic. This is bullshit." I can't help but blame myself; my mind has been all over the place in the last twenty-four hours.

Peyton frowns at me. "You ok?"

"I'm fine." I grab a random magazine and start flipping through it. It's full of celebrity red carpet pics, which just skyrockets my stress. Peyton pulls it away, pages crumpling.

"I thought you said this was routine."

There's no world in which I can school my expression quickly enough to fool her. Her shoulders sag. "Ethan…"

"Please, Peyton." My voice cracks a little. "Can we just wait and see what they say?"

"What are you imagining? 'Congrats, she's on the mend'?" Her tone is sharp, sad. "It's never going to be that, Ethan."

I stare at my hands, resting palm-up in my lap.

Finally, she sighs. "I'm sorry; that was uncalled for. I just *hate* seeing you do this to yourself."

"Doing what?"

"Thinking it's your job to control something that doesn't play fair, doesn't have any rules. There's nothing we can do but be there for her."

"There's always something. I just haven't found it yet."

She grabs my hand, pulls me to my feet. "Come here."

"Wait—"

"We'll only be a minute."

We follow the blue plastic signs through the clinic into the hushed, sun-drenched lobby of the main hospital. Peyton power walks everywhere with her soccer-player quads, so I focus on keeping up as she takes the steps to the second floor two at a time. The nurse's station is empty; no one stops us from sneaking down one of the long hallways flanked with patient rooms.

Peyton stops at room 242. The door's open, lights off, bed unmade. She hesitates, a strange look on her face, then goes in and sits on the edge of the bed.

"What is this?"

She studies the heart monitors and IV stand, the snarls of cables and sensors. "This is where my dad died."

I clearly remember the day her father collapsed from a heart attack four years ago. "Shit, Pey. I'm sorry." I sit down next to her.

She takes a deep breath. "I got the news in class and made it here just in time to say goodbye. If the traffic had been different, I wouldn't have been here at all."

"I sense a point coming," I say with a weak smile.

"How prescient of you." She bumps my shoulder with hers. "Look. I lost my dad in an instant. You're going to lose your mom tomorrow, and again next week, and again next month, over and over. Sometimes I don't know how you cope."

By pretending I have a choice in any of this.

"But Ethan, I got one chance to say goodbye. Some people don't get any. You get a hundred, a thousand; you get to make every one matter, find every possible way of saying *I love you*. Ugh—" Cheeks reddening, she swipes moisture from her eyes. "My point is, you're bleeding yourself dry trying to find answers that don't exist as those chances are passing you by."

Standing up, crossing to the window, she gives me a moment. But I don't know what to do with it, besides stare at the wall with a numb kind of pain eating at my heart. Whether I fight for Mom, whether I give up and "make her comfortable" as the doctors say, I'm always doing the wrong thing. So I just work harder, sleep less, give my mother more of myself, hoping that someday, someone will come by and tell me it was enough, that I can finally rest and everything will be alright.

"We have a trip planned," I say when the silence goes on too long. "A whole month, maybe more. Everywhere in the world she wants to see."

Peyton smiles. "June's so excited about it. She brings it up every time we hang out."

Except by the time I can afford it, it will be too late.
Unless.
Unless twenty thousand dollars just came out of nowhere.
Like a freak coincidence. Like a story you'd never believe. Like fate.

After I tuck Mom into bed that night, I help Ana carry her bags to the car. The silence feels heavy; after her appointment, the doctor told me Mom and I should start visiting care facilities before her needs go beyond what I can provide.

"I'll speak to my boss," Ana says as we stand by the car in the damp night air. "We'll find the most affordable option for you."

I shake my head. "She can't go to a nursing home. She's not ready. I'll pay anything, whatever it takes, to keep her home as long as possible." I'm just spewing words, promises I can't back up, and Ana knows it. But she doesn't argue, just gives me a motherly hug and climbs into her car.

I go back inside and stand in the doorway of Mom's room for a minute, listening to her even breathing, a sound which has always comforted me on a primal level. Tonight, it makes my throat clog up with tears I never shed. I kiss her lightly on the forehead and sneak back to my room.

Before I can think too hard, I dig under my bed and pull out a small cardboard box carefully sealed with wide strips of packing tape. I didn't have to label it because I could never forget what's inside. The sound of tearing cardboard can't drown out the voices in my head as I pry open the flaps.

It's Danny and the faint smell of his deodorant, my cousin and the happy, lazy years we spent together. Plastic Transformers we played with when we were ten. The paper air rifle target with the bullseye he scored at summer camp. My high school perfect attendance award, on which he scrawled "you're a loser" with a smiley face. His third-place swimming medal.

My mom and her sister both ended up as single parents, so Danny and I grew up as brothers. We shared a room for years when our moms rented an apartment together. I set the box next to me on the bed and pull out what I'm looking for: a battered scrapbook.

It's a shrine to Victor Lang. Danny hunted down every news story, every stat sheet, every magazine cover. He started swimming lessons at fourteen thanks to Victor, and always talked about the day they'd face at the Olympics, even though Danny kind of sucked at swimming. His big dreams always awed me, as someone who didn't really know how to dream at all.

I flip slowly through the pages, studying each one. It's a beautiful story: an unknown kid comes out of nowhere to win the junior national championship, unseating a world record set by a boy two years older than him. The announcers were yelling their lungs out as it happened—an iconic YouTube clip with eight million views, half of which came after the scandal.

At the end of that swim, Victor faced a crowd of frantic reporters without an ounce of fear. In response to the prevailing question—who *are* you and where did you come from—he announced that he was going to destroy the Olympic gold medal record in men's swimming.

He was a force of nature, consuming one record after another, eclipsing his rivals, achieving the impossible. He specialized in the most technically demanding stroke, the butterfly, and pushed until he could go 25, then 50, then 75 meters, without air. Sports analysts argued if it was possible to reach 100 meters or more and pointed out that his mind game was just as potent as his physical ability, if not more. He swam like he didn't care if he ever breathed again.

He was gorgeous, a bright flame, a perfect physical specimen. The first openly gay athlete to reach this level of fame, forcing everyone's homophobic grannies to admit that "some of those people are alright" when he asserted US dominance at every international competition.

In reality, I guess it was all a lie, a false promise that hard work and passion can make you invincible. Lying back on the bed, I close my eyes and wonder if Danny would still be alive today if he hadn't swallowed that promise hook, line, and sinker.

We drove five hours east to Lake Chelan once every summer, at the tail end of wildfire season. Aunt Cath and Mom and Danny and I shared a tent, while my uncle and his second wife towed in a camper. I always thought it was kind of an ugly place, dry scrub and rattlesnakes and smoke so thick in the air you could taste it.

Danny and I would get ice cream sandwiches from the camp store and eat them on the dock, watching little kids play in the shallows and waiting for one of the big boats full of college students to launch. They'd let us on and give us turns on their inner tubes and water skis. When we fell off, they'd offer us hard lemonade or beer and let the boat go where it wanted between the indigo sky and the bottomless water, talking about art and philosophy and sex.

That last year, Danny had just watched the 2001 Planet of the Apes for some sociology project and was trying to convince me that it had my favorite actor, Matt Damon. I told him Damon had never been in a fucking Planet of the Apes movie. So when the adults said they were driving down to town for some cell service, I said I'd go with them and find out what lookalike schmuck had actually starred in the damn movie.

Danny was pissed at me, so he didn't want to come. He needed to practice his butterfly stroke, he said. He had a seizure once, years ago, that doctors could never figure out and even though he was healthy as a horse, Aunt Cath never wanted him to swim unsupervised. My mom said she'd stay behind and watch him. Just in case.

Forty minutes later, we pulled into an empty campsite. I was holding a box of donuts on my lap—a jelly one for Mom, chocolate with sprinkles for Danny, maple log for me.

"Where did they go?" my uncle asked, getting out of the car. He called my mom's name, loud, then Danny's.

There was a splash, just one, way out at the base of one of the twenty-foot rocks kids liked to jump off. Blink and you'd miss it.

I dropped the donuts and started running as fast as I could. Even though I quit swimming lessons after one summer, I dove straight into the water.

My uncle dragged me out just before I drowned. He had to hit me in the chest to get me to start breathing. Danny was long gone; I never felt him, never saw him.

We found my mom on the other side of the campground, trying to get into some stranger's tent at the campsite we had three years ago. She didn't remember us leaving, Danny going for a swim, any of it.

When she found out, she fell on her knees and held on to me and came apart. Because I didn't know what else to do, I took her home, got her to a doctor. She forgot about Danny again, and this time she didn't remember. That's when I started lying.

But the rest of my family remembered, and they wrote me a letter saying that they couldn't forgive her. That if I wanted them in my life, I should have her committed to a home. I said I wouldn't.

I had only just turned eighteen.

Danny died two months before the doping scandal, so his album ends on a high, with Victor preparing for his first Olympics. But between the last pages, I find what I'm looking for: a sheaf of magazine clippings and computer printouts that I folded and hid away. The story of Victor Lang's fall. I don't know why I felt the need to add these, to ruin the dream. I guess I thought that things were going to end up ok and this would become just part of the story, an interesting chronicle about how a phoenix burns up and comes back to life. I thought Danny might appreciate that.

But the resurrection never came. I unfold a paparazzi photo of Victor on his way into a meeting with USADA and WADA reps. Sunglasses hide his face and his hair's a mess, but most of all I can recognize for the first time that uneasy, beaten posture in his shoulders that I saw at his house yesterday.

For a few extra seconds of speed, he betrayed his sport and cast a shadow over the whole Olympics as news outlets obsessed over his story and ignored the achievements of his teammates. He let down the entire world. And instead of trying to redeem himself, he crawled into a hole with his daddy's money and lost himself in drugs and ass. He deserves everything that's happened to him and more.

I crumple up the press clipping and throw it across the room. I've been broken, too. But I keep trying to do better every single day, because I don't have any other choice.

Maybe it's time for him to face someone he hurt.

I call the number on Werner's check, expecting to leave a message for tomorrow. I'm startled when a woman answers. When I explain myself, she says she's emailing me a contract and NDA. "Please print this, sign it, and take it to Victor's house for him to sign as well. If we receive his signature by tomorrow, then we'll process the paperwork and move forward."

"But—"

"Think of it as your audition." She hangs up, leaving me to stare at the phone, bewildered.

Even his own people don't want to go near him. This does not bode well.

There's still time to back out. All I have to do is go to my night job and leave the contract unsigned. But this isn't about me. It's about Mom, asleep in the next room, waiting for me to show her the world. It's about how badly Danny would want his childhood hero to redeem himself.

At least it's on the way to work.

Chapter 7

VICTOR

Some people think *hole* is the worst thing you can call your partner. It's degrading and cruel, telling them they have no value except as something warm and wet to come inside.

Maybe that's why I find it so comforting. It gives a name to the things I am; it simplifies something people like to make complicated. When I use it in my hookup app profile, it attracts the kind of men I'm looking for.

But there was one guy named Ian. He talked to me when he was down my throat, told me I made him feel good. Then he came on my chest and licked it off, which in some ways is the nicest thing anyone's ever done for me.

So maybe that's why, now that I'm panicking, I break my never-the-same-guy-twice rule and call Ian.

I made a mistake.

He shows up with four other guys I don't know. I wouldn't have let them in, but he had the gate code and the front door wasn't locked so I find them already standing around my living room when I come downstairs.

I stop and stare at him, and he comes over to put an arm around me, rubbing my shoulder through my thin t-shirt. "It's not like that," he says quietly. "We brought coke and music."

Except I think it is like that.

I lie on the couch upside-down, feet in the air and head dangling, while the strangers put on some beats and turn down the lights, arrange the coke on my coffee table. I'm not a drug addict, but I've done plenty of them and if I try, I can dig inside and find that light, recreational withdrawal that makes me want to do them again. I think I need to be high tonight, so I work on talking myself up to it.

Ian grabs my feet and massages the bottom of them with his thumbs. I'm so easy I can already feel myself getting hard. "I'm sorry if you're not cool with this. You just sounded like you were lonely and they were already with me and I figured, since we had the shit, we could share it."

I sit up and let him kiss me. "Hey, what if they leave and we sit outside? I'll make you a drink and you can watch me swim, and then we'll fuck on a lounge chair and fall asleep out there."

He stares at me. "You already on something, dude?" I shove him away with a foot to the chest and go back to watching upside-down strangers do lines off my table. One of them eyes me with a look that says he'd rather be doing them off me.

I roll over and accept someone's silver Visa. Just as I'm about to go to a place where whatever happens next isn't going to hurt so much, someone bangs on the front door. Everybody jumps and stares at me like I called the cops.

"Calm down." I don't know if I'm talking to them or the person outside. My body aches everywhere from swimming all day—I was trying and failing to beat even one of my pre-scandal records—so I limp painfully over and crack the door. I open it an inch further when I see who it is.

That pervert from yesterday crosses his arms and gives me a defiant look. He's wearing a red polo that's faded and a little too small. When he hears music, he tries to look over my shoulder.

"Are you here for your boot?" I ask. "It's still in there; you're welcome to dive for it." When I fidget with the hem of my shirt, his eyes drop and I realize I'm still at half-mast in my shorts. His face twitches and he stares down at his ugly black shoes as he speaks.

"I need to talk to you. Did your father tell you anything?"

"The fuck are you doing talking to my father?" I growl, but he presses his lips together and gives me a look that says he won't tell me anything until I let him in.

I push the door open and jerk my head. His shoulder nudges my chest out of the way as he stalks inside. He freezes, taking in the drugs, the five men staring at him. When he notices the credit card in my hand, he looks like I just slapped him.

"You can't seriously be surprised. Come on."

Ian comes over, bristling possessively, and puts an arm around me. "Who is this, babe?"

"I actually have no idea. What was your name again?"

"Ethan," he grumbles.

"You should leave, dude," Ian tells him, like it's his house.

Ethan smells weak. He's scared of water, scared of me. He talks quietly, has gentle, worried eyes. But when he wanted his card back yesterday, I gave it to him. And tonight, when he fixes his gaze on Ian, the guy lets go of me and backs off. "Whatever. But if he calls the cops, I'm coming after you, Victor."

Interesting.

He grabs my wrist, towing me down the hall into an empty room. Half the bulbs in the ceiling fixture are out, and dust coats everything, sticking to my feet. I wrench my arm away. "Rule number one. I touch you; you do not touch me. Ever."

Failing to hide an eye roll—he's surprisingly sassy for a square—he slaps a piece of paper in my hand.

NDA.
The undersigned agrees.
"You have thirty seconds to make me understand this." I lean against the wall and cross my arms.

He does a good job. Within twenty-seven seconds, I know exactly what my father thinks of me, how badly this guy wants money, how fucked this all is.

"Look." I balance on one foot, putting my other against the wall, where it leaves a dark smudge. "If this is about cash, I've got some nudes you can sell if you can get anyone to believe it's me."

His eyes darken. "I don't see why this is such a problem. You're already going to be at the event; I'll just stand next to you. Unless you're not planning to cooperate."

"I know this is hard for your earnest little brain to comprehend, but you have no idea what this is really about."

"Sure I do. Rich people getting richer. An unscrupulous brat making a comeback instead of taking responsibility." He looks sullen as I laugh. "I'm late for work," he snaps, shoving the contract at me. "Sign it and send it back to your father's office."

Pinching it between two fingers, I pull a lighter from my pocket. He watches incredulously as I ignite the corner of the paper and send fire crawling up through all my father's words.

Just before it burns my fingers, I drop it on the floor. When Ethan raises his foot, I stop him with a hand across his chest. The flame starts to die, then flares again as it catches the edge of an old, brittle floorboard. I hold him back more firmly as an orange tendril sways dangerously close to the wall, with its peeling wallpaper. I glance over and watch the flame reflected in his eyes.

Finally, when it's almost too late, I let go of him and he stamps the fire out. "What the hell?"

"You and Gray and my father can draft all the paperwork you want. Sign the deals, print the money. But I'm the one with the match, and I don't give a shit if the whole place goes down. So if you want to come in here and stick your hands in things you don't understand, just remember that."

He shakes his head, a strange expression on his face, voice low. "If that was true, Victor, you wouldn't be talking to me right now. I know what a cornered animal looks like." Walking to the doorway, he turns around. "Think of it as an opportunity to rehabilitate yourself."

I flex my hand at my side and imagine strangling him.

Stalking toward the door, he pauses for a second in the living room. It smells like desperation and the sweat of unfamiliar men. He looks at me, shakes his head, and leaves.

I cross to the door, then step outside into the fresh, peaceful dark and stand on my front step, watching him back down the driveway. As he waits for the gate to open, I walk on my bare toes across the cool concrete, following the path of his tires until I'm leaning against the gate, looking through the bars at his tail lights as they disappear.

I rest my head against the wrought iron, grip it in my hands. When I look over my shoulder, Ian's standing in the doorway, waiting for me. I turn back to the place where Ethan was, but he's gone.

Maybe you forgot something. Maybe you'll turn around.

He doesn't.

Ian whistles. "Come on. It's cold out here."

ETHAN

When I get home from Qwik N' Go the next morning, I wait until Mom's in the shower before calling Werner's assistant. "I'm sorry for wasting your time. I tried."

She sounds surprised. "It says here that he signed a couple of hours ago. Are we good?"

I lower the spoonful of Cheerios halfway to my mouth, remembering the weight of his arm against my chest as we watched the fire burn a hole in his floor. How small he looked in that house, with all those guys. How I spent my shift wondering if it was really ok to leave him there.

"I guess we are."

the mystery of you
is the story of my sins

Chapter 8

Ethan

Every once in a while, I get two blessed days off in a row. This time it just happens to fall on the day before and the day of the press conference. It gives me plenty of time to tear the house apart in anxiety. I put on a paint-stained wife beater and a backwards ball cap, blast some Metallica, and start digging through cabinets and closets that haven't been emptied since before my grandparents moved out.

I'm lobbing forty-year-old Tupperware into the garbage and slapping the floor in time to the guitar solo from "Battery" when I look up and realize Mom has left her puzzle to watch. She has a small, knowing smile on her face that I haven't seen since before she got sick. I switch off the music and study her from my position sprawled on the linoleum. "Am I being too loud?"

She shakes her head. "I like it when you're loud." As an afterthought, she adds, "There's someone at the door asking for you."

I scramble to my feet, wiping sweat off my forehead and checking my phone. Neither Peyton nor Ana texted they were coming over, so it must be a Girl Scout or a Mormon. I know which I'd prefer.

It's sure as hell not a Girl Scout.

The man in the charcoal suit is so tall our eyes are level even though he's standing down a step. He's clearly older than me, but not as old as most men you see in suits like that. He tips his head down slightly to cut the sun glare on his glasses and studies me, from my crooked Raiders hat to my filthy, ripped clothes. Over his shoulder I see what looks like an Aston Martin nosed up to the curb.

"Let's go for a walk," he says crisply, handing me a business card. *Gray Freeman.* That name rings a bell—Werner Lang's lawyer or something.

"I can't leave my mom alone."

"Five minutes."

"Are you here to condescend to, intimidate, flex on, or otherwise bully me?"

A smile tugs at his mouth. "That depends. Even if I am, it's too late to back out. The payment should be hitting your bank about," he checks his watch, "now."

"What?" I glance over my shoulder to make sure Mom is focused on her puzzle again. "I'll be back in a second." Pulling the storm door shut behind me, I herd Gray down the driveway until we're out of earshot of the house. "I haven't done anything yet."

"Think of it as a goodwill gesture. We can afford to be generous with tiny sums like that."

"So you *are* here to flex on me."

This time, he doesn't smile. His brow furrows as he turns and starts strolling down the sidewalk, expecting me to follow. "I have a suit in my car to deliver to you, along with a folder of personal information you're to memorize. It covers basic background on the Lang family and Victor's preferences, along with a cover story to go with the pseudonym you've been assigned."

When I hesitate, he turns around. "Victor and I haven't had a single normal conversation. Shouldn't we meet up and go over this stuff together, get to know each other?"

"Your job isn't to get to know Victor. Your job is to say the things written on that piece of paper and then disappear into the sunset."

"Are they going to say we broke up?"

"That's not your concern." He seems to relent a little. "Victor's the main attraction; no one will remember you. They'll assume that you're a secretive person or that he eventually moved on. It doesn't matter."

"Well ok, then." I'm feeling more and more alone, like I'm the only one who cares if this stupid plan goes right or not.

He crosses his arms and examines me again, more slowly this time. Feeling self-conscious, I try to adjust my hat without showing him my unwashed hair. But even though I look like I just crawled out of a hole, his expression when he finishes seems satisfied.

For the first time since I set eyes on him, he hesitates, like he's searching for words. "Be careful with him," he says abruptly, then starts walking back toward his car, which has attracted a lot of attention from people doing their Saturday morning yard work.

I should keep my mouth shut, but if there's one thing I can't stand, it's being made responsible for other people's carelessness. When I was seven years old, I panicked because the other first graders were goofing around during singing practice instead of doing the motions and my teacher wouldn't make them stop. She told me it would be ok as long as I concentrated on doing my part perfectly. During the performance, I messed up one time, just a little, and broke down bawling. I think she meant well, but I'm sick of the decent people in the world being expected to make up for the existence of the freeloaders. "Be *careful* with him? You do know he was doing coke in his living room with a bunch of creeps the other night, right?"

Gray's gait falters for just a second, but he keeps walking without a word. I can't help but admire the lines of the Aston Martin as he opens the door and pushes a garment bag and a folder into my arms. "A car will pick you up at five o'clock tomorrow evening. Call the number on my card if you have any questions."

When he pulls away, I realize all the people gawking at his car are now gawking at me. I hurry inside and open the folder, preparing myself to pull on another life like a spare jacket, a life where I was the kind of person—God knows who—that would catch the eye of someone like Victor Lang. If that imaginary person existed, I would have felt very sorry for him.

The next afternoon, after Ana arrives, I shave and spray on deodorant, then wash my hands carefully and open the garment bag in my room. Even though I skipped breakfast and lunch, my stomach is churning. I've never even *felt* fabric like the stuff under my fingers as I ease the jacket off its hanger, trying not to let it touch anything in my dusty room. The fact that they have all my sizes without asking me is some supervillain level shit.

The last time I wore a suit was to Danny's funeral, a wrinkled polyester hand-me-down that my wide shoulders nearly tore in half. I threw it in the garbage that night, one of the only things I've ever outright wasted. This tailored jacket hugs me in all the right places, while the light gray color makes me look impossibly sophisticated and somehow older. I have no idea what to do with the matching bow tie, so I leave it hanging around my neck as I pull on the surprisingly comfortable black leather shoes.

Ava was supposed to take Mom out shopping so I could leave discreetly, but when I emerge into the living room they're still sitting on the couch. *Shit.* Ava's eyes get round, and Mom bursts into tears.

"Mom, Mom, it's ok." I tug up the hems of my trousers and crouch in front of her, folding her hands in mine. "It's just me. What's wrong?"

The suit came with some kind of fancy handkerchief, so I pull it out of my pocket and hand it to her. She presses her face into the fabric, leaving smudges of mascara. "Baby, you look so handsome. You really are grown up, aren't you?" She sniffles. "Do you have a date?"

I seize on the excuse. "Yeah. Something like that."

"If Kathy Renfroe asks you to stay after to help clean the gymnasium, tell her to stuff it. Even the student body president should get to enjoy his own prom."

I stare at her for a moment, then pull her into my arms. I want my mom to tell me things are going to be ok. "I feel ridiculous."

She laughs, leaning back and taking my face in her hands, stroking her thumbs along my cheeks like she used to do. "Don't put your hands in your pockets and don't slouch. Stand tall and look people in the eye when you talk to them."

"Yes, ma'am."

And as I kneel in front of her, she straightens my lapels and starts knotting my bow tie. She can't have done that since my dad left when I was two, but her fingers don't hesitate for a minute. I make eye contact with Ana, who smiles sadly. It's one thing to remember and another thing to get lost in the past, but sometimes they bring you to the same place.

I see headlights through the curtains and scramble to my feet. "I love you, Mom."

She squeezes my fingers. "I know you do." And that's something I don't let her forget.

Victor

Fuck fuck fuck fuck.

Gray never even asked me if I would go to the tailor. He just stood me in my front hall and did the measurements himself with a fabric tape measure and a pen in his mouth. He didn't say a word as he examined the results, but his mouth was a flat line. As he carried my suit out the door, he paused. "Did you do coke again?"

"No."

He hesitated. He fucking hesitated. That sanctimonious asshole Ethan ratted me out, tried to turn him against me, and it fucking *worked*. I wasn't even lying; they snorted it all before I could get there.

I slammed the door in Gray's face.

When I got moved to the hotel penthouse last night to prepare for the event, Gray didn't check on me. And he sent one of Dad's grunts to return the outfit instead of doing it himself.

Now that I'm looking at myself in this suit, I want to call him back up here and tell him to burn it, to burn me, to burn the whole city, whatever he has to do to make this stop. It fits perfectly, and no matter how I stand in the mirror, I look weak. Small. Every day of the last six years written on my body for *everyone* to read. I imagine the Facebook comments, the tweets that are going to come from this:

God, he's barely recognizable.

He couldn't swim 50m if there was a mountain of coke at the end.

I take my jacket off and throw it at the mirror.

No wonder he needed steroids.

Get the man a fucking cheeseburger.

I'm going to be stared at, picked apart by strangers and, worst of all, by the people I used to know, and there are no doors I can close to stop it. I lie on my back, my arms thrown over my face, and listen to the strange, scraping sound of my breath. "You did this to me," I moan, squeezing my fists until my bones creak. I whimper it into the crook of my elbow. "You did this to me."

You were right, Gray. I can't do this. Please let me go home.

But he's not here.

*E*THAN

An anonymous black car with an anonymous driver delivers me to an anonymous security guard at the back door of a luxury hotel in downtown Seattle, like I'm a package of drugs in a crime thriller. I'm sure Victor would prefer me that way.

After examining my ID and making a phone call, the guard ushers me into a private elevator, swiping his card across a chip reader instead of selecting a floor. I assumed he was going to show me where to go and what to do, but he steps out as the doors close, leaving me to grip the hand rail and contemplate the depth of my mistakes. I stare at my barely-recognizable reflection in the sheet metal walls and try to imagine my face next to Victor's on the front page of some celebrity news site. *There's one for your scrapbook, Danny.*

The doors open on a soaring penthouse suite stained neon orange by the sunset outside a two-story wall of glass. Between the needle points of the skyscrapers, a burning sky sears its image into the waters of the Puget Sound, dotted by cranes and cargo ships. It's one of the most beautiful things I've ever seen.

It also looks like a frat house exploded in here. I kick aside a discarded pair of jeans, staring at the empty alcohol bottles and bags of chips, the underwear and wadded up towels and empty suitcases. There's a wet swimsuit hanging off the grand piano, dripping on the floor. "Hello?"

No answer. Something about the uncomfortable, heavy warmth in the room has me holding my breath as I cross to the window and crane my neck, looking right down the side of the building to the street forty floors below. My already weak knees almost give way in a lurch of vertigo and I step back, grabbing the edge of the piano.

"You shouldn't let me see what scares you." Victor is sitting on the railing of the lofted bedroom above my head, looking down at me with a crooked half-smile. "I'm compiling quite a list."

I feel like I've gone back in time six years, from his flawless black suit to the gelled hair to the sharp, clean-shaven jaw. When he swings his long leg over the railing, I spot the chain he always wore glinting at his throat. I could almost convince myself that I imagined the barefoot, tangle-headed wreck I met the other day, with his long shirts and short shorts and chaos in his eyes.

When I don't say anything, he jerks his head for me to follow and disappears. I climb the stairs, stepping around a few more empty bottles. He's lying on his back on the bed, arms stretched across the comforter. There's shit all over this room too, including a massive bottle of lube on the bedside table. Even before his career died, there were rumors about him, that he would let anyone do anything to him and like it. I used to tell myself they weren't true.

"Are we going or what?" I shift my weight uneasily, eager to get back downstairs, where I'm not alone with him. My phone vibrates, and I grab it without thinking, scared to see Ana's name on the screen. It's just Roy, bothering me about extra shifts.

"Cute girlfriend," Victor says next to my shoulder, like he teleported there.

I frown at my phone wallpaper. It's a picture Mom took of Peyton and I when we went to Pike Place Market. I'm holding an eggplant in front of my crotch while Peyton hoists two melons against her chest. We're blurry from laughing so hard—when you're permanently sleep-deprived, everything is funny. Peyton set it as my wallpaper and I never got around to changing it.

"She's not my girlfriend." I bite my lip, reminding myself not to give him ammunition.

"There's no need to be ashamed." He wanders into the bathroom and props his hands on the counter, meeting my eyes in the mirror. "You wouldn't be the first straight guy to be turned on by my ass. I was in a Buzzfeed quiz and everything."

"I'm not—" I seal my mouth and stare back in silence.

"You're learning."

When I follow him into the bathroom, he wraps lean fingers around the bony part of my wrist and stands on his toes, pressing his nose against the skin under my ear. It's cold. "You smell like dollar store hand soap."

"Do I look like I own cologne?"

In a boyish gesture that doesn't match his appearance, he pulls himself up to sit on the counter and prods lazily through a selection of bottles next to the sink with one finger. "Use this." He tosses it, forcing me to scramble to catch the cut-crystal vial. As much as I hate to admit it, it smells good—spicy and sweet.

When he seems satisfied with my application, he pats the counter between his thighs. "Here."

I freeze, alarm bells going off in my head, but he just waits. Tonight, his eyes should be picking up the warm tones of the hotel lighting, but they look hard and icy, almost iridescent, like the inside of a mollusk shell. His eyebrows scrunch together as I stand between his knees, ignoring the stir of discomfort in my core. "Do you style your hair with a vacuum cleaner?"

He slicks his hand with gel and grabs the back of my head, pulling it down so he can reach. I squirm as his impatient fingers snag in my hair. "Stop," he complains, wrapping one of his legs around the back of mine to keep me still. When he's done, I glance at the mirror over his shoulder and burst out laughing. "I look like a high school freshman on picture day."

He leans back on his hands, resting against the mirror. "At least now you won't embarrass me. You know what to say tonight?"

"Gray gave me the—"

"Nothing." His voice is cold and flat. "You say nothing. I don't want to hear a word out of your mouth."

"That's not what they told me."

One of his eyebrows twitches. "They're not here. You're my prop. I'll put my arm around you, maybe I'll hold your hand, whatever I feel like." He leans in, his thighs still bracketing mine. "I'll kiss you if I think it would look good." His eyes study me, bright now, his tongue working in his cheek as he tries not to grin. This close, I can see a hint of red, inflamed skin around his eyes, protected by his pale lashes.

Holding his stare, I force a smile. I won't play games with him. "Ok."

But I twitch when he dives for my mouth. He stops just short, his breath stirring against my lips, then leans back to drink in my expression. "Do you need to practice tasting fag mouth so you don't puke on the red carpet?"

"They'll just have to clean it up." I push him away from me, then turn around and walk through the bedroom, to the top of the stairs. When I glance over my shoulder, he's doing one last check in the mirror. He still has more of an athlete's body than most people ever will, but his bulk and presence are gone, like he was never a god at all. And as he studies himself, he keeps struggling to stand taller, to cast a longer shadow.

It feels good to see him like that. He makes me cruel, like a toxic cloud rotting away the good and leaving only the worst. "Are you happy you ruined your life for a body you couldn't even keep?"

He turns around. This isn't the old Victor or the new Victor. It's just a blank, nothing. But a second later, he flashes a smirk. "Are you happy you ruined your life for a mother who barely even knows who you are?"

He strolls past me, hopping down the stairs two at a time as I stand frozen, staring after him. "Never touch me again. I told you the rules."

I don't know what's worse, hearing my mom's name in his disgusting mouth or realizing that he knows about her at all, that his people are digging into the corners of my life and feeding him information that will force me to do whatever he wants.

Chapter 9

ETHAN

When we reach the bottom of the elevator, a security guard walks us to the private parking garage beneath the hotel. "You're going to go right out the exit and follow our SUV down the block. Pull up to the curb outside the venue, and their team will take it from there. No detours." He directs this at Victor with the same cautious precision someone would use to diffuse a bomb.

Forget the Lambos and Ferraris, the overcompensating rich-boy cars. Victor drives a *gorgeous* black vintage Jag, restored with all custom details. The dashboard looks like a space capsule, full of unlabeled dials and switches, and the engine lets out the smoothest, throatiest growl as we cruise onto the street. I slouch in my seat, watching Victor's hand work the gear shift and adding *ruining my chance to enjoy the most beautiful ride in the world* to the man's list of sins.

We both jump when his phone rings. He yanks it out of his pocket and tosses it at me so unexpectedly I fumble to keep from dropping it. "What am I supposed to do?"

"*Answer it.*"

"Hello?" I clear my throat, wondering who on earth I'm talking to. When I recognize Gray's smooth baritone, I flip the call to speakerphone.

"Someone leaked to the public; there are hundreds of people here vying to be the one who posts the first cell phone video of him in six years."

There's a moment of silence. Victor's grip on the steering wheel tightens. When he sees me watching, he flips me off. "So what?"

Gray sighs. "We're going ahead, but you need to stick to the security guards and do exactly as they tell you."

Victor snatches the phone from my hand and hangs up. He turns on the radio, even though we're only driving two more blocks. It's blasting Katy Perry, but I don't think he's listening. Craning my neck, I can see a swarm of people down the street, flashbulbs lighting up the night air. The security SUV inches its way forward, clearing a path to the curb in front of the conference center.

I flinch back in my seat as someone slaps the window. Crowd control is trying its best to manage the unexpected turnout, but people are slipping through the cracks and trying to grab the car. *This is insane.* He's a gay icon, the closest thing the sports world has to a rock star, and the source of one of the biggest controversies in sports history. I wonder how many of these people give a shit about Werner and his dating app. But he's playing the long game; he'll get a million downloads and another million hate-downloads every time Victor's face shows up on TV.

The situation gets more and more controlled as we near the center of the crowd, unruly spectators giving way to press cameras and reporters. I spot Werner and an entourage walking into the building. Victor edges the car to the curb and throws it into park. "You scared?" He's smirking at me. "You seem like a sensitive guy."

"Are you? You let every single one of these people down."

"That sounds like a them problem." He pats my knee. "If you're looking for my conscience, you're about ten years too late."

Someone opens my door and as I unfold from the car there's a *wall* of sound, so all-encompassing I feel like I've stepped into a thunderstorm, shredded by the lightning of camera flashes that keep burning into my retinas until I can hardly get my bearings. I don't know what to listen to or who to focus on, like I've just been let go after spinning in circles. Trying to get my bearings, I look over the roof of the car at Victor's blond head.

He's just standing there, stock still, gripping the top of the door. His pale eyes have almost disappeared behind dilated pupils that keep flicking, unfocused, across the crowd like he's looking for someone or everyone at once. His lips tremble for a second, like he's trying to breathe.

"Hey," I snap. He turns to me, blinks. "Get me the hell out of here."

So quickly I think I imagined the whole thing, he straightens up and flashes that dazzling smile, the one everybody knows, and the energy on the street skyrockets. People in the distance cheer, punctuated by some booing. He puts both fists in the air, grin widening. "I'm back, bitches!"

I stifle my eye roll just in time, remembering that I'm supposed to be in love with this idiot. I offer him a tepid smile as he circles the car. For all his threats, he barely brushes a hand against the small of my back as we climb the steps.

When we pause in front of the photo opportunity halfway up, I wish someone had told me what to do with my hands. We end up with our arms around each other's shoulders, more like best pals at summer camp than adult lovers, but no one seems to care. They're all obsessed with Victor, and the flashbulbs surge every time he brushes his hand through his hair or lifts it in a wave. All I can do is remember Mom's advice—don't slouch, make eye contact, smile. If she could see me now. She'd probably just laugh. It's her life's mission to get me to laugh more often; she says I have a tendency to forget.

I'm still blinking away the lights in my eyes, a fake smile carved on my face, as we enter a huge lobby hung with banners and dotted with reception tables. TV crews jog back and forth between side doors and the conference room, moving their equipment.

Gray appears out of nowhere and gestures for us to follow him. He keeps glancing at Victor uneasily, until the man bugs his eyes out at him. "I'm *fine*."

The conference room looks just like what you see on TV—a bunch of chairs facing a raised table in front of a *Lang Media* backdrop. Each seat at the table has a microphone, a bottle of water, and a sheet of paper. I pick mine up as a stage hand shuffles me into place at the end of the table, next to Victor. It says "Tanner Faulks" on the top—my pseudonym—along with a few lines printed in the middle of the page.

> *How did you two meet?*
> *We met through comeVa. On our first date, I actually spilled coffee on him. (Pause for laughter). It was love at first "Oh God, I'm sorry." (Pause for more laughter)*

> *What's it like to date a celebrity?*
> *Our relationship is like any other, despite the fame. ComeVa connects people for their personalities and interests, not who they are, and I'll always be thankful for that.*

Smooth.

"You shouldn't have to say anything," Gray explains over my shoulder, looking as cool and unhurried as ever. "But if something happens, this is your backup. Werner will come in and make the announcement, then Victor will field a few short questions, softballs."

I crane my neck to see Victor's sheet, but he tilts it away from me. "Don't cheat." He clears his throat and pretends to read. "'I'm really a side piece in my boyfriend's sugar daddy arrangement with my father.'"

Ignoring him, I uncap my water and drink half of it in one go. My chest is so tight the cold makes it ache.

The crowd in the room starts to thicken, the low murmur growing in volume, and I can feel eyes all over me. I distract myself by checking my phone under the table, answering the text from Roy: *I can work tomorrow.* I need to anchor myself to the promise that there's a normal life waiting for me on the other side of this.

Victor

I put my hand on the back of Ethan's chair and lean into his personal space. To the rest of the room, it looks like we're sharing an intimate moment. They can't see the flash of disgust that crosses his face every time I get close to him. "So. I was thinking."

"God help us all." He looks anywhere but me, focused on sliding his water bottle from one hand to the other and back.

"We should throw this."

The bottle stops moving. "Huh?"

"You've already gotten paid. Just sit here and don't do anything to stop me."

"What are you going to do?" His eyes flick to my face. They're the color of summer sun through a glass of whiskey. Even though he just shaved, his cheeks already look stubbled. He's so *ordinary*, a dull, rough around the edges day laborer who can't imagine anything more to life. And he thinks he has the right to judge me.

"That's not your concern. You're not part of this family."

He shakes his head. "If you have beef with your father, settle it somewhere else. I thought you'd be tired of causing a scene in front of the press by now." He looks over his shoulder, like he's searching for someone to tattle to.

His body goes rigid when I hook a finger around the side of his jaw and turn his face to mine. "Be still and keep your mouth shut. I have plenty of ways to ruin your life." Why did I think it was a good idea to tell him in the first place? Sometimes when I'm around him I do things I don't understand and I *really* don't like it.

Before he can answer, the lights come up and my father walks onto the stage in a shower of applause and flashes.

I hate bright places. Nothing good ever happens in the light. Last time I was in front of the press, I hadn't slept in so long I thought the sun through the skylights was God coming down to burn me alive. Everyone had the same question.

Why?

Why did you do it?

No, really, why?

No matter what words came out of their mouths, the real question was always *why*. I was supposed to say *no comment*, but I kept messing up and saying *I don't know* instead. Eventually I just sat in my chair, forcing my eyes to stay open until my vision was written over with white that turned into a purple smear when I blinked. Part of me hoped I'd go blind.

Something kicks me underneath the table, and I jerk back to the present. My dad's still talking, spewing marketing bullshit. Ethan slides his water toward me. I ignore him.

As soon as questions are announced, every hand goes up. Gray, standing next to my father, points to a woman in the front row, who turns to me. "So we want to know all about this." She gestures between Ethan and I. "What a surprise! What does finding love mean to you, after everything that's happened? And how do you navigate such a complex relationship?"

My mouth opens, ready to ignore the question and go rogue, ruin my father's day. There's so much I can say, so many ways to bring this castle down as long as I'm willing to bring myself down with it. I could send this room into chaos with about five words. But just like the thousands of other times I desperately wanted to say those words, they all stick in my throat, choking me.

Then Ethan stirs next to me, taps his mic. Some moron who hasn't been briefed turns it on for him and the sound of his amplified throat-clearing makes everyone on stage freeze. This isn't in his script, and no one has any idea what he's going to say.

"It's funny." He props his elbows on the table, scooting closer, his voice deep and a little rough, so different from anything you'd expect to hear in the world of multi-billion-dollar business deals. "I used to have a poster of this guy on my bedroom wall. My cousin and I took swimming lessons because of him. He watched me sleep." He knows how to pause for laughter even without prompts. "Then, of course, certain controversial events happened." Gray stirs uneasily. My father is watching Ethan like a hawk.

"And I think what I've taken from it after meeting Victor is that it doesn't matter who you put on a pedestal; they're going to disappoint you. None of us can be great—most of us can't even be good. But what I appreciate about comeVa is that it gave us the chance to meet as people, independent of our pasts. Now that Victor's put in the work to get better and is ready to apologize for his actions—"

Mother*fucker*.

"—he's incredibly excited to start a new phase of life in his family's company by representing the app that brought us together." He breaks my rule, reaching out and clamping his hand around mine. "You'll be seeing a lot more of Victor Lang, and I think everyone should give the app a look, too."

Flushed, he flashes a million-dollar smile and sits back in his seat as the room fills with applause. Gray, looking vaguely stunned, hurries to end the press conference on a high note, even though I haven't said a damn thing.

As the mics cut out, Ethan leans in and puts an arm around me, like any doting boyfriend would. As I turn and rest my forehead against his, I can see the smug grin playing on his mouth, the defiance in his eyes. "You're dead." I tell him with a smile, squeezing his shoulder.

He stands up, brushing himself off. "I'm out of here. I hope the rest of your life is hell."

Gray ushers us off the stage into a back hallway. "Take a moment, drink some water, then get out there and start circulating."

I savor the sight of Ethan's eyes widening. "Did no one tell you about the reception when you were planning your mic drop?" His cocky stature melts as I sidle up and grab his hand to keep mine from shaking. Torturing him is a welcome distraction. "Come on, dear."

My father appears, impeccable and powerful in a suit that cost five times the rest of ours put together. He's a tough old bull; no matter how many years pass, he never shows any sign of weakness. Or empathy. Or human emotion. I can feel Ethan twitch as Dad puts a hand on his shoulder. "Good job, son. I don't appreciate the improvisation, but you earned your pay." His eyes flick over me like I'm not there, and he disappears in the direction of the lobby.

Chapter 10

VICTOR

I stumble into the alley behind the convention center, gulping in humid night air that smells of garbage. Holding the door open with my hip, I crouch on the concrete and put my head between my knees.

The room was packed with people—next to me, behind me, constantly moving and churning like a dark ocean. *He* could be there. Security would have let him in, no problem. I'm deep in one of my nightmares, absolutely certain that I'll turn around and find him right behind me, except this time I can't wake up and crawl into tight, locked places where I feel safe. So I set my untouched champagne on a table and took off down a random hallway, weaving through silent, high-ceilinged spaces until I found an escape route.

I lift my head and rub my eyes, studying the backs of the buildings around me. The one directly across says *Cosmos Club* in tattered, blue letters. Clubs are built for disappearing.

The back entrance leads me down a long, grimy passage that opens onto the dance floor, if it could be called that. The place is almost empty, and I can see why as I take in the faded furniture and dated mood lighting. A couple of dancers, one girl, one guy, gyrate to music people listened to when I was twelve.

The bartender's eyes widen when he sees me. He turns around and stares at the news broadcast playing on the TV behind him, showing the front of the building next door. He looks back at me like, *hallucination, explain yourself.*

I chuck a wad of cash on the bar and put my finger to my lips. Studying the back wall, I point to the tall, smoked-glass vodka bottles. "Get me a new one of those, the whole thing."

Carrying my prize to a booth in the corner, I gulp down a generous sample, flinching at the burn. I stretch my arms out on the table, which is sticky and smells of Lysol, and rest my face in them. Time starts to warp and slip, disappearing in chunks when I close my eyes. I didn't sleep at all last night.

"Found you."

I squint up at Ethan's sullen expression, his crossed arms. "Good job."

"They didn't notice you're gone yet." When I don't move, he shifts impatiently.

I pretend to stand up, then grab his arm and pull him into the seat next to me. "I've always believed money tastes so much sweeter when you have to earn it."

He snorts. "You haven't earned a penny in your life."

I take another mouthful of vodka and slide it over to him. "Got me." He examines the bottle for a minute, then wipes off the rim and takes such a dainty sip I burst out laughing.

"You're drunk already."

"Not really," I wheeze, wiping my eyes. "You're just so fucking funny." The music switches to a song I remember, and I hum it out of tune, tapping the side of the bottle. Ethan studies the dancers. The girl has her tits hanging out, but he only has eyes for the guy, shirtless and sweaty. I prop my chin on my hand and watch him until he feels my eyes.

"What?"

"So you *are* a homo."

"I never said I wasn't."

I'm so tired and hungry. Groaning, I lie on my back on the bench seat and prop my feet in his lap, hanging an arm over my eyes. I smile against my elbow as I feel him squirm out from under me, perching at the very end of the bench. "So you're a virgin."

"No."

"How many?"

"One."

"So you're a virgin."

When he stands up, I stretch out to occupy the whole bench. "Can we go?" he complains.

"Be my guest."

"I can't leave you here."

"I believe in you."

The table creaks and when I look up he's sitting on the edge of it, looking down at me with miserable, stubborn eyes. "I'll wait here until you're ready."

I prop my head up so I can drink. "Let me guess. Your one partner broke your heart and filled you with internalized homophobia that has crippled your ability to love yourself, but someday you'll meet a manic pixie dream twink who will teach you to smile again and help you rise from the ashes."

A slow shrug wasn't the response I expected. "Nah. I'm good." When I raise my eyebrow at him, his nose wrinkles slightly. "I just didn't care for it."

"Didn't care for what? Relationships? Sex? Being gay?"

"It's all fine, I guess. For other people."

To his credit, he finally gets me to sit up. I study him, fascinated, then drop my eyes to his crotch. "Is your dick a shriveled-up piece of jerky? It sure didn't feel like it the other day."

He crosses his legs, glaring. "It works. I just don't feel like it."

"This ex…" Forgetting I'm in a suit, I pull my knees up and rest my chin on them, my eyes fixed on his. "And this is important, so think hard—did you fuck him or did he fuck you?"

"Oh, for God's sake." He stands up and heads for the door.

I grab for him and miss, toppling off the bench. "Wait! You can't withhold crucial information from your therapist! How am I supposed to fix you?" Stretched out on my back on the grimy floor, I can't stop laughing. Alcohol is a trip on an empty stomach with no sleep.

He comes back and pulls the vodka out of my hand. "You couldn't even hold it together for a few hours, could you?"

"And you couldn't help but fuck with things that don't concern you."

"Sorry I ruined your life goal of OD'ing in a dumpster."

His phone rings loudly. The guy forgot to silence his cell during a national press broadcast. I start laughing again, even though my stomach hurts like fuck.

As soon as he sees the name on the screen, he practically runs out of the club.

I stop laughing and pull in a shaky breath. I'm on my ass on a dirty floor, not sure where I am, not sure I can stand up. My body aches to dive into cool water, but I don't remember the way to my hotel.

This used to happen all the time, every Friday night, my team and I going hard until we couldn't remember our own names. Then I'd wake up alone like this, or in some stranger's bed, and I'd call *him* to come get me, because I didn't have anyone else to ask in the whole world.

I stayed in my house for six years so this would never happen again.

"*Fuck*," I groan, dragging myself to my feet. The room stabilizes enough that I can walk to the men's restroom. I puke up a trail of vodka and spit, nothing else. Shivering, I dig out my emergency cigarettes and light one, watching myself in the mirror. My nose is running; my hair has escaped its gel. Cig dangling from my fingers, I follow Ethan out the door.

Through the warm, still air I can faintly hear the crowd in front of the convention center, but it's quiet here. My phone vibrates with a text from Gray: *Where are you?*

Ethan's standing in the gutter with his phone to his ear, looking for a cab. When he sees me, he says, "I'll call you back."

"Cabs are for old people. Wait, I'll drive you." I dig in my pocket, but the valet has my keys.

His lip curls. "One, you're hammered. Two, I'm never letting you find out where I live."

"How the hell do you think Gray showed up at your door?" God, that really makes him mad. "Anyway, you can't leave." I prop my shoulder against the wall and go to take a drag, but I must have dropped my cigarette somewhere between here and the bathroom. "You need to take me back to the convention center."

He shakes his head. "I'm done. My mom needs me."

I'm gonna black out here in the street, alone. No walls, no doors to protect me. I fold my arms behind my head and look up at the slice of dark purple sky between the buildings. "Isn't babysitting head cases kind of your thing?"

He stiffens, takes a step toward me, eyes burning in the dark. "If being a sack of shit is a mental disorder then yeah, you're certifiable. You think I feel sorry for you because you're a fucking degenerate has-been? You're nothing; I'm *sick* of all this 'oh, he's special,' 'be careful with him' *bullshit*."

I blink. "Who said that?"

"You think everyone doesn't talk about you behind your back? Even your buddy Gray."

With a deep sigh, I push off the wall. "Big words for the guy begging to suck off my Dad for a measly 20k and a suit. At least I know how much to charge."

"Ok, that's it." He unbuttons his blazer and starts toeing off his shoes in the middle of the sidewalk. I have to duck to avoid taking a jacket to the face. "Give that to your father," he yells. I didn't know such a taciturn guy was capable of yelling. He strips off his shirt and lobs it after the jacket, standing there in his undershirt with his wide shoulders tensed. "And that one's for Gray."

I stare as he drops his slacks to reveal cheap, black boxer briefs. Instead of throwing the pants, he walks up to me in sock feet and drapes them around my neck. They're warm. He leans in until his face is close to mine. "And you can shove those up your ass."

"Melodramatic, but points for style," I call after him as he stalks away toward the nearest intersection. And just like that, he's gone, leaving behind a pile of clothes like he was fucking raptured.

I pick up the vodka that he left behind and sit on the curb, picking at the nasty-ass leaves stuck in the gutter drain. With my other hand, I pull out my phone and dial Gray.

Ethan

Even the permanent smell of Irish Spring soap in my house feels comforting as I sneak in the front door well after midnight. I'd smell it for the rest of my life if it meant never seeing Victor again. Mom's in bed, calming down from her panic attack, but Ana gives my sparse attire a weird look as I see her off.

I pull on some sweats and go for a piss. When I'm done, I catch myself just standing in front of the toilet, dick out, staring at my bathroom cupboard. My stomach aches and my head is pounding and my mouth tastes bad, even though I didn't drink. Most of all, I feel like I did years ago, before Mom and I got our lives in order: hanging on the edge of sanity and wired, like I'm going to be awake for days.

Slowly, I open the cabinet and dig through the half-empty dandruff shampoos and expired cold medicine for a small, orange bottle. I set it on the counter and stare at my name on the label. The one time I got desperate enough to see a psychiatrist for anxiety, he wrote me a Xanax prescription, which was the exact reason I didn't want to go in the first place. Like I needed an addiction on top of everything else. I threw it in the cupboard and never looked back.

Twenty-thousand dollars sounded like so much, but it's going to disappear in a second and we will always, always need more. You have no skills and no way out. You'll go on like this until Mom dies without even knowing your name, and then you'll be too broken to start over. You should have just let go, in that lake with Danny. Followed him to the bottom.

Digging out an old straight razor, I shave a flake off one of the thick, white pills. I'm scared; I don't like being drunk or high, even laughing gas at the dentist. I need to stay in control. But tonight, I need the fear to stop more. Wetting the tip of my finger, I put the flake on my tongue, rinsing it down with tap water.

Then I pad down the hall to Mom's room. She's lying in bed, curled in a ball, eyes open as she half-listens to the audiobook Ana put on. I can see dried tears on her cheeks.

As soon as I fill the doorway, she sits up and holds out her arms, tearing up again. Ana said that she panicked when she couldn't find me. I switch off the audiobook and turn out the lights, lifting the covers and sliding in next to her. She nestles against my side and rests her head on my chest. "You smell strange," she whispers. "Is it you?"

"It's me." I put my wrist to my nose in the dark, catching another whiff of Victor's cologne. I can't wait to wash it off and smell like sweat and dollar store hand soap again. "I'm here."

"I can't sleep."

Cradling her head, I roll onto my side and wrap her in my arms. "Close your eyes, ok?" When she obeys, I rest my face against her hair. There's an ache behind my eyes and in my chest, a tangled nest of fear and sadness, anger and self-loathing.

You did what you had to do. Now you never have to see those people again.

I wrap my cold hand around her warm one and squeeze, releasing all the tight muscles in my body. "We're going to go on a trip around the world, as soon as I save up," I whisper, reciting familiar words like a bedtime story that's new to her every time.

"Really?"

"Uh-huh. Where do you want to go?"

Her breathing steadies against my chest. "Where's that jungle temple on the mountain?"

"Machu Picchu? That's in the Andes. You think we should get a llama to carry our stuff up there?"

There's a smile in her sleepy voice. "I like llamas."

"After Peru, I think we should go to Costa Rica. Get a tan. Your turn."

"I want to see Baker Street." We used to watch stuff like *Sherlock* together, and Mom was always the first to guess the culprit.

"London it is."

She stirs. "Didn't you say Danny's in London?"

"Shhh." I smooth her forehead. "Keep your eyes shut. Let's take a train to France from London."

We're walking across the sands of Egypt, looking for the Sphinx, when she drifts off. Usually I sneak out, but tonight I just want to stay. I keep whispering, guiding her dreams from the desert to the snows of Russia, then the Great Wall of China.

"And if the steps are too steep, I'll carry you."

Listening to our heartbeats sync, I start to feel a slow, creeping kind of peace. I wish, as I disappear into the darkness, that I didn't live in a world where the only way not to hurt was to shut everything out and live among your dreams.

Chapter 11

Ethan

When I show up for my extra shift the next morning, Scooter and the boys are sitting around the boss's computer. They stare at me with wide eyes as I pull off my t-shirt and don my polo. "What?"

"It's not him." Daryl shakes his head. "You owe me three hundred."

"It *is*. He has the same crooked hairline." Scooter isn't in a position to be criticizing anyone's hairline. I lean over the desk until I can see the monitor, and nearly lose my balance. They're looking at a *USA Today* article featuring a massive photo of Victor and I on the red carpet. "Who's that?"

"What do you mean, *who's that*? It's you," Scooter protests.

I cross my arms and stare at him deadpan, targeting the uncertain tone in his voice.

"Think through what you just said."

"But you went to his house last week, right?"

I jab my finger at the article. "Did Bill Gates ask you out when you were transplanting his zinnias?"

"Pay up," Daryl snaps. "What a fucking stupid bet."

Ray sticks his head in the door. "Off your asses, guys. Ethan, wait for that shipment of fertilizer and help them stack it."

As the boys file out, I collapse in the desk chair and dry-swallow a couple of ibuprofen, praying it will erase the effects of last night. I scoot the chair closer to the desk and study the photo. It's surreal, like seeing my face glued onto a stranger. Victor looks amazing, bright and clean and confident and perfect, completely eclipsing me. They should have printed a shot of him hammered on the floor in that shitty club.

My heart sinks when I skim the article.

> *The return of the prodigal prince of swimming has broken the internet, but his handsome, mysterious boyfriend, Tanner Faulks, has blown it to smithereens. Everyone wants to know who managed to turn around one of the biggest falls from grace in sports history and teach him the power of love! The two made quite the sight on the red carpet, and Tanner's passionate endorsement of the app comeVa has kicked off over a million downloads since last night. If I could find a guy half as hot as either of these two, I'd say it's worth the subscription fee. We can't wait to see more of them as they kick off an ad campaign for the app.*

My first stupid instinct is to make an account and post comments insisting that no one is going to see more of his boyfriend ever again. Fortunately, the fertilizer delivery arrives and I focus on helping them stack the unwieldy bags. Going back to honest work—arms covered in dirt and an aching back—calms my racing thoughts.

When I walk back into the front office, Werner Lang is sitting in my chair like a Bond villain, reaching around Scooter's bikini girl bobblehead collection to scroll through the news article. I'm about to spin around and sneak back out, but the sound of the door alerts him.

"He was less than a block away," I stammer. I've already sent a loan repayment from the funds; if he wants his money back, there's nothing I can do. "I thought—"

"I don't know what you're referring to, nor do I want to."

I shut up instantly, wondering why Victor didn't tell his father that I abandoned him.

He taps the computer screen, distorting the picture. "Did you read this?"

"Yes."

"This is what it means to be powerful, Ethan. You opened your mouth and a million people downloaded the app. If they each pay five dollars a month to use it, you're now bringing in five million dollars a month."

My knees go weak, and I sit against the back of a desk.

His eyes narrow with a nasty gleam I recognize from his son. "And you accepted a single payment of twenty thousand dollars."

I swallow. "You've all made it very clear that you exploited me. I get it; I'm stupid. I didn't go to college."

He offers a dry smile, changing the subject abruptly. "They say he's beyond saving, that he can't love. What do you think?"

"I..." I massage the back of my neck, trying to ease my headache. "I have no idea. I never thought about it." But that's a lie, because something in the back of my mind has been turning it over ever since the article mentioned the word *love*.

Even after seeing the worst of Victor Lang, I can't bring myself to say he's a lost cause. I don't believe in lost causes. I still believe good always wins and love can prevail, which is fucking stupid when you think about everything that's happened to me.

"Your speech to the press gave you away." He smirks a little. "You think *you* could save him. It's nothing to be ashamed of. Gray says he's never seen him latch onto someone the way he has with you."

I never in a million years thought I could save him, is what I should say. Instead, I just stand there, listening to the bubbling of the dirty aquarium at the back of the office. The guys could walk back in at any moment. "Can I help you?" I prompt.

"As you've heard, we're off to Italy next week to create the campaign for the app relaunch. We didn't expect this, but people want to see both of you—"

I start shaking my head. "No. Absolutely not."

"One point five million."

I bite back a groan, grip tightening on the desk, fighting to stay cool. "You just told me I was worth five mil a month."

He chuckles. "Two million, and all expenses paid toward your mother's health over the next five years. I know a doctor in California, best rate of dementia reversal in the world. I'll fly you two down to see him. And if that doesn't work, we'll put her in the best care home in the country."

"You're lying."

He smiles for real, and it's just as soulless and conniving as his fake one. "It's less than one five-hundred-thousandth of my net worth. Do you understand how small that is?" He stands up. "It's time for you to decide how you feel about fate. Maybe a freak accident brought together the only man who can get through to my son and the only man who can give your mother the help she needs."

I know he's just saying what I want to hear, playing me like a fucking violin, pretending this is anything more than a ploy to add more billions to his billions. "No." But my voice is weak.

If someone's going to save that son of a bitch, it won't be me.

For some reason, that thought isn't as satisfying as it should be.

"Ethan!" Mom shakes my shoulder.

I lower my phone and crane my neck in her lap until I'm looking at the bottom of her chin. "Yeah?"

She points at the TV. "She set her oven timer for one hundred minutes instead of ten." The cooking show has framed a fantastic shot of the contestant happily chopping vegetables as a steady column of smoke rises from her oven behind her.

"Shit." I laugh when she pinches my arm for swearing. Unlike the woman on TV, Mom's a great cook—I have a fat stack of notecards where I've written down her best recipes so she can still make them when she forgets the original.

I half-watch the chef in question cry over her blackened dish while Mom's fingers run through my hair, damp from the shower. This is the one place I can always relax—except for today. I reach out and grab the remote, muting the show. "Mom?"

"What is it, hon?"

Groaning, I sit up and brush my hair back, folding my legs on the couch so I can sit facing her. "I did someone a...favor the other day. And now he wants another one, and I'm not sure what to do."

Her forehead creases as she frowns, concerned. "What kind of favor?"

I was going to lie again, but there's a chance she'll see me on TV or in a photo. And unlike Scooter, she won't have trouble recognizing me; I'm the only person she's never forgotten. Not yet.

I opt for a half-truth. "They were looking for models to shoot photos for an ad, and they liked me. They want me to go overseas for a week or two with them."

Her eyes widen in surprise, and I feel my face getting hot. "It's ok, you can laugh. Me as a model, right?"

She puts a hand on my cheek. "No, you're very handsome, when you try. The rest of the time you're a little messy." This time I laugh for real. "Do you want to go?"

I take a deep breath. "I want to stay here with you. But they said they'd pay our medical expenses—nurses, medicine, the best of everything. They said there's a doctor in California, a new one, and he's really good."

Her smile fades a little. She squeezes my arm, interrupting my rambling. "We've heard that before." We have. And that's just the stuff she remembers. I've lost more money than I would ever tell her on the next doctor, the next therapy, the next hope, all for nothing.

"Yeah, but—"

She scoots closer and takes my hand. "You're the best son anyone could ask for. But I've been thinking a lot, on good days, and I'm starting to come to terms with things. None of this is going to fix me, honey."

I shift, my chest going tight. "Mom..."

"I just want to enjoy you and our little life while I can, not drain all your resources, your future, trying to chase something that can't happen."

"I know." I pick at a loose thread on the couch cushion, unable to look her in the face. I'll say what she wants to hear, but I don't believe it. I can't. She's just making me even more determined to keep fighting. She thinks there will be something left of me when she's gone, but I've given her everything I am and the thought of losing not only her but myself is terrifying.

"If you want to go, you should do it for yourself, not me."

"I'll think about it." I stand up, kiss her on the cheek.

There are a few dented beer cans in the back of the fridge from the days when I had spare time to drink. I fish one out and take it to the back porch. The sun is setting in the remnants of a rain storm tattered across the sky. Our neighbor's massive dog throws himself against the fence, enraged that I dare to show my face.

I tip my head back against the side of the house and close my eyes. Maybe none of us can be saved. Or maybe, like Werner said, I've been handed the key to saving everyone.

Because Victor was right. Trying to fix lost causes has always been my thing. All of them except myself.

Chapter 12

Victor

All fifteen or whatever the hell of my suitcases are zipped up and piled together, taking up most of my bedroom floor. I tried to remember the old days, what I packed for a trip and what I left behind, but today I felt the panicked need to bring everything I own. It's all part of an intricate system for keeping myself safe and sane, and I don't know how to let go of any of it, even for a week.

I should be dressed in something beyond a Hard Rock Cafe t-shirt and briefs, but instead I crawl over the bags and into my rat's nest of a bed, a bare mattress topped with a mountain of blankets and pillows. I wedge my way underneath them and take out my phone. Nothing but a text from Gray—*Ten minutes away. Be ready this time.*

Sorry, buddy.

Chewing on a hangnail, I flick open the comeVa app. Ethan doesn't have social media—one of the reasons they hired him—but something told me to poke around in the app and yesterday I found him in a masterful piece of detective work, under the name Carter Lowe. Must be his middle name.

I open his profile again. *24, gay, loves animals and ultimate frisbee, secretly good at jigsaw puzzles.* I rub my fingers in my eyes and groan. He's *so* boring. God got halfway done making him, said *good enough*, and shat him out.

There's just that one thing, that niggling instinct in my gut, the question he refused to answer in the club last week. I want to pull him open and find out if there's anything hiding inside.

The first couple of pictures are typical crap—posing in front of the Space Needle, a selfie with some aunt's cousin's sister's dog.

In the last photo, he's leaning on a tree after a jog, clothes clinging to his damp body, his free hand tucked up under his shirt to show a hint of abs. He has one eye closed under his sweaty tousle of hair, the other squinting at the camera, and a half grin.

Squirming out of the blankets, I stretch onto my back and slide down the front of my briefs. I prop his photo on the windowsill where I can see it and hold the hem of my shirt in my teeth, my nipples hardening from even the barest breath of cool air on my chest.

And I just touch myself, persistently, aimlessly. I run my fingers around my navel, out to my hips, down the flare of my ass. I bounce my balls gently in my hand, run my thumb up the top of my hardening shaft. I rest my cock in my palm and squeeze it, rub the head. I'm half asleep and barely trying, just chasing what feels good, but my cock starts to thrum, thickening, my balls heavy and tight.

My body's an insatiable slut; it's so easy to turn on, any time, any way. Guys love it, but it's really a nightmare. I can't control my own body and the things it wants, the things it asks for, and I can't tell the difference anymore between fear and lust.

My head's just empty as I stare at the picture of him, alone in my room, sliding my hand between my legs to find my hole. Quiet, unconscious sounds slip from my throat as I play with it the way he probably could if I taught him.

Abruptly, I give up and curl into a ball, underwear around my knees, and close my eyes until Gray bangs on the door.

I pull on a pair of leggings and running shorts and a hoodie as he slots my bags into the car like a game of Tetris. He informs me that we need to pick up Ethan on the way to the airport, like we're operating a shuttle bus. "My father owns more than one car," I gripe, slouching in the front seat and breaking open the iced Frappuccino bottle he brought me.

Propping my sneakers on the dashboard, I stare out the window as we creep into a frumpy little neighborhood full of old trees and cheap cars and recycling bins lined up on the curb. Ethan's tiny brick house has a half-dead crabapple tree in the yard and a moss-covered roof.

"Go fetch him," Gray orders, taking away my coffee.

"You're kidding me."

"That's your punishment for making us late."

"Fuck you." I unfold from the car and limp up the driveway, avoiding the weeds and sugar ant trails.

The doorbell doesn't seem to work, so I open the storm door and kick the red-painted front door. I hop from one foot to the other, stressing out. I haven't visited someone's house in so long that I don't remember how it works.

A woman in her fifties opens the door. Her brown hair is braided and she's wearing a sweatshirt with cartoon cats sailing a boat. She beams at me. "You're here for Ethan, right?" For a second, I think she's going to recognize me, but nothing happens. I guess it's that thing, whatever's wrong with her. "Come in!"

"I—" I point mutely at the idling SUV at the curb, but she just waves me inside.

"He's almost ready."

I'm hit with that smell he had at the hotel. Old person soap and potpourri. There's a jumble of shoes in the entry, under a cross-stitch that says *Cats welcome, people tolerated*. In the living room, a puffy couch faces a brick fireplace and a TV playing some cooking show on mute. There's a huge table by the back door with a half-finished puzzle of a lighthouse.

"Can I get you a drink?" This woman smiles a lot, but she has sad eyes. I pictured a little old lady raving in a wheelchair, but she's just a normal person.

"Are you a model, too?" she asks, refusing to leave me alone.

"A model?" My lips twitch. "Is that what he told you?"

"*Hey*," Ethan half-shouts, like he's trying to stop a dog from pissing on a couch rather than greeting someone. He shoves his suitcase between his mother and me. I raise my eyebrows at him and enjoy the horror on his face from seeing me in his precious house.

Something warm tickles my legs, and I jump. The something mews and looks up at me with big, green eyes. "Uh, hi."

Mrs. Lowe sweeps the cat up and cuddles it to her chest. "Her name is Petunia. Ethan got her when he was twelve."

She seems to expect something from me, so I reluctantly poke Petunia's head. She purrs and rubs my knuckles. Mrs. Lowe holds the cat out to Ethan. "Kiss her goodbye."

A small smile cracks his mask and he gives the creature a peck on the head. "Ok, Mom," he says awkwardly, voice thick. "Ana and Peyton will be here for you, and you can call me whenever you want."

I stuff my hands deep in my pockets and wait to be elsewhere as he folds her in his arms and buries his face in her neck. I wonder if they've ever been apart this long in his life. It's kind of a relief my own mom just abandoned me.

"Wait." He squeezes her tighter, sounding scared. "I can't do this."

She gently pushes him away. "Go. I'll be ok." I stare at the plaster ceiling, looking for shapes. I find a horse and a cock. Then Ethan storms past me into the yard, carrying his bag, and I find myself standing alone with his mom, who has tears in her eyes.

"Okaay." I sidle for the door. "See you around."

"Wait, I forgot!" She runs into the kitchen and comes back with two small wax paper packets. "These are for you and Ethan, for the airport." They warm my palm; when I look inside, I see two gooey chocolate-chip cookies. When I was in grade school, the moms were supposed to bring cookies the first Friday of every month. My mom, being in Germany with her new family, of course left me without cookies. One of the girls in the class gave me hers, and they felt like this. Hot, heavy, a little oily. Good.

"I don't—"

"Take care of each other, ok?" When she reaches for my shoulder, I step back.

"You bet."

I pick my way across the muddy, crabapple-strewn yard back to the car, snagging shotgun before Ethan can. I pull on headphones and lean against the door, closing my eyes.

If my life is as strange to you as yours is to me, maybe I understand why you hate me so much. Rest assured, it's mutual.

On the freeway, I take off my headphones and hold up the cookies. "Your mom likes me."

Just as I'm about to toss them into the back seat, he jerks forward against the seatbelt, glaring at me. "Don't think about, speak of, or interact with my mother ever again."

"Understood. Please forgive me." I roll down the window and lob the cookies out onto the highway, watching the wax paper flutter away in the wind.

"Jesus Christ." Gray presses a hand to his head as someone behind us honks. "Victor, can we not?"

I roll up the window and grin at Ethan. *If that's how you want to play, then let's go. You're on my turf now. Good luck.*

Chapter 13

Ethan

You know you've arrived in life when you drive *past* all the losers in the airport terminal and cruise over to a row of private hangers. I've been pretending all week that I'm not scared of heights and speed and tight spaces. Now that I'm staring down a plane that looks way too small to make it across the state, let alone an ocean, I'm pretty sure I'm going to die on the very first flight of my life.

I freeze in the doorway of the plane, hunting for an excuse to turn around and run. Then something hits the backs of my knees so hard I almost fall over. Victor herds me expressionlessly with the edge of his giant bag, which he got to keep even though the crew forced me to surrender mine. "It's cold out here," he complains through the passport clamped between his teeth, even though it's a summer afternoon and he's wearing a hoodie.

The interior is all chrome, wood, and beige—I guess rich people would call it *champagne*. Four pairs of double-wide recliner seats take up most of the cabin. This might be a death trap, but that doesn't mean my long legs and wide shoulders won't appreciate the extra space.

"Good afternoon, sir." A stewardess interrupts my gawking, handing me a glass of white wine with a vaguely impatient smile and shunting me out of the way. I turn around to see Victor put his hand on her arm and murmur something in her ear. She lets him into the galley and he comes back with a full bottle of Riesling tucked under his arm.

Throwing his suitcase in an open seat, he circles me, eyes lit with mischief. "Where do you wanna sit? Everyone says window, but I think aisle is great for spending the whole flight wondering if we're losing altitude or if it's just your imagination."

"*Sit down.*" Gray stalks past, pushing us out of the way. "We're on a schedule."

As soon as Werner walks in, Victor's attitude evaporates. He slinks to his seat and pulls on headphones, tipping his bottle of wine down his throat.

I straighten up, trying to catch the old man's eye. I just need one word or gesture to acknowledge that he brought me here for a reason and they're going to take care of me.

He strides down the aisle without so much as a glance at anyone, through a door at the back of the cabin. I catch a glimpse of a table and some more seats before one of his staff members slams it shut. *Great.*

I take a window seat as far from Victor as I can get, and fumble my seatbelt with sweaty hands. Gray gives me a slightly sympathetic look before turning to a folder of paperwork in his lap.

I stiffen when the plane starts rolling along like a giant car, engines revving. The wine dries out my throat and makes me dizzy as my heart starts pounding against my ribs. I don't know how this thing gets into the air, and I don't want to find out.

The stewardess comes through the cabin, nodding at my seatbelt. Victor's eyes are closed, so she gingerly steps over his legs and straps in his bag. "Please stay in your seats until we reach altitude," she announces, though I'm the only one paying attention. "This plane has all the standard safety features; please let me know if you have any questions." Before I can open my mouth, she walks behind the bulkhead and sits down.

I *do* have motherfucking questions. What's a standard safety feature? How hard would it be for another passenger to throw me out of the plane mid-flight? The pit in my stomach turns into a yawning chasm.

The engines pitch up into a roar that sounds like they're about to rip themselves off the wings, and I feel myself tip backwards, pressed into my seat. One glimpse out the window, a terrible mistake, shows the world dropping away at a disturbing angle. I pry one hand off the arm rest to slam down the shutter.

The whole plane bucks, tearing a whimper from my throat. The stewardess doesn't even look up from her phone. Just as I'm telling myself to get it together, it happens again, worse this time, like we just dropped hundreds of feet. I grab my arm rest hard enough to risk cracking the plastic.

When I open my eyes, Victor's sprawled sideways in his chair, headphones pushed off one ear, watching me with a huge, shit-eating grin on his face. It just gets bigger when I point a middle finger in his direction. "Did you know sometimes they find wrenches and missing screws flying around the engine compartment?" he offers helpfully.

Shutting him out, I grab my phone and open the e-book Peyton loaded up for me, one of her favorites. It's a thriller called *The Wives Across the Street* or some shit, and it's not nearly interesting enough to overwrite my noisy thoughts.

What the fuck have you just done? She's going to need you, and you won't be there. You should have just worked harder, instead of trying to take the easy way by doing a deal with the devil.

When I look up thirty minutes later, after the new woman in town who is probably a ghost seduced the main character's husband, Victor's asleep. He slid onto the floor and wedged his back into a corner. All his limbs are wrapped around a pillow, his head tipped back, neck open, lips parted as he snores lightly. He took the athletic band out of his hair and pulled up his hood, loose curls hanging over his forehead.

Like this, he looks almost innocent. I have a weird urge to make sure no one disturbs him.

Something rustles, and I look up to see Gray sitting down next to me. He follows my gaze to Victor, and studies him for a moment. I think I hear him sigh. "I want to get started briefing you."

"What about him?"

He makes a gesture like something's flying into his ear, then out the other side. "You can pass it on later."

"That doesn't seem ideal." A shift in his eyebrows shuts me up.

"You signed up for this. You're not going to earn your pay sitting around posing for pictures." His voice drops. "Believe it or not, it's going well so far. He's asleep."

"He's not sleeping because of me."

Gray doesn't answer. He slaps a notebook in front of me. "Take notes. When we reach the Regale Naples hotel—remember that name if you get lost—tomorrow morning, you'll be meeting the director and going to a private room for some screen tests. Then we'll attend a formal luncheon."

I scrawl as fast as I can in my bad handwriting.

"You two have one job: keep your mouths shut and look like you're in love. The faster we finish, the sooner we can go home."

"And I'm supposed to make him behave himself. Did you not see him scatter my mother's parting gift across I-405?"

Gray ignores me. "If you're by yourselves, don't say *anything* but 'more water please' or '*non parlo italiano*'. Assume everyone is a member of the press trying to get a sound bite. And if someone on the street recognizes him, make a prompt and graceful exit. When in doubt, kiss, smile, and get the hell out."

"Just like that, huh?"

"Is that a problem?"

"Have you ever gotten paid to kiss a stranger?"

"Not since his gigolo days," Victor croaks, pushing his hood out of his eyes. "He had a monster dick but they fired him because he thought dirty talk was telling someone how to do their taxes."

Pretending he didn't hear, Gray takes my phone off my knee and types into it. "That's our emergency security line. We don't anticipate many problems in Italy, but we're always prepared."

He gets up, giving Victor a warning look and disappearing into the chamber of important people at the back of the plane. Victor yawns and stretches like a little kid, then crawls out of his nest and flops into the seat facing mine. He strokes a long finger along the lines of my notebook. "Good boy doing his job." There's a nasty smile in his sleep-thick voice.

On the far side of the cabin, the evening sun burns orange through the windows. It's time for Mom's herbal tea. I left instructions for Ana but she can't call me if she has a question. *She's a caretaker, of course she can make tea.*

"You know what?" I pitch the notebook across the cabin, watching the pages flap and scatter. "Who fucking cares. Just leave me alone." I lean my head against the wall and try to fall asleep.

There's a pause so long I think he left. "This is about the cookies, isn't it?" He sounds weirdly proud, like he came up with an insightful observation. He has the emotional intelligence of a piece of tree bark. "They have cookies in Italy, you know."

"Will you fucking *stop*. I don't give a shit about cookies." When I open my eyes, I see that he's propped one of his black and gold sneakers against my seat, directly between my legs.

"Why are you such a loser?" he asks conversationally, bouncing his heel so my whole seat wobbles. "I looked at your dating profile. There isn't a single interesting thing about you."

"I don't have time to be interesting."

"Why not?" He focuses on picking a loose thread out of his hoodie cuff.

"Some people have to work for a living." Sick of the jiggling, I grab his shoe and hold his foot still.

He doesn't look at me, but the corner of his mouth twitches up. "Don't touch me. Some people have interesting jobs."

"I was going—"

When I stop, he glances up. "You were going to what?"

"I'm not telling you a single thing about me."

He stretches the thread tight and bites it off. "If I picked a boyfriend, he wouldn't be boring. We'd have all kinds of secrets and lies."

"He sure as hell wouldn't be with you for your personality."

He hesitates a split second. "Obviously not, with an ass like mine." Putting his foot down, he leans forward and grabs a fistful of my hair, using it to turn my face to one side and then the other. "I'll keep you for now, but you're going to have to figure out how to entertain me."

Since I can't touch him, I just stare at him until he lets go. "Are you really him?" I ask, studying this manspreading puddle of athleisure in front of me. "Are you really *the* Victor Lang?"

His eyes look so tired. "I ask myself that all the time."

Victor

I guess I doze off in the seat across from Ethan, which is weird because I can never fall asleep unless I feel safe. When I jolt awake out of a bad dream, he's still across from me, watching a movie on the fold-out TV. I don't want him to look at me, so I pull my hood down over my face and curl up in my seat, folding the hem of my shirt around my fingers again and again, threading my finger through a small hole, making it larger.

"Supper, gentlemen?"

Ethan's eyes widen when the stewardess offers him a crab salad; I think he expected cardboard trays of sludge. I shake my head when she tries to serve me.

When she offers drinks, Ethan asks for a rum and coke. He should be careful drowning his sorrows on a plane. He still looks pale and queasy.

Taking swigs of my wine, I watch him pick at the salad. "She could probably microwave some chicken nuggets if it would make you more comfortable."

He takes a deep, sulky pull of his drink. "Aren't you hungry?"

"Mmm." I put my feet up on the seat next to me and try to ignore the smell of his food. Gray was supposed to give me a protein bar from his bag, but he's still in the back and I'm sure as hell not opening that door.

Ethan turns his movie back on and chows down his salad, examining bits of crab and sun-dried tomato on his fork like he's never seen anything like it before. When he sees me looking at him, he nudges the TV screen until I can see it too. He's watching one of the movies with all the superheroes mixed together. Even without sound, I can zone out and watch people blast each other with particle effects and martial arts kicks. I recognize Spiderman and The Hulk from my childhood, but I don't know much about them or why they're working together. Even so, when the movie ends, I sit up incredulously. "Wait, seriously?"

He pulls off his headphones, scraping up the last few pieces of lettuce. "What?"

"Are they all dead?"

He gets a mischievous look in his eye. "Yeah, all of them. There will never be another superhero, ever. Audiences rioted in the streets."

I arch my eyebrow. "That's fucking stupid."

Ethan orders another rum and coke as the stewardess takes his plate.

"Don't show up in Italy sloshed," I warn. *Or I'll have to face it alone.*

He looks pointedly at the half-empty bottle of wine hugged against my stomach. Wordlessly, I hold it out to him. This time, he forgets to wipe the rim before he drinks. He starts another movie, one with a lot of guns.

And wouldn't you know, I fucking fall asleep again. He's dangerous for me.

When I wake up, the lights are off and the cabin is empty. Heart thudding, I crane my neck and look for Ethan, then climb out of my seat with a groan. I need to pee, but the bathroom door is locked. *Found him.*

I kick the door. "Open up."

When no one answers, I kick it harder. "Come on."

I could find the stewardess or Gray, but something tells Ethan isn't going to want that. Sighing, I dig a credit card out of my wallet and start jimmying the lock. I manage to shunt the latch out of position and yank the door open.

Well then.

Ethan's curled into a ball against the wall, half-asleep, half-sick, arms wrapped around himself. The toilet's full of vomit. His hair's a mess, his skin pale.

"Hey there." I wedge myself into the bathroom and sit cross-legged on the cold rubber floor next to him. He can barely open his eyes. "You're a mess, aren't you?"

He groans and grips the edge of the toilet, but I don't think there's anything left in him. Eventually he lies back, closing his eyes again.

"I know it's scary," I hum quietly. "I know." I grab some paper towels and wet them, straddling his legs and holding the back of his head. I clean off his face, his full lips and stubbly cheeks, until he's good as new.

"Come on, big guy." There's no way I'm picking him up, but I get his arm over my shoulders and hoist us both to our feet. He moans grumpily. "God. You're heavy."

Waking up a little, he lets me guide him down the aisle and lower him into a seat. Leaning against the bulkhead, I watch him try to get comfortable. I know he hurts. I know he's thirsty. Because I've been here, too. I dig around the galley for some water and put it to his mouth, tipping it gently until his throat moves. This time I wipe off his lips with my thumb. There's a cupboard with blankets at the back, so I pull a couple out and throw them over him. He's going to feel like hell tomorrow.

I fold myself into the seat next to him and open the window shade, looking out into the night and the darker night beyond, knowing there's a sun, moon, and stars out there somewhere that I can't see.

If only someone had done this for me. If only.

But I don't deserve the same things as him. He's a simple, pure person, made of cats and cookies and little brick houses full of afternoon sunlight. I'm made of mud and broken things, deep water and suffocation. I pinch my nose and hold it tight shut until the pressure behind my eyes goes away. I need to be swimming right now, free and untouchable, outrunning the dark.

Ethan

I dream of a warm weight against my shoulder. I dream of a voice, very close, quiet as wind on a still day. "I lied. I like how you smell."

When I open my eyes, sun pours through the window into my lap, warming my stiff fingers. I'm alone in the cabin, but the seat next to me holds someone's body heat. Pain occupies the space where my memory of last night should be. My mouth tastes like sick.

A door opens, and Gray taps my shoulder. "Buckle up for landing."

Blinking the grit out of my eyes, I scoot over to the window and watch the clouds part over Italy. My chest drops when the plane banks, but I focus on the huge, sparkling sea and rocky coastline. I flex my jaw to ease the pain in my ears.

Victor doesn't deign to appear until I can count the trees along the roads that wind through olive-colored hills. He's freshly showered in tight-ass black jeans and a white shirt with a gold designer logo that highlights his tan. Pulling a beanie over his tangled hair, he slides into his seat and rests his forehead against the bulkhead wall in front of him. The bone at the top of his spine peeks out the neck of his shirt, and the sleeves hang loose around his biceps. He hiccups a couple of times, then buries his head in his arms and holds his breath until they stop.

I hate that I look for him whenever he's not here. I hate the relief when he appears, like all the bad ways he makes me feel are the only anchor I have.

bend me to the shape
of everything you've lost

Chapter 14

ETHAN

Even the sky looks different here, high clouds and morning sun silvered with a shimmering haze that makes everything feel ancient. Mom and I always promised we'd see the world together, and for a minute I forget that she's not here and point at a mountain looming on the horizon. "That's Vesuvius, right there," I say in wonder, quoting the in-flight map.

Victor shoves past, almost knocking me down the stairs to the tarmac. "Thanks, PBS special." I imagine the volcano exploding in a cloud of ash, coating us in lava. Watching Victor burn to death and then sleeping forever sounds worth it.

Feeling dazed and a little nauseous, I follow Victor toward a row of three black cars, idling as if wasting even a second would bring civilizations crashing down. I spot a glitter of press cameras at the fence a few hundred yards away, and Victor puts up a hand to block his face.

Werner gets into the first car, Gray into the passenger seat of the second. Victor shoves himself and most of his luggage into the back like a hoarding dragon, leaving barely any room for me. I shut the door and search between Louis Vuitton carry-on bags for the end of my seatbelt. It's tempting to throw a few out the window as we pull out of the airport gates, show him how it feels.

Gray turns around in his seat. "It's go time now, boys. You're *on* at all times, except in your room."

Victor looks sullen and squinty in the bright morning, long, dusty lashes framing his pale irises. When he sees me watching him, he sticks out his tongue and mimes stuffing two fingers down his throat.

"Love you too." I turn to the window. Where the Pacific Northwest is all dark pines and fog, the light in this place sparkles across dusty, sunbaked grass and tawny stone buildings. Between two hills, I catch a glimpse of the sea, bright as a jewel. With a rustle, Victor sits up and stares intently, hunger in his eyes. His knuckles flex where he's gripping his seatbelt. Maybe that explains what's wrong with us—the same endless void that terrifies me calls to him.

I turn on my phone and dial Mom, before remembering she's asleep. *Landed safe. I love you.* I hope that if she was scared, she fell asleep holding the t-shirt I left her. I text Peyton: *Have her call me when she wakes up.*

It's actually kind of peaceful in the car, swooping around the curves with the sunlight moving across my skin, listening to a radio DJ speak a million miles an hour in a language I don't know. Then Gray takes a call on his cell. "Damn." He speaks briskly to the driver in Italian, then turns around. "You won't be able to settle in before we meet the director and board members." My eyebrows go up as the car slows and pulls into a gas station, splashing through puddles on the dirty concrete. "Go inside and change. Your suits are in the trunk."

"Seriously?" Victor slides down in his seat until his knees are curled up against his chest. "It's gross."

"Do you want us to make out in front of the cashier on the way?" My snark surprises all of us, most of all me. Victor can't stifle a giggle.

Gray looks at me like *not you, too*. "Hurry up."

We've entered an urban area on the edge of Naples, and it smells like gas and burned tires as I climb out of the car. Traffic flows steadily past, just like it does everywhere else in the world. The air clings to my skin, slides along the sweat at the back of my neck. When the trunk springs open, I rummage around and pull out two garment bags, hanging them awkwardly over my arm. There's no way to be subtle about this.

The speakers in the convenience store are blasting an Italian pop ballad that's way too cheerful for the bad lighting and floors covered in dirty shoe prints. The cashier, a large, oily man, doesn't look up or remove his borderline pornographic magazine from the counter.

Victor catches up when I stop in front of the only toilet, a small tiled room with sticky yellow patches on the floor. "Wait here." I hand him his suit. "I'll go first."

He shakes his head, eyes skimming around the store uneasily. The shelves are tall enough to block the view of who's coming in or out. "I'm not standing out here by myself while you change."

When I look uncertain, he elbows past me, stepping gingerly over the urine stains. I latch the door and carefully hang our suits on the hook on the back. That damn song goes on and on as I face the wall and pull down my pants.

These suits are lighter colors, cut differently, like rich European guys from movies. The unfamiliar way the fabric caresses my skin reminds me of the press conference. "You gonna be ok?" I ask the cracked, taupe tile in front of my nose.

His belt rattles against the floor; I risk a quick glance, trying not to notice the way his underwear hugs the tight curve of his ass. He's balancing in bare feet on top of his sneakers, squashing them flat as he unfolds a pair of socks. "Why wouldn't I?"

Our voices sound loud and tinny. "You shat the bed about five minutes into the reception."

"That was a warm-up. I can do anything now. Book me to read to some kindergarteners, shit, put me on *Sesame Street*."

I turn around, buttoning up my shirt. "I'm serious."

"So am I." He stands there with his lower lip in his teeth, watching my chest disappear behind the white linen. His dress shoes are still in the garment bag, so he does a weird hop-shuffle to scoot his sneakers closer to me without touching the floor. He grabs the ends of my tie, and I swat his hands away.

His jaw tightens and he jabs his finger against the base of my throat. "*No touching rule*. Are you stupid?" His voice sounds strained. I hold up my hands, trying not to put him even more on edge.

He goes back to looping the pieces of black silk around my neck, frowning in concentration. "I know how to knot a tie," I protest, watching his eyebrows furrow. They're thick, and darker than his hair.

"Then do mine."

I slide my arms under his and try to figure out how to do the knot backwards. "You're just going to say it's shit and do it over."

He smiles, but doesn't say anything. We stand side by side in the mirror, transformed from worn-out travelers to suave businessmen. Kind of. I try to smooth my hair down with some water from the tap.

"Yeah, sorry. It's hurting my eyes." Victor pulls his tie apart and starts over. Grabbing my stuff, I leave him behind. He bumps into my back halfway across the shop, hopping on one leg as he pulls his other shoe on and grabbing my shoulder for support. I wonder what the difference is between touching and being touched, why it matters so much.

When we get back to the car, Gray looks relieved and slightly surprised, like he was afraid we had made a run for it. I wish I had thought of that.

As we pull back onto the street, I let myself believe things are going to be ok. For a minute there, in that bathroom, you could have convinced me Victor and I were on the same side. Two fucked-up boys against the world.

Then we pull up to the Regale Naples hotel, a nine-story structure of stone and wrought iron bathed in late morning sun. Across the street I can see a marina bristling with little masts and the tops of yachts. I turn to ask Victor about the building that looks like a castle from *Game of Thrones*, but I follow his stare to the crowd of reporters clustered around the front door of the hotel. Gray looks pissed. Talking into a radio, the driver pulls right past the entrance and around the block.

The air gets cold as we turn down a stone ramp into a claustrophobic underground parking garage that looks like dwarves carved it out with picks. When we idle to a stop, Gray jumps out and opens Victor's door. Victor is clutching his largest suitcase in his lap, almost too big for him to carry, but Gray refuses to let it leave the car. "They have bellboys for a reason."

"Fucking *fine*."

As they head for the elevator, I tap the driver's shoulder. "Uh, thanks."

He smiles. "*Maledetti giornalisti*."

"And these bags." I pull the zipper on one of the suitcases open a little and see a swimsuit, big surprise. "They're definitely all going to his room, right?" I don't want to be around him if any of this shit goes missing.

"*Si*, do not worry."

Gray is holding the elevator door open for me, but he doesn't get inside. "Werner is waiting at the top. I need to run some logistics." He leans in and looks at Victor, sounding unexpectedly kind. "Be good. The more you cooperate, the faster this will be over."

Something crosses Victor's face in a flash, an expression I almost miss. He looks like he just got punched in the gut. Then he grits his teeth and stares at his reflection in the mirrored walls.

"We're so not prepared for this," I realize as we start to rise toward the lobby.

I notice that the eyes of his reflection are looking at me. "You're such a fussy little bitch." He sounds hoarse. Gray's words seem to have destroyed his fragile mood. "You're giving me an ulcer."

"Look," I cross the car and lean against the wall next to him, studying his profile. "We want the same thing. You're going to work with me, right?" Like an idiot, I hold out my hand.

He looks down at my palm between us, then back at my face. "I don't know." Taking my hand in his, he traps it against his chest and leans in, lowering his voice. "Did you fuck him or did he fuck you?"

For a second, I blink, struggling to remember what he's even talking about. The question he mocked me with at the club. I yank my hand away and wipe it on my pants. "Asshole."

Chapter 15

ETHAN

The elevator opens on an ornate, classical lobby with columns and towering potted palms and paintings of the view across the street.

As if he's nothing but thrilled to be here, Victor straightens up and flashes that heart-slaying, crooked grin. An easy confidence carries him into the lobby, where he shakes his father's hand, then kisses both cheeks of the Italian woman next to him.

"Welcome Mr. Lang, Mr. Faulks." For a second, I don't recognize the name of my alias. "I'm Emi, director Campagna's assistant. If you'll follow me this way, we'd like to do a quick screen test before lunch so our commercial crew can assess your complexions and heights for cinematography and wardrobe."

She ushers us through the lobby and down a dark-paneled hall. Worry tugs at me when Werner doesn't follow. I thought we'd be under constant supervision, to provide a safety net in case we mess up. Apparently, we're on our own.

As if on cue, Emi turns around and walks backward down the hall. Since I'm in front, she zeroes in on me. "We're preparing lunch. Does Victor have any allergies I should phone down?"

Shit. I've never seen him eat *anything*. I'm starting to realize a lie this complex would be impossible to perfect in the time we were given and everyone but me knew it. They just didn't tell me, because they knew I'd back out.

I glance over my shoulder, but Victor is walking ten feet behind me, looking at his phone. I can tell by the set of his mouth that he heard the question but has no interest in helping me out.

"Shellfish?" I latch onto the first lie to enter my head.

"Ah, that will be no problem."

I picture Mom's cookies bouncing under the wheels of a semi. The question Victor asked in the elevator. The way he always seems to be able to pull me in just enough to hurt when he lashes out again. "Alcohol gives him severe reflux. Coffee, too. Please only serve him water." Victor looks up, alarmed, and I smile at him.

"Understood." Emi pulls open a pair of double doors that lead into a conference room with high ceilings and massive chandeliers.

The first wave of jet lag hits me as everyone in the room looks up from what they're doing to stare at us. I can feel my face getting warm. Crew members go back to adjusting a white backdrop lit by a bank of LED panels, while a man in light-wash jeans, sandals, and an infinity scarf comes over to shake our hands.

"I'm Sansone Campagna, the executive director of the marketing campaign." His thick accent caresses each syllable. "You are both well after your journey, yes?"

Well might be putting it strongly, but I just nod.

"Never better," Victor adds, scrunching up his eyes instead of smiling properly. He grabs my hand, and I realize his palm is just as sweaty as mine.

"If you don't mind, please stand in front of the camera as we make some adjustments." One of the production staff moves a light out of the way so we can access the backdrop. Everyone sneaks glances at us, ready to see the love story that broke the internet, the one that's going to make them all millions.

I pull in a deep, shaky breath. This isn't about them and their money, and it's not about the blond brat next to me and how much I hoped he would be just like the idol I always admired. This is about doing whatever it takes to provide for my family, and no one's going to take that from me.

As we stand side by side, watching Campagna take notes and flip settings on the massive DSLR pointed at us, Victor shifts his weight until his shoulder is pressed into my side.

No. I'm not going to carry you through this. I lean away, crossing my arms and leaving him alone with his hands shaking a little, breathing shallowly, eyes fixed on the camera lens.

Victor

Be good. The more you cooperate, the faster this will be over.
Oh, Gray. I'm always good. You have no idea.

Campagna clicks the shutter on the camera a few times. An assistant swoops in and fixes Ethan's damn cowlick. She eyes my mop of curls, but decides that's a fight she can't win without reinforcements. "Looking good," Campagna calls. "Tanner, can you stand behind Victor and put your arms around him?"

"Sure." Ethan turns to me. His autumn eyes look swollen and bleary, his hair wet where the assistant spritzed it. I expect him to grab me, but he hesitates. "Is it ok?"

I stare at him. No one has ever asked. I've never been allowed to make this choice. "Fine," I mumble.

He stands behind me and rests one elbow on my shoulder. He's always so strong and stable, like he's anchored solidly to this earth, like he could keep me from floating away.

Campagna smiles and clicks his tongue. "No need to be coy. Get intimate." I can feel Ethan sigh before his arm slides around my chest, tugging me back against the warm wall of his body. His jaw rests against my temple.

"The fans are going to love this."

For six years I've made sure that nobody could look at me. If I could've blindfolded the fuck partners I brought over, I would have. Now my picture will be published across the world and anyone will be able to stare at me, dissect me with their eyes. *He* will see it, I have no doubt of that. He'll study my face and wonder why I'm letting someone else touch me when I belong to him, like he never taught me better.

I can feel every pair of eyes on me like a finger probing my skin. One of the production assistants turns to his friend, voice so low I can barely hear. "Does he know his boyfriend…" he drops into Italian, but I catch *"un po' di puttana." A bit of a whore.* Someone snorts. I catch his eye and wink, but the way his face flames doesn't help the cold feeling in my gut.

"Quiet on set," Campagna demands, but he's smiling a little.

I pull away from Ethan; he lets me go. "What did they say?" he whispers.

"They said you have something hanging out of your nose." I turn to Campagna. "We finished?"

"*Sì*, for now. Do you want to see?"

"I don't get paid enough to look at my face."

The doors to the room are heavy as I shove them open, like they want to keep me in. Chills run through my body.

Fight or flight, except I can't.

Go home, except I can't.

Dad and Gray and Ethan, the people I should have been able to trust, are dragging me into the light and cutting me open so everyone can see what's inside.

I head for the nearest restroom. Everything in this place is gilded and antique, and I half expect the toilet to have a pull chain. There's a narrow gap between the side of the toilet and the wall, a little smaller than me. After turning off the light, I fold my shoulders up, wedge myself in, and hug my knees to my chest. Just for a minute, I can finally breathe.

The door pops open; I *forgot* to lock it. A shadow blocking my way out. That's the worst nightmare, the one I stay awake all night to avoid, and my heart is beating so hard it throbs in my vision by the time Ethan gets the light on. He blinks as I stand up. "What are you doing?"

"I aim better in the dark." My voice won't stay steady.

He looks like the stress is causing him physical pain. "I knew you couldn't do this. But you need to pull it together, because we don't have a choice."

I cross my arms and look him up and down. "Why not?"

"Because—"

"Because I'm your meal ticket to a bunch of cash."

"Come on." He leans back against the door. "It's for my mom. You met her."

"And I'm sure she'd be cool with all of this. I bet you told her every detail of exactly why you came here."

His face darkens. "Don't." Pushing off the door, he walks right up to me, as close as he can get without touching. I stare at the top button of his shirt, refusing to back up.

"Look at me." He has no idea how bossy he sounds. And I obey, immediately, because I was built to be good. Meeting his eyes, I notice that they turn down a little at the outside corners, which makes him look very gentle and serious. "What can I do to get you to communicate with me?"

I break into a big grin. "Did you fuck him or did he fuck you?"

He throws up his hands and walks out. In the doorway, he pauses and looks back. "What did those guys say about you?"

He'll look it up eventually, when he gets his phone on hotel Wi-Fi. I just shake my head. "Word of advice: never trust a guy who wears an infinity scarf post-2009."

When he's gone, I lock the door behind him and lean against it for a long time.

Big windows line the private dining room, overlooking views of the sea and the castle. They're propped open to let in the smell of climbing roses and the calling of gulls. My skin's on fire, like an addict, from being stuck away from the water for almost twenty-four hours.

The lunch setup is a full-on blowout—white tablecloths and crystal and rows of polished cutlery—to impress my father and the other board members who have joined him. Now that they're being bought out by an American, all the local comeVa employees are fighting to keep their places in the new world order. Ethan's eyes widen as he walks in.

If there's any doubt about who's really important here, it becomes clear when Ethan and I are shunted to the end of a table while the big men with money sit in the middle. I don't mind; I like the cool air on my back. While everyone else has wine glasses, a lonely cup of water sits by my plate, just like Ethan ordered. *Joke's on you. I wouldn't have drunk their wine anyway.*

Waiters in black and white bring out bowls of clear, rich broth and a profusion of salad. I pick up my bowl and dump it into Ethan's, almost overflowing it. "Hey," he complains as I add my salad to his.

"Hope you're hungry. Anyone who doesn't clear their plate is an ungrateful asshole."

Ethan hesitates, hovering his hand over the selection of forks and spoons. "What do I use first?"

I click my tongue. "I thought you were prepared for this trip."

"Very funny." He picks up the dessert fork, studies the rest of the room uncertainly, and puts it back down. "Everyone else has started eating. Just tell me."

"Did you. Fuck him. Or did he. Fuck—"

He buries his face in his hands. "Jesus Christ. He fucked me, ok?"

"Ah." I sit back, tapping my finger against my chin. "There's your problem."

"What?" He shakes his head, then picks up the three forks and fans them out in front of me. "Which one?" It's not hard, just fucking left to right, but he's so easy to fluster.

"I never said I'd tell you."

His jaw tightens. "No one will notice if I do it wrong."

"Keep telling yourself that."

"You want me to beg?" The man's need to be in control, to do things *correctly*, is beyond anything I've ever seen.

I prop my chin on my hands and look up into his angry face. I drop my voice, soft in my chest. "There's no reason for me not to help you. The answer's on the tip of my tongue. I just don't feel like it." His tired eyes ignite as I smile at him. "How does that make you feel?"

"You're a piece of shit."

"Yeah?" I study his lean face, all the little scars and weathering of working hard jobs in tough conditions.

"Someone needs to—" He cuts off, presses his lips together, but his expression is dangerous, something I've never seen on him.

"Needs to...what? Teach me to behave?"

I want him to crack. I want to hear him call me fucked up, a slutty little bitch, because that's the language I understand. Because I can sense something in him, something he doesn't even recognize himself, like the ripple of water before an earthquake—he's built to take control, not offer it up. And maybe I'm doing this just to humiliate him, but deep down I want to know if being hurt by someone who hates you makes cleaner, sharper wounds than the hideous scars love leaves behind.

His eyes drop to my mouth as I smirk. "What would you do to me right now if all these people weren't here?"

The answer is clear in his eyes, but he doesn't speak. My body's humming, because I only play games I already know I'm going to win. Under the tablecloth, I skim my hand over his thigh until my knuckles find it, a bulge forming in his slacks.

I remove my hand and wipe it on my napkin. "Like I said. There's your problem."

The fire in his eyes disappears in the space of a blink, and he slowly takes the salad fork I offer him, biting the inside of his cheek. If looks could wipe someone off the face of the earth, I'd be space dust now. "Whatever you're trying to prove, it's bullshit." He stuffs some arugula in his mouth, no dressing, before starting on his cold soup. "And even if it wasn't, it doesn't make any difference."

"Ok, honey." I tip my chair back against the wall and rest my arm on the windowsill, sneaking my hand out into the clean salt breeze. I can feel the moisture in the air, clinging to my skin, calling me.

Chapter 16

ETHAN

My thighs are still aching as I finish off two portions of steak.

I don't understand what Victor did to me. I don't understand the urges that torched my body. And I don't understand why my cock, an emotionless, unresponsive piece of equipment I pump out once every couple of weeks, is awake and begging for the human train wreck making my life miserable.

I don't want to understand.

Before I gave up on relationships, I dreamed of finding The One. He would be kind, sensitive, intelligent. We would hit that perfect balance of independent and supportive that leads to optimal mental health and happiness. Our fulfilling sex life would teach my body to want the things it was supposed to want, to do what it was supposed to do.

I wouldn't feel insane every time he leaves the room and scared every time he comes back. He wouldn't infect every single thought in my goddamn brain. He wouldn't have me counting the seconds until his next insult because hate is the strongest emotion I've felt in six years. Jet lag must be making me loopy.

As I scoop up my last bite, Victor watches the meat glistening on my fork with glazed eyes. As far as I can tell, he refuses to eat and then throws a fit because he's skinny. Trust rich people to create their own problems.

Campagna swings by our table, flashing a very white smile. "This afternoon light is to die for. The official photo shoot will be later this week, but can we get some spontaneous shots? We've sent some clothes to your room." He speaks to Victor instead of me, and I remember that word he was snickering about—*puttana*—and the way everyone looks at Victor, like they're eager to see him degrade himself all the ways the rumors say. It makes me feel...God, I don't know. Petulant. Possessive. Things I wouldn't be feeling if I weren't sleep deprived.

"We'll be there," I say pointedly, and he glances at me like part of the table just talked. When Victor smiles like a shark and puts his hand on my shoulder, I remember just in time that I'm not allowed to pull away.

Campagna's lips twist as he thanks us, and I'm pretty sure he's starting to see through our sitcom levels of bad acting. Whether that information is profitable enough to use against the Lang family is another matter. Fuck, I'm already starting to think like them.

Victor flicks his unused napkin onto the table. "*Ciao*, bitches." Out of the corner of my eye, I see Gray hand him something that looks like a snack bar, which he stuffs in his pocket as we leave.

"Luxury hotel" definitely means something different than it does in the States, as I discover when we crowd into an elevator that looks like it was built by Leonardo da Vinci. It even has one of those flimsy cage doors, allowing us to see all the rusty nooks and crannies of the elevator shaft as we ascend. I could swear I see bats sleeping in the shadows.

It's not until Victor produces a key to one of the heavy wooden doors on the top floor that it sinks in—we're sharing a room. I open my mouth to suggest that I'd rather sleep in a hall closet, then close it again. He'd probably take me literally.

The room is strange but inviting, sun-bleached with creaky parquet floors and antique furniture that looks like it will break if I sit down too hard. A small balcony invites guests to take in the harbor from a pair of plastic chairs covered in a patina of crusty, white salt. Mom would love to sit out here with a scarf around her hair and write postcards.

When Victor slams the bathroom door hard enough to knock one of the paintings on the wall crooked, I turn around and realize there's only one bed. A queen, at that. Sighing past my gorged stomach, I sit weakly on the edge of it and look around for a couch, a pullout, anything.

Golden dust swirls lazily through the air when I move. The quality of light in this country is like nothing I could have ever imagined, like a fairy tale. It's not helping me stay awake. My head throbs as I pick up the phone on the bedside table and dial the front desk. "Hello?" I lower my voice to avoid goading my demonic roommate. "Do you have rollaway beds, or cots or something? Could I have one sent to room 8C?" I screw up enough courage to add "*Grazie*," hoping I didn't say something insulting.

Pulling out my cell, I double-check the time and ring Mom's phone.

"Ethan?"

Everything tight in me melts away. "Hey. You'll never guess where I am right now."

"Where?"

I step back onto the balcony. It's getting hot and sultry, and even I can feel the call of the cool water. "Naples. Overlooking the Mediterranean."

She squeals, happier than I've heard her in so long. "I can't believe it."

"There's this castle right outside the hotel. I need to go find out what it's called."

"Can you send us pictures?"

A hand wraps around mine on the phone. Victor squints irritably up at me. He must be wearing the outfit Campagna provided: a black t-shirt and white jeans, Gucci sneakers. "Hurry up. I want to get this over with."

I push him away and mouth *fuck off*. "Of course I can. I'll—"

He grabs the phone faster than a snake striking. "Going into a tunnel *kshhhhhh* bye." Then he drops it off the balcony. We both watch it bounce off the grass into an oleander bush. I spread my hands wordlessly.

"If you feel half as shitty as you look right now, you're already jet lagged as hell. The sooner we do this, the sooner you can go to sleep."

I follow him back into the room, where his luggage has somehow exploded over everything. I pick up one of the swimsuits draped over the desk. "I see what this is about. You can't go swimming until after the shoot."

He yanks it out of my hand and sits on the edge of the bed with it cradled in his lap, like I just wounded one of his children. "Your clothes are by the sink."

I sigh at the gauzy white t-shirt and gray chinos. Letting the whole world see my nipples is exactly the conclusion this day needs. As I dress, I notice a protein bar wrapper in the bathroom trash. *Gotcha*. I want to feel judgmental, but I mostly just feel relieved. And like all my other feelings today, that annoys me.

Victor already has the door open when I come out, bouncing it from one hand to the other. He shakes his head at my outfit and turns to go.

"I'm not some kind of sadist, you know," I blurt at his back.

He doesn't turn around. "I know."

"Then what were you trying to prove at lunch?"

He walks off down the hall, nearly shutting the door in my face. In the elevator, he weaves his fingers in the cage door. I'm about to point out how dangerous that is when he says, "You'll figure it out. Or you won't."

"I'm not here for your entertainment."

"Ok." His soft shirt bunches as he shrugs his shoulders.

The photographer waiting on the front steps of the hotel has an assistant with him. While she works on untangling Victor's curls, I hunt through the garden for my phone. It survived the fall, so I text Mom that I'll call back later.

The reporters have gotten bored and left, which makes the security guard who follows us at a distance seem redundant. I don't realize how tired I am until we start to walk; my mouth tastes sour, my throat hurts, and every time I blink it's a fight to open my eyes again.

Warm two- and three-story buildings crowd the narrow streets, shading wide, clean paving stones. Mopeds nudge their way between cafes and flower shops and apartments. We emerge right by the sea, on a path divided from the water by a low stone wall streaked with seagull droppings. Colorful flower pots lined with moss hang from the ornate iron lamp posts, and the castle looms in the background. Victor hops up on the wall and balances, hand shading his eyes as he watches the slow roll of the surf.

I've never hated something so beautiful so much, tortured by sleep deprivation and not allowed to enjoy any of it. And I don't entirely know if I mean the view or him.

"Sit on the wall together, *per favore*." The photographer hoists his camera with its long lens. "This is perhaps for two pages of a magazine." He spreads his hands to indicate *wide*. I blink uneasily, trying to focus as I put my arm around Victor like we're posing for a Christmas card. His body, just a little smaller than mine, fits almost but not quite perfectly against my side. He smells bright, the cologne he gave me at the press conference. I probably smell like Listerine and sadness.

"More, um, hot, please." Our director hunts for English words, looking unsatisfied.

My brain fills with an unwanted image of us stripping off our shirts, and I'm so deliriously tired I can't get rid of it. I've never been high, but maybe this is what it feels like.

"Fuck's sake." Victor squirms away from me and grabs my chin, pulling our foreheads together, holding me there as the camera clicks. His eyes pick up the yellow haze of the afternoon sun and the pale blue of the shadows below us, mixing them into colors as impossibly elusive as he is. I can see traces of salt on his dry lips just before he rolls them into his mouth to moisten them.

When the photographer tires of this pose, he points over the wall, where a jumble of unsteady-looking rocks slopes to the water, which picks away at the smooth, wet stone with hungry little gulping sounds that turn my stomach. "I want a clear shot."

Victor vaults the wall and looks at me expectantly. A warm breeze keeps trying to pick his curls out of the gel, return them to their natural chaos.

I shake my head. "It's not safe."

He waits, unimpressed, hands hanging loose at his sides as the wind ripples his black shirt against his body. The silver chain around his neck is all crooked, and he's frowning into the sun, and suddenly he's so much bigger and smaller at the same time, not a monster but just a guy, just a human, hot skin over weak bones. But at the same time, he looks like a wild mystery, a fey god of the sea.

"If you don't get over this wall, I'll fucking fire you," the god complains.

And so I climb after him, trying to hold my shaky balance. When my foot slips, he grabs my arm. "Come on, big boy."

The photographer's assistant comes back with a packet of fried balls from a stand across the street. "Arancini." She hands them to me. "Feed them to him or something cute."

"Really?"

They feel greasy against my palm, and the rich smell makes my overly-full stomach clench. The camera's already firing again, catching all the candid moments as I contemplate how little I want to try and put anything into this psychopath's mouth. Then I notice his face. He looks helpless, staring at the food like it's going to crawl down his throat and kill him.

In an explosion of feathers and wings and whatever the hell's inside an arancini, a gull cannonballs my hand and makes off with as much of the food as it can carry. The rest scatters between the rocks.

And you smile. The first one I've ever seen.

Not a TV smile or a fuck you smile or a smile that hides things, just a quick bubble of laughter from his chest. "Your face," he says, eyes glittering. There's sweat on my skin and on his, and the air smells like vinegar and warm stone, and I'm losing my mind. I want to make this moment belong to me and no one else, to put my hands all over him, to make him pray my name.

"*Merda*." The photographer glares at me, like it's my fault he wasted his money on the food. "Can you just kiss?" I stiffen. This is a worse idea than the food. The worst idea. I can see Victor's eyes assessing, face blank.

"Holy shit," a woman's voice drawls. "Victor, is that you?"

Chapter 17

ETHAN

Victor's head snaps up. He almost falls.

Two women about our age in short, brightly-colored summer dresses stop behind the photographer, squinting at us. When the one on the right takes off her sunglasses, I realize the two of them look exactly the same. I never would have recognized them walking down the street, but seeing them next to Victor pulls everything together: Katrina and Rachel Garrel, the identical twins from Victor's old swim team. They went to the Olympics without him, ignored in favor of non-stop news coverage of his scandal, and didn't even medal. I always felt sorry for them.

"What the hell?" Victor climbs over the wall and pecks both of them on each cheek. "What are you doing here?" He shifts from one foot to the other, glancing up the promenade every few seconds and scratching at the back of his neck, which is starting to burn.

The one I'm pretty sure is Katrina pulls out a long, white cigarette. Victor cups his hand around the end and lights it for her in a gesture that tells me they've done this many times.

"I can't believe this." Rachel grabs Victor's wrist, swinging it childishly. "*Babe*. I thought we'd never see you again." She has a flat, strident Boston accent; their team lived and practiced at a compound in New Mexico, but their coach pulled a lot of members from old money families on the East Coast.

"Is—" Victor hesitates. "Are you—"

Katrina rolls her eyes and tucks a strand of hair behind her ear. "We're on a fucking bonding trip before Worlds," she says past the cigarette. "And yeah, Alek is here. God, you're still obsessed with each other."

Thanks to Danny, I'm a walking encyclopedia on this team. Alek Simmons was Victor's main rival, son of their world-renowned coach, Clint Simmons. Coach Simmons proved that he had no knowledge of Victor's doping, allowing him and his team to carry on and try to put the pieces back together, but they've never escaped Victor's shadow. Most of Victor's records were disqualified after the fact, but they're still the stuff of legend, and the world has watched Alek try and fail to beat them many times.

Victor shrugs, like he doesn't care, but it looks rehearsed. The photographer, sneaky bastard, lifts his camera to capture the moment for what would undoubtedly be a big headline, but Rachel swats at his lens like it's a bug. "No, no. Shoo."

He gives up and checks his phone. "I have enough for now, gentlemen. *Buona sera*." Hoping this means I get to go to bed, I scramble over the wet rocks and join the others on the path.

"Who is *this*?" Katrina tips down her sunglasses and scans me from head to toe. Her red lips turn up at the corners as she offers a languid hand.

Before I can respond, Victor steps between us and pushes her hand away with a warning smile. "That's mine. Don't touch it."

Her mouth forms an O, then she throws back her head and laughs. "You're a brave man," she tells me over Victor's shoulder.

"It's fine," I say stupidly.

"I can't imagine being in a relationship with a professional cum dumpster." Katrina blows smoke at me, the sour tang blending with the smell of drying seaweed.

Her sister slaps her arm. "Don't be so gauche. Obviously they have an arrangement." She puts her arm around his waist; instead of retreating, he rests his nose in her hair and grins dryly at her words. "You absolutely must join us tomorrow night, Vic. We miss you. The rest of them are no fun when they're high. Besides," Rachel adds, taking his free hand, "you have to say hello to Alek. He won't believe this, of all the places in the world. It's fate."

I'm staring at their exchange in a kind of confused fog, trying to understand how Victor's demeanor changed in the blink of an eye and why they're allowed to touch him, when that word snaps me out of it.

Maybe fate is recursive—the mention of fate can, itself, be fate, signposting the steps our unlikely journeys take through the universe. Or maybe fate is a word people invoke to manipulate those who are desperate for meaning.

"I'll think about it." He keeps glancing over his shoulder uneasily.

"We're looking for gelato." Katrina wrinkles her nose. "Have you seen some?"

"Maybe down the way," I cut in, pointing along the path and hoping they'll leave. Rachel grabs my hand, startling me.

"Let's all go." She winks at Victor. "Victor's treat."

"So that's why you want me to come." His hoarse voice doesn't match his laconic, teasing smile. No one bothers to contradict him.

A thick silence falls as we walk, punctuated only by the clicking of the girls' heels, and I'm relieved when we spot a gelato stand surrounded by rusty tables and chairs.

Katrina insists on ordering for everyone, and comes to the table with four cones balanced between her fingers and napkins under her arm. My light green gelato has chocolate shavings mixed through.

Rachel shares a rickety chair with Victor, pressed up against him, and I think back on interviews with the team when they were clean-cut teenagers with eager, earnest faces. A few people made crazy claims, stories of parties, drugs, and sex—not with each other but just about anyone else. I always hid those rumors from Danny. Maybe that was a mistake.

Victor holds his vanilla cone like it's a microphone and he's being forced to give a speech he didn't prepare. Rachel puts her finger on the bottom of the cone and pushes it towards his mouth. "Come on. It's yummy."

His nostrils flare. "If you want it so bad, you eat it." In one quick movement, he grabs her cone and replaces it with his, then jumps up and dunks her ice cream into the nearest bin before walking away toward the sea wall with his hands behind his head.

She shoots me a sympathetic look. "He hasn't gotten any less touchy, has he?" Licking his cone, she trots after him. I watch them stand side by side at the wall, talking.

"Where did you two meet?" Katrina asks, putting out her cigarette on the edge of the table.

"His garden," I say without thinking, distracted by the ice cream melting down my knuckles. When her brows furrow, I add. "Party. His garden party."

"Ah." She purses her lips skeptically. "I thought he was a recluse."

"They were small parties."

A slow smile tips the corner of her mouth. "Lucky you."

"He's coming tomorrow night," Rachel announces loudly, dragging Victor back by the arm.

"Thank God," her sister drawls.

"Victor," I say warningly as he slides down in his chair and rests his head against the back, staring up at the sky.

"I can't wait." His throat bobs as he speaks.

Rachel does exactly what I've been wanting to do all afternoon, ruffling her fingers through his hair until the untidy curls start to reappear. "Seriously though, our local dealers, they're super nice, super cute. We'll have to buy extra shit for you, so can you make them happy? Get us a discount?"

Victor blinks at the cotton-puff clouds passing overhead. His voice is almost slurred, like he's falling asleep. "Sure. Whatever you want."

"Unless," Katrina shoots me a conspiratorial look, "your boyfriend doesn't—"

"Nah. He doesn't give a shit."

Nauseous and aching all over, I get up and throw away my half-eaten cone. I walk to the gelato stand and buy a bottle of water. As the owner fetches it from a cooler, I turn to study Victor stretched out in his chair, fidgeting the silver ring on his thumb over and over, defenseless, his wariness turned into apathy. He just nods as they talk about whoring him out to strangers, then closes his eyes, his lashes sweeping against his cheeks.

"*Signore.*" The shop owner taps the water bottle against my arm, sounding annoyed. "You are sleeping?"

Putting the cold, damp plastic against the back of my neck, I look back at the two girls leaning toward him, hands all over him, his still, still body. "Yeah, I think I am."

VICTOR

Oh, God.
Please let me wake up.
Please tell me they're not here.
Please don't do this to me.

Chapter 18

ETHAN

After he bids goodbye to the twins, we retrace our steps to the hotel. "You know you're not sneaking off to some party tomorrow, right?" I ask irritably. "We're not in high school."

He doesn't answer, and neither of us speak again.

The sun hasn't set, but I can't keep my eyes open for another minute. Victor grabs a swimsuit and bangs the door to our room behind him on the way out. I search the place, my heart sinking when I can't find the promised rollaway bed. I triple check under the bed, in the closet, everywhere, before calling the front desk.

"Room 8C?" the woman asks. "Ah, *si*, I take note here that Werner Lang canceled the bed a few hours ago. He says there is only one couple, so they do not need a cot. *È corretto?*"

"It's fine," I mumble, resting my head in my hand. "Sorry."

I grab two pillows off the bed and a spare comforter and blanket from the closet, dragging them into the bathroom. Making sure the clawfoot tub is dry, I line it with the comforter. The little bathroom smells like lavender and gets perfectly dark and quiet when I shut the door. Stripped to my boxers, I climb into the tub and pull a blanket over me. Werner can suck it unless he wants to come here and drag me out himself. I'm asleep before I can finish my thought.

God knows how many hours later, I jolt awake with a strangled yell as freezing cold water douses every inch of me. Coughing and shivering, I sit up and rub my stinging eyes.

Victor switches off the shower and studies me in the light of his phone flashlight. His eyes look wide in the dark, his pool-wet hair tousled. The tattered edges of his oversized gray t-shirt hang around his muscular thighs, and when he fidgets I realize he's not wearing anything else.

I turn away and start trying to dry myself with the corner of my blanket. "What the hell?"

He doesn't answer until I look at him again. He's chewing on his lower lip; it's flushed and a little swollen, like he's been at it a while. "This isn't a bed."

"It's my bed. Get out." I intend to lock the door when he leaves. Fuck him if he needs the toilet in the night.

"Not any more it fucking isn't." He flips the shower knob again, drenching my bedding and forcing me to scramble out so quickly I almost slip. He points at the queen bed in the other room. "Let's go."

"No." Water coats my trembling skin and runs down into my boxers.

Knowing he's going to get his way, he pads back to the bedroom and climbs into bed. I fight with everything in me not to check how much of his ass is showing under that shirt.

Grumbling under my breath, I hang my bedding out on the balcony to dry and hunt for some towels. I'm pretty sure the asshole hid them, because I can't even find a solitary washcloth. My teeth are starting to chatter.

I stand next to the bed, studying its shape in the dark. Victor's just a lump, the duvet pulled up over his head. His breathing sounds slow and steady, like he might have fallen asleep. Gingerly, I slide off my wet boxers and perch on the edge of the mattress, planning to drip dry until I can put on clothes.

According to the clock, I only slept a couple of hours in the tub—nowhere near long enough to heal my body from the walking, the jet lag, the anxiety. My eyes drift shut and I catch myself just as I start to fall over. This happens two more times before I give up and crawl under the covers, staying right at the edge of the mattress with my face toward the door.

Even with the windows open, it's quiet except for the sighing of the sea. Victor stirs behind me, sheets against skin, a small sound in his throat.

Behind my eyelids I find only the sight of him standing on the sea wall, arms out, made of things that scare me and things I want that have never had a name. We're in the same bed, a foot apart, neither of us dressed, all of me against all of him, and I realize, mortified, that I'm getting hard. *Again.*

Biting the edge of my tongue, I stare at the shape of a dresser across the room, a mirror above it reflecting nothing but darkness. I think about paying taxes on two million dollars, about how I should vacuum the spiders behind my bedside table when I get home, about who might win the current season of *Bake Off*. I breathe through the ache in my groin and it starts to fade.

Until the mattress shifts under me. Until a warm tongue tastes the water beaded along the back of my neck. My body, so wound up it's about to snap, shudders and I let out a tight, needy sob.

Hot breath on my skin, the barest brush of cracked, sun-bitten lips, and then he's lapping thirstily, long licks from the base of my neck to my hairline. I fight to keep quiet, air hissing through my nose, but then there's a sigh, the softest wet sound, and when he sucks on the protruding bone at the top of my spine I moan.

"You were so jealous," he breathes, kissing softly, relentlessly, up the side of my neck, taking the lobe of my ear between his teeth. "You don't want to share me, do you?"

"That's not true," I grit, gripping my rigid cock. I jerk myself dry and rough, my balls slapping my fist, the bed creaking slightly.

He nuzzles his cheek against my dripping hair like an animal leaving a scent. "You're mad that everyone knows how good I am except you."

"No." It hurts. I pump my hips into my palm.

"You…want…to…know," he whispers, kissing along my shoulder between each word, sloppy, all tongue, "how good I could be for you." His teeth scrape my skin for just a moment. I can feel the soft fabric of his t-shirt sticking to my back, but no other part of him touches me.

My breath catches in rhythm with my hand and I wonder, wildly, if this is why everyone's so obsessed with sex, this unspeakable feeling. I want to fill my hands with the golden skin I've been staring at all afternoon, but when I try to roll over he grabs my hip, holds me in place. I don't think he means to, but I can feel his fingers straying, exploring my ridges and dips in spite of himself, and just that hint, the promise of his skin against mine, undoes me.

When I start to come, a sudden, raw explosion, his hand slips between my damp thighs and traps my balls, twisting them too hard. My orgasm lances through me like I've been stabbed—my choking sob into the sheets, the light behind my eyes, the *pain*, the worst and best and most shameful come of my life.

Victor

Don't turn around. Don't touch me. Don't speak.
Don't go.
Fall asleep between me and the door. Give me your dreams, the dreams of someone who has never done anything wrong.

You tasted good. You sounded even better. But I'm not what you deserve. I just needed to make sure you'd stay here, between me and the door. And I don't know any other way to ask.

Sometime in the night, you climb out of bed and put on a shirt, some shorts. I watch you go, because I'm not asleep, and I expect you to leave. Maybe for good. Maybe, after everything I've done, it was this that drove you away.

But you don't leave. You pull back the sheet and climb in next to me.

No one ever comes back for me. Until you.

Ethan

I wake up on my back, tangled in sheets. Last night returns to me in moments, memories of breath and sweat and skin; I wouldn't believe it happened at all if it weren't for the clearer recollection of scrubbing dried cum off my stomach at three in the morning.

When I sit up, I feel a tug on my shirt and look down. Victor has lost his pillows and sheets, balled up in a tangle of limbs in the middle of the mattress, his t-shirt pushed up under his armpits. I see the curve of his ass, part of a soft cock under one of his long legs, ribs rising and falling with uneven breaths.

It doesn't feel right to look, so I drop my eyes to his hand, which is wrapped tightly in the hem of my shirt, gripping so hard his knuckles are popped out and flexed. Not wanting to break open the quiet morning, I lie down again and close my eyes, pretending to sleep.

A few minutes later, he shifts his weight and coughs, sits up, mumbles *fuck*. The tension on my shirt disappears. A pause—I think he's looking at me. It's so quiet I can hear his tongue moving in his dry mouth. Something in the air feels heavy and wrong today, like the pressure change before a tsunami.

He coughs again and stands up, shuffling across the room.

"Don't go to the party," I say suddenly, keeping my eyes closed.

"Jealous," he mumbles, voice sleep-thick and scratchy.

"No," I lie.

I hear the synthetic rustle as he pulls on one of his swimsuits, then the door slams. Opening my eyes, I reach out and press my hand against the bed where he lay, feeling his warmth. I roll over and bury my face in it.

What the fuck is wrong with me. I take the coldest shower I can stand. Our schedule looks empty today while the crew sets up for a big shoot, so I pull on loose jeans and a Sounders jersey Peyton got me for Christmas. I drag one of the balcony chairs into the sun and curl up in it, flipping through the photo album on my phone in an attempt to ground myself.

This is who I am. This is where I live. These are my people.

Life isn't that complicated, even when we try to make it so. Good and bad are more clear cut than we like to admit. Victor betrayed his sport, derailed his teammates' careers, stole world records that shouldn't have been his, and did it all with a smile, knowing his daddy's money would shield him from serious consequences. Now I know he also used illegal drugs and blew countless strangers with no thought for the millions of young fans who looked up to him. If there's anything he's good at, actually good at, without the help of steroids, it's manipulating and using people.

Look what he's already done to me.

I can't stand to see his face right now, so I dig through his wallet on the side table for a handful of euros and head out into the street, determined to finally find out the name of that castle.

Chapter 19

VICTOR

I want to swim in the sea, but the streets aren't safe anymore. Ethan needs to go with me; if I run into my team again, his hate is the only force strong enough to keep me from going home with them.

Unfortunately, Ethan has disappeared in one of his self-righteous fits. I hunt for him upstairs and in the dining room, the lobby, the garden. I want to ask him which part of yesterday he's angry about and how long he's going to stay that way before we can go. But I guess he grew enough of a spine to explore town without me. Fuck him.

In the kitchen, I ask the chef to scramble me some eggs while I watch. By the time I get the bowl to my room and lock the door, they've gone cold. I sit on the floor next to the tub and shovel them in, thinking about all the bad things that are going to happen at the party this evening because Ethan wasn't here to take me to the sea.

I put on my speedo and swim laps in the pool for hours. It's not the same as the ocean; I want the dangerous invitation of the waves to give up and let go, to find out once and for all if there's a warm, welcoming place deep below all that weight of water.

Fat men with hairy bellies and newspapers doze on deck chairs as I execute length after length of perfect butterfly stroke. People don't recognize me often now, not after six years and most of the muscle gone, but sometimes when I'm swimming someone notices the rhythm of my stroke, the one that belongs only to me. Not today.

My body's numb when I climb out and wrap myself in a towel. I check all the hiding places again, my bare feet leaving wet trails through the hotel. No Ethan. I check my phone. Nothing from him, nothing from Dad, nothing from Gray.

I'm not needed.

Just as I'm about to put it away, a text from Katrina pops up. *We've already started. Hurry up.*

Just like it used to be. When no one needed me—my coach, my family, the press—no one wanted me, and when no one wanted me, I lost my mind. Until the team made me a home where I was always needed.

Get the drugs for Friday night.

Blow the guy who can get us in the club.

Pay for the week in Majorca.

Because I need to be needed. I need to be told what to do and hear how good I am when I do it. And after a while, I became so needed that I broke myself in unspeakable ways just to hear that praise, and now I have nothing but an empty shell and the knowledge that I should probably gather my courage and end myself.

No one notices or calls after me as I walk to the street and hail a white cab. *Do I actually want to get high?* I wonder as I tell the driver the address in Katrina's text. I don't think so. But that choice was made for me the minute I got into this car. I'm needed, and I don't have it in me to say no.

As the taxi starts to move, I look around one more time for Ethan. He'll glare at me in loathing and tell me I'm not allowed to go. But he's too late.

The cab drops me off at an apartment building halfway up the hillside, crammed tight along a winding street where the breeze has a hard time reaching. The strip of sky over my head is turning yellow. There's a thin, dirty black dog on the street, staring at me. I hold out my hand, but he growls and runs away.

A sagging metal staircase takes me to the second floor, where one of the doors throbs with the sound of bass.

Katrina opens the door on my knock and smiles slowly. Whatever she's smoking already has her eyes glazed. She pulls me inside by my wrist. I can't see properly in the dark, and the room is full of people I don't know. It smells like their sweat. My heart batters at my ribs like a panicked bird about to get its neck snapped.

She presses a cold beer into my palm and leads me to a corner where the rest of the team is lounging, empty bottles everywhere, white powder on a mirror on the table.

A tall man with the body of a god and eyes as black as his hair sits up, eyebrows raised incredulously. I'm the only one who notices the shock, the cold and creeping fear of seeing a ghost he promised himself had been exorcised forever, along with its unspeakable secrets.

Surprise.

As his face darkens, I know he's about to take it all out on me.

He was the closest thing I ever had to a brother. Our hair and eye colors made people call us all sorts of stupid things—the yin and yang of swimming, the angel and the demon. Until everyone lost interest in Alek because he just couldn't keep up with me. My downfall gave him what he needed: an open playing field where he could write his own legacy as a great athlete. I don't blame him for what he did to get there. But even with all the training in the world and all his father's hopes on him, he never rose past the middle of the pack.

Katrina pushes me onto the couch next to Alek, and he throws an arm around my neck, using his thumb to turn my face toward him, studying me. "I can't believe it."

"The gang's back together!" Rachel enthuses, propping her feet in her sister's lap. Katrina just watches, waiting for the train wreck we all know is coming.

I study my beer, then pull out of Alek's grip to set it on the table. "It's the greatest day of my life."

"I forgot how uptight you are before you get going." Alek smirks.

I rest my head against the back of the couch, tugging down the shorts that keep riding up my thighs. "Your dealers wanted to fuck me?"

He laughs. "Not yet. We've got time." Up close, I can see the turmoil behind his eyes. He thought our story had been closed for good and put on a shelf to rot. "Tell us what you've been doing all these years," he demands.

"Yeah." Rachel's rubbing her nose in a way that tells me they've already sampled the goods. "Your ban finished three years ago. Why didn't you come back?"

It's hard to breathe, packed in here with the bodies and the music and the memories. "I don't know."

Alek shakes his head. "You piece of shit. You don't know?"

"You can't talk to him when he's like this." Brushing off her pink romper, Katrina stands up and gestures to Alek, who drags a bag of pills from his pocket.

I don't think I want to be high. But I can't make my mouth say the words, because anything has to be better than going through this sober.

Katrina opens the bag and straddles my lap, resting her hand on my chest. She wrinkles her nose. "God, you're, like, wasting away."

Her fingers land lightly on my chin.

The rules. No one touches me. I don't—

"Open up, baby. Don't pretend you don't want it."

I stick out my tongue, and she puts the pill on it. I probably should have asked what it was. Too late. She prods her finger into my mouth to make sure I swallow, so I stick my tongue out again to show her.

Yeah, America's best and brightest young team of stars was fucked up one way and down the other. We were like an incestuous little den of stoned vipers. The press would have shit themselves. Oprah would have taken back her invitation.

"Did you know I was here?" I ask her, studying her blue eyes.

She laughs, chasing a couple of pills down her own tongue with my rejected beer before she stands up. "I forgot how paranoid you are. You remember how Coach always takes us somewhere before a big competition? Bribing us to do our training. Of course we didn't know you were here."

Alek examines me. "He's paranoid because you have to watch your back when you're a fucking cheat."

"I didn't cheat you out of anything." My awareness starts to fragment, like I'm thinking double instead of seeing it. "You swam like a quadruple amputee during the games."

Katrina giggles. "You *did*."

"You didn't even place," he snaps. He turns and grabs a big handful of my side, making me jump. "I bet you think you could come back any time and Dad would throw me aside in favor of you. Even in this condition."

"I really don't." I meet his eyes, willing him to remember the long, long path we've walked together. Something like guilt flashes across his face, but it twists into cruelty.

"Why don't you ask him?" Every nerve in my body screams as he pulls out his phone and opens his father's contact. I haven't spoken to Coach since the day he testified against me in front of a committee of the US Anti-Doping Agency. Our eyes met across the room. Then he turned his back and walked away. If I ever saw him again, I'm scared of what I might do to myself.

"Wait." My voice sounds weak.

He ignores me, getting on his knees by the table and frowning in concentration as he arranges a line of coke down the phone screen, right across the call button. "Here." His eyes dance with malice as he holds it out. "They have good stuff in Naples; try it."

"God, Alek, you're such an asshole." Kat's mouth tips up a little at the corner. My blood's in the water, and they're all sharks.

I may not know better than to take pills I don't recognize, but I do know not to mix them with coke. Unfortunately, no one's here to stop me. The rug scratches my knees as I kneel next to Alek. He puts a steadying hand on my back. "Ready?"

"Go, go, go," Rachel chants unsteadily, and some idiots in the rest of the room pick it up without any idea what they're cheering for.

The shit burns, and there's a lot of it. But when I tip my head back, it's all gone and the phone is not dialing the ghost of Victor's past. Danger in his thin smile, Alek takes his phone back and wipes it on his jeans. And now that it's way too late, it finally sinks in that I've broken all my rules and I'm about to be helpless in a very unsafe place.

"I'll be right back." Trying not to touch anyone, I stumble through the room into a shitty little half bath that probably has roaches sleeping in the mold behind the toilet.

I lean over the sink and stare at my red eyes in the mirror, trying to count how long I have until the drugs switch my brain off, wondering if I've burned the only bridge I have left.

Perching on the edge of the toilet, I fumble through my phone, trying to Google the number of the hotel. It's hard to read when the letters rearrange themselves every time I blink, but the picture looks right.

"Regale Naples. *Come posso aiutarla*?"

Why is he saying words that aren't words? I slide a hand down my face. "Huh?"

"How can I help you?"

"I need to talk to Ethan." I'm sweating and cold, my thighs gripping the porcelain.

"I'm sorry, sir, I don't—"

"Can you call my room?"

"Do you know your room number?"

I close my eyes, searching. The thoughts are all falling out; that information's long gone. "Please." My voice cracks. "Call Victor Lang's room."

Pause. "One moment, sir."

Listening to a tinny rendition of Mozart, I slide onto the floor and pull my knees up, resting my forehead against them.

The door knob rattles. I want to scream.

"I gotta shit," a girl's voice complains, and I relax a little.

"Shit off the balcony."

"Prick."

A door shaking on its hinges, my heart in the back of my throat, choking me.

"Victor, open up."

No.

But I always do. It doesn't matter if the door has a lock; no doors are safe as long as I can open them from the inside.

Hurt me once, shame on you. Hurt me twice, shame on me. Hurt me a thousand times, I must have done something to deserve this. I was born wrong.

"Hello?"

Looking around, confused, I remember there's a phone to my ear. His stupid motherfucking voice, dumb and uptight and warm and low...

"Come get me."

Everything goes quiet for a second. I wonder what he's doing up there. Eating room service? Talking to his mommy? Jerking off?

"Where are you?" He sounds worried.

For a second my stomach clenches like the drop of a roller coaster because I have no idea. "One sec." I open the text from Katrina and read the address out loud. "Hurry up."

"How am I supposed to find—"

"For two mil you'd better fucking figure it out."

"I'm not your bitch," he grouses. The contempt in his voice pours cool water on my overheating brain.

"If you say so." I hang up so I don't have to listen to him decide if he's coming. My legs are shaking as I stand up and limp back to the living room to keep an eye on Alek, in case he changes his mind about calling Coach.

Fighting a trip hurts too much and finally I shut my eyes and let go, pretending it's eight years ago, the night after I broke my own world record in the 200m butterfly. We all camped out in Alek's room and got wasted and played *Mario Kart*. For a few hours, we were almost happy.

I don't know how long it is before something touches my shoulder. I lash out, connecting with flesh. My vision comes back when I sit up and puke on the floor. Ethan's standing there, bathed in purple light, holding his arm where I punched him.

"I didn't think this would be your kind of thing," Katrina teases, but he doesn't pay any attention to her. He crouches down, avoiding the puke, and studies my eyes. His hand cradles the side of my face, breaking my rule. "I need to come down," I croak, shivering as I push his arm away.

Eyebrows furrowed, he straightens up and takes in the rest of the party—the drugs, the mess, the depravity. He doesn't belong here, and I can see the disgust and anger on his face.

He disappears into the crowd without a word. I collapse back into the scarred leather upholstery. I don't blame him; if I came across a piece of trash like me, passed out in some filthy apartment whose address he doesn't even know, I'd leave him to die.

But when I blink, he's back with a fistful of paper towels, carefully mopping up my vomit. He has honest hands. Shoulders built outdoors. He doesn't deserve the shitty life he has.

His fingers squeeze my shoulder, helping me sit up. "Come on."

"Rules," I groan, shrugging him off. "You don't *listen*."

Standing up feels easier when I know he'll catch me if I fall. "Did you bring a coat?" he asks, like he's picking up his toddler from daycare. I start laughing and can't stop. "Ok, we're going."

Alek blocks our way out of the apartment, leaning against the door with a fresh beer. The threat in his eyes tells me I haven't seen his worst yet. He smiles coldly. "Before we leave next week, I'm swimming to Capri. Care to race?"

Ethan butts in. "Where's Capri?"

"Off the coast, oh, eighteen miles or so." Alek is talking to Ethan, but he's focused on my reaction. God. I've gone that far before, in my prime. In my current condition, Alek knows it would be insanity. He's so desperate to beat me at *something*, even a cheap, meaningless victory.

When I open my mouth to refuse, Ethan cuts across me again in an overbearing growl. "That's insane. Besides, that's not what we're here for."

"Ah," Alek murmurs, smirking at me. "I see how this works."

"Sounds fun. I'll do it," I snap, enjoying the pure frustration in Ethan's eyes. "Have Kat text me the details." With great effort, I coordinate my limbs to carry me out the door and down the steps to the street.

"Which one's mine?" I kick the tires on all the cars until Ethan unlocks one of them.

"Very funny." He pries my fingers off the driver's side door and scruffs me, guiding me around the car and pushing me into the passenger seat. His hand squeezes the spot where my neck meets my shoulder, and his free fingers grab my chin, forcing my face up toward his. I guess I've lost the privilege of having rules; I make a mental note to punish him for this when I'm sober.

His eyes flick between mine, though I'd bet money he has no idea what he's looking for. "What have you taken?"

He pulls his hand away when I go to bite it. I pray for him to snap, grab my hair, to make me feel...I don't know. Small. Because then nothing can be my fault. But of course he doesn't.

"Coke." My smile is more like a grimace. "I didn't ask if it had mix-ins."

"And?"

I hold my fingers a few centimeters apart. "This big, white. One or two, I'm not sure."

Worry creases his face. "Do I need to call Gray?"

"You're the one that will get iced, not me."

He sighs. "Don't die in my car."

Chapter 20

Ethan

I keep thinking I know what hell feels like, until I discover that things can *always* get worse. The day started out good. That castle is called *Castel dell'Ovo* and I found a postcard of it from a nearby gift shop before walking as far as the sea path will take me and eating a delicious sandwich of herb-stuffed pork from a food stall.

All that seems distant now. When Victor called, I started to panic and make stupid decisions. I convinced Gray to give me the keys to the car we took from the airport under the pretense that I had forgotten something inside—a ridiculous excuse that he would have seen right through if I didn't have such a do-gooder reputation.

Now I'm edging a large, expensive car through narrow Italian streets in the dark at the speed of a narcoleptic granny, trying not to get pulled over. I'm sure the half-unconscious man splayed in the seat next to me, out of his gourd on illegal substances, would make a policeman's night. All I can do is drive and pray Victor isn't going to stop breathing.

"I like your face when you're scared," Victor mumbles hoarsely, startling me. He wriggles around in his seat and curls his arm up under his head so he can stare at me. His blown-out pupils hide all but a sliver of his pale irises. I want to punch him.

Kicking off his sandals, he spreads his bare feet on the dashboard. "I can do whatever I want and you can't tell my father without getting fired. Too bad neither of you geniuses thought of that."

I'm too focused on navigating to answer. The lit windows of cafes and restaurants send warm patches of light through the car, across his skin, as we drive past.

When I don't say anything, he closes his eyes. His voice is so slurred I'm struggling to understand him. "What could I pay you to turn against Dad? If we both walk, he'll be screwed. Then I can figure out how to get out of his contract."

"You can't pay me anything, because he owns all your money," I answer dryly.

He makes a sound that I think is supposed to be a laugh. "If he didn't?"

"I don't fantasize about impossible things like unicorns or your father liking you or me being able to trust you."

Silence. I round a corner and, instead of the hotel, we're looking at a small beach and the moonlit water.

Victor comes alive, instantly, and tries to climb out of the still-moving car. I slam the breaks and hit the power locks as he grabs the door handle and shakes it. "I need to practice for Capri," he rambles. When he fumbles the lock open, I flip it again. He throws his shoulder against the door, but his reflexes are too fucked to outmaneuver me.

Finally, he just rolls the window down and hangs his head out, letting in a humid breeze that stirs in his hair. The outline of his strong shoulder blades protruding from his tank top looks like broken wings. They used to carry him faster and further than anyone else on earth. As I watch him watch the water, I have a strange feeling that if Victor went out there now, into the night sea, he'd never come back.

Impulsively, I ask him something that's been bothering me for a long time. "Why do you hate being gay?"

"I never said that."

"But you do. I can tell from the way you talk about it."

Keeping his elbows propped on the open window, he looks over his shoulder at me, eyebrow quirked. "Because I hate gay people."

I'm so confused I don't speak for a minute. Finally, I manage to find words. "You were, like, the poster boy of the future of gay rights. Out and proud since before puberty, so compelling that everyone put aside their prejudices to cheer for you. I idolized you." *And thirsted for you.*

He brushes hair out of his eyes, flashing a smile that doesn't reach any other part of his face. "I never asked for this body, the things it needs. I never consented to it. And of all the exquisite fucking hells I've known, this sexuality has been at the heart of the very worst." Turning away, he rests his cheek against his arm like he's too tired to hold himself up any more. "So you'll have to learn to live with it. Unless you think you can fix me. I know you like to fix things."

Heart pounding, I throw the car into drive and roll up his window, forcing him to slouch back in his seat. "Be careful what you wish for."

From this angle I can barely see his lips twitch. "In case you haven't noticed, I bite."

Scanning the available roads, I pick one that goes uphill. "I'm pretty tough."

"Mmmm," he hums, distracting me as he reaches up to grab his headrest and stretch, arching his long body. "Not last time I tried."

I just shake my head, willing my dick not to betray me.

By the time I find the hotel, he's cogent enough to walk by himself. I text Gray that I'll return the keys in the morning and breathe a sigh of relief when we're both locked in our room. He hisses in pain when I turn on a lamp, so we get ready in the dark. I don't have a choice about sharing a bed with him, but from now on I'll do so fully clothed.

He brushes his teeth while I piss, because I don't have the energy to shut him out of the bathroom. "Promise me you won't see them again," I say, tugging up my sweatpants.

"I'll have to, for the big swim," he mumbles past his toothbrush.

I cross my arms and lean my hip on the counter next to him. "That's another thing. Are you completely insane? You'll drown."

He shrugs. "Maybe that's the point."

"Don't."

Spitting and rinsing, he strips off his shirt and wanders into the bedroom. "Why would you agree to it, anyway?" I call after him.

"Because you didn't want me to."

I throw up my hands. "That's the thanks I get for coming to get you?"

"That's the thanks you get for thinking you have any right to me just because you jacked off in my bed." He's sitting tense on the edge of the mattress in blue striped boxer briefs, like a sleek, skittish seal in the silvered moonlight, poised on the edge of a rock, about to dive in and disappear.

I lie down and yank the covers up. "Be careful. Just because you got me off doesn't mean I'm on your side. I'm not losing my two million just because you're a crazy fucker with no soul."

He doesn't answer.

As I stare at the ceiling, struggling to wind down, his words ring in my head. *Unless you think you can fix me.* When Werner hired me, he tried to make me think this could be fate, that I was somehow destined to be the one thing Victor needs.

But I've heard the word *fate* way too many times in the past two weeks, always from people trying to get me to do something for them. I'm starting to think the universe is just a pinball machine with eight billion balls going at once, flying around at random, hurting and being hurt with no reason and no purpose. The last few days—my whole life, in fact—would make a lot more sense that way. I can stop trying so hard to make anything I do matter.

After I fall asleep, I dream. I dream that I'm cuddled up to the big black lab I had as a kid, but she's shivering like crazy and making awful whimpering sounds. She's thin and beat up and no matter how tight I hold her, she won't calm down

When I open my eyes, I'm sweating and the room smells like smoke. It's still dark, the gauzy curtains swaying gently over the open window with just the occasional sound of a motor in the distance. I throw off the covers and look out the window to the balcony.

He's there in nothing but his underwear, sitting on the iron railing and smoking. When I open the door, he glances up and his eyes look ghostly under the shadow of his brow. Smoke slips between his lips as he studies me like he's never seen me before. I realize he's sitting so far back on the railing that one tan foot hooked around an ornamental iron swirl is the only thing between him and a nine-story drop into the middle of the street.

I stop, holding my breath, not sure if I'm overreacting. The atmosphere feels off, dangerous, like all his smugness disappeared along with the coke high. Watching me, he deliberately takes his hand off the railing and crosses his arms, the cigarette held up between two fingers. "You know the Bible?" he asks. His voice sounds reckless.

"...do I *know* the Bible? Shit, it's a little obscure, but I think so. Or maybe I just saw the movie."

His lips twitch, but his eyes stay dull. "It says man is made from dust, to work the earth, and in the end he'll return to dust."

"Ok. So?" If he's talking, he's not falling.

"I've always believed I came from the water. It speaks to me. It keeps me alive, and I always thought it would take me back." He looks over his shoulder, at the sea, and I risk a couple of steps toward him.

"I have no idea what you're talking about."

"When I go, I thought it should be by drowning. That's why I don't breathe when I swim, because if the water wants me, it can have me. But maybe this is better—"

When he turns around, I'm standing directly in front of him and he sucks in a quick breath. I take the cigarette from his hand and put it out on the railing. "Are you going for lung cancer instead?" We both look at the empty pack balanced next to him. "Should we walk down the street and get more?"

"God." He rubs his palm fretfully against his forehead like a tired little kid. "I don't smoke."

I want to grab him, but something tells me he should come down on his own. I wish he would tell me what happened at that party.

"I saw some weird shit in here." Almost tripping over furniture in the dim room, I head for the minibar. I switch on a lamp, creating a pool of yellow light, and pick up a bottle of something labeled in Italian. "I have no idea what it is. Let's try it."

The corner of his mouth tilts, but his eyes don't change. They're like the burn you get from pressing your skin against ice. I force myself to look away. Even though I just decided it isn't my fate to save him, even though he tries to convince me he isn't worth saving, I can't help myself because I'm not sure there's anyone else in his life who would.

I pop the cap on the bottle I'm holding and dig up some glasses. "I don't see any ice. I can go find some."

"For God's sake." Relief floods me as he slips down from the balustrade, every movement smooth and fluent like he's made of water, and walks on bare feet across the carpet.

He takes the bottle, and tips it straight to his lips. A second later he starts coughing and shoves it at me, splashing my t-shirt. "It's just sparkling water, you fucking idiot."

"Oh." I examine the label again. Victor throws himself into a chair and rests an arm over his eyes. "*Acqua minerale*." The way he snorts into his elbow tells me my pronunciation is as poor as my translation. "Do you want something else? There's plenty to choose from." I guess his father's paying for it all.

He puts his feet up on an ottoman and refuses to answer. The arm that's not over his eyes lies open on his lap, the vulnerable inside of his wrist exposed where it flows into his wide palm. I can imagine the soft, sensitive skin if I put my fingers there, the relentless pulse of someone whose body keeps fighting even when he doesn't want to live.

Forcing myself to look away, I lie down on the bed and reconnect my phone to the hotel Wi-Fi. One new email: *Have you bought our souvenirs yet?* Despite everything, it makes me smile. Peyton informs me that she'll accept anything in Italian leather and that the weather has been surprisingly excellent, sunny most days. We came up with a slapdash code language to describe my mother's condition as Peyton helped me pack.

The mattress creaks when Victor flops face-down into his pillow.

I scan the rest of the email. "Hey, someone from my mom's church gave her and Peyton Mariners tickets, right behind home base."

I brace myself for a disgusting comment, but he doesn't say anything. Opening the attachment, I chuckle at the photo of the two most important women of my life hugging each other, laughing. Peyton has a pint of beer and Mom is waving a blue foam finger. I set it as my lock screen.

He rolls his head sideways and his hard fingers pry my phone from my hands, a blue glow highlighting his face as he squints at the picture. His thumb smooths across the screen, unconsciously, like he's trying to touch them, their smiles, the salt-tang wind in their hair. He stares for so long, perfectly still, his breathing slow and deep, that I think he's fallen asleep. Then he buries his face in his pillow again and shoves the phone at me.

I can barely hear his muffled voice. "Did they win?"

"The Mariners?" I could have sworn I misheard him. "Yeah, I guess they did. For once."

"How much?"

"What, you're a baseball fan now?" Sliding my phone into my pocket, I stare at the back of his head, waiting for him to twist my words, the knife in my gut. He doesn't say anything. "Four to two," I concede, as a siren passing below the window breaks the dense silence.

I trace the faint ridge of his spine with my eyes. His skin is like poured honey. Shifting a little, he clears his throat painfully, and I notice one of his hands is fisting the duvet, like he did with my shirt last night.

For some reason, I keep talking. "The food sucks at the stadium, but it's fun to go. Once it gets dark they turn on all the lights, but the roof is still open to the night sky." The tension in his knuckles relaxes just a little, so I ramble, saying whatever comes to mind. "The breeze comes through, right off the water. By the sixth inning everyone's stuffed with garlic fries and kind of quiet, content. And when the ball pops up into the stands, way faster than you'd think, you always wonder if it's going to brain someone."

When I run out of things to say, he just lies there, motionless, until I give up and climb under the covers and wonder if I imagined the whole thing.

About thirty minutes later, he sits up. He thinks I'm asleep. I watch carefully, ready to get up if he heads for the balcony. Instead, he gathers his pillow and all the remaining blankets from the cupboard. He carries them into the small, empty closet and drops them on the floor. The door slides shut, and I hear a sound like he's wedging something against it and in that moment, I remember a door in his house, the bolts. My stomach curdles.

You had everything. How could you do this to yourself?

Suddenly, I don't feel well. I roll over and curl up in a ball, pretending I'm at home. Even mowing lawns with Scooter sounds like heaven right now. Anything but this sinking realization that I'm in over my head and I've just remembered I can't swim.

Chapter 21

Victor

At breakfast the next morning, I say a few quiet words to the waiter. When he brings all the plates of sausages and eggs, he hands me a little plastic carton of strawberry yogurt. My happiness as I peel the top back and lick the creamy bits of strawberry off my spoon dies when I realize Dad's glaring at me like I just embarrassed all of our ancestors. Since it's already too late, I cross my legs in my chair and make eye contact as I run my tongue up the spoon.

A woman from the film crew stops by our table, leaning between Ethan and I to show us the plan for today's commercial shoot. "The story is pretty simple. You two have just met and Victor is taking you out on his yacht."

Ethan's face pales, and his eyes search out mine. "A boat?"

"It's ok." I poke his knee with my finger. "The Mediterranean is only about five thousand feet deep, and it's never choppy except for windy days like today."

The assistant gives me a weird look as she hands me the schedule. "The yacht is perfectly safe. Please be at the dock by nine o'clock so we can get started on hair and wardrobe."

"I'll be joining you today," my father announces from across the table. "This is our relaunch ad; it needs to be perfect." My skin crawls.

As the assistant walks away, I wad up her document and stuff it into my empty yogurt container. I stand up, nudging Ethan's chair with my foot. "Let's go." It's not until I reach the door of the dining room that I realize he's not behind me. My father and my fake boyfriend have their heads together; every time Dad says something, Ethan nods.

My hand tightens on the door, and I regret not leaving my stomach empty. I'm so hungover that I take out my sunglasses and slide them on.

Is he the reason you came to the party? Is he the reason you didn't let me fall?

Of course he is.

No one comes for me unless they want something.

And you want money a fucking hell of a lot more than you want anything I have to offer.

He doesn't look at me as he passes and leads the way to the cars waiting outside. There's a hint of sunburn on the back of his neck and arms that reminds me how sweet he tasted.

The day is beautiful but uneasy, bright sun with a breeze that's just too strong for comfort, sending clouds scudding across the blue sky. A huge, cream-colored yacht with teakwood accents rocks slowly at mooring, dotted with film crew setting up their equipment.

Ethan hesitates at the bottom of the loading ramp. "What's she called?" I ask, nudging him with my shoulder. "Titanic Jr.?"

"That's the best you could come up with?" he grumbles as we take off our sneakers and put on deck shoes. Dad and Gray are immediately escorted to a shaded dining area, while Ethan and I head to a room inside that has been converted into a wardrobe. The blue shorts they hand me fit very tight, and when I start to button up the shirt they gesture for me to leave it open. It's hard not to laugh at how awkward Ethan looks in white pants and a navy-and-white striped polo, but at least he gets to wear real clothes.

Sansone Campagna, dressed in yet another infinity scarf, shakes our hands. "Welcome on board, gentlemen. We're about to push off. I want to get a shot of your backs as you watch the land recede."

Those last few words have Ethan looking queasy again. He stands as far from the railing as possible without ruining the shot.

"We're supposed to like each other, remember?" I hook an arm around his waist as the engines purr to life and the water below us starts to churn. Naples, green and gold, spread wide across the hills, moves steadily away from us. If I turn I can see Capri as a dot in the distance. It really is a hell of a way to swim with nowhere to rest.

Ethan's hand finds the spot where my shirt rides up on the back of my shorts. "Why do people have boats? They're awful." He's sulking like this isn't one of the most beautiful sights in the world.

"You love to fucking suffer, don't you? If you don't have enough reasons, you make something up."

Just as he's about to answer, Campagna ends the shot. For the next hour, we're herded all over the boat—sit here, sit there, look at the water. It's almost relaxing. Ethan smiles a few times, for real, forgetting where he is, and I pass the time waiting to see if it will happen again.

For the first time, I think maybe I can do this. Maybe I don't need to fight.

"Let's have Victor do some still shots," Campagna calls out. "To drive social media engagement. Tanner, you can go ahead and sit down for lunch. We'll only be a minute."

My photographer leads me along the deck, then turns down some steep stairs into the cabins. I hesitate, glancing back to where Ethan is climbing down from the sunbathing area near the bow. He gives me a sharp look, a Dad look, that says *just do what you're told*.

We walk so far it feels impossible, like we should be outside the bottom of the boat, into a huge berth with a king-sized bed illuminated by a bank of studio lights. I stop in the doorway and dig my toes into the thick carpet.

"Can you sit on the edge of the bed?" the guy asks, fiddling with his camera.

"What's this for again?" I bite my lip, studying the room.

He sighs. "Social media. We need some pictures to draw people in, get a lot of shares and likes so they follow the link to the app."

I swallow, pry my fingers off the door frame. *The more you cooperate, the faster this will be over.* The mattress sinks under my ass as I sit down. "Like this?"

He leans over and tugs open the front of my unbuttoned shirt, until it's almost falling off one shoulder. "And can you," he prods my knee, widening my stance. "Lean back on your hands, don't smile. Perfect."

The shutter sounds deafening in the stuffy room. There aren't any windows, and the bright lights are heating up my skin. I squeeze a fistful of the comforter.

"Now lie down on your back." My stomach starts trembling deep inside me, and I tense my muscles to hide it.

"Did, uh, did my dad approve these?"

"Uh-huh. We showed him all the concepts." He's busy changing settings. "Sex sells best on social media, especially when the celebrity looks like you." I think it's supposed to sound like a complement.

"Mm." I'm losing the ability to talk. Lying back on the bed, I close my eyes as he fusses with the way my shirt should drape. Then he kicks off his shoes and steps up onto the bed, one foot on either side of my hips, pointing the camera down at my face. *Click. Click.*

"You ok?" He stops, frowning. I'm shaking all over, so hard he can feel it.

"Seasick," I croak, scrambling out from between his legs. I almost knock a light over as I run into the tiny attached bath and lock the door. I dry heave into the toilet and sit back against the wall, staring at nothing, unable to stop shivering.

There's a place I go. The water is emerald green and has no bottom so I can just sink and sink and sink. As long as I keep sinking, as long as I don't come up for air, no one can reach me there.

I don't know how long it is before the door rattles. Holding my breath, I stand up slowly. "Victor," Dad growls. "Open this door."

You know you've fucked up when they send God himself down to yell at you.

I wipe my mouth off on my sleeve and shoulder out the door past him. He glares at me as I sit on the edge of the bed and button up my shirt. "Your participation in this ad campaign is not a matter of opinion. If you don't, I will prosecute you for breach of contract and leave you alone, unprotected, with nowhere to go."

Hot, painful emotions I can't identify or control spark behind my eyes. I point to the lights, the bed, my voice louder than I've ever dared to be with him. *"You knew this was going to happen."* The look in his eyes makes me bite my tongue. I try again, quieter. "I'm looking into your eyes right now, as my father, and asking—" I slide off the edge of the bed, onto my knees where I belong "—*begging* you to let me go home. Please."

A long, long silence. We're so deep in the boat I can't smell the dusty sunlight or hear the water. My father clears his throat. "Your personal problems have nothing to do with me. If you can't cope, maybe you should have considered your life choices more carefully."

I make a sound like he just kicked me in the chest.

"It's time for lunch." The old man strolls out of the room, knowing I have no choice but to follow.

Ethan's eyes narrow when he sees me approach the two large tables, set under the shade of the upper deck and arranged with fruit, pastries, thin shavings of meat and cheese—absolutely nothing pre-packaged. I'm carrying a cigarette I bummed off of two crew members I caught taking a smoke break on the way up. Even though I don't want it, I need something to do with my hands.

"Your dad spoke to me just now." He sounds upset. When I take a pull instead of answering him, he fidgets. I study the horizon through my sunglasses as the wind whips the smoke from between my lips. "I get that this shit isn't exactly fun, but you're making things harder for everyone. You said *I* like to suffer, but you're the one turning a free vacation and some glamor shots into the ninth circle of hell."

"What exactly did he tell you?" I ask softly.

"You got pissed and walked out on the photo shoot."

"Ah." A dry laugh bubbles up in my chest and I raise my voice. "Is that so, Werner?"

My father looks up from his plate, and Gray turns around to stare at me. I hold Dad's eyes, but I'm talking to Ethan. "What if I told you he was fucking with me? Setting me up to fail? Who would you believe?"

He hesitates. Whatever's in my chest where my heart should be cracks. "Got it." I throw my cigarette down and grind it out on the decking. "I get it."

"You want me to be honest?" He's trying to speak quietly, but I know my dad can hear. "God knows I've tried, but you have never given me a single reason to trust you. You live in some insane dream world and I can't *afford* to stay there with you, whether I want to or not."

I can't breathe, air spasming in my lungs, but I keep my lips pressed together so Ethan doesn't notice. Suddenly, I get why he's so afraid of the ocean. There's nowhere to go.

Dad nods to me, smiles. He still knows every way to hurt me, to punish me for all the shame I've brought him, by taking the only things I care about.

Pushing my chair back, I get up and start walking, hunting for any part of the yacht where I can't see cameras or people. On a quiet bit of deck at the stern, I settle down on the warm wood and hang my legs over the water, resting my chin on the railing. Flecks of sea foam hit my cheeks, and the rumble of engines fills my brain until there's no room for thoughts.

Ethan

It takes a little convincing, but after I film a few extra shots by myself Campagna agrees that we have enough to call this day a wrap. The way the deck tilts as the yacht sluggishly turns around makes me swear never to set foot on a boat again.

Staying as far from the railings as I can, I hunt through the ship until I find Victor's hiding spot. He scrambles to his feet, shaking his head. "No. If you wanna fucking see dry land again, you will turn around and walk away."

He looks as queasy as I feel, eyes haunted, and a sliver of doubt forces its way into my convictions.

I hunt for words, struggling to fuel the righteous anger that brought me here. "We need to get some things straight. I'm not going to be the rope in a tug-of-war between you and your father. He gave me a job to do and I came here to do it."

His smirk-shaped mouth turns up at the corner as he stands there, shifting his weight with the movement of the boat. "I mean it. Go away."

The sleep deprivation, the stress, the gnawing feeling I might have made the wrong choice—it all spills out in a rush of words. "This is what I mean. You're always running away, hiding, getting high. You threw away a legendary career over a suspension because you couldn't admit you were wrong." I thump my fist against my chest. "I have problems, too. Big ones. And it hurts but I fucking face them."

Despite his warning, he approaches me. Before I know it, he's walked me backward until my ass is pressed to the railing, trapping me there. His cheek brushes against my neck as he speaks into my ear. "People need you, Ethan. They look for you when you're not there. You can sleep at night." I can feel him breathing hard against my chest. "Is that not enough for you? You have to come here and *use* me to get more? Drain me dry?"

I try to move, but he grips the railing on either side of me. His words in the car last night come back to me, words I forgot too easily. *Remember, I bite.*

"Look. It was a bad day, but it's over; we're going back to Naples."

"Careful." He tilts down his sunglasses, looks up into my eyes. Today, his look light blue, like the furthest away part of the sky. "We're not there yet."

I look over my shoulder at the uninterrupted water. "I don't see any icebergs."

Catching the tip of his tongue in his teeth, he smiles at me. "Too bad there's only one life boat and you're the least important person here."

Too quickly for my mind to process, his hands collide with my chest and send me backwards and upside down into the warm sea. Panic and water wrap around my limbs, heavy and weightless at the same time, and in a flash I'm back in Lake Chelan, half-conscious, choking on lungfuls of water as I try to search for Danny below the spot he disappeared.

My head breaks the water and through blurry eyes I see Victor standing there, watching. I'm too scared to feel scared, like I'm already dead and looking back at how it happened. And of all the regrets I feel for myself, my mom, my friends, there's one more that I can't quite understand. Something that tells me maybe fate was real after all, that I might have been the only person who could reach him, that I'll spend the last minutes of my life wishing I had listened to the part of me that knew he was telling the truth.

Water fills my mouth as I go under, but I fight my way back to the surface just in time to see him take a life preserver off the wall and toss it lazily in my direction. He ties the other end to the railing, lets out a shrill whistle between his teeth, and walks away.

By the time the crew sounds the alarm and pulls me in, I have the white plastic ring clutched to my chest so tightly they have to pry it out of my hands.

Chapter 22

VICTOR

In the hotel lobby, Gray pulls Ethan aside to talk to him. He stands and listens, one hand on either end of the towel guarding his neck and shoulders from his still-wet hair, his eyes tired. Gray points at me. "Come here."

"I'm good, thanks." I grab a fistful of foil-wrapped biscotti from the coffee station and head for the elevator.

It's quiet in our room except for rustling and chewing as I inhale one packet of cookies after another. I'm so fucking hungry. Outside the protection of my house, no one cares if there's food I feel safe eating.

I need to go home, which means finishing the commercial and swimming to Capri without dying. If I'm going to be strong enough to do either of those things, I need to eat and sleep. And if I'm going to sleep, I need a way to get rid of the nightmares that have been tearing me apart since Katrina first called my name on the street outside.

Turning my bags inside out, one by one, I hunt for the Ambien I stuffed into one of my socks. When I get to the end of the last suitcase, I sit on the end of the bed and bury my head in my hands.

After I get my breathing under control, I grab Ethan's duffel and start hunting through his thrift store t-shirts and the stack of travel brochures he's been collecting for his mom. An orange bottle falls out of his spare pair of sneakers. Fumbling the lid off, I check the label. Xanax. The first good thing to happen to me today.

I dump six into my palm, then hesitate. Pushing one under my tongue, I put the others in my pocket and drink from the bathroom tap. When I hear the elevator reach our floor, I go onto the balcony and scoot into the far corner, where I can't be seen from the window. The chilly stone turns the bottoms of my feet numb.

Ethan shuts the door behind him and sighs. "Victor?" He sounds completely drained. "Are you in here?"

Biting my lip, I watch the lights flicker to life in the castle by the harbor. I try to imagine him dead in the sea, how it would have felt to leave him there. Whether it would have hurt less to watch him die than it did to listen to him agree with Dad. I don't have names for feelings, just *good* and *bad*, *pain* and *not pain*, and none of those describes the way my chest cracks apart whenever he looks at me.

When I hear him open the closet door, I close my eyes. The boy has been paying attention, watching everything I do. "Victor?" Whether he's angry or worried or pleased, he always says my name carefully, like it matters.

Finally, the bed creaks. My plan is to wait until he starts snoring and sleep in the closet again, but the Xanax takes over and drops me right into that deep, deep water.

Tonight, *he* finds me there. Hands holding me down, a voice in my ear, fingers in my mouth. I gasp awake, aching and cold. According to my phone, it's only two o'clock in the morning.

Nights are too long, but I hate the days, too. There's no good time to be alive.

Trying to bring feeling back to my legs, I hobble inside. He's sprawled all over the place, mouth open, chest rising and falling so steadily it's hypnotic to watch.

I step up onto the bed and walk across the mattress, settling cross-legged right next to him. My dream still has me by the throat; I'm afraid he'll feel the pounding of my heart through the bed.

I nearly jump out of my skin at the sound of footsteps in the hall. It's not him. It's not. I scoot closer to Ethan, until my knee bumps his side, and reach up to brush a lock of hair off his forehead. *I'm sorry I scared you. Are you having good dreams? Can you let me in?*

A nearby door opens and my adrenaline skyrockets. My hand hovers above his shoulder, about to wake him up, but instead I reach over and pick up his phone.

I enter the passcode I've watched him use. There's that photo, his friend and his mother in front of a baseball diamond. I chew my knuckle, smiling a little as I flip through his photo reel. Every third picture is an accidental shot of the idiot's shoe or the crotch of his jeans. I text myself the best view of his bulge and one other, just him sitting in his truck with his arm out the window, unaware of whoever took the photo.

His texts are just about boring enough to put me to sleep sober—endless messages to his mother, his friend, asking what's up, what he's going to make for dinner. He found a puzzle at the thrift store; he's running late to trivia night; he dropped a ceramic planter on his foot and needs to buy frozen peas to ice it. He has one of those match-three jewel games at level 2321, probably from working some boring night shift. Sighing, I press the phone to my forehead. I can't wake him up.

You can't belong to someone like me. I'm an infection in your world.

Desperate to stop looking at him, I crawl around in the dark until I find my speedo and a towel. The door creaks, but he doesn't stir. It's time to start practicing for the last race of my life.

ETHAN

An uneasy feeling wakes me up just after two. When I stretch my arm across the bed, it's empty and cold. "Shit." Sitting up, I switch on the bedside lamp. Bed, closet, bathroom, all deserted. That's when I notice my Xanax bottle thrown haphazardly in the top of my bag.

I get up and dump them on the table; there should be thirty, since I've only had a fraction of one. When I only count twenty-four, it feels like someone threw ice water on my face. He was already on the edge, and we pushed him too far today.

He could be anywhere, but I have to pick one place to look. It's not hard. Without changing out of my pajamas or putting on shoes, I forgo the elevator and take the stairs, struggling not to slip on narrow steps that are definitely not OSHA compliant.

Sure enough, when I reach the outdoor pool surrounded by colorfully-lit beds of tropical plants, there's a dark body disturbing the water, all alone under the wide stars.

I can still taste salt water raw in my throat from this afternoon, so I stop a safe distance from the pool's edge. Victor's head comes up and he tosses back his hair, running his hands through it. He blinks when he sees me.

"Get out of there," I demand.

"Why?" I think he actually means it. He wipes his nose like a kid, squinting at me.

"Because you're on six fucking Xanax. You'll drown before I can even get you to the hospital."

He shakes his head, holds up one finger. "I told you before. If the water takes me, then it's time."

When he threw me in the sea, I just felt numb. Numb and hurt. Now I feel what I should have felt then, a white-hot flash of anger, pushing me a few steps closer to the pool. "Do you ever *think* before you do anything? I'm sick of rescuing you."

"Then don't. My father will still pay you. Maybe he'll adopt you." He sinks until only his eyes are above the water.

I risk one step closer, even though my stomach twists. "I wish I had asked for your side of the story today. I've been thinking, and I don't—"

He turns his back on me and strikes out in that beautiful, reckless butterfly stroke that experts have spent years analyzing. The spark of anger turns into something deeper, a feeling of pure, impotent frustration at a world where things won't go right, no matter what I do. It reminds me of the day my relatives called to tell me that they were cutting off my mother and me, and nothing I said could change their minds.

Pulling off my shirt and sweats, I step off the edge and land waist-deep in the shallow end. The scrape of my feet against the tiled bottom provides an anchor to keep me from panicking as I wade deeper. Victor hits the wall, twists under the water, and almost swims straight into my chest. He comes up, coughing, face to face with me. I can tell I've finally surprised him.

He inhales sharply when I grab the back of his neck, my wet skin slipping against his. "I'm done playing around with you," I growl, gripping tighter, feeling his skin dent under my fingers. "I have you figured out. Your games aren't going to work on me anymore"

We're both panting, noses almost touching. His eyelids flutter under droplets of water, his pale eyes fixed on mine as he leans just a breath closer.

"Pay attention," he whispers. His hand traces along the waist of my boxers. The coaxing pressure of his fingers on my back pulls our hips together and I realize we're both already getting hard, so fucking desperate. "I'll show you how to take what you want, how to own me. I'll teach you how to hurt me."

I open my mouth to say that's not what I want. But then I realize it's not true. When I hesitate, he seals my mouth with his, not gently, devouring, his tongue assaulting mine like he's trying to climb inside of me. Before I can react, he breaks the twisted echo of a kiss and puts his wet lips against my ear. "Don't let me up until you finish."

Then he's gone, water closing over his curly hair. His hands trail down my body and it makes my cock ache so deeply I want to cry. He tugs my boxers around my knees, one of his hands groping my ass, the other circling the base of my shaft. A trail of bubbles breaks the surface, then

I gasp as hot suction gulps down my cock. My hands find his hair instinctively, and his grip on me tightens. He doesn't work up to it; I'm all the way down his tight throat as he swallows hard enough to make my knees weak and jerks off the length he can't fit in his mouth.

I'm trying to convince myself that I'm still a good person, that those seven words—*I'll teach you how to hurt me*—didn't blow open the locks inside me that no amount of sweetness and love have been able to touch. But as two of his fingers slip into my ass crack I realize that all the dreams I haven't been able to remember this week, the ones that disappeared as soon as I opened my eyes, they were all about this.

A car honks loudly on the street outside, piercing my daze, and I realize he's been down there a minute, maybe longer, without easing up. "Ok," I gasp, fumbling through his hair, trying to grab his shoulders. "Come up."

When he feels my hands, he holds me tighter and tips his head back, taking me deep, his tongue grinding along the bottom of my shaft. "God," I groan, miserable and desperate. And yet I can't make myself stop him because as fear takes my breath away, as his body starts spasming in a fight for oxygen, pleasure *sears* through me and I unload into the warm cavern of his mouth. The feeling of him swallowing, sucking down my cum like water in a desert, pulls my orgasm out until I feel like I'm the one drowning.

After what seems like forever, his head breaks the water. He's wheezing as he reaches for the wall and clings to it, goosebumps standing out along his back.

"I hate you so much," I breathe, ashamed, staring through bleary eyes at the wall of plastic-looking palms hiding us from the hotel.

"You weren't trying hard enough," he manages between gasps, forehead pressed against the wall.

"Excuse me?" When he glances at me, his eyes are glazed and his lips are flushed and wet. "I wasn't trying hard enough to drown you?"

He grabs my hand and pulls it under the water, presses it to the bulge in the front of his speedo. Closing his eyes, he starts grinding against my palm with slow jerks of his hips. "Tell me I did a good job." His voice is cracked and soft, throat wrecked.

"No." But I don't move my hand. I can hear soft whimpers in his throat as he thrusts. "This isn't normal."

"That's the point. No one has this but us. Isn't that why you're here?" His head falls back, hips moving faster. "Oh God. Shit."

I want him to finish so I can go back to bed and pretend this never happened, pretend he isn't right about me. When he stops moving, I look up. He's resting his head against the wall, forehead scrunched like he's in pain. "Hey." He doesn't open his eyes. "Are you ok?"

"I'm sorry," he breathes, words coming slowly. "I don't think I can. I'm not—" He shivers. His eyes when he opens them are windows to a hurt I can't even grasp.

I pull myself up to sit on the edge of the pool. "Come here." The first time he tries to get out, his weak arms collapse. I help him with a hand under his armpit.

Leaving him there, I grab a pile of towels off a table and lay one out over the nearest deck chair. I put the other one around his shoulders. When he catches his breath, I pull him to his feet and guide him to the lounger, sitting next to him. "It's ok," I say, not even sure what I'm talking about. "Do you need some water?"

"Tell me—" He swallows painfully. "Tell me you hate me again."

I hesitate, frowning, and he leans forward, resting his elbows on his knees and cradling his head. "Please."

Closing my eyes, I search all the corners of my mind, everything he's said and done, all the pain he's caused, the way he's turning me into something I don't understand. The lounge creaks as I lean toward him until my lips almost touch his damp hair. "I do hate you. I really do. I think you're a bad person."

"Uh-huh?" He sounds so tired, so hopeful.

"I hate you, Victor."

"Promise?"

"I'm never gonna stop."

At last his stiff, exhausted body starts to relax.

Chapter 23

ETHAN

My phone rings when I'm showering the next morning. Victor doesn't look like he's going to move any time soon, just a pile of blankets, so I pull on a hoodie and duck into the hall, pacing on the worn, flowered carpet. "Hey, Peyton, how are you?" I'm hoping she doesn't ask how I am, because I don't have an answer.

She doesn't ask. "She needs to talk to you."

My heart sinks. "Yeah, ok."

Mom's voice trembles when she picks up the phone. "Ethan?" It kills me that I'm not there to hold her.

"Hey," I say gently, keeping my voice cheerful. "I was going to call today and ask you what you'd like for a souvenir."

"I had a bad dream about Danny," she whimpers. "I wanted to check on him, but I can't reach him. And when I called Cath, she didn't answer either."

I sit on the windowsill at the end of the hall, an old-fashioned radiator digging into the underside of my thighs, and close my eyes. "They're completely fine, Mom."

She sniffles, and it breaks my heart. "It was a really bad dream. I was so scared when they didn't answer."

"Dreams can't hurt you," I lie, gently, remembering the look in Victor's eyes on the balcony.

"Can you come home? Why did you go?" That question hits me like a fist. The deeper I crawl into this crazy world, the more I forget that I'm here to collect my money, get Mom to that specialist, and watch her get better. Because she's going to get better, no matter what anyone says. And the man currently sleeping in my bed has no place in my peaceful, precious world.

"I'm going to get you an awesome present today. But I can't tell you what it is."

"Because I'll forget." I flinch. She doesn't mention it often, and I'm never sure how clearly she understands, but sometimes it spills out.

"No," I tease lightly. "Because I haven't found it yet, silly."

We talk a little while about nothing, until I can hear the smile come back into her voice. With the sun on my shoulders and the faint scent of smoky, floral candles, I can pretend I'm in my living room at home, watching football while Mom knits, free from Victor's chaos. What scares me the most is that I'm not entirely happy about it.

Since I'm up, I descend in the elevator to get a quiet coffee in the breakfast nook I spotted last night. Trying not to disturb the middle-aged men with their newspapers, I grab an espresso and sit by the window. It looks out toward the pool, and I feel shame heat my face as I watch an employee scoop leaves out of the water.

The chair across from me creaks and I look up into Gray's studied, permanently disapproving expression. He always looks perfect, not a hair out of place, suit pressed. Staring at me over the rim of his cup, he sits back. "How is he?"

Everything flashes through my mind—the team, the coke, the balcony, the yacht, the pool—and I freeze, wondering which one he's trying to get me to confess. "Why are you asking me?" I say finally. "You're the one who's known him for years."

His eyebrows furrow. "He seems to trust you."

"I'm not sure that's what I'd call it."

A ghost of a smile. "You have his attention, and that's the best any of us can hope for." After a long moment, he speaks again. "I want him to make it through this alive. Please come to me if you need help."

"I have a question."

"Hm?" He looks a little surprised.

"What's wrong with him?"

His frown isn't quick enough to hide the split-second hesitation. "He passed a clean bill of physical and sexual health right before the trip."

I stiffen, wondering why he felt the need to be so specific, but he doesn't seem to notice. "You know that's not what I meant."

Drinking the last of his coffee, he sets his cup down firmly. "To be frank, Ethan, I wish to God I knew. Over the years I've known him, he's changed in front of my eyes from what you saw on TV to...this. There are gaps in his life, blanks, things that don't make sense. But he won't tell me."

My heart's beating faster. "Like what?"

He catches himself. "It's not my place to share. If he truly trusts you, you'll find them for yourself. And maybe you'll get deeper than I could. Will you tell him something for me?" He stands up, dusting himself off, and lowers his voice. "If he's ever ready to talk, I'm here. And if it comes down to father versus son, I choose him."

"You should tell him yourself," I point out, but the man is already gone.

VICTOR

"Where are we going?"

Ethan turns around with a peeved expression and sees me sitting at the bottom of the hotel steps, legs stretched out in the sun. I'm driving the doorman and the valet crazy. I can't stand being inside, but I'm not brave enough to go any further on my own.

"*We're* not going anywhere. *I'm* going to spend a long time choosing sentimental souvenirs for my mom at the most boring shops imaginable."

Leaning back on my elbows, I grin at his blatant attempt to shake me off. He's getting a tan that looks good with his white Henley and tan shorts, like a closet cosplay of a rich European.

I can still hear his voice in my ear, quiet and honest. *I hate you so much.* Catching sight of him is becoming an obsession; when I look at him, I see something bright, a flame I can use to burn us to the ground.

"Where to first?" I put on my sunglasses and scramble to my feet. He's close enough that I have to look up into his face. Something has changed. He's not hiding anything from me now because we made the hate real, wove it like a covenant between our bodies. As long as he's here, nothing bad can come near me because there's no room for anything but him and me and the ways we hurt each other.

A little too fast, he turns around and walks away, unfolding a big, floppy map of the city. He acts like he's trying to lose me, but every time I get too far behind, he slows down a little. It's nice not to have to pretend we're together, just for a few hours.

I follow him past a church with faded flowers painted on the pillars and up a hill with way too many steps. He stops someone to ask for directions, trying out his limited Italian vocabulary. Since we got here, his confidence has skyrocketed while mine has plummeted. Maybe that's why I'm slowly losing the ability to function without him.

Finally, we turn down a narrow pedestrian street full of graffiti and cheap merchandise, overhung by balconies and full of the sound of pop music from one of the apartments. Just like he warned me, he takes fucking forever in every store while I sulk in the entry until the shopkeepers kick me out for blocking the flow of traffic.

At last, he emerges with a puzzle of one of the castles we walked past and a small, camel-colored purse.

"Are you finally satisfied?"

He drops the bag in my arms. "If you're so desperate for something to do, carry these."

"You should know better than to trust me with things I don't care about."

I'm kind of relieved when he doesn't walk toward the hotel but instead leads the way into a bright, cheerful square ringed with cafes. I make a beeline for the big fountain in the middle, sitting on the edge and putting my hand in the blue water, picking out moldy coins and throwing them back. In spite of what I said, I put Ethan's bag between my feet where it can't get splashed.

"Victor." I can usually ignore my name, but not from his mouth. He's standing next to a gelato cart, looking at me thoughtfully. "Come here."

Jesus fuck those two words in that voice do something to me. I pick up the bag and walk over to him, glancing down at the open bins of gelato in the display. "I don't want one."

He ignores me, pointing at an almost empty tub of chocolate. "Do you have a fresh one? Can you open it here?"

The guy gives us a weird look, but disappears and returns with a full tub. He throws the old one away and wrestles the new one into place. Ethan watches me as the man cuts a plastic seal off the lid and peels it open, revealing untouched ice cream. "Two of those, *per favore*." He pretends not to notice me staring at him as he hands me a paper cup and a spoon.

We sit side by side on the edge of the fountain, close enough for our knees to touch, and Ethan waits for me to take a bite before he digs into his own. "Good, huh?" It's one of the best things I've ever tasted.

When I'm scraping my spoon around and around the bottom of the cup, trying to get the last drops, he clears his throat. "Is it, like, a germ thing? 'Cause I get that. But maybe you should see someone about it."

My body tenses up. "Did you buy me this to make me talk to you?"

"No." Running a hand through his hair, he frowns. "Gray said—" He stops instantly, but it's too late.

"You've all been talking about me again? Did you get Dad's opinion, too?" This doesn't feel good. I hate not feeling good.

We didn't notice the sky getting darker, and Ethan jumps when the first raindrop hits the edge of the fountain. "You already know everything," I lie, watching tourists run under cover and the food stands drop their shutters. "I cheated. I got caught. I'm not sorry. And I'm not a good person. Every bad thing you've ever thought about me is true, and if you keep pushing me I might do something worse."

If you knew, you'd never look at me again. I wouldn't even be worth your hate.

When I meet his gaze, he's studying me like I'm the most important exam of his life. His voice is almost too quiet to hear over the patter of rain on concrete. "I don't know if I believe you."

I drop my ice cream cup on the ground and his eyes widen as I grab either side of his head. This is so important. I need him to understand. "Don't you get it? If I'm not a bad person, then what we have, you and I, it doesn't exist." My fingers curl against his skin. I look at his lips, parted, wet with rain, then back to his warm eyes. "Is that what you want?"

For you, this is just a detour, a blip. For me, this is everything. I didn't know what it meant to feel safe until you hated me.

He doesn't have an answer. I stand up, untangling his shopping bag from my feet.

"Where are you going?"

"I don't know."

He starts to get up, but I hold out my hand to stop him. "I don't need you to rescue me again."

Chapter 24

ETHAN

It's like I said: maybe we're just a bunch of helpless, mindless pinballs set loose in a machine the size of the planet. Collisions happen. Ones we never saw coming. Ones that send us spinning out of control.

That's not what I'm thinking about when I follow Victor, staying far enough back that he doesn't notice me. I'm thinking about the stray cats I used to feed as a kid. If one of them wouldn't eat, I'd ask around the neighbors for a new treat to try. And eventually, I'd find something that brought even the most skittish stray right up to my hand. That's how it felt to watch Victor eat his gelato. It was a perfect memory and I wish I hadn't ruined it.

It's getting dark, and I'm soaked through. Victor hasn't stopped walking up and down random streets, hands in his pockets, his wet button-down clinging to his narrow ribs.

When the front door of one of the apartments along the road opens, letting out a spill of warm light, I don't think anything of it. Someone comes out, locks the door with a jingle of keys, turns around to grab a bicycle leaning against the side of the house.

Victor stops dead, like he got turned into a statue. So I stop, too. A motion-activated light on the front of the building flicks on, bright pricks of rain falling through its yellow beam, and illuminates the stranger's face.

Just like too many times in the past two weeks, I recognize someone I've seen on TV, in sports magazines, on major news sites. A stocky man with receding hair and a square jaw—Victor's old coach, Clint Simmons. It makes sense, knowing his swim team is in town, but something about the way he appears with no warning out of the dark feels strangely shocking.

Clint looks rather shocked himself. I can't hear what he says, but he offers his hand to Victor with an uncertain smile. From what I remember reading, they parted on very poor terms. But unlike Victor, some people move on.

Victor takes a step back, hands hanging stiffly at his sides.

I move close enough to hear over the steady hiss of rain. "I've missed you," Clint says. He sounds emotional, like he might start crying. Victor was like a second son to him. "I've wanted to see you for years, to put the past behind us."

When Victor doesn't move, he sighs and picks up his satchel. "You know where I'm staying now. Think it over; you're always welcome."

As he pushes his bike past Victor, he gives his bicep a gentle squeeze before getting on and riding away.

Victor stands in the middle of the street for an absurdly long time, just staring at the house, until a moped comes down the hill and almost hits him. The driver screeches to a stop, wobbling dangerously, and unleashes a torrent of furious Italian directly into Victor's face. I hold my breath, waiting for the explosion, but Victor just listens in silence before turning and walking unsteadily toward the center of the city.

I stop and wait under an awning as he goes into a small liquor store and emerges with a bottle of vodka. It's like deja vu. He leans against the building and chugs it until he's forced to double over, coughing. Sliding onto his ass on the wet concrete, he just sits there, taking deep pulls from the bottle.

Here I am, shivering in the dark, watching a fully-grown man melt down because he can't face his own guilt. And as angry as I am, I'm also desperate to go to him. I want to be his shelter from the rain. I want to make him look into my eyes and remember that I'm the only one who's allowed to hurt him.

You're so bad for me, and I don't know what's going to happen if I can't get free of you.

Just as I force myself to leave, an old soft-top Volkswagen pulls up to one of the nearby houses and a man climbs out, holding a newspaper over his head like an umbrella. Victor scrambles to his feet and calls out to him. They stand next to the car arguing for so long that I'm about to intervene.

Finally, they step into the shelter of the man's entry and pull out their phones to perform some kind of transaction. Shaking his head in disbelief, the man hands Victor his keys, grabs a handful of junk from the backseat, and goes inside.

It appears that he just bought a random car off the fucking street. Every time I think nothing can surprise me anymore, he comes up with something even more insane. Money really can accomplish anything.

He leans against the dark green vehicle and finishes off his vodka before fumbling the driver's side door open and starting the engine.

The headlights blind me as I break into a run, smacking my hands against the hood before he can start rolling. He jumps, staring at me like I'm some kind of mythological creature, then sticks his head out the window. "Move."

"No."

He taps the accelerator, but I dig my feet in and stare him down. It's a dangerous game to play with someone this drunk, but some part of me knows he isn't going to hurt me. "Come with me and sleep this off. In the morning, we'll give the man back his car. And someday, you'll thank me for this."

He throws the empty bottle at me, missing by a mile. "Fucking *move*," he screams, his voice cracking. He's never raised his voice before.

We lock eyes, both of us frozen with shock as the bottle explodes on the pavement. He slides down in his seat, eyes wide, like he thinks I'm going to pull him out of the car and beat the shit out of him.

When I grab the handle of the driver's door, he tries to hold it closed. I reach through the open window and wrap my fingers firmly around his wrist. "Victor. Hey."

For the first time, it's like he actually sees who I am. With a whimpering sound in his throat, he lets go of the door. I open it and crouch down on the wet street, looking up at him. I don't know what to say, so I just say his name again. My tongue likes to say his name.

"I'm leaving," he says hoarsely, slurring his words. Looking around, he points in a random direction that I think is meant to indicate *away from Naples*. "I need to go." His eyes are begging me to understand.

When I shift my weight, he stiffens, grips his seat like I'm going to drag him away. He looks like a puppet that's having its strings cut one at a time but still trying desperately to function.

If I don't take him back, they have every right to end my contract. Hell, they have the right to send police after me. But when I think about what might happen to my mother if I got arrested, I think about what she would do if she were in my place right now. What she would tell me to do.

Groaning, I stand up and tap his shoulder. "Scoot over. I'm driving."

don't cry
my top-down sun-out summer boy

Chapter 25

ETHAN

The guy who owned this car must have been shorter than he looked. The whole creaky wreck rattles and squeaks as I adjust everything—seat, mirrors, steering wheel—and wish Victor had at least chosen something made in this decade. I pull away from the curb and into a roundabout, picking up speed.

The seat behind my back already feels wet, and there's water dripping off Victor's hair onto his nose. "Can we swing by the hotel to get a change of clothes?"

"No."

"But—"

I manage to slam on the breaks before he gets the door open and one foot on the ground. He's breathing hard, like he scared even himself. He glares at me, pale eyes cloudy. "Either you're on my side or you're not." His chin tips up.

"Fine. Get your fucking feet inside." I'll figure out what to do later, after he's asleep.

Thankful for the quiet night roads, I follow signs that seem to take us out of the city. I'll never find the way back without help.

He tilts his seat back and slumps down, eyes lidded. Every once in a while, his throat convulses as he swallows. His damp tank top has twisted around, exposing all of one thick pec and dusky nipple, but he doesn't seem to notice.

As the city thins out, I catch more and more glimpses of cypress trees and pale hillsides. Something touches my knee, startling me. He's watching me, eyes anxious. "Stay by the sea," he whispers.

"How am I supposed to do that when I have no idea where I'm going?"

Sitting up, he reaches across me, all his movements tentative, like he's waiting to be hurt. He rolls down my window. "Just listen to it." The rain has stopped, and the breeze in my hair feels warm.

"Ok." I can't hear anything, but I need him to relax.

After a few minutes, his eyes start to drift shut and flutter open again. At last he rolls onto his side with his back to me and stops moving.

I think the sea is to my left, so I keep taking random left turns until I'm on a road where the waves can be heard clearly, with little petrol stations and closed fruit stands whipping past.

Our petrol looks full, thank God. I don't have enough euros for a tank. I don't have a shirt or a toothbrush or the charger for my cell. I don't even have the assurance that I'm doing the right thing. I'm lost in more ways than just streets I don't recognize and towns whose names I can't pronounce.

I decide to drive until I know what to do, until any of this makes sense. An hour later, I realize I'm way further from Naples than I intended to go. I slow down, looking for any sign of a hotel, a town, anything. Aside from boarded-up shops and the occasional crumbling beach house, I haven't seen anything for miles.

Making an abrupt decision, I turn into a narrow lane that winds between huge vineyards until I spot a gravel pull-off almost buried in a thick hedge. Branches scrape the roof as I park and listen to the engine tick, trying to catch my breath. The air smells sweet, and I've never been anywhere so quiet.

With a groan, Victor rolls onto his back and stares out the windscreen. The moonlight makes his eyes bright but doesn't give them any life. He looks like a ghost, barely held to the earth at all.

I clear my throat. "Let's sleep for a few hours, sober up." Reaching over him, I snoop through the glovebox. Underneath an atlas, which I take to examine in the morning, I find two oat bars in foil wrappers. "Score."

Setting one of the bars by his elbow, I open the other and take a big bite. "It's like wet, expanding sawdust." I'm starving, so I finish the rest even though it makes me gag.

Ignoring me, he wriggles deeper into his seat and closes his eyes.

I toss and turn, trying and failing to get comfortable. I can't tell if Victor's asleep or not, but after staring at him through half-closed eyes, studying the tint of his skin in the moonlight, I take off my jacket and drape it across his bare shoulders.

I roll up my window, reach across to do the same to his, lock the doors, and close my eyes. I thought it would be hard to sleep, but I already feel so lost in a strange dream that moving deeper is an easy matter after all.

Sometime before morning, I jolt awake, convinced that the Italian equivalent of a redneck axe murderer is tearing our car to pieces. The suspension sways crazily to the sound of cracking, snapping plastic.

Something is suffocating next to me, the gulping of someone who needs to scream but can't get any air. Victor kicks the door again, as hard as he can; in the moonlight I see some part of the body panel shatter and send pieces bouncing off the ceiling.

I grab his shoulder without thinking and he just about decapitates me with his elbow. He scrambles away, pressing his back to the door, gasping.

"You need to breathe," I say stupidly, my heart hammering against my ribs.

"Can't—" It's the only word he can force out, and for all that he brags about drowning, in the flash of his eyes in the darkness I can see that he's terrified to find no air in his lungs.

I grope blindly for understanding. "Did you have a bad dream? It's not real."

He closes his eyes and forces in a wheezy breath. "The door...was locked."

"There's this handy little switch, you know, that doesn't involve putting your foot through the door."

At that, I see a spark of life in his expression. "Did you..." He fights to speak clearly, like he's about to say something terribly important. "Pack...the Xannies?"

I flop back in my seat, rubbing my palms against my eyes. "No, Victor, I did not pack you *drugs*. You didn't even let me pack a dry t-shirt."

The corner of his mouth twitches. "Fuck...you." He sags against the door, and I can see the sweat sheening his skin. He's shuddering and his breath keeps catching and he's coming apart—weak, dehydrated, confused, too full of alcohol to get control of his body.

He's my stray. This afternoon, I fed him for the first time. I remember my favorite kitten, the small one who got sick from being lost outside in winter. My neighbor told me to come into her living room and lie on her couch. She set the kitten on my chest to warm her up. I lay there for two hours without moving, my hands cupped around the fragile creature, feeling it fight for life.

Twisting my body in the cramped car, I climb over the center console into Victor's seat. He pulls back, jaw clenching; I can't tell if he's scared or being stubborn.

"Slow down." I meet his eyes, and his brows furrow.

"I—" His breath catches painfully and he presses a hand to his chest, gritting his teeth. "Jesus Christ."

I draw on everything I've learned from comforting Mom. "You know you're safe, right?"

My heart sinks when he shakes his head slowly. Fuck, he's so far gone.

I take one of his hands where it's gripping the door. It's cold and clammy, sweaty between the joints, and yet this is the first time I've really noticed his hands and they're gorgeous, absolutely perfect. I wrap my bulky fingers around his long ones and squeeze gently. "I'm here. Feel me."

Slowly, like he's concentrating, he presses his other hand to my chest, splaying his fingers wide, feeling it rise and fall. Suddenly, I know what to say. "You're stuck in a car with the person who hates you more than anything else in the world. Whatever you're afraid of, it's nothing compared to me."

His luminous eyes flick to mine. Shifting his weight, he slides down beside me and rests his ear over my heart. I stare at the ceiling, willing my body to stay calm. His bulk gets heavier as he relaxes, warmer as he takes on my body heat.

I prop one hand behind my neck so I can look down at his dirty blond hair and slide the other up under the hem of his tank top, rubbing slowly up and down his spine.

My muscles start cramping and aching after an hour, but I force myself to stay perfectly still. I distract myself trying to name all the places I'd rather be than here, alone in a strange country, crushed under the weight of a 180 lb man having a nervous breakdown. When I realize how short the list really is, I start to wonder if I've made all the wrong turns in life.

Chapter 26

ETHAN

When I open my eyes, he's sitting against the back wheel of the VW in the sharp, gold light of sunrise, smoking. For someone who doesn't smoke, he's sure been doing it a lot.

My muscles scream as I stand up and stretch. I hear a sound on the other side of the stone wall, and when I climb up to look there's a goat from God knows where trying to pull apart a thick tuft of grass.

"Hey there," I coo, holding out my hand. When it glares at me and runs away, Victor snorts softly. We're so far from the main road I can't hear a whisper of traffic. There isn't a single house that I can see in any direction.

"It's time for you to explain why the hell we're out here chasing goats instead of eating breakfast at our luxury hotel," I complain.

Victor exhales smoke, squinting at nothing, the sun turning his lashes white.

Victor

I wake up without words.

When I was younger, even though I was in hell, I used to be able to smile and say whatever people wanted to hear. Now I'm too weak to fight that hard.

I'd be dead this morning if Ethan hadn't taken the wheel. I don't know if it would have been intentional or a drunk accident, but that doesn't change the results. This sun would be rising on a sea cliff with a broken safety railing, warming the water over my head.

Ethan sits on the hood of the car and opens his atlas. If we don't know where we are, we can't know where we're going. I close my eyes and let the world come to me in pieces—gravel crunching under my ass, the burn of smoke in my lungs, my dry mouth and pounding headache. My life is no more, no less, than this.

"Let's go," Ethan says. "I have a plan."

I shake my head.

"We're going the opposite direction from Naples, just for a little bit." That gets my attention. I point at the map. "No, it didn't help. Get in."

Who needs Xanax when you have an earnest, demanding Ethan bossing you around?

I stay seated, watching him until he widens his eyes at me impatiently. "Let's go. I have a plan."

We bump back down the lane to the main road. Beyond a row of bleached-looking olive trees and the canvas top of a fruit stand, I can see the glint of water on the horizon. My skin aches for it.

Ethan parks across the road and gets out. I stay in the car and watch him buy two apples and two oranges and two bottles of water. He dumps it all in my lap and keeps driving. As we pull into a real village, a cluster of sunbaked houses with fishing nets stacked outside, I scrape an orange rind with my thumbnail and smell it.

He parks in an empty lot off the central plaza and shakes one of the water bottles in my face. "This had better be half empty when I get back."

I throw the water in the back seat and frown at him as he walks around the car and up to a group of teens. They talk for a long time. I think through all the ways he could be setting up a trap, waiting to betray me and take me back to Gray. Or Coach. But he's never been able to lie to me.

I don't understand what he's doing, and I hate things that I don't understand.

When I don't get out of the car, he comes around and opens my door. "We're going to see a Roman ruin."

The fuck? I raise my eyebrow, but he ignores me, pointing east of the village. "It's up there."

Scrunching deeper into my seat, I point west, toward the sea I can't hear anymore.

"We'll get there eventually, I promise."

Everything sways a little when I stand up, but then I feel better. I follow him back to the plaza, warm stone under my feet. If he looks bad, clothes wrinkled, hair standing up, stubble on his chin, I must look worse.

I'm too tired to do anything but plod after him, watching my legs get dusty as we follow a chalky shoulder of the road out of the village and into the countryside. Ten minutes later, I can see a field dotted with broken pillars and arches. Dirt paths weave into the distance among half-fallen walls and informational placards and grass laced with patches of dandelion. It's so hushed, just a few elderly people wandering around.

I don't like thinking about the past. They're all dead. For someone who wants to die, I'm awfully afraid of being dead.

The cramped, chilly visitor center creeps me out, but Ethan marches inside and I can't let him out of my sight. While he talks to the employees at the counter, I stare at a map on the wall, trying to figure out if there's anywhere to swim nearby.

I jump when he hangs something around my neck from behind. When he sees my glare, he looks sorry.

It's a plastic box with a speaker and a number pad, attached to a green lanyard.

"They're audio guides." He's in his fucking element. "Have you never used one?" When I shrug, he narrows his eyes. "Have you never been to a museum?"

I'm pretty sure that's a family vacation thing. I wouldn't know. But Ethan forges ahead without waiting for an answer. Outside of all the pressure and scrutiny, he seems to have come alive.

My audio guide bumps against my chest every time I take a step. Birds hop between the broken stones, pecking the ground, and the sun bakes my shoulders. Some of the broken paths have mosaics, jumbles of dark tile I can't decipher. Ethan has his audio player to his ear as he walks, the breeze stirring his hair. He turns in a circle, pointing at things. "There's a small temple, a council chamber, and a market." Apparently, I'm going to get the full tour, whether I use the guide or not. A field trip with Miss Frizzle-Ethan wasn't what I expected from today.

Ethan

"This is a taberna," I ramble as we approach a half-broken wall. "They were small shopping stalls built into the ground floor of dwellings. Based on carvings found inside, this is thought to have been a book shop run by two men named Justus and Felix."

"It's a rock." I haven't heard his voice all day, and it startles me. It's hoarse and fragile and somehow comforting.

"Everything's rocks, if you think about it. All of human history."

He sits on a broken pillar, rotating slowly to face me as I examine the foundations. "You think they were fucking?"

"All my straight friends carve their names on the wall of their shared bedroom."

He smiles, quick and unexpected, like when the gull stole my arancini. All kinds of tension I didn't know I was holding flows out of me. His face closes off again, but at least I know there's someone in there. For the rest of the tour, he walks a few feet behind me as I tell him facts from the audio guide he's spinning around his finger. He pretends he's not listening, but I think he is.

Chapter 27

ETHAN

It takes an hour and a half to reach the far end of the ruins, backing onto an overgrown field. I expected him to revolt halfway through, but he just trailed silently after me, biting at a bit of dry skin on his lip.

Feet aching, I sit down in a patch of sweet-smelling wildflowers and pull the fruit I bought from my pocket. "My mom would love this place. This is going on our travel list, if I can manage to find it again."

Victor stands there with his hands in his pockets for a long time, staring into the distance, as I peel an orange and take a bite. "Damn. This is the best fruit I've ever tasted."

Slowly, he folds his legs under him and sits next to me, taking the segment I offer. The sun is bleaching his tousled hair. He takes a bite, and the juice runs over his palm and down his wrist. Absently, like a cat, he licks it off in long strokes. He's like a piece of lazy Italian summer that has been locked away in the dark for too long. He slides the fruit onto his tongue, sucks on it, and I catch myself staring at his juice-stained mouth. When my eyes return to his, he's watching me expressionlessly, but his lips move as he swallows.

"It's dangerous, isn't it? Even for you," Trying to change the subject, I blurt something that's been on my mind for days. "To swim to Capri."

After a long pause, he nods. He pulls up a handful of grass and starts trying to braid the pieces together. He's clearly never done it before. I'd show him, but my hands have always been too big.

"Then why would you do it?"

"Why wouldn't I?" he says quietly. "For you? You think you're special?"

"No." I stare at my hands. "I just don't get it. Do you miss your team that much?"

A strange, tight laugh bubbles out of him, and he flops onto his back in the grass. His chest rises and falls, and I sigh. He's impossible.

I dig in my pocket and pull out the sunglasses I bought in the visitor center. These are round and hipster-ish, because the only other option was bug-eyed Lance Armstrong wannabes.

Something flashes next to me and Victor lies back down, sliding my sunglasses over his eyes. "I paid for those," I gripe.

"They look stupid on you."

"I liked it better when you weren't talking."

"I'll cancel my swim to Capri," he suggests, wrinkling his nose, "if you can tell me what you want from your life."

"That's easy. I want to take my mom on a trip around the world."

"Bullshit."

"Excuse me?"

He sits up and tips the glasses down until I can see his eerie eyes. "You've made helping people your personality so that you don't have to come up with your own. If your precious friend never told you that, she's doing you a disservice. And if you're not going to be honest, then I'll do the race and I'll think of you while I'm drowning."

I should be angry at him, tell him he's wrong, but I can't.

Standing up and shading my eyes, I turn in a circle and take in the scenery all around us—silvery trees, sweeping hillsides, the hazy air. I can hear bees in the grass and a hawk way up above our heads. I want to stay here forever and I want to go home. I never want to see him again and I can't stand to look away.

"Say it," he demands quietly.

"I don't have time to think about myself. But sometimes I wake up and I'm just *made* of want. I don't even know what for. It's all caught in my chest in this big snarl, but I can't pull it apart. And it hurts."

"You should see someone if that lasts more than four hours."

I aim a kick at his head and he rolls over in the grass, laughing, his shirt riding up over the smooth, olive skin of his hips.

On the long walk back through the ruins, I catch him with the audio guide to his ear as we pass the home of the two definitely-fucking booksellers.

Because we don't have any fresh clothes and I'm about to go crazy looking at his shoulders in that tank top, I stop in the gift shop and buy two of the only shirts they have. Victor holds up the bright blue tee, grimacing. "'Keep calm, I'm Roman'?"

"I didn't write them."

I watch out of the corner of my eye as he changes, struggling with my fragile grip on control. Untouchable Victor drove me crazy, but this version of him, fey and docile and so breakable—I don't know what to do with him and I don't have names for the things I want to do.

"So," I begin hesitantly when we're both in the car, motor running. I see him stiffen out of the corner of my eye and I fall silent. I can't force the words out. So instead I say, "Won't your father be panicking by now?"

He shrugs. "If they've noticed I'm gone."

This is the part where I ask him what happened last night, why we're here. I think he can sense what I'm about to say, because his jaw works and he looks out the window from behind my sunglasses.

"We can't stay out here forever," I say finally. "If I let Gray know where we are, I guess we could wait another day."

He clears his throat, his voice cracking. "Can we go to the sea tomorrow? Then I'll go back."

"I don't have money for lodging, and I'm not spending another night in the car."

He taps his wallet. "I've got it."

I spot a larger-looking town on a far hillside, like a miniature Naples, and navigate toward it, pulling over at the first hotel I see on the outskirts. It's a sprawling compound with only ground-floor rooms, woven among a lush garden full of the sound of running water. The walls are peeling and a bit dirty, but it's peaceful.

The woman at the front desk speaks very little English, but she knows exactly what to do with Victor's gold card and hands us two iron keys on a ring, like we're about to open up a castle dungeon.

The keys worry me a little, but once we get the stiff lock open the room behind it seems nice enough, with modern, if dated, conveniences. There's a box of chocolates on the TV stand and a vanilla-scented candle burning, which Victor blows out immediately.

He sits on the corner of one of the two queen beds, studying everything judgmentally. At the end of the circuit, his eyes meet mine and he holds them for a few beats too long.

We both know what's coming, as inevitable as a storm on the horizon. What I don't know is what the consequences will be.

"Let's find dinner before it gets dark," I say too loudly. His shoulders sag a little and I remember that he won't eat anything at the restaurants or cafes. Then I have an idea. "Come on."

"Where?"

"I need to make a call, then food."

He rubs absently at the dirt streaked on his thigh. "I can stay here."

I kick his sandals across the floor toward him. "Let's go. Hurry up."

Luckily for me, it only takes a five-minute walk down the hill to find what I'm looking for: a grimy convenience store with football posters in the windows. Victor wrinkles his nose. "I'm good, thanks."

"I work in one of these, back home," I say. "Night shift."

"That's tragic."

"You're a snob."

His shoulder bumps mine, in our stupid matching shirts. "Duh."

He walks a little way down the street as I tap Gray's number in my contacts. I'm kind of relieved when his phone kicks me to voicemail. "I'm babysitting your child," I inform him. "I'll return him tomorrow. He fusses all the time, but I've managed to entertain him."

Hanging up, I dial Mom. "Hello?"

"Ethan! You didn't call last night."

"Sorry. There were things...happening."

"Are you ok, hon? You sound funny."

"I saw some Roman ruins today." I try to change the subject. "They were beautiful."

"Are you still..." she hesitates. "Are you still doing that job?"

"Yeah."

"With that boy?"

I'm startled. "What boy?"

"The one who came to our house. With the pretty eyes." I'm stunned that she remembers him.

"Yes, that's him."

She sounds strangely confident. "Good. He was important."

I turn around and look down the street. He's standing in the middle of the road, sunglasses pushed up on his forehead and his head tipped back, staring at the twilight above the buildings. He looks thin and lonely, lost, like he could be wiped out in a second. I'm always looking for him now, unable to stand not knowing what he's doing or who he's with. "What do you mean?"

She speaks hesitantly, searching for words. "Everyone seems the same to me sometimes, a blur, like looking at the world without glasses on. It's happening more and more. But I could *see* him. He felt real. Like you. Like he was always meant to be right there."

My heart's beating a little too hard. I thought I had a choice about what happens next, but maybe she's right and it's been here the whole time, waiting for me.

"I love you, Mom."

When I hang up the phone, Victor's standing nearby, hands in his pockets. I jerk my head toward the shop.

"Do we have to?"

"I'm going to teach you how to be a poor person."

Victor

The paint on the walls is flaking and the lights flicker, but it's not that bad inside. The old man at the register nods at us without a word. A tiny television behind the counter has on a football match which draws most of his attention.

Ethan picks up a basket from next to the door. "I've brought you to a mecca of pre-packaged food. You can eat every fucking thing in here."

"I'm not an eight-year-old picking out snacks with his mommy."

He just shrugs and wanders off, weaving into the shelves where he knows I can't see him without moving from my spot by the door.

There really is a lot of stuff here, in colorful packages with pictures that make my mouth water. Finally, I pick up a cucumber-flavored sports drink, a microwave breakfast sandwich, and a small bag of salt and vinegar chips and place them in his basket, hoping he won't notice. He doesn't look at me, just keeps collecting one of every chocolate bar in the place.

As he scans our food, the cashier keeps giving me weirder and weirder looks. He says something complicated in Italian that I can't follow, and Ethan shrugs. The man windmills his arms, like he's paddling, then points at me. "Victor Lang," he enunciates past his heavy accent.

I forgot I was someone to be recognized.

When I nod, his face lights up and he digs under the counter, pulling out an Italian sports magazine that has nothing to do with me. He taps the cover hopefully, offering me a pen. Ethan eyes me.

"*Si*," I mumble, scrawling my name. I freeze when the man offers his hand and a blinding smile. No one has asked to shake my hand since my career went down in flames. But it doesn't seem to bother him. When I take his hand, he squeezes it tightly. He pulls out his wallet and shows me a picture of a little boy in a swimming cap. "My son," he says carefully. "We watch you swim."

"Thank you," I croak. "I mean, *grazie*."

He holds up his phone and the counter digs into my hips as I lean across it to be in his selfie. I don't have a smile in me, so I throw up two fingers instead.

I wish everything in my career had been simple, like him. Swimming and the people who love swimming. That's all I ever wanted.

We carry two big plastic bags of junk food into the sunset-purple street. After today, I know every inch of Ethan's back. The way his shirt rides his shoulder blades, the tan that's deepest at the base of his neck, the cowlick on the back of his head. I study them again as we climb the hill to the hotel.

My nerves are buzzing as I walk in the shadow of his strong, easy gait. Many people have loved me, with many kinds of love, and that love has been all the worst days of my life, all the darkest nights. I've learned to shut myself off, to do everything that's asked of me without feeling a thing, and I can't stop because my body's only purpose is to be used. But he's not here to love me, and that promise has filled me with a dangerous hope.

Chapter 28

ETHAN

I hand Victor the remote as I arrange our haul on a wobbly table next to the tiny microwave. "Find something good."

He sits cross-legged in the middle of one of the beds and flips through channels we can't understand. When he stops on something that looks like news, it starts playing an ad for comeVa and he rapidly moves on. He settles on a show where people are demolishing a kitchen and bringing in new tile, arguing loudly over what looks like curtain swatches. I chuckle. "My mom's obsessed with these shows."

"I watch them sometimes, in the—" He cuts off and presses his lips together, glances at me. I think I know what he was going to say, but I don't want to be right.

As his sandwich heats up, I dig a gold-wrapped candy out of our bag and examine it. "*Gianduiotto*?"

"It's Italian for 'you're a man-child who bought his weight in dessert for dinner'."

"This is amazing," I mumble through a mouthful of rich chocolate. "I need to get, like, seven hundred of these to take home."

Passing Victor his dinner, I perch on the end of the other bed and open a bag of chips. A low whistle makes me turn. He pats his bed, next to his knee, his big eyes careful on me.

The mattress dips under my weight and he has to grab his drink to keep it from falling over. "Tables exist for a reason," he complains.

"You've never had a movie night?" He shakes his head. "A bed picnic?" He pulls a face. "A sleepover?" His eyebrow twitches, and he shakes his head slowly. His breathing seems unsteady

"Now you have. Hope you're having fun."

He tilts his head, pretending to consider. "The food is shit, I can't understand the TV, and stuff keeps spilling."

He's such a fucking brat and I can't keep my hands out of his hair for another second. It's still warm as I run my fingers slowly through the tangle, like it's holding the sun. "You're impossible to please." His eyes half close as my thumb brushes his cheek, finds the corner of his mouth.

He rolls his head, pressing it into my palm. "That's not true," he murmurs. Eyes fixed on mine, he kisses my palm, the inside of my wrist, achingly slow with his chapped lips.

I grip his jaw in one hand and climb on top of him, shoving him deep into the mattress as I claim his mouth, stroke by hungry stroke, tilting my head sideways to get even deeper. He clings to me, a fistful of my shirt in each hand, making helpless, longing whimpers, the most vulnerable I've ever heard him. And I can feel in his body the moment that he finally lets go and gives me all the power, all the control. It's terrifying.

I break the kiss, gasping, and roll over to lie next to him, pulling him against me. "I've never done anything like this before," I breathe against his neck. "I'm not some kind of macho alpha top. I'm scared I can't give you what you want." I'm scared my body won't cooperate, that I'll hurt him, most of all that I'll break whatever strange connection we built between us today.

His fingers find my hair, rub the back of my neck, trail down to trace my lips as he looks up at me with eyes full of lonely, distant stars and, so far behind them he isn't even aware of it himself, something unbroken. "Your body knows what to do," he whispers. "It's already part of you."

I kiss him again and again because I can't stop, tasting the memory of mint gum on his lips, mumbling my words in between kisses. "If I made you think I'm strong, it's not true."

"I already told you." He takes my hand, wraps it gently around the base of his throat, his fingers woven through mine. "I'll show you how to hurt me."

My forehead rests against his. "I don't want to hurt you." But I'm so hard it feels like my shorts are about to tear open.

This time he moves my hand to his chest, pressed over his heart. It's thundering against my palm. "I've been fucked more times than I could ever remember. I've been used, passed around." He swallows. "But deep down, you think that no one in this world can give it to me the way you can. You think you know how to fix me, how to make me as good as you." His finger brushes my bulge, trails along it as the corner of his mouth turns up. "You're gonna have to prove it, because I don't believe you."

The words wake up something inside me, urgent and powerful. Twining my fingers in his hair, I tip his chin back and kiss along the hollow of his throat. "Take off your shorts," I say against his warm, perfect skin. If my body knows, I'll follow it anywhere.

Faster than I've ever seen him obey me, he's fumbling with the tie on the board shorts he's been wearing since we ran away from Naples. He kicks them around his ankles and his cock springs up against his belly, long and straining. I sit up and pull off my shirt, then spread his knees for me, sit between them. I kiss the head of his cock and rub my nose through his trimmed nest of blond, musky-smelling pubic hair.

"Wait," he frets. "You don't have to—"

He shuts up when I climb his body and take his face firmly in my hands. "I don't care how any other asshole fucked you, Victor Lang. If I'm going to do this, I'm gonna do it my way." My thumb slips into his mouth and he grips it in his teeth, eyes wide. "I'm the one you're wet for, right? Not them. Because they don't hate you like I do." He nods.

Returning to the foot of the bed, I spread his legs further, holding them still, and run my tongue up the bottom of his shaft, from balls to tip. He arches into my touch, moaning. "No one's ever done this to you before, have they?" I ask, stroking his thigh.

"No." He whimpers when I pull him into my mouth. He tastes wild, dark and feral and good. I suck him as hard and tight and flushed as he can get as he watches me through pleading eyes, sprawled on his back with his arms over his head.

When I return to his mouth, he licks the taste of himself off my tongue, running his hands all over my body. "Let me take care of you," he begs.

He scrambles across the bed as I stand up, throwing off his shirt and lying down on his stomach in all his naked glory.

Unlike the night in the pool, he takes his time. He hums in his chest, nuzzling me, kissing my length, then lapping at it just like he licked the orange juice off his wrist in the field. He slicks it all wet for him and I can tell he's very, very practiced as he works me into his mouth and teases me crazy with easy swirls of his tongue.

Doubt claws at the back of my mind. This is all new for me, but he's done this hundreds, maybe thousands of times. No matter what I say, I can't make myself believe I have anything special to offer.

Then he pops off and looks up at me with hopeful puppy eyes, resting his forehead against my thigh. "Talk to me, please. I love hearing you talk to me. Tell me how good I make you feel."

If this is what flying felt like, maybe I wouldn't be afraid of it.

"Roll over."

He knows exactly what I want; he's panting for it as he stretches out on his back and hangs his head off the edge of the bed. "That's right." I brush my fingers across his exposed throat, then gently open his mouth and push inside. I'm scared of hurting him, but he wraps an arm around my leg and pulls me closer. His Adam's apple bobs and his whole body tenses, his nostrils flaring. "Damn," I breathe. "Do you know you're the only person I've ever been inside? The only one that's made me this hard?" He moans through his nose.

I run my hand down his chest, play with his stiff, dark nipples as I start thrusting into his mouth. "You can take me all the way, can't you? I love seeing your lips stretched around my base." He's sweaty and shivering, his cock bouncing against his stomach as his throat fights me.

He's so beautiful.

When I was sixteen, I watched Victor on TV and he smirked, glanced at the camera with those pale eyes, and my core twisted and ached. That flutter in my stomach, like a prophecy.

Sexual attraction has always felt performative to me, like I'm acting out the reactions I know I'm supposed to have. I didn't like bottoming, but more than that I couldn't figure out why I was supposed to invest in this thankless connection when I could just focus on Mom and Peyton and the love in our little found family. My body slowly went into hibernation, waiting for the day when it might come across something it recognized, that twist and ache, something it was made for.

Now my body is *burning*. For tonight at least, we've built a safe place together, one with walls strong enough to keep out the dark. This man has given himself to me and, until we go back to Naples, I'll make sure he knows he's mine.

I pull out of his mouth and crouch, kissing him upside down, fondling his hair. "That's right. You're perfect. Now show me your ass."

The cheap bed creaks as he clambers on his hands and knees, stroking himself in irregular jerks. His ass is round and tight, flawless, with that impudent speedo tan line across the tops of his cheeks. He twitches and inhales when I spread him with my fingers and blow lightly on his hole.

It's so small, like it can't even fit my little finger, and my nerves flare up again. I don't know what I need to do to make this good for him.

Your body knows.

Maybe it does, maybe it doesn't, but right now I know what it wants to do. I tease my tongue up his crack and lick his hole, swirling a wet trail around it. "Fuck," he hisses, and I wrap an arm around his hips to hold him still. I nuzzle my cheek against his ass.

"You're so sensitive. You act tough, but I barely have to touch you to make you cry." He holds his breath, tries to be quiet because he's a contrary little shit, but when I probe his hole with my tongue he breaks down, half-whimpering, half-laughing.

One second I'm grinning, the next it feels like my heart is breaking. Out of a thousand men, none of them have put his shaft in their mouth or licked his hole, anything tender and giving. "No one's been good to you, have they?" I whisper. I massage his hole with my thumb, up and down, circles, feeling the tight rim loosen up a little. He doesn't answer, but I feel one of his hands wrap around my leg, hold on. "I'm gonna erase them all."

When I work the tip of my finger in, not sure how far or fast to go, he groans, "God, yes," and bears down suddenly, pushing back onto my hand. Before I know it I'm inside him, gripped by firm, velvety walls as hot as a fever, and all the blood in my body rushes to my cock, thrumming and gorged and leaking more than I ever have before, dripping down my shaft. He holds out his hand and circles his thumb, showing me how to warm him up.

But when I try to take my time, make it easy for him, he whines impatiently and tries to spiral his hips against my hand, shove me deeper.

"You like it in there?" He breaks off in a shuddering gasp when I try curling my fingers, hunting for the way to pull him apart. "Then hurry up and show me how that big cock feels pushing me open." He shoots me a goading smile, knowing exactly what it will do to me.

Victor

"Shit." Ethan sits back, pulling his hand out of me as I vocalize my displeasure. "We don't have lube."

I spit impatiently on my palm and rub it down my crack. "Done."

He arches an eyebrow, unimpressed and so stubborn. "That's ridiculous."

It's all anyone's ever given me. I'm used to it. But I don't think he wants to hear those things. I scoot across the bed, open my wallet, and throw a pre-lubricated condom packet at him. "Happy?"

"Get over here."

His cock is arched with need, and I jerk myself gently as I watch him roll on the condom. My whole body tingles to feel his firm thighs pressed against the backs of mine, his thick head right there, ready to fill me up.

His body fits mine like I was made for him. I arch my back and spread my knees as he works his way in with short, careful thrusts that send sparks shooting along my skin. Then he's all the way inside, his heavy balls dangling against my taint, and I want him to stay there forever, just stretching and holding me open so perfectly.

"You're tight as hell." His voice sounds strained, like he's on the edge of control. "You're the best fucking thing I've felt in my life." Slowly, he rolls his hips, grinding them against my ass, rubbing his shaft against the edge of my prostate, and I can barely see. He kisses my back, each shoulder blade, runs his tongue up my spine as he makes me wait, enjoys the feeling of me desperately trying to rut against him. His hand grips the back of my neck to keep me still as he takes his time.

"You're gonna kill me," I groan. "I don't think I can hold it. Please touch my cock, let me—"

"Wait," he breathes, pulling out of me. "Turn around."

I hesitate.

Don't look at me. Not when I'm weak. I'm scared of what you'll find.

"Let me see you," he hums, and I can't say no to him. I'm shaking as I roll onto my back. He hooks my knees around his hips and pumps his cock into me, faster this time, and pretty soon it doesn't matter what he sees or doesn't see because I'm lost to everything but him, a shipwreck on his shore.

I can feel him start to spasm as he pounds me, his cock swelling, and I wait for him to come, pull out, turn his back on me, and go to sleep.

He stops, breathing loud. He presses his face into my neck, his nose brushing my frantic pulse. "You're so good, baby. You're gonna come for me."

Sliding his hand between our sweaty bodies, he jerks me fast and fuck if this isn't his first time but he somehow knows right where my prostate sits, exactly how to grind his tip against it. I come so hard my jizz splatters the wall above my head.

Before I can even come down, he puts his elbows on either side of my head, his chest slipping against mine, and *fucks* me, biting down hard enough to leave a mark on my shoulder as he comes.

We're both gasping as he collapses next to me, and I study the light fixture over my head, covered in spiderwebs.

This is the part I hate the most. It's cold after sex, empty, a mess leaking out my ass, and I always feel small and dirty as I watch my partner go for a piss, get dressed, and leave. I keep an extra-large hoodie by my bed that I pull on as I curl up in a ball, waking up hours later in the dark with my bare ass sore and my thighs sticking together.

I don't want to see the moment where he loses interest in me, where all that heat we've built day after day leaks away and he's done with me. Because for all the shit I say, I'm the one who's weak. So I roll over on my side and bury my face in my arms, trying to slow my breathing.

I hear him get up, walk to the bathroom. I close my eyes so tightly I see lights.

His hand runs down my side, lingers on the swell of my hip. Gently prying my hands away, he tips my face toward him and wraps his lips around mine. He kisses the tip of my jaw, my ear, and slides his arm under my head where I can smell him and feel his bicep move against my cheek.

His knee slips between my legs, supporting them as he runs a warm, damp towel down my crack, along my thighs, up my stomach.

I haven't cried in ten years. I'm never going to cry again. "Stop." Rolling onto my back, I push him away. "Calm down. We're a couple of lost causes that fuck each other, not lovers from some regency romance you keep under your pillow at home."

He studies my face for a long moment, looking a little hurt, then gets up and tugs on the covers. "Scoot."

After he switches off the light, we lie side by side in bed listening to the sprinklers hiss past the window again and again. His breathing deepens into sleep, but I can't even get my eyes to shut. I remember how it felt in the car, when he let me fall asleep on his chest.

I slide under the covers, where I like to hide. But tonight, I'm not alone down here. Gingerly, I stretch out my hand and find the muscled curve of his back. I can't stop myself from wrapping my arms around his hips and pressing my face into his rough, sweet skin.

I'll move before he wakes up.

Chapter 29

VICTOR

When I open my eyes he's on his back, reading a text on his phone with my arms still clamped around his middle. My right shoulder, stuck underneath him, is numb and sore as hell. I sit up and swing it around, hissing in pain.

"Gray's pretty rude when he's mad," he says. My laugh turns into a dry cough.

"So we're going back today?" I can't fight it forever; I'll just have to hole myself up in the hotel, where I can't run into Coach again.

He looks pleased with himself. "I got us one more day." When he meets my eyes, his smile fades a little. "Now you *want* to go back?"

"I don't know, ok?" I throw myself out of bed like a total drama queen and yank the carafe out of the coffee maker so hard it falls on the floor. "How the fuck do you use one of these shitty things anyway?"

He shakes his head, making me even angrier. "I'd say you woke up on the wrong side of the bed, but I don't think you have a right one."

I dump some water in the carafe and throw the can of instant coffee at him. "Make this."

Sitting on the edge of the bed, I pull on my clothes and watch him baby the pot until the drip starts. Why does the sun have to be so bright? "I'm just saying," I blurt out, "maybe it's for the best."

"I'm not following." He smells the Roman ruins shirt and frowns before pulling it on.

"We've fucked it all up, right? So let's just get it over with."

His eyebrow arches. "Has anyone ever told you you're really high maintenance?"

"I'm being serious." I frown at my knees, picking at an old scab. The bed shifts as he sits down next to me.

"So am I."

"You're gonna make me say it, aren't you? This...*that*," I wave my arm at the bed, "that was it. The part of the chick flick where the guy and the girl realize they don't hate each other anymore. Where the clock starts ticking down to the fucking 'I love you'."

"Well—"

I cut him off. I'm boiling over inside, desperate to get out of here and never come back. "Let me make this very clear." Standing between his knees, I grab his hair and tip his face back, jabbing his throat with my other finger between every word. "I. Do. Not. Love. You. I will never love you."

"Cool," he says, narrowing his eyes at me. "Because I pity any fool that thinks it's a good idea to fall in love with you."

"The shit you were saying last night—"

He holds up his hands. "Dirty talk. It's all horny bullshit."

"If you so much as *think* the word 'love', I will take you back out on that yacht and hold you under the water myself."

"Not if I poison your food first. Oh wait, that wouldn't work."

It's such an unexpectedly dark joke, coming from him, that I let go of his hair and start laughing. "That was pretty good."

He grabs the front of my shirt and kisses me, rough and demanding. His amber eyes are heated. "What have I told you a million times?"

"You'll always hate me."

"Who else can promise you that?" He smirks when I relax a little and tousles my hair. "That's right. So we're going to have one perfect day, just us, and no one can tell us what we are or aren't, because we know. We wouldn't be here if we didn't know."

"I regret giving you a taste of power," I snark, pouring sludgy coffee in a cup, tasting it, and throwing it away. "You're all cocky now. I said I liked you when you were scared."

He chews the inside of his cheek, trying not to smile as he looks out the window into the garden full of roses and the occasional big, orange butterfly. "I guess that means we'll have to go to the beach today."

Ethan

We walk to the convenience store from last night, but the cashier who got Victor's autograph has been replaced by a bored teenage girl. She scans our sandwiches and drinks, along with two cheap t-shirts from a display in the back. Mine is gray and has the logo of the national football team, but Victor's says *Italian Princess* on it in green, white, and red.

"What?" he gripes when I make a face.

He catches me ogling him as he changes his shirt outside the shop. Grinning, tongue in his cheek, he arches his back and pulls his new shirt on extra slow, letting me appreciate how carelessly low his shorts are hanging off his hips. "Your turn."

"Unlike you, I don't strip in the middle of the street."

We're able to use the atlas from the glovebox to take us fifteen minutes out of town, heading steadily downhill through a bunch of tiny, picture-perfect farms. Victor's eyes light up when we pull into a car park in front of an endless stretch of sand and sea.

Before I can even turn the car off, he's gone. I lean back and watch him sprint across the sand, a streak of gold and blond that charges straight into the blue water and disappears.

Feeling like a grouchy old dad trying to corral his family on a day out, I change shirts and wrap our snacks up in the old one before sedately following the dirt path through scrubby grass until my feet dig into warm sand.

Aside from a few beach umbrellas and people walking their dogs, it's quiet. I wander in the direction with the fewest people, hunting for a comfortable spot to spend the day not swimming. Maybe I'll finish Peyton's book, find out if the adulteress was a ghost after all.

I find a little alcove under the hills lining the beach, a big log surrounded by a snarl of driftwood someone must have cleaned off the sand and stacked here. Satisfied, I settle down in the shade, wishing Victor hadn't stolen my sunglasses.

Taking out my phone, I check for messages from Mom. Part of me wants to call her, tell her she was right. The boy with the pretty eyes is important. He's real. And right now, I'm having a hard time convincing myself he wasn't meant, from the beginning of fucking time, to be right here.

My thumb is hovering over the *call* button before I remember that all of this is a dream—the wind that smells of cypress trees, the fragile white shells catching the sun. In approximately twelve hours, we're going to wake up and start counting down the minutes until we pretend this never happened. Until we try to forget.

So instead I open the camera and turn around to frame a photo of myself in front of the blue water. A tired grin, a thumbs up. I send it off and put my phone away.

He comes loping up the beach an hour later, dripping everywhere, holding his dry clothes in one hand. "You look like a grouchy old dad up here."

"I even bought sunscreen." I wave the green bottle. "For those of us without perfect tans."

Digging in his shorts, he pulls out a cigarette and tucks it between his lips. "Here." He claps his hands together and I toss him the sunscreen. He shakes his head at my look. "I didn't light it today. Baby steps."

His big, lean hands work along my shoulders and down my back, pausing occasionally so he can kiss or nip the back of my neck and squirt more sunscreen on his palm. He moves slowly, kneading at my muscles, and his fingers keep straying to places that don't need sun protection. While he works, I open my wallet on my lap, hunting for a place to stuff my last few euro bills.

"Hey." He leans over my shoulder, using one finger to flip through the contents of my wallet. "You still have it." When he holds up Danny's card, the holographic stripe flashing in the sun, I have to bite back the instinct to grab it away.

"Of course I still have it. It's important to me."

"Really?" He flops on his back in the sand next to me, holding it over his head and studying himself, six years younger and so much more innocent. Or so I thought; now I'm not so sure. I can see in his eyes that he doesn't like looking at it. "Why?"

"I told you all this before, when we first met." When he opens his mouth, I hold up my hand. "Let me guess: you don't remember anything that doesn't interest you."

He waggles his eyebrows at me. "Tell me again. I like listening to you talk."

But when I try to say the first word, there's something thick and painful blocking my throat. I close my mouth again, confused. "Sorry, I—" My chest contracts and suddenly my eyes are threatening to fill up and it's so strange, because this hasn't happened for years. Something about Victor makes me raw, everything so close to the surface.

He squirms until his head is resting on my hip as he keeps turning the card around, front and back, upside down, like somewhere he's going to find an answer that explains how we got here, what happened to us.

"My cousin was obsessed with you. He had an entire scrapbook dedicated to you."

"Oh, boy." He closes his eyes. "Usually they're thirteen-year-old girls."

"He drowned a couple of weeks before the Rio Olympics." He doesn't say anything, but his eyes open and find my face. "He wasn't a strong enough swimmer. My mom had her first dementia episode and wandered away from the lake. I don't know what happened exactly, but he was gone before anyone could get there. I almost drowned trying to save him."

"That's why you hate the water." His voice sounds flat, matter-of-fact. When I look down, he's watching the surf.

"Anyway, the last thing I promised him before he died was that I'd get this card signed. That's why I came after you in the first place."

The silence goes on for so long I regret bringing it up at all. Finally, he sits up and rubs the salt breeze from his eyes, pushes his hair back. "You got a pen?"

"No."

He sighs. "Trust you to make this hard." Before I can answer, he hops to his feet and jogs down the beach, stopping to pester every single sunbathing couple and sandcastle-building family until he comes back with a battered ballpoint pen with no cap. He scribbles it on his palm until the ink begins to flow.

"Ready?"

I don't feel ready.

Then I imagine Danny's face if he could see us right now: his surrogate brother and his idol, chilling on a beach together.

Some stupid, stupid part of me thinks, *Maybe he knew this would happen.* Because something about this place and all the years that led me here makes it impossible to hold onto my pinball theory of the universe. I need today to mean something, even if that makes me a fool.

"Here." I spread the card carefully on my knee, holding it in place. Victor scrawls his name and sits back, chewing on the end of the pen.

"I don't know what the fuck people do at this point," he says, frowning. "I'm not gonna pray or some shit."

I'm drained, like I could lie down and sleep for days. "I don't know either."

Crouching in the sand, he props his chin on his knees. "You think he'd like to stay here? The view's pretty good." He bites his lip, flushing a little under my gaze. "I don't know. If it was me, I'd be happy here."

"Ok."

We spend an hour carrying random shit to the top of one of the hills with the best view of the water—rocks, shells, some flowers Victor found in a crevice of driftwood. I dig a little hole and, after holding it for a long time, put the card inside and bury it. He helps me stack up a makeshift cairn and then sits next to me, letting me exist in the silence.

Eventually, he clears his throat. "I wasn't happy," he offers, like it's some kind of exchange for the piece of my life I let him see. "All I ever wanted to do was swim. Fast and far. Then everyone got weird about it, my coaches, the press, and all anyone wanted me to do was show up on TV and make them money. I never said the right things, so people told me what to say and I said that. And I guess you saw, but my team was toxic as shit." He picks up a rock and throws it across the sand. "Nothing turned out the way I thought it would, but it was too late to get out."

"Is that why you did it? To get out?"

A strange expression works its way across his face, then he smiles bitterly. "I don't know. Maybe."

Shutting down the conversation, he stands up and brushes sand off his ass. He's been swimming in his briefs this whole time. "Let's spend the night out here. We can make a driftwood house."

"Are you *volunteering* to spend the night outdoors?"

"I'm volunteering to watch you build me a house and then let me sleep on you so I don't have to touch the dirt."

I'll never forget the rest of that afternoon, even though nothing significant happened at all. We built a shitty shelter that fell over three times before we got it to stand up. I read Peyton's book while Victor swam. Sometimes he would run up the sand, look at me for a moment as if making sure I hadn't vanished, then run away again.

We were high on the freedom of not being in love. Love has borders, limitations. A million movies and a billion books have charted its course. We chase it because we already know how it makes us feel, and once you're in love, your only choice is to fall back out of it again.

Hate is intimate, endless, obsessive. Addictively co-dependent. You can't disappoint someone who believes in the worst possible version of you. You can only memorize them, every hope to break, every vulnerability to tear open, until they're your everything and you're their shield against the nightmares that you made for them. And now that I've tasted it, I'm not sure I could ever go back, even though I know it's wrong.

At some point, I drift off on my back in the sand, waiting for him, and when I open my eyes, he's crouching over me. He tips his head toward the ocean, the bright horizon in his eyes.

"Come on."

"I don't want to."

"Come on." His hand slips through mine like an electric shock. I've never held someone's hand like this, fingers threaded together, and he feels so incredible that he could lead me anywhere and I'd never let go.

We walk together down the sand, to where it's wet and bubbling. The people in the distance with their umbrellas and plastic buckets have gone home, and we're the only ones left.

My heart flips when the surf touches my feet, and my hand tightens around his. He rests his chin on my shoulder and I can feel him smile. "It's ok. This whole world wouldn't be here without water. It protects me. It's always protected me."

His shirt flutters around him in the breeze and, just like in Naples, he looks like an untouchable god of the sea. But this time he's mine to touch.

He leads me deeper, until the water's around my knees, shifting the sand under my feet. I shudder, but he holds on. "Shh. Just listen to it. Let it touch you." I close my eyes, then yelp in protest when a swell rushes up to my waist. "Getting wet's the hard part," he says. "After that there's nothing to lose."

And so I follow him deeper, to my chest, because I want to know how it feels to have nothing to lose. He squeezes my hand whenever it's time to jump over a wave. The water is cold and rough around me, and it's all too much when a wave slaps my face, fills my mouth with water. I let go of him and move to solid ground, secretly proud of the progress I made.

Victor stays in the water a minute longer, diving under the waves and coming back up, tossing his hair back. He lets the next wave carry him to me, stumbling on all fours, laughing.

I shove him when he tries to wipe his sandy hands on my clothes and we tussle through the shallow water. He wins, just like always, and throws his arms around me, rubbing dirt down the back of my shirt.

"You did good," he breathes, burying his face in my chest. I can feel him catching his breath, his warmth. I can feel that he's happy.

I remember the bathroom in his house in Medina, pitch black and smelling of sweat and fear. The fucking dog bed. The bolts.

I pull him in, fitting his tousled head under my chin. I can't hold him tight enough. "Please tell me what happened to you," I say into his hair. "I'll fix it. I promise."

He pulls back, puts his hands on either side of my face, studies me. I can already see his answer in his eyes. "No, you won't."

He kisses me, on his toes, lips coated in salt. He sucks on my tongue until my knees go weak. When I push my hand down the front of his shorts, he grins. "I had you pegged from the moment we met, pervert." He rocks his hips into my palm.

I push his hair away from his face, grip the back of his neck. "And I always knew you were a twisted little brat."

He looks so happy it kills me. "I was put on this earth to ruin your life," he breathes in my ear.

"Fucking right."

Chapter 30

ETHAN

I'm shocked that the shelter didn't collapse on our heads in the night. Sun filters gently through the gnarl of driftwood, throwing bright flecks on my hand where it rests against the sand. Victor isn't here, but my body is still warm in all the places I curled around him.

I sit up, muscles protesting, and squint into the blinding sea. His head surfaces, a long way out, followed by the effortless arch of his back, the forward drive of his shoulders. I wonder if he's practicing for that awful, insane suicide mission of a swim.

Yesterday afternoon I saw a shuttered coffee stand at the foot of the path to the beach. As I walk in that direction, I force myself to follow the edge of the surf, close enough for the biggest waves to wash over my feet.

If I practice, maybe someday he could take me out with him, past the breakers, and show me what it is he loves so much.

Fortunately, the shop's canvas cover has been rolled up to reveal a sleepy young barista. He looks happy to have a customer. "Cappuccino, *signore*?"

"*Si*, thank you." I hold up two fingers. Steam curls in the air as he forces lids onto two Styrofoam cups.

With a pang, I hand him three euros and drop all the rest into his tip jar. Our joyride is over, and I won't need cash anymore.

When I get back to the shelter, the hot cups burning my palms, Victor's lying spread-eagle on the sand, eyes closed and panting, with water droplets clinging all over his skin.

"You're going to be filthy when you stand up," I say, and he smiles without opening his eyes.

"Then I'll just go back in again."

Sitting down next to him with a groan, I press one of the cups against his bare shoulder until he grabs it. He rolls onto his side, head propped on his hand, and hisses in pain as the coffee burns his tongue. Of course he immediately drinks more instead of waiting.

I take the lid off mine and fan it. "Did you sleep?"

He nods slightly, eyes fixed on a family carrying armfuls of towels and plastic buckets.

"Did you dream?"

The breeze plays with his curls as he picks up a small, gray shell and starts breaking pieces off of it, lining them up in the sand, burying them. "I don't dream when you're touching me." He says it quietly, sounding more sad than happy.

I want to know what he dreams about. I want to know what demons chased us here in the first place. I want to invite them to chase me instead, because he's worn out from running so far and I'm strong enough to take it.

But today is not the day to ask.

He wedges his cup in the sand and reaches out, running a finger along my knee, tracing each of the bones. He trails his finger up my leg in a slow, wavy pattern, back and forth. When he gets to the long, diagonal scar

I got from side-swiping a wooden fence on my bike as a kid, he strokes his thumb along it. I watch as he continues up to the hem of my shorts, spreading and smoothing his fingers underneath, gripping a handful of my thigh and squeezing.

"It's going to be ok," I say.

He huffs a sharp, dry laugh. His eyes, tinted with the soft violet of sand at sunrise, mock me. "And how do you know that?"

"Because I won't let it be any other way."

Stretching his arms over his head, he rolls forward all the way to a standing position, looking down at me. "I'll be right back."

I watch him walk into the waves, fall into their arms. Finishing my cappuccino, I dump the rest of his away and slot the cups together.

That's when it hits me: he didn't see the coffee prepared, but he still took it from me and drank. I don't understand, but it feels important, like that last stray, the most feral one, the one that had been kicked and attacked and starved, pressed into my leg and purred for the first time.

Cradling his cup in my hands, I watch him gallop up the sand, shaking himself off.

"What?" he says. "You're looking at me weird."

"Let's go."

"I want to put the top down," he announces when we reach the car.

I shake my head. "Those things are a pain in the ass. Quit stalling." Now that it's really time to go back, no more excuses, I just want to get it over with. I want to get yelled at, move on, and start the process of convincing myself that I'm ready to go back to a normal life.

"Top down, top down, top down," he chants, bouncing his hands off the soft top in time to his words. He pumps his fist when I give in. The car is old, practically vintage, but the convertible roof seems to be a recent modification. When I hold down the button on the dashboard, the roof hums and begins to retract, folding in on itself.

Three-quarters of the way through, it rattles to a stop. Pushing the button again makes a horrible grinding sound. "Piece of junk." I gripe. "Now we have to drive around like this."

The VW creaks and sways and I realize Victor is climbing onto the back.

"Hey—Jesus Christ." I grab my head in both hands as he jumps on the half-folded roof. He stands on top of it and stomps on the arms holding it on either side. With a few ungodly snapping noises, it crumples up like a run-over umbrella. Satisfied, he vaults into the passenger seat and looks at me expectantly, resting his chin on the top of the door.

"Let's go."

"I can't believe you," I complain, climbing in and yanking my seatbelt into place.

He puts on my sunglasses and stretches his arms straight up, wiggling his fingers in the fresh air as I pull out of the car park. "It's not like I was going to keep this thing once we got back."

"I would say that's the most privileged sentence you've ever uttered, but I'm confident that's not true."

Scrunching down in his seat, he props his legs on the dashboard and opens the atlas I gave him to navigate. "I don't keep track."

I almost wreck the car watching him as he hunts through the maps and runs his finger across the page, trying to find where we are. His thick eyebrows are pulled together in concentration above his glasses, his lips soft as he mouths road names to himself, hair whipping in the breeze. He looks like a character in one of those coming-of-age movies about summer and puppy love.

Victor

Once we have a direction, I flip through the radio stations. All the music is sad, ballads and opera, and I switch it off again. We're winding through hills now, climbing higher until we can see wide, smoky views of the countryside. I want to stop and look, but I'm scared that if we stop I'll never have the courage to start again.

I'm entertaining myself by pulling pages out of the atlas and trying to fit them together, like a puzzle, when Ethan hits the brakes. Two reddish-brown does are standing on the road, looking at us with their ears all alert. I put my feet down and get up on my knees on the seat, looking over the windshield at them.

They start to cross with dainty little steps. "Shit," I breathe when a perfect baby fawn comes out of the grass after them, kind of wobbly and scared but trusting. I look down at Ethan. "You see that?"

He nods. His enthralled face makes it obvious that he's crazy about animals.

"Follow your mommies," I call to the fawn when it hesitates, confused. Ethan's hand brushes the back of my leg.

"I don't think that's—"

"Shhh. They're a lesbian couple taking their new baby for a walk. Don't be an asshole."

He smiles, even though he's trying not to.

When everyone's crossed the road safely, we start moving again. "You know," Ethan says, glancing at me. "I love animals. I always wanted to be a vet."

Crossing my legs, I study the side of his face. "You said you didn't know what you wanted."

"It's been six years since I had to drop out of school to take care of my mom. I forget about it sometimes."

"So what, you wanna be like a horse vet or one of those neighborhood clinics?" He looks surprised that I'm interested. I guess I just want to be able to close my eyes when I can't sleep and imagine exactly what he's doing.

"I would have a clinic that works mostly with animal shelters, rescues, people that rehabilitate strays."

"That doesn't sound profitable at all."

He laughs. "Shut up. I know." After a pause, he clears his throat. "What about you? If I could think of something, surely you can, too."

"I—" I close my eyes, rub my face. Being honest makes my nose itch. "I wanted to swim in an Olympic pool. A real one. I never got to."

"Oh."

I can read his mind. *If you wanted it so much, why did you throw it away?*

"Does that mean you're going to try and qualify again?"

I bark a laugh. "No way. It's over."

"Past regrets don't count as dreams."

I'm skin and bones and swimming and pain. Those are the four building blocks of me: I'll never be anything more. You can't plan your future when you don't have one.

"I'll be the sexy receptionist at your clinic. And secretly, I'll be your sugar daddy who pays all the bills because you're a fucking soft touch that just wants to cuddle strays."

His smile is a little impatient. "Seriously, though. What do you want?"

Want

I want

I don't want to talk any more.

Chapter 31

VICTOR

I lean over and kiss his brown bicep where it's stretched out to hold the wheel. I flick my tongue against the faint salt taste of his skin.

Pushing up the sleeve of his t-shirt, I kiss the tip of his shoulder, nuzzle my face against it. He swallows, grip tightening.

Reaching up the leg of his shorts, I palm his cock and start lazily jerking it. His protest trails off into a hungry sound and the car wobbles a little.

I rub my thumb hard over his slit. "Concentrate. Distracted driving kills."

"You're a little shit," he mumbles, but when I stop moving my hand he shifts his hips pleadingly.

Breathing slowly through my nose, feeling my own dick throb, I grind him between my palm and his leg and he says my name in a fragile voice I like and drifts toward the center line.

"You've got such a fat fucking head," I tell him, teasing the edges of it. "It stretches out my mouth, fills up my throat." I push up his shorts, his cock laying heavy against his thigh. "Look at it. My tongue's gonna get tired playing with that, but if you tell me to keep going I'll lick it all over until you're crazy, until you blow."

The suspension bounces as he swings the wheel and barrels up a dirt road, shady and overhung with trees and the sound of late summer birds. I can smell the dust settling around us as the engine goes quiet. We stare at each other, his eyes glazed and his needy panting.

It's not enough to blow him.

Standing up on my seat, I step across and straddle his lap and his hands go straight to my ass, pull down the back of my shorts so he can palm my bare skin. I trail my fingers through his short hair, our noses touching as I drown in his eyes. He looks up at me like I'm God and I finally came to tell him all the secrets of the universe.

I fuck with him, leaning in for a kiss and pulling back at the last second, grinning, until he lunges up and seizes my mouth, grabs the back of my neck as he fills me with his hard tongue. His lips are rough and they always bring mine to life, tingly and sore.

You will never forget me.

Every one of your dreams will have a ghost that looks like me.

Every man you fuck will taste like me.

Lifting his hips, he pulls down his shorts, then yanks mine around my knees. Our erections touch, mine long and pale, his dusky and thick. He spits into his palm and jerks them together as I brace my hands on either side of his head, watching them swell, watching his hand milk and smear our precum into a shiny slick along our shafts.

Then he lets go and kisses me again, messy and deep, and his fingers tease along my ass crack. Instinctively, I spread wider, open up for him, because I know what he needs and he knows what I need. "Good," he whispers. "Get it ready for me." I stick out my tongue and he slides his middle finger all the way into my mouth, lets me suck it.

I rest my head against his shoulder as he works his wide, wet finger into me, my legs shaking. There's nothing in the world like that feeling of being forced open, filled up, opened more, filled more. I'm making obscene noises, thrusting, trying to get him to give me another finger.

When he does, I sit up and grab the sides of the car and ride his hand, head thrown back to look at the endless green leaves, all rustling like they're trying to tell me something. He runs his tongue up my chest, holds me still with his free hand and sucks my nipples, bites me hard. My hips jerk against his fingers and then he curls them against the perfect spot just once, twice, like no one has ever done before, his hand wrapped around the very core of me, and the world explodes behind my eyes as cum sprays my chest.

"Fuck," I groan, resting my forehead against his, quivering as he empties me, leaves me open. He runs his hand up my back and holds me still. Eyes locked on mine, he jerks himself in slow, hard pulls, daring me to look away.

The wind brushes across my body and his, tickling my damp skin. In his dark, warm eyes I find the reflection of the sun filtering through hundreds of branches, specks of gold moving and shimmering as the leaves flutter. His hand comes around to rest on my cheek, his thumb stroking the tender, exhaustion-bruised skin under my eye.

And I see it. The echo of my own thoughts. *You will never forget me. Every man you fuck will taste like me.*

I nod to him.

Then I turn my face and kiss his palm and he shivers under me, coming all over his belly with a deep, throaty whine.

We rest for a while, just as we are, because this has to last us forever. When I wad up my t-shirt to wipe us clean, he says "Wait" very softly.

He turns me over and lays me on my back along the seats. Every part of my body fizzles and sparks as he lies on top of me, heavy on my legs, and starts gently licking away the cum on my chest. He takes a long time, trailing his tongue over same spots again and again until every hint, every taste of it is gone. Then he rests his cheek against my chest.

When I tap his shoulder, he crawls up until his abs are level with my mouth. I hold his thighs still and lap it all away, the good, good taste of him, writing my name across his body with my tongue.

I tip my head back to look up at him. "You're inside me now."

"I know." He sits up, straddling my chest.

"Am I inside you?"

He runs his fingers through my hair. "Taste and see."

He parts my mouth and lets me explore his tongue, the mystery of it. I can taste us both, tangled together, rich like a dark wine.

"Don't forget this," I tell him as we sit naked in the car, my back against his shoulder, and listen to the faint sound of goats bleating, carried on the wind. Because for every mile we travel closer to Naples, the foreboding in my chest is getting deeper.

*now that I've touched you in the dark
I would know you anywhere*

Chapter 32

ETHAN

After a lot of arguing, we parked the piece-of-junk car in front of the original owner's house and left the keys on his doormat. As if he's going to want it back smelling faintly of cum with no roof and an empty petrol tank.

My head hurts and every part of my face feels dried out, my tongue stuck to the roof of my mouth, but I tell myself it's just from driving with the top down. I want to buy a cold bottle of water on the fifteen-minute walk back to the hotel, but all the groceries and cafes we pass are shut. Victor says it's for *riposo*, the Italian version of a *siesta*, but it gives me the eerie feeling that the city is some kind of set that closed down when we left and hasn't yet realized we've come back.

At the top of a steep hill, we pause. There's a chest-high wall, and Victor climbs on top of it, straddles it while I stand on my toes and prop myself up with my arms.

Among the dense clusters of buildings, I can see shocks of green and orange and purple where people keep their small gardens—a tree, a pot of flowers, an umbrella, the pieces of a tranquil, ordinary life. Behind me, cars flick past down the tight street, inches from clipping my shoulder.

"So," I begin, less because I have something to say than because I wish I knew what to say.

The heels of his sneakers bounce against the wall as he swings his legs, knocking loose bits of crumbling plaster. "Don't talk any more."

Then he jumps down and we keep walking in silence. It's warm without the countryside breeze, and a light sheen of sweat coats the back of his neck.

Jogging to catch up, I reach out and touch his wrist where his hoodie sleeve ends, the soft spot where his pulse sits. I can feel him tense as I lace my fingers through his.

"You're pathetic," he murmurs, not looking at me. "We agreed to stop this once we got back to Naples and you can't even last ten minutes." His grip tightens and he runs his thumb over my knuckles, back and forth, tracing each one.

"I'd consider this more Naples-adjacent. All the locals agree the city line starts somewhere around the Regale Hotel."

He snorts a laugh in spite of himself, shaking his head.

"Are you scared?" I ask, suddenly. "About coming back?"

"No." His grip shifts uneasily in mine.

"Because I told you I won't let anything happen?"

He chuckles drily. "You say fucking stupid things. No, you know me." He reaches out his free hand and trails his fingertips along the yellow, graffitied concrete. "I don't give a shit about anything."

"Cocky *and* a liar. Where have you been all my life?"

"In your nightmares," he deadpans, and we both crack up.

No one meets us when we arrive at the Regale Naples, and that's when things start to fall apart.

I gave Gray our arrival time, but the lobby is empty except for a retired American couple in matching tropical button-downs. I'm about to point them out to Victor, but he crowds my elbow, tension rolling off his body in waves. Bringing him back here feels like a betrayal, but I don't know what the hell else I was supposed to do with him.

"*Mi scusi...*" A woman in the hotel uniform taps my arm. "I've been asked to direct you to Werner Lang's room upon your arrival, on the third floor."

The elevator ride is silent except for the rattle of the cage and squeak of the cables. Victor opens the front-facing camera on his phone and squints at it, fidgeting with his hair. I start to feel that familiar pinch and grind of anxiety in the back of my head, the suffocating sense of helplessness.

When we knock on the end suite on the third floor, a muffled voice says, "Come in." I glance at Victor, but he doesn't look at me.

I'm braced to get glared at, yelled at, asked for explanations. But no one even looks up when we enter. The suite has been rearranged into a kind of office-slash-command-center for Werner's business dealings. Heavy velvet curtains black out the windows, leaving the air dim and cool, with a dry smell like paper and mothballs. Gray and Werner are fixated on a small laptop on Werner's desk.

The atmosphere crackles ominously like the second before a lightning strike as Gray straightens up and examines us. "Have a seat, gentlemen."

Instead of sitting next to me, Victor drags his chair to the opposite end of the desk before slouching into the plastic seat. When I shift positions, I can still feel his dried spit, traces of cum on my chest. He won't look at me.

"We have a situation." Gray shuts the laptop, and the stress in the lines of his face makes my chest go cold. Werner's stormy, slate eyes watch me as Gray picks up a sheaf of papers and tosses them into my lap. I hear a rustle as Victor stands and the soft shift of his breathing when he comes to look over my shoulder.

The top page appears to be a printout of some kind of web forum, the kind that's full of anonymous users who make the news for doxing people or distributing illegal porn.

It isn't until I hear a faint, strained moan in Victor's throat that I read the title of the forum thread, timestamped this morning.

Victor Lang never used steroids — I have proof

"In three hours," Gray continues quietly, "this has received almost thirty thousand responses, ranging from incredulity to outlandish conspiracy theories about Russia secretly owning the World Anti-Doping Association."

I fumble through the pages, trying to read a thousand things at once.

"What's the proof?" Victor asks, voice stretched so tight it's about to snap.

I jump when Werner explodes. "Nothing! In all of that bullshit, there's not an ounce of proof. They're a bunch of freaks wanking off in socks in their mothers' basements."

"The original poster has not released any public proof," Gray inserts in a more measured tone of voice. "However, at least five mainstream news outlets have picked up this story. Now tens of thousands of forum users are coordinating an effort to unearth and examine every piece of information associated with Victor's life in the hopes that they'll be the one to uncover some kind of vast conspiracy."

"I don't know who the fuck's still interested in you," Werner growls. There's confusion in his voice, like he can't fathom how someone could remember Victor's existence when he had no problem forgetting all about his son.

Gray perches on the edge of the desk, massaging the bridge of his nose. "As far as we can tell, the photographer from your first day in Naples leaked a photo of Victor speaking to Katrina and Rachel Garrel. Speculation that Victor was planning to rejoin his old team and make a comeback has sparked a lot of attention."

"How dare you speak to those girls without telling me?" Werner snaps at Victor. "This is your fault."

Bristling, I get up and step between Victor and the two men. "Hold on. Did he dope or didn't he?" Everyone's staring at me, faces blank and impossible to read, and I feel like the room is shrinking around me. "If he did, then there's no evidence to the contrary. And if he didn't, why wouldn't you want that to come out?"

A hand clamps on my arm, twisting me around until I'm staring down at the cold fury in Victor's eyes, his clenched jaw. "Sit down and shut up," he hisses.

"I—"

"Shut the *fuck* up." He shakes me a little. "This is not your concern."

I yank my arm away, the back of my neck burning, and focus on straightening my rumpled shirt.

Gray clears his throat. "Victor's original dope test was valid, and there shouldn't be any proof indicating otherwise. *However*, the temperature of public opinion can change very quickly, and we have decided to temporarily suspend work on the comeVa advertising campaign. We don't want our stock impacted." He raises his eyebrow at me. "Satisfied?"

Fuck, no.

"In the next day or two we will decide whether or not to indefinitely postpone the campaign, in which case, Ethan, we will be sending you home early while Victor stays here with us."

"Jesus Christ." Victor grabs the papers from me and throws them on the desk, where they scatter like a flock of birds. "Why the hell doesn't everyone just leave me alone?" He storms out, slamming the door.

I glance awkwardly between the two men. "I—"

Everything's going to be ok.

How do you know?

I'll make it so.

But I can't find the words to fix this.

"Get out of here," Werner snaps.

"Until we have a plan, neither you nor Victor should leave the hotel. I'd also suggest beginning to pack your things." Gray gestures dismissively. "We'll be in touch."

In the hall, I draw a shaky breath. The more I think about how tight my chest feels, the more constricted it gets until I have to crouch down and put my head between my knees.

I told him I'd protect him.

And within five minutes, I failed.

I'm as useless at saving him as I am at saving Mom. And I've broken just as many promises.

Victor

He finds me at the pool.

Part of me wants him to jump in like he did that night, block my way, grab me hard enough to hurt and tell me he's in charge now. But he just throws himself on a lounge chair and closes his eyes. Finally, I climb out and stand at the foot of the chair, staring at him.

"I can hear you dripping," he says finally, without opening his eyes. I don't answer.

I like his body all stretched out, in a black tee that molds to his pecs and jeans tight enough to remind me that I never got to feel his thighs around my head. But today it makes me feel shitty instead of good. I crouch down, studying him.

"Why are you sulking?" I ask. I'm sulking because thirty thousand anonymous strangers are trying to ruin my life. But I don't know what his problem is.

"Because I'm depressed."

I sit on the lounger next to his, letting the sun dry off my back. We're alone except for the sound of leathery tropical leaves rubbing against each other in the wind.

"Don't be depressed," I say. It sounds weird, but I can't think of a different way to tell him what I want.

Finally, his eyes crack open and he looks at me. "Don't sleep in a closet."

I look at my hands, clasped between my knees. "I get it. Sorry."

"I'm the one who came here to apologize." He meets my eyes, but I look away.

"I don't want you to apologize."

"I told you I'd protect you when we came back, and I couldn't do it." He pauses. "You didn't have to yell at me, though. I was trying."

I sit on my hands so I can't touch him. "Please don't try."

He's silent until I look at him again. His eyes are burning with all kinds of things—frustration, confusion, need. "Victor," he says. Just that. My name.

I run my hand through my wet, tangled hair. It's getting damaged from all the chlorine and salt water. "I'm fine. You can go home and protect your mom."

I guess that wasn't the right thing to say, because his face just collapses and he turns his head away, toward the pockmarked concrete wall of the hotel.

"I don't think I really help anyone; I just brute-force my way through life, telling myself I'm doing the right thing." His chest rises and falls rapidly. If we were still in the countryside, I'd take his hand and make him feel my heart beat until he calmed down, like he did for me.

"I'm not going to sit here and argue with you." I stand up. My head is throbbing. Picking up my clothes, I take my sunglasses, the ones I stole from him, and slide them onto his face. "Don't get sunburned."

As I walk away, I imagine for a minute that it was a real goodbye, that I can't turn around and see him right there because he's on a plane to Seattle. I try to really believe it. Running my tongue over the tang of chlorine on my lips, I pretend it's the taste of his last kiss, the one he sneaks in because he can't stop himself. I wonder what my final words to him were, whether they were mean or funny or stupid. What he said back.

Jesus Christ, I'm falling apart.

Pulling on my shirt and shorts, I go out and smoke on the front steps of the hotel. I'm supposed to be quitting; I told Ethan I would. But I can't drop more than one addiction at a time.

After ninety minutes, I work up the courage to leave the hotel property and wander down the street in a direction I've never been before. It's the hottest day of our trip so far, every stone surface baking and shimmering, and the air smells of herbed fish and cotechino sausage as the whole neighborhood dusts off their grills.

I stop outside a small grocery with crates of figs and lemons on the sidewalk. It's packed, and I'm scared to go inside.

I don't have very many ideas, so I have no way of knowing if this one is good or not. But I want to find out, so I pull up my hood and duck through the door.

Grabbing a basket, I open the notes app on my phone with my other hand. It's a messy list full of typos because I type too fast and never read it back.

-animals
-oranges
-mariners b-ball
-gelato
-that chocolate that starts with a g
-licking around the head
-complaining

It goes on and on. I've been making it for a long time. There's a lot of food; the man likes to eat.

It's the shape of you, as best I can make it. I had to be good at forgetting, to protect myself, and now I can't remember anything. I put it here, so that when you're gone I can rebuild you again every time I forget.

I've almost deleted the list a couple of times, because it doesn't seem like the kind of thing you do for someone you hate. But today, I'm glad I kept it.

Chapter 33

Ethan

For the first time on the trip, I grab some shorts and head for the hotel gym. I run until my legs give out and lift until my arms are numb, trying to find my center again. Going from sunshine and sleepy mornings and freedom to a claustrophobic, angry world where I have no power has sucked away all the confidence Victor found in me.

Thoughts of Victor bleed into thoughts of my mother—*none of this can fix me*—until it's driving me insane.

I chug a bottle of water and shower in the attached locker room, standing under the hot stream with my forehead resting against the slippery tile wall. It reminds me of home, scrubbing the shower as I wash myself because there's literally no other time. Ever since Danny's accident, there's been a weight on my chest that never went away, a constant push to try *harder*, until I forgot that it hadn't always been there.

Then those seven words—*I'll teach you how to hurt me*—turned into the best three days of my life and I could *breathe*. Now it's back, twice as heavy, like a punishment.

You've made helping people your personality so you don't have to come up with your own.

If I can't even do that right, what's left of me?

I stay in the shower a long time, telling myself that when I walk out Victor will be sitting there, waiting. He'll grin and say, "Look at you, all wet. Don't fucking touch me like that," eyes daring me to do it. I'll grab him, smear water on his face and mess up his hair, and then we'll just walk out of this place and forget it ever existed.

He's not there, but a text from him is.

Hurry up.

Where? I'm busy. I have no interest in continuing our conversation by the pool. In fact, the next three days will be easier if I just avoid seeing him at all.

Then he texts me a photo: he's lying in the hotel room bed on his back, head hanging off the edge, shooting down the length of his naked body, one hand displaying his hard cock.

We agreed that what we shared in the car would be the last time. We promised this was over, because obsession and hate don't share with *anything*; they can't survive on twice-a-week sex and dates on the weekend.

It should have been the last time. But there's a long way between "should be" and "is", a lot of places to get lost in between. The elevator can't get me upstairs fast enough.

But when he opens the door, he's dressed—kind of. A pair of sweats hangs low on his hips, making it clear there's nothing underneath. He's shirtless, just his chain necklace caught up in his clavicles. A smirk teases at his lips.

I step inside and slam the door, backing him up until his legs hit the edge of the bed. Then I stop, because there's no mattress. For the first time, I look around the room.

The mattress, piled with blankets and pillows, sits on the floor in front of the TV. There are about ten thousand snacks on the floor next to it, in a messy pile.

"Surprise," Victor deadpans. He's trying to look cool, but he seems nervous. "Yippee. I'm so fucking fulfilled by thinking of someone besides myself. So exciting. So romantic."

There's a microsecond where we both freeze at the last word. I clear my throat. "You found all the food I liked." He's watching me hopefully, and there's such a softness he doesn't know I can see behind the bravado in his gaze. When I run my fingers through his hair, he closes his eyes. We're both so desperate for touch, even after a few hours, that it feels as potent as the first time. "What's the occasion?"

"It's the one day of the year that I'm nice. Like a reverse *The Purge*."

"Lucky me." We both grin, and the lingering awkwardness disappears.

He jumps on the mattress with both knees like a kid and turns on the TV. There's a DVD menu featuring Harrison Ford's young, smoldering face.

"My favorite, the classic *Indiana Jones I predatori dell'arca perduta*."

He laughs at how I mangle the name. "I think it's an Italian dub with English subtitles. It's the only thing they had at the shop." He grabs my legs and unbalances me, pulls me down next to him. "You should see it; it's a fucking bootleg CD with the name written on in permanent marker."

For the next two hours, we gorge ourselves on junk food and make fun of the extremely dramatic Italian dub track and how badly it matches the actor's expressions. Victor has never seen the film before, which makes it even funnier. I catch myself watching him instead of the movie, drinking in the glow of the TV on his tawny skin. I could sit here for a year, just touching him, every flawless inch of him, and never get tired of it.

My workout starts to catch up with me around the time Indy finds the ark. Victor prods me and I realize I've dozed off, propped against the bed. "I need you awake to tell me what the hell is going on," he complains.

I manage to keep my eyes open long enough to see his reaction to the face-melting scene. His jaw drops, then he busts up laughing, glancing over at me. "The fuck just happened?"

The next time I wake up, the movie is over and he's nudging my shoulder.

"Sorry." I swallow, squinting at him. "I'm tired."

A shiver runs through me when he cups my face in his hand the way I usually do to him. His hands are so intoxicating to me, refined but strong with a wide palm and big knuckles and the spaces between his fingers made to fit mine perfectly. "It's going to be ok," he murmurs.

I lean into his touch as his thumb strokes my eyebrow, my cheek. "I was wrong. I say a lot of shit I can't back up. I know I shouldn't, but I want it to be true so bad I convince myself."

To my surprise, he chuckles softly. "I know."

"I don't think it's going to be ok."

"Maybe not."

I tense up, start to pull away. "I'm not sure *I'm* going to be ok."

"Shh," he breathes. "I know." He tugs my shoulder until I'm lying down with my head in his lap. His fingers run through my hair, trace my jaw.

"I want to be the one who keeps you safe, the only one that hates you right." It's all spilling out, and I can't stop it. Without the fear of hurting someone you love, there's no limit to what you can say. "But it's harder to be strong here."

"Listen." He tips my head until I'm looking up at him, like Mom does with me while we watch TV. "Give me your phone."

It's probably not a good idea, but I would do anything to stay here even another minute, before we run out of chances to break our *one last time* promise. He takes both of our phones and runs to the balcony. I sit up. "*Victor.*"

But it's too late. He chucks them over the railing and suddenly I lose the will to worry any more. He grins at me as he yanks the corded phone cable out of the wall. "Now no one can bother us, not tonight."

I shake my head. "It's called knocking on the door."

"Shut up." He tackles me, throwing me on my back into the pillows with him sprawled all over me.

"That's how you wanna do this?" I try to hook his leg, flip him over, but he's like a squirmy fish, laughing breathlessly as he escapes. Wrestling turns into hungry grinding and humping and kisses with too much teeth as we fight for who gets to be on top. In the end Victor wins, trapping my thighs under his knees and raising his fists in victory as I lie there, panting. We're both ridiculously hard in our pants.

He leans down and kisses me deep, over and over. He presses his erection to mine and rubs them together with smooth pumps of his hips until I moan.

"Victor," I say against his mouth.

He chases another kiss, then sits back, watching me. I run my hand down his chest, the body I marked as my own, erasing everyone else who has ever touched him. Sliding my fingers under the waistband of his sweats, I stroke the soft skin of his hip. "I'm sorry."

His head tips like a curious puppy, but his voice is rough and needy. "Why?"

I'm scared to say it. Part of me expects him to get up and leave. "I don't think I can hurt you tonight."

His eyes cloud a little, and the corner of his mouth tips up in a sad, strange smile. "God, you're so soft tonight. My soft boy."

He takes my wrists, pins them gently over my head, and kisses me again. He tips my chin up with his nose and sucks on the line of my throat. "You don't have to hurt anybody, baby," he whispers. I feel like I'm dreaming, losing my mind. I don't know this Victor. I'm not sure he does either.

"But that's what we do. That's all we have." I whimper when he slides down and laps at my hard nipples.

"I have an idea, ok? A game." He rests his chin on my chest, looking up at me, still holding my wrists down. "We'll fuck every night until you leave, and every night we'll pretend something different. We'll try on all the different ways we could be together in all the different universes and realities. And maybe we'll find the one—" he cuts himself off, buries his face in the hollow of my throat.

Finally he continues, voice muffled. "And it won't matter if things fucking suck during the day, because we'll know that we're coming back here."

I pull my arms free and prop myself up on my elbows. "This is the opposite of pretending nothing ever happened."

He crawls back up my body, eyes lidded, and puts his forehead against mine. Right now, his irises are the color of the moon. "It hurts too much," he whispers. "I need to quit you slow, or it's going to kill me."

I sit up and push him against the side of the bed, pulling his sweatpants down until his ass is hot in my hands and his cock, glistening with trails of precum, stands proud between my thighs. "What game are we playing tonight?"

He leans back, drinking in my face like he's looking for an anchor, something to give him courage. His lips work for a moment, his breath catching, and I can feel his heart beating fast. "I—" He looks away, makes a sound of frustration in his throat. "Fuck."

Then he grabs my face in his hands and kisses me breathless and somewhere between the strokes of his tongue I feel him speaking into my mouth.

"Tell me you love me."

I pull back. It feels like a train hit me, just wiped me off the face of the earth, and I have no idea if it's good or bad or right or wrong. For a second, I go dizzy, like I'm going to puke. "What?"

He's watching me with his chin tipped up, warily, lust and fear tangled together all through him. "You've thought about it, right? You want to say it. You think that if we were in love, maybe all this shit would work out; we could go back to Seattle and have a fucking normal relationship, get married, start a fucking family. Some part of you is mad at me for not being able to love you like that."

"I don't know." I want to understand the shape of love, not because I think it might be better than hate but because sometimes I wonder, just for a second, if it might be another name for the same feeling. "I don't want to make you uncomfortable."

He pulls me against him, arms around my shoulders. "I can take it; it's just a game. Tomorrow we'll try something else. This is your chance." His lips brush my forehead. "See if you can change my mind. I bet Gray told you I'm clean, right? So tell me you love me, then fuck me sweet and slow, bareback, until I've got your cum running out of me."

I groan at his words, my whole body aching in time to the throb in my cock.

He's so tense, braced for it, but I make him wait. As the humid Mediterranean wind drifts through the curtains and the moon shines in on us, I take him gentle and deep until he forgets all about words and when we come at the same time, me in him and him in my hand, I cover his body with mine and tell him I love him, just once, just to try the sound of it on my lips.

He doesn't say it back, doesn't say anything, but I don't need him to.

Because it's just a game.

Victor

I don't want to touch him that night, after we fuck. I want to practice sleeping alone, so that when he goes home I don't lie awake for weeks, going insane.

But my body wants what it wants and when I wake up in the night we're wrapped around each other, my face in his neck, his legs between mine. I roll over and put my back to him again, telling myself to try harder.

In the morning, I've laced my fingers through his and pulled his hand under my head to use as a pillow.

I'm lost, and my heart's a broken compass that will never get me home.

I shake him awake so early the sun is barely starting to come up, the sky pastel and trailing cotton-candy clouds.

"Are you ok?" He sits up, rubbing his eyes. His hair is everywhere, his face puffy and squinty, and I wish I could add it to my list so I never forget it.

"I'll drop out of the race to Capri, if that's what you want."

He wakes up the rest of the way in an instant. "Really?"

It's not some huge gesture. I'm not ready anyway, and maybe I don't feel like dying this time.

I narrow my eyes at him. "Don't make me repeat myself." I start hunting for my phone, and he laughs, all deep and throaty.

"Our phones are in the oleander bushes."

"Shit."

We both get up and pull on pants, stumble down the long, steep staircase. It smells sweet enough out here to give me a headache, and the dew on the grass soaks our bare feet. Once I find mine hanging out of a bush, we use the flashlight to find his. He looks over my shoulder as I text Kat: *Tell Alek I'm out. And I hope your plane crashes on the way home and scatters flaming pieces of your bodies across the Atlantic.*

I'm still jittery from last night, all the crazy things I said, so I pass the phone to Ethan. "You do it."

His lips quirk as he deletes the last sentence and hits *send*.

When we're back upstairs, crawling under the covers, Ethan whispers, "Thank you."

"I'll text him back if you don't shut up."

My head finds his chest and he rests his palm gently against my forehead. His skin is cool even in the thick, sweaty air. "The mouth on you." He's smiling, and so am I.

I don't mean to fall back asleep, but it happens before I can stop myself.

Chapter 34

ETHAN

Someone bangs on our door at 6:30 AM—not a room service tap, but full on hinge-rattling pounding. "Get up," Gray's voice demands, muffled through the thick hardwood, "and open the door."

He rattles the handle so hard I'm scared he's going to break it open and barge in on us stark naked in bed, Victor snoring on top of me with his legs wrapped around mine.

As Victor makes irritated sleeping animal noises and rubs his eyes, I pull on jeans and throw a pair of sweats at his face. There's nothing I can do about the snacks and pillows everywhere, the mattress on the floor, or the faint tang of cum and sweat in the air, aside from throwing open the windows on my way to the door. If Gray doesn't know exactly what's going on as soon as he walks in, I sure wouldn't hire him as my lawyer.

My passive-aggressive "Good morning" is cut off as Gray shoulders past me. He steps over Victor, who is still fighting with his pants, and turns on the TV, flipping the channel wordlessly until he finds BBC News, broadcasting in English with Italian subtitles.

"...completely unexpected turn of events," the broadcaster picks up mid-sentence, "the World Anti-Doping Agency is opening an investigation into swimming star Victor Lang's 2016 Olympic doping record, where he tested positive for multiple performance enhancing drugs and earned a three-year suspension. Their spokesperson announced that they received a 'credible' anonymous tip, possibly from one of the online communities that has—"

Victor hits the power button on the TV so firmly it almost falls off the back of the table. He stands there for a moment, not saying anything, then turns and starts fishing through his luggage for a shirt like nothing ever happened.

I open my mouth, but I have no idea what to say.

"I've been on the phone with the WADA and USADA since four o'clock this morning," Gray announces in a steely tone, watching Victor's back as he tosses clothes all over the floor. "In ten minutes, we're leaving for the hospital."

Victor spins around, holding a pink t-shirt to his chest, his eyes dark. "Why?"

"You're giving them a blood sample."

He takes a step back. "No, I'm not."

Gray merely raises one eyebrow. He seems even less interested in anyone's bullshit than usual.

"What's the sample for?" I ask. "It's not like he's doping now."

"They are trying to confirm that the original blood sample belonged to Victor."

I blink. When the scandal broke, everybody wondered if there was a mistake in the lab results—inaccurate levels or a false positive. Suggesting the blood belonged to a completely different person poses questions that have never even crossed my mind.

"I'm not doing this," Victor repeats, pulling on the pink, scoop-neck tee, which has a gold leopard-print pattern that would be absurd on anyone else. He looks pleadingly at Gray.

"Funny, I don't remember asking you." Gray's voice is dry. His brow furrows. "Is there something you'd like to share with the class, Victor? Help me help you."

"Of course the sample belongs to me. I shouldn't have to go through all this bullshit just to *stay* guilty."

Gray turns to me. "Ethan, you're going home the day after tomorrow. This commercial won't be released for a while, if ever, and there's no need to keep you from your family. I'll get you your boarding documents later today." He pushes off the desk. "Downstairs in five minutes, both of you."

When the door shuts behind him, Victor picks up one of his bags and throws it against the wall, scattering underwear and headbands on the floor. He's breathing hard.

"Victor." Ignoring me, he crouches down to lace up his sneakers. "Do you have a thing about needles or something?"

He snorts derisively.

"Then I don't understand. If the sample is yours, then I assume you'd want to clear that up. If it isn't, and you know it isn't..." I trail off as his back stiffens.

"Listen." He doesn't turn around to face me. "That fucking inquisition, back in 2016, it was a nightmare. The press, the articles, the testimonies. I was getting death threats; I couldn't set foot outside." He rubs his hands down his face. "The thought of dragging all that shit back, all these insane people on the internet, the predatory reporters... All for nothing."

"I see." I stare at my hands and try to convince myself that I believe what he's telling me.

Stuffing his phone and wallet in his pockets, he opens the door. "Come on. Let's get this over with."

In the elevator, our eyes finally meet. "Two days," I say.

He studies the ornate design of the elevator ceiling. "Uh-huh." Biting my lip, I turn my focus to a faded copy of the hotel restaurant menu attached to the wall.

"Hey," he says as he unlatches the cage door at the bottom. His face is pale and his eyes look red from lack of sleep. "Two nights. Remember?"

I nod.

Victor

I am a little scared of needles. I'm more scared of hospitals. I slept in an ER waiting room once, trying to work up the courage to ask them for help. In the end, I called *him* to come get me, because I couldn't do it, and I told him I was sorry.

In the car on the way to the hospital, Ethan puts his hand flat on the seat between us and I do, too, our pinkies about an inch apart. After hearing him say "I love you," I was honestly terrified that I'd never want to touch him or come near him again. That I had tainted him. But he's just the same, that solid, gentle presence that keeps my soul tied to the ground.

"This is a hospital?" he asks incredulously when we pull up to an ancient building with pillared arches and sweeping staircases. He digs out his phone as he follows me inside, nearly tripping on the steps. "God, it's from the sixteenth century."

"That's why I didn't want to come." I hold the door open for him so I can postpone going inside. "They stick a leech on your arm; it takes hours."

A tall, blond man in a suit stands up when we enter the waiting area and offers his hand to Gray. "I'm Patrick, WADA. I'm just here to collect the documentation." His voice has a Canadian lilt. One minute I'm asleep in Ethan's bed, the next I'm in a fucking hospital with a WADA goon waiting to collect my blood.

Before Patrick can speak to me, I push past Ethan and follow signs around the corner to the nearest restroom. Inside the men's toilet, I lean my weight against the wobbly door so no one else can open it and pull out my phone. I can't feel my fingers as I fumble to make the call.

"Victor?"

"Dad." I close my eyes. "Do you know what's happening? Where I am?"

"I just heard." He's fucking furious; I can hear it in the harsh grate of his voice. "The messes you fucking make, Victor."

"I know," I whisper. "It's my fault. I'm sorry." He always said I should become stronger, because great people become legends by embracing their hardships. Instead, I broke. He's never forgiven me for disappointing him.

"Did you talk to that Ethan boy? I heard you two were all over half the country."

"No."

"He's a very moral person, sees the world in black and white. He wouldn't be able to wrap his head around this if it got out. He'd never look at you the same."

"I—" I clear my clogged throat. "I know. He has nothing to do with this. Just pay him his money and let him go home."

"Does that mean you'll do as you're told from now on? Like we agreed?"

"I will. But Dad, the WADA rep is fucking *standing* out there, waiting for the paperwork. What do I do?"

"Just give them your blood and come back to the hotel."

"Dad..." I pull in a deep, shaky breath. "Are you sure—"

He hangs up on me.

The nurse that takes my blood doesn't speak much English, but she's gentle, the first person today not to yell at me. To her, I'm just another patient. When she notices I'm shaking a little, she hands me a bottle of water. She gets the needle in without me feeling it and fiddles with the small vials until they fill with dark blood. Watching them makes me sick.

She insists on walking me back to the waiting room. When she sees Ethan jump up like a fucking idiot, his eyes all worried, she smiles and pats my arm. "Ask him buy you espresso; feel better."

"*Grazie*," I mumble, pulling my sleeve down to hide the cotton pad attached to my arm with adhesive strips. Gray and Patrick are at the administrative desk, so I step close to Ethan and lower my voice. "The nurse says you owe me an espresso for being a brave boy."

He fights a smile. "Were you a brave boy? I thought I could hear you complaining all the way out here." But he puts a hand on my arm before remembering and pulling it away. "I saw a cafe across the street. Wait here."

I lean against the wall, itching for a smoke, as he asks Dad One and Dad Two for permission to go outside. Not being allowed to roam freely shouldn't bother someone who didn't leave his house for six years, but I was just getting used to exploring a bigger world than the inside of a dark half-bath. I guess once Ethan leaves, I won't have a reason to go anywhere.

We cross the cobbled street to a grotty cafe with unstable chrome-and-plastic furniture. Ethan orders a cappuccino and buys me a sealed bottle of iced coffee. He frowns at me as I pick at the bandage on my arm.

"Don't say 'That wasn't so bad now, was it'," I grumble as he sits opposite me.

"I wasn't going to," he lies. "But I still don't get it. Why would someone doubt your test results?"

I've been thinking ever since I got off the phone with Dad, and I know what to say. "Athletes can adjust the timing of their steroid doses to give clean blood work. I was good at it. I passed the first Rio dope test."

He sits up, startled. The air conditioner over our heads is broken and keeps making a cyclical thudding sound, farting out bits of cold air.

"But someone lost the sample and I was pulled for a second test. I didn't pass." He doesn't know enough about the system to realize I'm making shit up. "So I'm guessing someone found a record of the clean test result and freaked out, thinking it was a big cover-up."

"Oh." He looks deflated. "When are today's results going to be ready?"

I wish I knew. I feel like I'm being eaten alive from the inside. "Do I look like I work in a hospital?"

His moody October eyes study me. He didn't have time to shave this morning, and he looks about as scruffy as he did in my backyard when I dragged him out of the pool. "You know that you can tell me anything, right?"

I put my head in my hands. "Yes. You've made that abundantly clear."

Ethan

I don't know what I was going to say next, but it probably would have been something brilliant, the one thing he needed to hear to open up to me. Before I can say anything at all, a voice behind me exclaims, "It *is* you."

Victor's head whips up, glaring at someone over my shoulder, and I turn around to see a girl probably five or six years younger than us with a messy ponytail and a backpack on her shoulder.

"I've been watching you for a while," she announces, seemingly unaware of how creepy that sounds. "I was trying to make sure it was you."

Victor spreads his hands sarcastically. "Happy?"

"Have you been reading the forums?" The intense blue eyes behind her thick glasses are completely fearless even as he stands up, shoving his chair back.

"Fuck off." She doesn't move. "Come on, Ethan," he snaps. "Let's go."

I'm not sure what comes over me. "Go ahead. I'll be right there."

He widens his eyes at me. "*Ethan.*"

"Shit, dude, calm down. I have to pay for the drinks." I take out my wallet and start shuffling through it for his benefit, until he storms away and climbs the steps to the hospital. Then I put my wallet away, because I already paid for the drinks.

Everyone lies. Even you, even me.

Eyeing me cautiously, she lowers herself into the seat opposite and sticks out her hand. "I'm Nicola."

"I'm Ethan."

She suppresses a smile. "I heard. So Tanner is just an alias?"

Fuck. After the last twenty-four hours, I'd completely forgotten Tanner ever existed, along with most of the rest of the world. "I—"

"It's ok, I won't tell."

I study her, wondering why I couldn't have been this confident at her age. "You wanted to tell us something about the online forums?"

She glances at the spot where Victor disappeared and lowers her voice. Rain starts to spit down outside, bouncing off the cafe awning. "I'm one of the people trying to research his past. When I heard he was in Naples, I wanted to say hi and offer to send him any information we find, in case he was framed and needs evidence."

My skin prickles. This feels wrong, but I can't bring myself to leave. "Why do you think he was framed?"

She hesitates and sighs, playing with the discarded cap of Victor's drink. "A lot of information around him seems to be missing, things that should be easily accessible. It just feels off."

A strange wave of relief washes over me. I've been driving myself insane for weeks—no, half my life—wondering what happened to Victor and why none of it quite adds up. Hearing someone tell me I'm not crazy makes me do things I probably shouldn't have done.

Nicola hoists her backpack on her shoulder and stands up. "Aren't you going to threaten me and tell me to stop?"

I grab the receipt from the coffee and flip it over, pushing it toward her. "I'm going to ask you to exchange phone numbers so you can call me if you find something. Preferably before it goes public."

Trying and failing to hide her excitement, she scrawls her number down and hands me the scrap of paper. "Text me if you want. But this is too big; I can't promise to stop the release of information."

The sound of a car engine makes me look up. Our ride back to the hotel has arrived. As Victor follows Gray down the steps, he looks around for me. His eyes focus on Nicola and he stops walking for a minute. Then, before I can even stand up, he slides into the car and says something to the driver. He and Gray argue for a second before the car pulls away, leaving me sitting there with my mouth open.

"Uh...sorry." Nicola looks guilty.

I shake my head. "It's just another Tuesday with him. I guess I'd better start walking."

Chapter 35

ETHAN

It takes me half the day to get back to the hotel, not counting getting lost for an hour. By the time I climb the front steps of the Regale, my feet hurt and I'm dripping with a miserable combination of sweat and warm rain. Most of all, I'm furious that Victor would rather waste an entire quarter of the time we have left together than cooperate with me even a little.

Like a fucking reflex, like I can't help myself, I immediately start searching for him. I tell myself that I just want to yell at him, but it's only partly true.

After trying the room, the pool, the breakfast nook, and the front steps, the last and most unlikely place I check is the empty dining room. Just as I'm about to leave, a waiter wiping off tables calls out to me. "You are looking for your, ah, partner?"

"*Si.*"

Smiling a little, he gestures for me to follow him into the kitchen. Five or six chefs are bustling between large, gleaming prep stations, trimming thick cuts of beef and peeling potatoes bigger than two of my fists put together. At the back of the kitchen, he points me down a small passageway of red brick full of shoes and buckets and empty boxes set aside for recycling. The savory air of the kitchen wafts through into a clean, quiet alleyway.

Victor is sitting on the back step, playing with a puppy.

I've heard girls joke that a man with a dog makes their ovaries explode. I don't have ovaries, but if I did, Victor and a fluffy white puppy with crooked ears would just about do the job.

The cooks must have given him the handful of fatty meat trimmings he's using to coax the dog to spin in circles and hop up on its hind feet. "Look at you," he croons under his breath. "You're so smart. Smartest fucking dog in Italy, yeah?"

It shies away when he reaches for its head, so he offers another piece of meat and scratches it gently on the back until its nub of a tail wags so fast it almost knocks itself over.

My foot scuffs the threshold and Victor turns sharply, eyes wary. The puppy backs up and yaps at me, bristling. It's scruffy and thin enough that I'm certain it's a stray.

I hesitate, caught between having too much to say and not enough, between anger and how good it feels to see him like this.

"Dude, you're fucking scaring him. Sit down." He taps the clay-tiled step next to him and I settle down, our shoulders not quite touching. Victor drops a slimy bit of raw meat in my palm and I hold it out, but the dog won't come. It swivels its back end around until it's pressed against Victor's knee, glaring at me.

A huge, goofy grin stretches his face. "That's right, buddy. He's mean; don't play with him." I catch myself staring at his profile as he tickles behind its ears and lets it chew on his knuckles. He looks softer from this angle, the curve of his cheek, less hardened against the world.

"What's his name?"

He purses his lips, looking troubled. "I've never named anything before. Have you?"

"Did you never have a pet?"

He sits very still for a moment, then reaches over gingerly and lifts the puppy into his lap. It squirms against his chest, but doesn't struggle. "Someone gave me a dog once." I can barely hear his voice. "But I was bad, so they took it away again."

"You were 'bad'?" I ask incredulously.

He presses his lips together. His face relaxes a little when the puppy nips at his chin.

"There's no secret to naming," I say. "Just pick whatever you want."

"Can I call it Rio?" His ears flush pink at the tips. "That's what I wanted to name the other dog. I know it's stupid."

"Hi, Rio," I say to the dog. "Can I be your friend, too? Or just him?"

"Just me." Victor buries his face in Rio's fur. "I don't share."

"Did the test results come—"

"No." He cuts me off, still not looking at me, and all the frustration of that long walk back flares in me.

"Would you even tell me if they did?"

His shoulders tighten. "You don't trust me?"

"Not really." I flex my hands in my lap. They want to hurt him every way, to punch out his lights but also torment him until he's crying under me.

He puts Rio down and throws the last scrap of meat, watching the dog tear away after it. "I'll tell you about the test when you tell me what the hell you talked about with that internet stalker."

"Dude, she wanted to help. She's like an inside line, so we learn about everything they dig up."

"Godamnit, Ethan." He rubs his face roughly. "There's nothing to dig up. I know how desperate you are to prove I'm a good person, to tell yourself you were the one that saw through the mask." He kicks the toe of my sneaker with his. "News flash: I'm still not a good person, no matter how many times you ask. No matter who you pay to fabricate shit that will make me look that way."

"I didn't *pay* her for anything. All I'm trying to do is help you."

His face hardens. "You want me to be honest with you when you lie like that? Don't pretend you did it for anyone but yourself and your savior complex. Am I your next mom? You couldn't help her, so now you're obsessed with me?"

It's not even the worst thing he's ever said, but it stings the deepest. I stand, so he has to lean back to look up at me. "I told you once that you've never given me a single reason to trust you. You say so much shit to me that sounds so good, like we really have something, but that's the one thing you still haven't done. Not once."

He shakes his head slowly, a hard smirk twisting his mouth as he gets to his feet. "You're the one who thought there was something to trust in the first place."

As he pushes past me and disappears, it sinks in that those could have been our last words to each other. It's only a matter of time before stupid promises and pointless games can't hold us together in the face of this.

The depression my anxiety spawned yesterday gets heavier and heavier as I waste the rest of the day. I call Mom, hiding the edge in my voice, and get a slow start on packing my things.

After that, I lie on my back for a long time, dozing in and out of a sulky, aching sleep, wishing I had the energy to at least go sightseeing. And with every minute that passes, I get angrier at this whole mess, bitterness climbing up my throat to choke me until I want to start hitting walls and pretending they're that prick's face.

I finally get my energy back just as it's starting to get dark. Even though my feet are still killing me, my body is begging for something physical, any way to vent frustration. Since I don't have anything better to do, I put in earbuds and change into running shorts before making my way outside and stretching on the quiet front steps in the twilight.

As I settle into a jog, most of my attention is focused on remembering the landmarks I pass, so I don't get lost on the way back. Between my concentration and the earbuds, it takes me almost thirty minutes to realize there's another runner fifty feet or so behind me. If they were a serial killer, I'd be bloody chunks in the trunk of their car by now.

I slow a little, glancing over my shoulder, and recognize the flash of pink and the shock of light, curly hair. The fucker can't leave me in peace.

In a burst of energy, I pick up my pace. Before I can think about it, I start making abrupt turns, one after another, half-trying to lose him and mostly succeeding in losing myself. Sometimes he's closer and sometimes he's further away, but he's always somewhere behind me.

I'm so focused on looking for twisty streets where I can shake him off that I don't notice it's completely dark now. I take out my earbuds and listen to the rubber slap of my sneakers on pavement, the rush of my breath, trying to hear his footsteps.

There's a new edge to the night, the excitement of a chase burning through my blood, igniting my anger into something heady. When I emerge from a tangle of alleys, he's no longer behind me and I slow to a walk, gasping.

I stop, hold my breath. Nothing.

Just as I turn up a narrow, dark street, hoping it will lead me back the way I came, a body flies out of the shadows and slams into me, throwing me against the nearest wall hard enough to send pain shooting through my shoulder.

Victor circles me, trying to catch his breath, eyes bright on me as I drop into a defensive crouch. I realize a second too late that he's cornered me in a dead end and I've backed right into it. We stare at each other, panting, bodies tense and buzzing

I feint to his right, then dodge to the left at the last minute, trying to throw him off balance. My foot slips on the damp cobbles and he goes for my legs, like he's going to wipe me out. I have to jump to get clear, stumbling away. "You don't want to fuck with me tonight," I growl.

He charges, his shoulder barreling into my chest as he slams me into the wall. His body's all over mine, rough, sweaty, searching for my mouth, shoving me every time I move.

"Tonight we're doing it like we fucking hate each other. Like it used to be." He groans when I grab his junk through his shorts. "Tell me how you want to hurt me. Tell me how I make you feel like shit."

I grab his shoulders and spin him around, face-first to the dirty concrete with all my weight against his back. "That's right," he hisses as I yank down the back of his shorts.

Anger and helplessness and desire melt together into a white-hot, burning chaos that has no name. "Why does it have to be this way, Victor? Why do you fucking do this to me? Why am I not fucking good enough?" I push my face roughly into his neck, working at his hole with a dry finger, rubbing my erection against his ass.

He tips his head back, exposing his neck to my teeth, and forces a hand into my boxers, squeezing my swollen cock, stroking it raw and desperate. "Because I don't need your help. I want you to leave me the fuck alone and never come back."

We fuck silently and viciously in the dark, scraping against the wall, all hard heat and struggle. Then we run back to the hotel without speaking, go upstairs, and do it again.

I give him exactly what he wants, sucking him off and then pushing his face down into the bed, pounding him, making him wait so long to come that he's frantic but too angry to beg which makes me blow so hard my balls ache like hell. I throw him onto his back and make him fuck my fist until he comes all over himself with a hoarse sob.

We fall asleep on opposite edges of the bed with a wall of pillows between us to stop our treacherous bodies from seeking out the comfort neither of us deserve. But when I wake up in the morning, he's asleep with his arm sticking through the pillows, holding on to my shirt. And I don't know if he did it in his sleep or when he was awake.

One more night. One more way to pretend. One more game that doesn't feel like a fucking game anymore.

Chapter 36

VICTOR

When I wake up, it's mid-morning and most of his stuff is packed, stacked by the door except for the things he needs tonight and tomorrow. He's sitting on the balcony with his phone and an espresso. I notice that he has tidied my shit up as well, which feels more like a pointed hint than a favor.

He looks through the door at me when I start getting dressed. "Hey."

"My ass hurts like hell."

"Fancy that." He sips his coffee.

"You know I'm going to throw this stuff everywhere again as soon as you're gone."

"Yeah, but at least I don't have to look at it."

I'm not angry any more, just tired and sad. And I just hate him the normal way, the dark, possessive throbbing of my heart that makes it impossible to think about anything but him. We didn't fix anything, but I'm a master at fucking away the ache.

After I get dressed and pull on a headband to keep my hair out of my eyes, I turn in a slow circle, studying the empty room. I don't like it this way, like he's so excited to leave that he's already mostly gone. I sit on the floor and start throwing shit out of his duffel bag until it's empty.

"Hey!" I hear the deck chair scrape as he scrambles up. He comes in and starts grabbing stuff away from me, re-folding it.

I toss two t-shirts and a sweatshirt on the bed. "Pick which one I get to keep."

He hesitates, straightens up with a wad of clothes in each hand, studying me. He pouts at the clothes I laid out. "But I really like those."

"I know. It's gotta hurt, or it doesn't mean anything."

He stands next to me without touching me and considers them. Finally he points to the sweatshirt, a kind of ugly orange one with a Harley-Davidson on it. I hand it to him.

"Put it on. Make it smell like you. Have you ever even sat on a motorcycle?"

"Maybe."

I raise an eyebrow at him. "You're too square. Why do you even have this?"

"I went through a *Sons of Anarchy* phase."

That makes me laugh, loosening up my stiff face. Digging through his luggage one more time, I snag his Raiders hat for good measure and put it on backwards. He snorts. "Raiders fans would eat a pretty boy like you alive."

"I know. You've demonstrated." I wink, enjoying the way he can't not blush.

"What do I get?" he asks, sitting on the edge of the bed and obsessively tidying the mess I made. I look down at my black hoodie draped over the desk—my favorite, with the thumb holes. It has my scent baked into it, even when it's clean. "This. You can wear it jogging and get all sweaty in it."

"Then what?"

"You can imagine me telling you how nasty you are, then licking you clean."

He shifts his hips restlessly, then pulls his focus to the hoodie I just gave him. "You got two things," he complains.

I shake my head at his needy expression. "How about this?" I pull down the waistband of my jeans so he can see the thong I'm wearing underneath. His eyes go huge.

"Good enough?"

"I don't know. I can't exactly wear that."

"Fine, I'll keep it." I grin when he makes a protesting noise.

Flopping back on the bed, he switches on the TV, flicking through channels. By the time we both remember why that's a bad idea, it's too late.

"We received confirmation just a moment ago from the WADA that they have closed their investigation following clear evidence that Victor Lang's 2016 test results were accurate and correctly administered."

I don't know how Dad does these things, and I don't want to know. Ethan mutes the TV and sits back, disappointment so obvious on his face, but I don't have the energy to yell at him again. I wish I could give him everything he wants, but I can't live with being the one who gives him the last reason to leave me.

"That's it, then." He looks at me probingly. "Is that it?"

"I think so."

Gray shows up about fifteen minutes later. "Victor, you and your father are giving a press statement in an hour and a half, endorsing the results of the investigation and encouraging your fans to move on." He hands me a script. "Memorize this, quickly." His eyes shift to Ethan. "You're staying here."

"Wait, what? No." Ethan sits up. I can't get enough of those flashes of protectiveness, even when they drive me insane.

Gray points at him, pinning him in place with the gesture. "You are no longer a part of this situation, starting tomorrow. No drawing attention to yourself."

"I'll be fine," I say soothingly, avoiding his eyes. What's another lie when you're already drowning in them?

Ethan

When Victor leaves to memorize his script, I'm left alone in the hotel room with a pile of packed bags, an ache in my stomach, and a phone number burning a hole in my pocket. Unable to stop myself, I pull my phone out and text Nicola. *You saw the news this morning? Does that mean you guys are finished?*

I get up to pass time until she answers, but my phone buzzes before I've taken two steps.

No. There's something weird going on.

I knew it. I've always known it—that creeping feeling when I look at him, all his neuroses, the way he refuses to tell me anything about his past. The thought that I could finally *understand* starts eclipsing any guilt I should be feeling.

What do you mean?

This time there's a longer pause. *How deep down the rabbit hole do you want to go?*

I'm staring at the question, trying to figure out the answer for myself, when she sends another message. *You could help us get some answers.*

How?

Can you get into his father's office?

I groan and get up, pacing around the room, listening to the creak of the old floors and trying to stretch out the muscles Victor and I screwed up last night. This isn't curiosity or well-intentioned information gathering. It would be a betrayal.

I feel like I can't decide without looking at him one more time, giving him one more chance to do the right thing. At least that way I'll be able to ignore the guilt.

Let me think about it.

The chef working in the kitchen smiles at me and pushes a bowl of discarded bread crusts across the worktop.

"*Grazie.*" That simple gesture of kindness feels overwhelming, making me think of home and all the people I miss.

Victor and Rio are sprawled against the side of the building. He's reading his script out loud to the dog. His eyes flick to me, but he pretends not to see me.

"Would you like a study partner that speaks English?"

"No."

"Ok." I sit down next to him and start tossing bits of bread to the excited puppy. He hops around on stumpy legs, chasing each crust I throw for him. It's sunny back here today, sleepy and warm.

Like we're a pair of magnets, impossible to resist, Victor slowly slides down the wall as he reads until he's leaning against my side. "'I've made peace with my past and dedicated myself to a meaningful future,'" he mumbles.

"Wow."

"I know."

He pulls out a cigarette and lights it, and today I don't have the heart to scold him.

"I can talk to Gray, see if he'll change his mind about letting me come. I could at least sit in the holding room with you."

"Why?" My least favorite word of his.

"So you're not alone."

"I'm going to be alone for a long time. It's practice."

"Victor." I kiss his hair, unable to stop myself. "Don't shut down on me. We're on the same side."

He sits up, blowing smoke across the shafts of golden light. "Are we? Because I think you're about to ask me again to stop lying and tell you the truth and I'm getting really fucking tired of it."

"Do you *want* things to get better?" I snap. "Or is starving yourself in a fucking dog bed in a bathroom everything you thought it would be?"

His breath catches as he turns on me, eyes helpless. "Don't say that," he murmurs, voice ragged. I think he's trying to be angry, but all I can hear is how close he sounds to breaking.

"I can't take it. I can't be with you if I have to watch you do this to yourself and never even know why."

Rio sits up, looking between us as if he's wondering why we fight every time we come to visit him. Victor unfolds from his sitting position, flinching slightly, and shrugs my hand off him. "You're not with me. We're not together. I think you'll be fine."

As he ducks inside, he brushes his hand once, lightly, across the back of my neck.

Slumping against the wall, I delight Rio by scattering all the rest of the bread on the ground. I take out my phone as he gobbles it noisily.

Everyone's going to be gone for a couple of hours. Tell me what you need me to do.

Chapter 37

ETHAN

Werner would probably fire all the staff in the hotel and burn it down if he knew that the woman at the front desk let me into his room just because I'm in the same party as him and claimed that I was supposed to fetch something he forgot.

Even though I know they're all lined up in front of the press right now, I still walk across the carpet on my toes, like someone might hear me. My instructions were extremely specific—*snoop around and take pictures of anything interesting*. This feels absurd to the point of being embarrassing, like a kid pretending to be a spy.

His laptop and paperwork aren't on his desk any more. All I'm able to learn from a first pass of the room is that he likes to drink grapefruit-flavored sparkling water, according to the contents of the garbage.

I tug on the desk drawers—of the four, three are empty and one is locked. I kneel on the floor, fidgeting with the mechanism. I'm sure the key is safely in his pocket, but this desk feels old and loose around the joints, and I've worked in construction, as a handyman, and as one of those guys who drives around getting peoples' keys out of their cars. It only takes me a few minutes to figure out how to lift the drawer off its rails and use a letter opener to slide the locking mechanism out of place. If I'm pretending to be a spy, I'm a pretty badass one.

Staring at the thick row of file folders, I really wish Nicola had told me what to look for. I'm not sure she knows herself. Double-checking the time, I start flicking through page after page of irrelevant financial records.

I almost pass the envelope. It's blank except for an address in the upper left corner, but I recognize the word *ospedale*—hospital. Someone has opened it and taped it shut again. Trying not to rip the flaps, I slide out a thick card covered in what looks like medical information. Among the Italian, I find Victor's name at the top. Trying not to get too excited, I take a photo of it on my phone and put it back.

After I return everything exactly where I found it, more or less, I take the stairs to the ground floor and settle down in the back of the breakfast nook, trying to calm my shaky hands with coffee and a view of the pool. Once I've caught my breath, I text the photo to Nicola. *This looks important.*

Thank you. I'll get back to you once I've had a chance to look into this.

Before I delete our text history, I send her one final message. *You guys are scary, you know that?*

Never doubt the power of the internet.

As I sip my bitter coffee, I contemplate if forcibly dragging someone to safety whether they want to or not really counts as saving them. Something tells me it doesn't, but I'm in too deep to back out now.

In less than twenty-four hours, I'll be gone. It won't matter if I saved Victor or not. If I ever want to know what happens to him, I'll have to read it in scraps on the internet like everyone else. I'll spend the rest of my life wondering if he's ok and how I can live without the pieces of me I gave to him.

And maybe the part of me that's melting down, that's doing absurd things like yelling at him and pretending to be a spy, has a lot more to do with missing him than with my overactive sense of justice. Unfortunately, there's nothing I can do to fix one of those two things.

When I glance up, Gray and Werner are passing on their way to the elevator, without Victor. Gray catches my eye, and he gives me a *look* that has me scrambling out of my seat.

When I finally reach the top floor, the door to our room is unlocked. "Victor?" The bed, the bathroom, the balcony, all empty. My stomach flips as I check over the railing of the balcony, just in case.

Then I notice the closed closet door. When I try to open the slatted wood accordion panels, they rattle but don't move. "Victor, it's me." I pull harder.

"Fuck off." He sounds choked up, soft.

I sit down with my legs stretched out and my back against the door. "What's wrong?"

He doesn't answer.

"Did the press conference not go well?"

"Did you watch it?"

I should have watched it, not fucked around breaking open desk drawers. I should have seen he wasn't ok and waited at the door for him to get back. "No."

Silence. I nudge the door with my shoulder. "What happened?"

"They..." His voice cracks. "They yelled a lot of questions, and I didn't know what to say. It was just like 2016, and there were so many people, and you weren't there."

I turn sideways against the door, resting my cheek against it, and slide my fingers through the gap at the bottom. "And this is what you do when you're scared?"

"It's safe," he murmurs. "No one can find me."

"Except me."

The barest hint of a chuckle. "Except you, you nosy fuck." Then I feel his fingers tracing mine. "Are you all packed?" he asks finally.

"I guess." I take a deep breath. "Victor, are you sure we can't work this out? I don't think I can live thirty minutes from you and never see you again."

"My dad told me we're going to move back to New York once this is over."

"Oh."

He chuckles again, with no humor, and squeezes my fingers. "You're in deep, aren't you? Wake up."

"What if I did love you? Would that change anything?"

He lets go of me, and I feel the door shift as he rests his weight against it. His voice gets closer. "Love is such a fucked-up thing, Ethan. The person you love tears you apart, crushes you, owns you until you turn into whatever they want you to be. I think I'd rather never see you again than have you love me."

I close my aching eyes. "Ok, so I don't love you. Why can't we just keep going the way we are?"

"What do we even have? It's not natural. The real world doesn't let things like us survive."

"Damn it." I punch the floor so hard my bones ache. "If it needs a fucking name, I'll find one for us. I'll come up with a whole new feeling if that's what it takes."

He huffs a soft laugh. "You would."

Turning around, I tug on the door again. "Let me in, please."

After a long moment, I hear him move out of the way. I accordion the door open, climb inside, and shut it again. Faint sun filtering through the slits in the door gives just enough light to make out Victor's shape, back pressed against the wall, the floor padded with blankets and pillows.

It's so claustrophobic and, just like the bathroom at his house, it smells of despair. It hits me suddenly how fucking *long* he's been doing this. All the days I spent with the sun on my skin, all the nights I dreamed in the breeze from an open window, he was here.

I hold out my hand in the dark, and he takes it. When he shifts, I can see faint reflections of light in his pale eyes.

"Welcome to hell," he says—I think it's meant to be a joke, but it doesn't sound like one. Then he crawls over and leans against my side and I stroke his hair, teasing the curls back from his forehead, loving the way they catch in my fingers.

"You're a good person," I say. "I want you to know that."

I can feel him shaking his head. "I promise you I'm not. Let it go."

He exhales softly as I take his face in both my hands. "You don't understand. Look at you. Look what you've fucking done to me. How can you not be perfect? It's not possible."

For a long moment, he doesn't move or breathe. I hear him swallow, throat moving against my palm. "Is that why you've yelled at me twice in the last twenty-four hours for ruining your life?" His mouth curves into a smile and he noses against my fingers, kisses them so softly I can hardly feel it.

I lean forward and find his lips in the dark. "I guess you're as perfect as a little fucking brat has any right to be. Lucky for you, I have a weakness for brats."

Chapter 38

VICTOR

For the first time, there's someone with me in the dark. He fills the space with his body heat and the smell of dollar store hand soap and Italian sun.

You always come back for me. Even when I beg you to stop.

"Let's get room service," he says. Then he catches himself. "If I go get it for us, if I watch them make it, is that ok?" His nose tickles my ear.

I nod. I never imagined I could trust someone like that again, but I do.

"I'll be back." He opens the closet door and offers me a hand, pulls me up against his chest, like I'm some kind of damsel in distress, but I don't really mind. "Think about what we're going to pretend tonight."

The last night. The last-last night, for real this time, no more take-backs. What do you even do with that?

I turn on the TV because it's too quiet, but I'm careful not to touch the news channels. Just a nature show with some shiny, green-headed ducks and a narrator that keeps saying things like *magnificent* and *rare* in Italian. I should save Ethan's sweatshirt for when he leaves, so I don't start overwriting his scent, but I can't stop myself from lying on the bed with my nose buried in it. I'll ask him to wear it again tonight.

Eventually, he comes back with two plates of fettuccine alfredo. "I realized I still haven't had a real Italian pasta dish."

I hesitate when he hands me the food. This might be the most trust I've ever given anyone in my life. When I take the first bite, I can see the happiness in his eyes and it makes it easier to ignore the panic in my chest and keep eating. It tastes so good I'm scared I'll make myself sick, so much rich food after so long.

"Did you figure out what we're doing?" he asks, wiping up the last few bites on his plate with a piece of garlic bread.

I chew on the inside of my cheek, staring at my lap. "Not really." *Nothing seems right.*

"Maybe—" he hesitates, and I'm scared he's going to start talking about love again and ruin whatever we have left. "Maybe we shouldn't play around tonight, pretend to be something. Maybe we should just *be*."

"Ok." For some reason, that makes my heart thump against my ribs.

We put the tray of dirty plates in the hall and lock the door.

I grab Ethan's sweatshirt and a thick blanket and head to the balcony. Leaning on the railing, I look across at the harbor lights, the skeleton shadows of boat masts, and the decorative lamps on the sea wall stretching miles in either direction. Then I tilt my head back and study the stars. They're faint here, pale freckles across the face of the sky, but there are so many of them.

Ethan nudges up behind me, his lips brushing the back of my neck. "I've never been anywhere so peaceful," he breathes. "I don't have to lie awake and play 'is that a backfire or a gunshot'."

Draping my blanket over himself, he lies down in the biggest lounge chair. He lifts up the corner and gestures for me to crawl in next to him.

Our bodies fit together perfectly, every hill and valley contoured to each other like we were one person who got broken in half before we were born.

His hand slides down the back of my jeans and his fingers curl around the waistband of my thong, his thumb brushing slowly back and forth across my bare flank, and we just let go of everything, melting into the kind of silence that comes when every word in the universe has already been said.

ETHAN

"I always wished I was a star," he murmurs into my chest, half asleep. His breathing rises and falls slow against mine and his soft hair tickles my neck.

"A ball of fire careening through the void that's probably dead by the time we see it?"

He shakes his head. "No one can reach them; no one can touch them. They're alone. But they're not lonely."

"How do you know?"

"Because I wouldn't be lonely, if it were me." He slides his hand under my shirt and spreads his chilly fingers against my stomach. "And because you'd be the star next to me."

"What if I don't want to be a star?"

Abruptly, he sits up and crosses his legs, his thigh pressed against mine, the blanket falling off his shoulders. "Maybe that's it. Everyone else is down here fighting and fucking, all the things we have names for, and we're just...out there, where it's quiet and still. And even if we never touched again, we wouldn't be alone."

Something elemental and painful swells in my chest as I reach out and touch his neck, run my fingers along his jaw.

"I don't hate you," I say.

He climbs into my lap. "And I don't love you."

Slowly, like we have all the time in the world, he strips off his shirt, then mine, and I run my hands over him until I've touched every inch of his skin. I pull off his jeans, drop them on the concrete, and continue exploring him until he's aching and shivering. He's half hard, but I don't get him off; I just let him have his turn.

Brow furrowed in concentration, he runs his thumbs across my nipples, around and down until he's cupping my ass. He kisses my thighs and even slides off the chair and kisses my feet. It tickles, and he busts up laughing when I almost kick him in the face.

The chair creaks as he climbs back on top of me and noses along my clavicles, my neck, while I nuzzle his hair like a dog. We give each other every possible last kiss, so that our dreams have plenty to choose from.

And if this has to be the end, maybe that's ok, because this is absolute and forever, no thoughts or words, just us. If love can see us now, it must be ashamed that it has nothing to offer.

You tore me open and put me back together but you kept something for yourself. You won't give it back, and now I belong to you.

He makes it easy for me to forget. He's done it before, so many times. I forgot about the bad things he's done, forgot why I came on this trip, forgot my own name. And now I forget about the secrets and the lies, all the people hiding the truth and all the people digging it up.

That turns out to be a mistake.

Chapter 39

ETHAN

I'm not important anymore, so I'm relegated to coach class on a regular plane, which seems petty. At least they're driving me to the airport instead of making me pay for my own cab.

Victor isn't there when I wake up on the balcony, my back killing me. His swimsuit is gone, too. I lean on the railing and examine the bright sea, trying to spot his head out between the breakers, but I can't.

I gather my stuff slowly, stalling and waiting for him to come back, until Gray drags me downstairs and practically throws me in the car.

At the front door of the hotel, he offers me his hand. "We'll be in touch regarding your payment and your mother's needs."

"Ok."

When I shake his hand, he holds on a beat too long. "And thank you for what you've done with him. He really is improving."

"He's not a dog." I pull my hand away, irritation flaring in my stomach. "He's done as much for me as I have for him." Until it comes out of my mouth, I realize I hadn't thought about it that way before. At the start of this trip, I felt like I was holding him together with sheer force of will. But he's the one who woke up the strength in me, who always knows exactly what to say to bring me alive. Who gave himself to me like no one ever has—smart-ass mouth, terrible attitude, and all.

"I will tell him that you said goodbye. *Buon viaggio.*"

"And good riddance." I say. "You people are insane."

He smiles ever so slightly. "Indeed."

I feel sick as the driver opens the back door of the car for me and we pull out onto the street. After everything we shared, he decided to run away from the hardest part and make me face it alone.

The driver throws on the breaks so hard I snap against my seatbelt. "*Cazzo!*"

Victor's standing in the middle of the road, hands out, panting. His eyes meet mine through the windshield, and I can see relief in them. He runs around the car and scrambles in next to me. He's still wet and wearing a swimsuit under his shorts. When the driver recognizes him, he swallows his curses as Victor taps the button that raises the partition between the front and back seats.

"Where were you?" I snap. I'm trying to stay mad and not look at the curve of his throat as he leans, back, sweaty, breathing hard.

"Swimming." His eyes beg me to understand, to forgive him for running away.

I don't have time to be angry with him. He's here, and that's what matters.

"You freaked me out." I sulk, staring out the window. And just like I hoped, I feel him slide over to sit next to me. I can smell mint gum on his breath; he must be trying not to smoke.

"We've got twenty minutes; you're king for the day. What do you want to do?"

I want you to make me understand how I can watch everything go back to normal, all of this fading away just like the water closed and smoothed out over Danny's head, like he had never been there at all.

"Can we just chill? Pretend we're bored and lying around on the couch on a Saturday afternoon?"

He snorts against my shoulder. "I don't think the driver's going to be cool with what I would do to you on a couch on a Saturday afternoon. But yeah, come here."

He puts an arm around me and pulls out his phone. I slide down until my head rests against his shoulder as I watch him browse. The fingers of his other hand play slowly along the soft hairs at the back of my neck.

Flicking through random websites, he shows me dumb memes and pictures of dogs until he gets a smile from me. He's the only thing in this world that makes my head go quiet, who unwinds that tight knot in my heart.

I turn, press my face into his chest, my nose against the collar of his tee, his soft skin. "I can't." I breathe. "I fucking can't."

He rests his cheek on the top of my head. "I know, baby. But you have to. It's gonna get better, I promise. You're really strong."

"What about you?"

"Nothing can hurt me."

"That's not true."

I can feel him shaking his head. "Just let it be true, ok? You're going to drive yourself crazy."

When I sit up, I realize we've already arrived at the airport. I take away his phone and wrap my fingers around his. I can feel his pulse irregular in his wrist, and the dampness of the sea still clinging to his skin. On one continent I have a mom with a disease I can't fight, about to be put in a care home, and on the other I have a man who owns every single part of me but doesn't trust me with his secrets. And I'm in the middle, useless to help either one of them.

"Victor, just talk to me. It's our last chance. Tell me the truth; it doesn't matter what it is."

His jaw tightens as he works nervously at his gum, not looking at me.

"What else can I do to be good enough?" I feel like I'm suffocating; I wish I had stashed the Xanax in my carry-on.

As the car pulls up to the curb in silence, I let go of his hand. "You'll meet a guy, someday, and he'll get to see all the parts you're hiding from me. And you'll let him keep you."

I yank the door open, step out into the noisy crowd with my heavy bag on my shoulder. A second later, before I know what's happening, he's out of his seat and pressing me against the side of the car, on his toes, his hand tight around the back of my head as he pulls my face into his shoulder like he's never going to let go. My duffel hits the concrete.

"Please don't say that," he groans, deep in his chest. "Tell me you wish you'd never met me, that you'll never think of me again, anything but that." His fingers work into my hair, cling to my neck. I can feel his heart pounding against mine.

Finally, I gather my wits enough to wrap my arms around him and tug his narrow body tight to me. I put my lips against his ear. "I didn't mean it. Listen, you know I didn't."

"I wish you wanted anything else from me. I'd fucking die for you if you asked me to."

"I don't want you to be dead. I just want to understand." Like I did in the car that night, I slide my hand under the back of his t-shirt and run my fingers gently up and down the smooth, warm slope of his spine.

He fists my shirt in both hands. "But it's not simple like that. I need time, maybe years, to figure out how to make you understand. And you're leaving in an hour."

"Just start with one thing, one small thing." We're fighting to find names for feelings that shouldn't exist, blundering along like good intentions are enough to patch together everything that's broken. "I'm right here. You have all the time in the world."

VICTOR

I don't.

My phone vibrates in my pocket, against his thigh, then again, over and over until I pull out of his arms, my heart already sinking.

A string of news notifications, five, ten, sprawling down the screen. I set the app to alert me whenever an article goes up with my name on it. *Victor Lang, Victor Lang. Anonymous source—blood sample—allegations—photos.* Then a text from Gray pops up. *Get back here, now.*

We stare at the phone, then at each other. In the space of a breath, I'm back in a world where I have no voice, no control, where I throw away everything I care about before it's taken from me. He told me I had time to make him understand, but it's already too late.

My whole body hurts. I can't see what the press has found this time, but some part of me already knows it's bad.

"Victor," he says warningly, his voice cracking, but I break for the car, throw myself inside, and flip the locks. He stands frozen, staring after us as we drive away.

Know that you're the only one I'd ever tell. Take that with you, if it can comfort you like I couldn't.

*hold me under
(never let me go)*

Chapter 40

VICTOR

I pull my knees up to my chest and rest my face against them as the airport grows smaller in the rearview mirror.

Opening the top news report, I mute the video and read the subtitles.

> On the heels of the WADA and USADA closing their investigation into the case of swimmer Victor Lang, their anonymous source has publicly posted images of Lang's medical records which indicate that the original 2016 blood sample does not, in fact, match Lang's most recent blood sample. Because the original sample is no longer available for DNA testing, we are unlikely to

> *ever know its true identity.*
> *The WADA spokesperson has expressed awareness of the allegations and reopened the investigation.*

I squeeze my eyes shut, breathing shallowly through my mouth as my head spins. How the fuck did this happen? Dad, of all people, would never mess this up. He has too much to lose if someone finds out just how much he's hidden to save his own ass.

Like the worst kind of dream, the video just keeps going when I open my eyes.

> *Another anonymous source contacted several major news outlets to distribute a compromising photograph they claim depicts Victor Lang, although this cannot be verified. Due to its disturbing nature, the photograph has not been made public and will not be broadcast without further investigation.*

I'm hyperventilating now.
What did I do wrong?
What the fuck have I done wrong to deserve this?
All I did was be born.
Is that it?

Ethan

I walk to my gate in a daze, not sure where else to go. Sitting as far from other people as I can, I scroll through one news report after another that tells me everything and nothing at the same time.

The blood test results should bring me some kind of satisfaction, but I can't stop thinking about how close I got to hearing the words from his own mouth, remembering the way his lonely eyes burned as they looked into mine.

The TV on the wall over my head plays footage of Victor from the press night in Seattle, climbing out of his Jag. Now that I know him, I can see the terror hidden behind his bright, charming smile.

When the news anchor turns her attention to the mysterious photograph, I fumble out my phone and text Nicola. She answers immediately.

The photo? Yeah, I have it.

Send it to me.

This time, I wait for almost five minutes. *You owe me*, I fire off. *I gave you that blood test.*

Chill. He's your boyfriend, right? You might not want to see this.

Victor

When I convince the driver to pull over at a service station and tell him to buy himself a coffee, I walk around the back of the building and crouch against the concrete wall in the cold wind, trying to steady my hands long enough to connect to the Wi-Fi and open the message boards, firing off private chats to every member I see.

The photo

The photo

Where is it

Where can I see it

While I'm waiting for a reply, I call Ethan, even though I know it's too late. I'm convinced he won't answer, but the other end of the line clicks. He doesn't say anything; I can hear him breathing. Maybe he's waiting for me to do the right thing.

"Whatever this picture is, it's not me. Don't look at it. They're desperate. It's a fake and they're setting me up." I'm losing the fight to keep my voice calm.

There's a long silence. "If you're not going to tell me the truth, fine, but the least you can do is stop lying to me."

"Ethan—"

He hangs up.

The first person I contacted responds. *I'm not supposed to distribute it. What do you want? Anything.*

Dick pics?

I would laugh if I wasn't about to cry as I pull down the front of my shorts and struggle to get myself half-hard. The photos keep coming out blurry because I'm shivering so much.

I guess they're good enough, because he says, *One minute.*

ETHAN

I want to see it.

I look out the window at the huge, taxiing jets and the pale sky. All the overhead announcements are in Italian, flowing together into a soothing stream of syllables I can't follow. When my phone vibrates, I don't look at the screen. I savor the last long moment before I do something I can't take back.

VICTOR

I drop my phone and the corner bounces off the asphalt, cracking the screen. I remember everything about the day they took that picture, pain and cold and dark, the hazy snatches of my nightmares. Breathing is something I used to know how to do, but now it's a mystery.

He's looking at it. Right now.

I put my head in my hands and scream into the asphalt.

ETHAN

They can't tell if it's Victor, because the person's head isn't in the photo. Just a neck-down, rear view of a naked man. He has one hand on the wall for support, the other hanging limp.

It's an ugly photo—stark, washed out lighting with a yellowish tinge and a blinding reflection off the gray tile on the wall, like someone took it with a flash in a dark bathroom.

Between his thighs, below his naked ass, you can see a glimpse of his balls hanging down, the tip of a flaccid cock.

There's an ungodly bruise on his ribs, purple and sickly yellow wrapped around his side. His wrists are bruised, too, mottled dark blue. And there's dried blood in his crack.

Another text from Nicola covers up the picture. *Someone found this in the cache of an illegal porn site that got taken down years ago. The guy who found it claims the shirt on the floor is a custom jersey Victor used to wear, but I don't know. And either way, I'm sorry.*

They can't tell if it's Victor, because the person's head isn't in the photo. But I can.

It isn't until I'm on the curb outside the airport looking for a taxi that I realize I left my duffle under my seat in the boarding area. I don't bother going back for it.

I've tried Victor a dozen times, but he won't take my calls. When my phone rings, I snatch it off the taxi seat. "Victor, I—"

"Sorry, it's Nicola."

My stomach drops. I'm struggling to imagine how this day gets more nightmarish, but I think I'm about to find out. "What?"

"Do you remember how you asked me to contact you before information goes public?"

"Yeah. So far you're doing a terrible job."

She tries to offer a pity laugh, but it falls flat. "Look. Someone noticed Victor's name in a database of old legal records and went digging. Really deep, into the kind of stuff no one's ever supposed to find. I think everything's about to get blown all to hell and I'd feel like crap if I didn't give you a chance to see this first."

"So just to clarify, this is *worse* than the fake dope test and the torture porn?"

She doesn't answer.

"Jesus. Cut to the chase, ok?"

"I can't..." she sighs. "I can't say it. Just see for yourself. I'm going to send you an encrypted link to view; it will delete itself in an hour."

"This is going to go public soon?"

"I don't think I can stop it. And Ethan? Make sure you go somewhere private before you open the link."

She hangs up before I can protest again. The link comes through a minute later. I'm tempted to open it in the cab, but something in her tone makes me wait.

When we reach the hotel, I sprint upstairs, hoping to find Victor in our room, but it's dark and empty. Since his things are still where I tidied them instead of thrown everywhere, I don't think he has been back.

I sit on the edge of the bed, breathing hard. The link opens onto a list of video files. Six of them, thirty minutes each. Holding my breath, I tap the first one.

"My name is Victor Jakob Lang. It is the, uh, the fifteenth of July, uh, 2016." The simple video shows Victor, in a suit, sitting in front of a beige wall. Based on the date, this would have been a month before Rio, before the dope scandal.

His clothing and hair are as immaculate as ever. He also looks like he hasn't slept in months. The dark circles under his eyes are so pronounced it looks like someone punched him. Then, to my horror, I realize that someone has; the skin around his right eye is puffy and blue, and a broken blood vessel stains the white of his eye red.

A stack of paper sits in front of him, but he doesn't look at it. He keeps hesitating and glancing off-camera for information or reassurance.

If I thought the Victor I met in his pool four weeks ago was broken, it's nothing compared to this. His empty eyes never stop moving, and he flinches at every little sound. He's bouncing his leg, fidgeting with a pen, and sometimes he reaches up to finger his black eye, wincing. His strained voice can barely be heard over the ambient room noise.

He stumbles to a stop after saying the date, and someone off-screen murmurs something I can't make out. He blinks, then takes a deep breath. "I wish to state for the purposes of this deposition..." He trails off, closes his eyes. The person off-camera speaks again, and he twitches. His voice is a whisper. "I wish to state for the record that Coach Clint Simmons has been abusing me for four and a half years."

As soon as the words leave his mouth, it all makes so much sense. The pieces come together so clearly that, even though I'm in shock, I hate myself for not figuring it out sooner.

"In twenty, uh, twenty twelve, after Junior Nationals, Simmons invited me to his home in Las Cruces, near our team's compound, to, um, give me a gift. He, uh." Victor blinks rapidly, staring at nothing. "He." He looks at the person off-camera. "Can I—"

Someone whose face I can't see comes around and sits on the table, facing him. She puts her hands on his shoulders and speaks quietly, then gives him a hug. When she turns around I realize she's just some legal assistant, an employee of whoever's recording the deposition.

He did this all alone, with no one but a stranger to hold him. Jesus Christ. I think of all the times he went on TV in the months before Rio, his untouchable smile. He didn't just suffer alone; he suffered alone in front of millions of people who could probably have helped him if he had found some way to tell them.

Victor swallows and his voice gets stronger. "He touched me and made me touch him and he, uh, he told me that professional athletes and coaches do this stuff all the time and everyone would make fun of me if I talked about it."

I pause the video and put my head in my hands. I can't stand to listen to any part for more than a few seconds, so I skip around at random through the files. In just five minutes, I hear enough to scar anyone for life.

The last meal I ate is rising to the back of my throat. Then I remember that there are six fucking videos, three full hours of footage, and I do puke, right in the garbage can which is still full of wrappers and bags from our floor picnic.

He just talks and talks, the emotionless monotone, the fractured stammering and long hesitations. He explains everything in childish terms, like his brain got stuck the day his coach first touched him. If he was "good," the man took him to nice hotel rooms in the city and treated him gently. But most of the time he was "bad", and he was beaten, raped, shared with other men, photographed for images like the one Nicola sent me earlier.

When he got old enough to fight back, his coach started drugging his food and trying to convince him, through never-ending mind games, that they were in love.

I remember how hungry he always looks, how he won't touch anything that he hasn't seen prepared or sealed. His absolute terror of the word love. The way he told me that the water has always protected him. I want to throw things, to hurt someone, to curl up in the bed and never get out.

By the end of the last video, his voice has worn down to a scratchy rasp. He's staring at his lap now, never looking up, talking so quietly it's hard to hear. When he finishes, he turns to the woman off-camera with tortured eyes. "Was that ok?" he breathes. "Can you use that?"

"Thank you, Victor. You did well."

He puts his arms on the table and buries his face in them. I can't tell if it's agony or relief.

But in the end, all of those words meant nothing. None of this ever went public. Someone, somewhere had the power to silence him, to take away his voice and shut the bright summer boy away, alone in the dark.

Chapter 41

VICTOR

Alek answers my call immediately and accepts my last-minute request to race to Capri.

After the driver drops me off in front of the Regale, I think about facing Gray, trying to say goodbye to the only person besides Ethan who ever looked at me like I mattered to him. Just like everyone six years ago, he's going to ask me *why*, in a voice that tells me exactly how bad I've been, how deeply I've fucked up. And when I say *I don't know*, he's going to shake his head and walk away because who the fuck lets something like this happen to them?

Instead, I wander to a random park. I lie down on a bench for the long afternoon, counting the clouds, feeling their shadows cool across my face as they pass over the sun. A jet purrs thousands of feet above me and I wonder if Ethan's on it, looking out his window.

I have a headache from the heat, sweat running from my temples into my hair. I pull my phone out of my pocket to call the whole thing off. There's another notification from the news app. *Victor Lang Sex Scandal*. Maybe he'll watch it on the flight, maybe after he lands.

I'm so goddamn tired.

Without opening the report, I get up and climb the nearest hill. After bending double to catch my breath, I climb on the top of the highest wall, holding a post for balance, and throw my phone out over the shimmering clay roofs.

Then I sit around in the shade, smoking, until the sun goes down. A cab drives me to the beach right at the heart of the Naples waterline. If it weren't dark, I'd be able to see Capri.

The twins have managed to pull a car onto the dark sand, headlights spilling out across the scrubby grass, and they're sitting in the back, drinking and watching Alek stretch in his wetsuit. I don't have one with me, so I'll borrow one of his, even though it's too large. The drunk girls whistle as I strip down and change in the night wind with the loud surf.

It's very lonely here, not at all like the beach I went to with Ethan, where we buried his cousin.

I should stretch too, but at this point I'm not sure I care so I just stand and watch Alek. He ignores me until he's finished, then straightens up to study me. "You already look worn out."

"Lucky you, maybe you have a chance."

He shakes his head. "You can't trash talk me looking like that." But even so, there's a note of doubt in his voice. That's how good I was, back then. There was nothing I couldn't do.

"I saw the news. Things are getting fucked up, aren't they?" Behind his bravado, he sounds almost scared.

I remember the two of us at thirteen, fourteen, sixteen, helping each other through practice, suffering together, being happy together. He couldn't do anything to protect me from his dad, but when we weren't fighting like dogs he always came to check on me. He made up games to distract me, or took me swimming in this little lake by the compound, or lay on his couch next to me playing video games, anything to get me through another day. We were only rivals because of his father. When he started doping, I was the one who sat on the bathroom floor with him and told him it was going to be ok as he took his first dose and tried not to cry.

When I broke down just before the Rio Olympics and tried to expose Coach, Alek told me he would testify against his father, that he even had proof. I may never know what the proof was or who caught us, whether it was Coach protecting his career or my father hiding the fact that he put the status of a famous son over stopping the abuse, but Alek backed out and my deposition was buried.

As if to buy his silence and punish me, Coach forced me to swap my negative dope test for Alek's positive one. When I begged Coach to change his mind, he asked me if I really wanted the whole world to know how twisted I was, the sick things I had done for him.

I never blamed Alek for letting it all happen. If he spoke up, he'd lose his career, the only thing that mattered to him. He wanted to know how it felt to be the best in the world. His dad had trained him to want that his whole life. I couldn't expect him to throw away his future for someone else, especially when I was never brave enough to save myself.

He hops into the surf and waits for me. Rachel offers me a swig of her beer, but I shake my head. I take a minute, walking a few paces up the sand and back, testing my lung capacity, getting my limbs moving. I stop and look up at the stars.

I'm sorry.
A lot of people say they were put on earth for the person they love.
I always thought I was a mistake, because I can't love. I was put on earth for no one.
Now I know I was put on earth to break your heart.
But I hope that's better than never having it at all.
I told you, the water protects me. And if it asks for me back tonight, that's how it was meant to be. You'll be ok.

I dive into the shallows, get my hair wet, and paddle out to where Alek is waiting. It's impossible to get my bearings in the dark beyond a general direction.

It seems like this should be an important moment, the moment where I let Ethan go, the moment where I return home to the place I was always meant to be. But it's just cold waves, an ugly car in the sand, and Rachel bouncing up and down on the shoreline. "Ready, set, GO!"

Alek takes off, because he's always been too hot on the start, no matter how far the race is. I start steady, try to fall into the rhythm where I don't get tired. But within an hour I know I'm not going to make it. This is the part where it's not too late to turn around, swim back. But I don't know what's back there, and I do know what's in front of me.

Ethan

Victor still hasn't answered my calls. For a while I wait, watching the sun go down outside the window and feeling the air become chilly. On an impulse, I go down the street to the spot where the cabs idle and ask one of them if he can call the other drivers in the area and see if they've driven a man my age with blond, curly hair. When one of them answers *yes*, it feels like that intangible, maddening fate that has been teasing at me for weeks, pulling my life apart.

I pay extra for the other driver to pick me up and take me to the same place he took Victor. "Where did you go?" I ask as soon as I get in, hanging between the front seats to try and understand his broken English.

"To the beach near Posillipo." The words slap me across the face. "I ask him why the beach at night," the driver complains, taking a sharp turn, "but he no answer."

"Please go as fast as you can."

When he bumps 8 km up on the speedometer, I put my hand on his shoulder. "Sir, I will pay your fucking speeding ticket, hell, you can tell them I forced you at gunpoint and I'll go to jail for you, just please hurry up."

He glances at me with a chuckle, half-bemused and half-concerned, and floors it. When we pull up on the road above the beach, I see the headlights of a car down on the sand and I feel like I might vomit again, if there was anything left in me.

I throw everything in my wallet at the taxi driver and sprint down the beach path in the dark, tripping on rocks and sliding on loose sand.

When I get there, it's just Katrina and Rachel, high in the back of the car, and endless miles of empty sand and water.

"*Fuck!*" I run into the surf, as deep as I dared go with Victor's hand in mine, and try to see him. If he could hear my voice maybe he'd come back.

"They left two hours ago," Katrina calls out.

Shivering in my wet clothes, I come into the bright circle of the lantern sitting on the bumper between their knees. "If he gets tired before they go halfway, he can still turn around, right?"

Kat lights a cigarette that the breeze keeps trying to put out, and offers it to me. I shake my head. "Honey, I saw the look in his eyes. He's not coming back." I don't know if she means back to this beach or back alive, and I'm starting to think there's no difference.

"God." I sit heavily in the sand, the grains cutting into my skin. "This can't be happening."

Rachel yawns, and I look up at them accusingly, impotent anger searing through me. "Did you two *know* about what happened to him? All those years?"

She blinks. "Know what?"

Kat looks between us uneasily, smoke trailing from her nose. "I don't know what you're talking about, but...I always felt like he and Alek hid stuff from us. And I don't think it was good." She narrows her eyes at me. "Does this have to do with all that weird news this afternoon?"

I can't tell them, not now, not his last secret. So I shake my head. "Forget it."

I want to fight back like I always have, to force the universe to give me a way of fixing this. But it's Chelan all over again, the day where I learned that in the end it doesn't matter how hard you try or or how deeply you desire, the day I've been running from ever since. And just like that day, the inexorable, black water has no answers for me. I stumble back to the edge of the sea and sit down, staring at the trail the moon leaves across the waves.

He's sitting in the dandelions, among the ruins, wearing my sunglasses. He tips them down, catches my eyes with his. The hint of a dare in the tilt of his lips. "Say it," he breathes.

Sometimes I wake up and I'm made of want.

It's all caught up in my chest and I can't get it out. But this time I know what it's for.

And it hurts. God, it hurts.

A hand on my shoulder makes me jump. Rachel crouches next to me, leaning into my shoulder, and offers her palm, a couple of white pills. "This really sucks for you," she says. I think she's trying to be nice. "These help."

When I hold out my hand, she gives them to me and offers me a bottle of water. I roll them around under my thumb, scared to lose control.

When there was no hope and no salvation and nothing else he could do, this is how he dulled the pain.

I wonder what he saw when he was high. I wonder if he found answers.

I wonder if he ever saw me.

If I've lost him here, maybe I can see him again in a world where you don't have to be dreaming to be happy.

Before I can stop myself, I slide the pills under my tongue and drink the water, feeling them come apart in my throat. I lie on my back in the sand and look up at the stars. The ones he promised me weren't lonely.

By the time I remember my mom, that I need to go back to her, that I'm all she has, something's wrong and I can't move any more, even when I hear the girls calling my name urgently, arguing. I'm drowning, deep, and maybe now I'll discover the things he says to the water, and what it says back to him.

Chapter 42

VICTOR

I think it's been five hours. It's so dark, the water blacker than black, and the stars go from horizon to horizon. I don't know where Alek is, and I'm exhausted. I stop, treading water, even though I know it will only make the trip take longer.

I can't feel my body any more, and I keep fucking up my breathing and taking in mouthfuls of salt water. Rolling onto my back, I go into a dead float, water teasing around my ears. I should be panicking, I guess, but there isn't anything to worry about.

I can clearly remember my father's words. Ethan sees the world in black and white. He won't be able to wrap his head around it. He'll pity me, because he's a nice person, and the day he pities me is the day I die. And I'm pretty sure that's today.

All I get to choose is whether I let the water have me or end up curled in the bottom of an airless closet where I can't smell the sea.

Experimentally, I close my eyes and let myself sink until my head is under. The water is so heavy here, forceful, the pressure of billions of gallons, and the deeper I go the heavier it will get. It cradles me, waiting for me to make up my mind.

The only time Coach couldn't touch me was when I was swimming. And now, if I stay, it will protect me from all the ways Coach and Dad will twist the truth and re-bury the secrets. I already went through that once; I can't do it again.

My head breaks the surface and I gasp, toss my hair back. I start swimming again, aimlessly, like I'm trolling for the best place to let go.

Ethan comes to me slowly, like I'm starting to drift off and dream, first in pieces and then all at once, his hands and his shoulders, his face and his smile.

I never thought I could be saved, but you came so fucking close.

I don't hate you.

And I don't love you.

The Ethan in my head looks at me with his whiskey eyes hazy and his brows furrowed, his full lips sullen. For the first time in my life, I don't have to struggle to remember. He grabs the back of my head, pulls me close. "If you wanna fucking die," he whispers, "then come back and let me do it myself."

I laugh stupidly, bobbing around in the sea, and for some reason, I keep swimming. In the end, I can't deny that man anything he asks for.

I genuinely don't think it's up to me. I don't think I can make it. But I'll try.

At seven hours, I start blacking out in the water. My body keeps swimming, the training of a champion, but I'm barely there anymore. I

fucking tried, and honestly, I got further than I expected. That's going to have to be good enough for Ethan, the demanding, needy asshole.

When something grabs me I lash out instinctively, trying to remember if there are sharks in the Mediterranean and wondering why this shark has such soft teeth.

"Hold still, for fuck's sake," Alek gasps in my ear, wedging his shoulder under my arm and treading water for both of us. I rest my head against his, shaking and trying to breathe as his powerful arm locks around my waist.

"Look at you," I pant. "You've been practicing while I was gone."

He shoves me away from him in the water, then swims up behind me and wraps his arm around my chest. "Stop moving." I can feel how hard his heart is pounding, as he drags us both through the water. "Tell me when you feel like you can take a turn."

After thirty minutes, I tap his shoulder. "Be honest with me," he says as we switch places. I feel him sigh as I stroke out, the quiver of his exhausted muscles. "No one else will tell me straight. Am I good enough, or not?"

I've followed his career. A bronze in Rio, middle of the pack in Pyongyang. He tries so hard, but you can't learn talent. "You're a good swimmer, but you'll never be great. And now the one time you could have beaten me, you came back for me."

He's silent for a long time, until we switch places again. We circle in the water, fumbling to feel each other in the dark. "I don't want to do this anymore. The fucking guilt every time I think about you, and for what? To come in fourth or fifth my whole life. Dad was bullshitting me when he said I could become you." His arm slides under mine, keeping me afloat. "Do you think we could ever be free of him?"

"You, maybe." I hesitate. "I don't know about me." Everything that made me want to be free has slipped through my hands today.

Neither of us speaks until we've switched places four or five times and the sluggish sun has climbed high enough to show us Capri, startlingly close, like it was sneaking up on us. We break apart and swim separately for the last hour, hitting the shore at almost the exact same time.

I collapse face-first in the sand, and he sits next to me with his head between his knees, dripping.

Out of nowhere, he says, "You do know it wasn't your fault, right?"

I sit up and stare at him as he runs his hands through his wet hair, over and over, until it's standing straight up.

When I don't answer, he glances at me. "Is it my fault my dad touched you?"

"No."

"Why not?"

I dig up a handful of sand, like my palm's a shovel, and draw shapes in it. A square, a star. "You were a scared kid. What were you supposed to do? You tried your best."

"Exactly," he says with finality, his voice rough in his chest from exhaustion.

When I realize what he's trying to tell me, I stand up and walk to the edge of the water. It washes my filthy feet clean, sighs for me as I crouch down and rest my forehead on my knees and try to wrap my mind around the idea that maybe Ethan could still want me after all, that he'd understand I did the best I could.

"I have old videos backed up on my phone, stuff I took when he wasn't paying attention. If I show them to a lawyer, will you help me end this?"

"Ok." I hold out my fist, like I used to do, and he knuckle-touches me. "Ok."

We both fall asleep on the sand for an hour and wake up sunbaked and covered in grit, sore as hell. We rinse off in the water and walk up to the nearest road. A man driving a truck full of fruit crates stops at our raised thumbs, staring at our wetsuits, and gives us a ride to the ferry.

On the way, he lets me use his phone to call Gray. "Where the *fuck* are you?"

"Capri. You should try it sometime. It's lovely." I hold the phone away from my ear so Alek and the fruit guy can laugh silently at the stream of swear words and scoldings pouring out of Gray's mouth. When he pauses for breath, I cut in. "Did Ethan land safely?"

Silence. I put the phone back to my ear and lean away from the other two, lowering my voice. "Gray."

"I don't know. When I was looking for you, I called him about a dozen times to see if he knew where you were, but he never answered."

Dad was right all along; he can't stand to look at you. Or even speak to you.

"Ok. Can you come get us on the ferry? We don't have any money."

He curses at me some more and hangs up.

The fruit guy gives us each a banana and leaves us sitting on the curb in our half-stripped wetsuits looking like two freaks. By the time Gray shows up, we've fallen asleep again, leaning side by side against a shady wall. He wakes me up by kicking my leg.

When he sees Alek, he sets aside his planned lecture and ushers us onboard in silence. Alek stretches out on one of the benches inside, and I follow Gray up top, to the railing, where it's so windy his perfect hair gets all mussed up.

He turns his back to the rail and examines my face. I've never seen such pain in him. "Why didn't you tell me?"

I look down at his shoes. "I'm sorry." If Ethan doesn't want me, Gray won't either.

When he doesn't answer, I glance up. His eyes are still sad, but the corner of his mouth quirks. "I didn't know you even knew how to apologize."

I cough a weak laugh. "I don't." When I lean on the railing, he puts his arm around my back and for once I don't mind being touched. "Gray?"

"Yes?"

"Alek was a witness; he has proof. Will you be my lawyer? I know my dad pays you a lot, but—"

My voice cuts off as he pulls me against him in a tight hug, my wet, sandy body staining his pristine suit. "Jesus, Victor. You know that all I've ever wanted is for you to be ok. I hate myself for missing all the signs; I was so fucking stupid."

I pry myself away and stare out over the water. "Careful, your feelings are showing."

Watching the spray around the prow of the boat, I try to imagine a world where the men who hurt me aren't free. Where they can't get to me. Where I'm not the loser who doped, or the sack of flesh who let himself get raped, but just me.

It's so overwhelming I want to go inside and shut myself in the nearest dark space. I'm a pile of broken pieces held together by scars that will never heal. How do I make a life when I've never had a chance to know what it means to live?

Ethan would know. But he's gone.

When we reach the far shore, all I want to do is go to bed. Gray forces both of us into the back seat of a car, and on the way to wherever we're going I use his phone to call Ethan another ten times. I double check his flight information and run the time zone calculations again and again. He's been on American soil for hours. Long enough to turn on his phone. I don't even need to see him or have him accept me; I just want to hear his voice and tell him that I didn't drown because he fucking haunted me into staying alive.

Gray drives us not to the hotel but to the nearest hospital.

"Gray," I whine, hanging between the seats. "I'm fine. Alek's fine. This is stupid. *Please* let me sleep."

"You're both getting checked for exhaustion, dehydration, hypothermia..."

"It's the Mediterranean in July."

Alek elbows me. "Maybe they'll give us sick IVs and let us sleep in there."

It feels good to goof around with him again, to see him smile back. It makes me wonder if certain things can be healed after all.

Chapter 43

ETHAN

When I open my eyes, I'm in a clean bed in a white room that smells like hand sanitizer. I try to move my arm, but there's needles stuck in it, tubes trailing away to a bag hanging by the bed.

A woman in a blue uniform bustles in and opens the curtains; she looks surprised when she sees my eyes open. "You're awake. How do you feel?"

My tongue is stuck to the roof of my mouth, puffy and raw. "Where am I?" I croak.

"Two girls called 113, said that you were unresponsive. When the ambulance picked you up, they weren't there. You had a bad reaction to some stimulants in your system, and your body started shutting down.

But you're going to be fine." She checks a chart hanging at the foot of my bed. "Are you Ethan Lowe? We only had the ID found in your wallet."

I nod painfully and the room kind of shimmers around me, making my stomach churn. Taking random drugs because you got your heart broken is some emo teenager level shit. I struggle to sit up, and she helps me raise the head of my bed. "Take it easy. Is there someone we can contact for you?"

Shaking my head, more carefully this time, I watch her check my vitals and take the IV out of my arm. "Can you turn on the news?" I don't know if it's too early to be reporting a drowning from last night or not.

"Rest a few more hours," she tells me as she leaves, "and we'll see if you're ready to be discharged."

I swing my legs off the edge of the bed and look down at the ugly, paper-thin hospital gown. My clothes are on a chair in the corner, but that's a long way to walk. At the sound of a phone ringing, I look up and realize my cell is sitting next to the table with my wallet, with Peyton's name on the screen.

"Jesus Christ," she gasps when I answer. "Where are you? I was supposed to pick you up from the airport five hours ago and you just dropped off the face of the earth."

"I'm sorry I scared you. I didn't get on my flight."

There's a moment of silence. "Ethan? You sound like absolute shit. What's going on? Is this about what's been on the news, about that swimmer guy? They were saying some crazy stuff, E, like sex trafficking or some shit. Is everyone ok?"

"I...I have to stay here longer." Even if Victor's gone, if it's too late to find him, maybe there's something I can do to get any kind of justice for him. "I'm so sorry. I know Mom is having a hard time."

"One sec." I hear the faint sound of Mom's voice in the background. I don't think I can talk to her right now without breaking down completely, sobbing like I'm five years old. Peyton's voice is a little wry when she returns. "June wants you to settle a bet for us."

"Huh?"

"You and this, uh, boy with the pretty eyes, so to speak."

"Yeah?"

"Are you guys a thing?"

When I don't answer, she groans. "June, I owe you so much money."

"Wait, how the hell does she know?"

"How should I know how mom senses work?" Her voice gets gentler. "Stay as long as you need to. We're ok. But you need to take care of yourself and him, ok?"

I would, I think as I hang up, *if I hadn't already fucked it up*.

In another one of those moments that could be fate or just a bunch of ricocheting pinballs, I hear a familiar voice from somewhere down the hall. "I *told* you you couldn't get hypothermia in the fucking summer, you paranoid asshole."

It's a good thing the nurse removed my IV, because I would have ripped it right out of my arm on my way to the door. My legs don't get with the program, and I have to grab the door frame to keep from eating it face-first into the floor. Victor Lang is standing with his arms crossed in front of one of those gross hot-beverage vending machines, kicking it because it won't give him coffee.

At the commotion, he glances over his shoulder. He looks pale too, his hair a mess, moving gingerly like every muscle hurts. His eyes go huge at the sight of me in my hospital gown with IV tape still dangling from my arm.

"You're..." He swallows, hesitates, looking everywhere but at my face. Taking one step closer, he stares at the dark needle-bruise in the crook of my elbow with the faintest whine in his throat, like he can't stand to see me hurt. When he reaches out to brush his thumb across it, my skin burns all over.

At the last minute, he backs up against the vending machine and wraps his arms around himself, biting the inside of his cheek. His voice is trembling too much to manage his old who-gives-a-fuck snark, but he tries. "Aren't you supposed to be in Seattle right now?"

Victor

I'm not ready. I haven't braced myself to watch him give me a pitying look, to tell me he's really sorry for what I went through and he hopes I get the help I need, maybe recommend a therapist.

"You fucking left me behind," he accuses, his voice all raspy and ragged. "You let me think you were dead."

"To be fair, I didn't know I wasn't until a few hours ago." I try to sound cocky, but my voice is weak. He's giving me hope, and I wish he wouldn't. "Why are you here?"

"I tried to come after you." He sounds petulant now, and it makes me want to smile. "I ran out of the airport like a fucking movie finale, took the taxi, tracked you down, and it was just a beach with those damn twins and their damn drugs I'm apparently allergic to, and—"

"Holy shit," I say. "Slow down, dude."

I can't hear what he's saying because all that's playing in my head, over and over, is *he came back for you*. I remember the very first night I touched him, when I was just trying to get him to stay between me and the door, to protect me from the dark.

No one comes back for me. Until you.

Then I realize the guy is kind of, sort of crying, trying to hold it back, and he's barely able to stand up straight. "What the hell." Shaking my head, I lead him back to the bed and make him sit on the edge. I stand between his knees, and he rests his face against my chest. "What's the matter with you?" I murmur. "You're so fucking soft all the time. You can't cry on me." I kiss his hair, slowly, because maybe there aren't any more lasts and we can finally take our time.

"I'm not crying," he grumbles, throat all gunky with tears. He pulls away and looks out the window, wiping his cheeks. "Why did you go?" he asks. His eyes beg me not to lie any more.

"I didn't want you to stop." My voice isn't much louder than a whisper as we both stare out at the cut-off tops of the oak trees in the hospital garden, the pale sky patterned with contrails. "I wanted you to keep hating me and needing me and annoying the shit out of me. But I figured when you saw what I really was, you'd either be disgusted or feel sorry for me, and I honestly don't know which would kill me faster. I thought I'd save you the trouble."

He shakes his head. "I only feel sorry for nice people."

"Thank God." I sit down next to him, because I'm tired, too. "And I'm sorry. I guess. If that's what I'm supposed to say."

"You're so good at this." He chuckles.

I grab his chin, turning his face from one side to the other. "Now who's gonna apologize for this mess, Mr. Don't-die-on-me? Fucking *allergic* to drugs? Only you." I touch the bruise on his arm and when he flinches, I bring it to my mouth and kiss it too gently to hurt.

Handing him his clothes, I let him hold onto my shoulder as he pulls them on so we can go home, even though I don't know where that is anymore.

As he straightens up, someone raps hard on the frame of the door.

"Victor," Alek calls, and his voice is urgent, scared, in a way my whole body recognizes. His eyes tell me how sorry he is. "The hospital called him to pick me up."

"What were you thinking, Alek?" Alek spins around as Coach grabs him by the scruff of his neck and shakes him. "I brought you here to rest up for Worlds, not destroy your body."

When he sees me staring at him, he lets go of his son. His pale blue eyes meet mine and I freeze, just like I did when I saw him in the street that night. Ethan's head snaps up from where he's tying his shoes.

Clint's face doesn't waver at all, which means that if I turned on the news right now I'd see headlines about the online leakers admitting that they faked the images and videos, clips of me at the last press conference talking about good my father's been to me, how sorry I am for what I've done, how I have nothing to hide. Powerful people don't have to be afraid of things that they can get rid of with money.

"You swam too, Victor? I didn't think you were that foolish." He steps into the room, and I stumble back until my ass hits the hospital bed.

His eyes study me, taking his time, and he nods. "It's too bad about these wild rumors. I'm sure we'll all be happy to denounce them and move on." I know he's flexing, just here to intimidate me, to make sure I don't talk to anyone. But it's fucking working.

An absolutely feral growl tears from Ethan's throat and before I can blink he slams Coach against the wall so hard that the clock above the door falls down with a crash. "I'm going to fucking kill you," he snarls, in a voice I never imagined he'd be capable of. Alek's eyes are bugging out of his head, and my heart is pounding so hard in my throat I can't breathe.

Ethan looks over his shoulder at me, and I see the truth in his eyes, pure and absolute. He would never pity me. He fucking worships me. And I believe he would kill for me, if I wanted him to. He'd probably cry his eyes out and spend the rest of his life beating himself up about it, but it's the thought that counts.

That mental image is endearing enough to give me the strength to get off the bed. I come up behind Ethan and put a hand on the back of his neck. "Hey, big guy. Give me a turn."

Coach coughs and straightens his polo as Ethan steps back. He glares at me again, the weight in his glance like hands on me, years upon years. "Your boyfriend seems to be having trouble distinguishing fact from fiction, Victor." My name in his mouth always destroys me. This is it. Six years of doors and locks and dark corners, of hunger and loneliness and renting out my ass just to feel. It was all to avoid this moment.

"It's too late," I say, but my voice is all tangled up in my dry mouth. Ethan's fingers lace through mine, so tight I think he's going to fracture something. "I have proof this time, proof you can't touch, and the best lawyer in the world." I make sure not to look at Alek. If his father knew that he was going to testify, God knows what he'd do.

Coach moves toward me and no matter how hard I try I can't stop myself from backing away. "The reason no one ever helped you is because no one would let something like that go on for so long if they didn't want it." He looks at Ethan. "Have you thought about that?" Alek makes a strangled sound, but I beg him with my eyes to keep quiet, to save it for the courtroom.

I'm not sure I'm strong enough to hold Ethan back as Coach walks away. Alek follows his father, his tall back rigid. "He's scared," I say over and over. "He's just scared. He's going to lose everything. Let him be scared. That's better than hitting him."

Ethan stops yanking on my hand, but his eyes are an absolute inferno. "Baby," I sigh. "You already saved me. It's gonna be ok."

Then my legs give out and I land on my ass on the hospital floor and I can't get any air at all, the worst it's ever been, like I'm going to die right here. Every part of me needs to crawl into the smallest space I can find.

A warm body sits down next to me and Ethan pulls me into his lap, drawing all my limbs together tightly in his arms. "Ok," he breathes into my hair. "Listen. We're gonna go into the country again, just us, where no one knows who you are. We can go as far as you want, and we can swim wherever you want."

Oxygen wrenches and claws in my chest like it's a foreign substance that's going to destroy my body. I'm shivering so hard that he keeps having to adjust his grip on me. Through a blur, I feel him take my hand and slide it up under his t-shirt, digging my fingers into his skin, the throb of his heart. "I was thinking," he says in my ear, low and gentle. "Maybe I'm ready for you to teach me how to swim. What do you think? What stroke do you think I'll be best at?"

My teeth are chattering, but I finally force the words out. "Doggy paddle."

His chest bucks under my hand as he laughs. "That's mean."

I headbutt his shoulder. "You wouldn't have me any other way."

Chapter 44

ETHAN

"Come and get it! Come *on*!" Victor runs back and forth across the park, waving a scrap of chicken we bought from the restaurant across the street. Rio just sits in the grass, staring at him, his stubby tail thumping the ground, until Victor collapses on his back with a groan. "You lazy little shit."

He throws the chicken away, and Rio dives on it happily. "You know you're just reinforcing his behavior," I comment from my position in the shade, looking up from the sequel to Peyton's favorite book, which I'll never tell her I bought.

"Stop being right; it doesn't suit your face." Victor hops to his feet and swoops in on me, grabbing my bag of chips and popping a handful in his mouth.

"Hey!"

He holds it out of my reach as I lean across him, until I grab the front of his shirt and kiss him, licking the salt and vinegar from his lips. "You know," he mumbles, his voice hitching when my hand slides down the back of his shorts, "You're just reinforcing my behavior."

When I pull back indignantly, he sticks his tongue out with a grin and escapes with my snack. He slumps down in the grass next to Rio, and I watch his eyes drift shut as the puppy gnaws on his fingers and tries to climb over his chest.

In the week since Victor's deposition video leaked, he's been avoiding the news while Gray works on collecting Alek's testimony and analyzing the video recordings he's been hiding for six long years, in case he ever found the courage to use them. When it's Victor's turn to testify, his words won't be buried again. Gray says they might even implicate the other men who were involved in Clint's abuse.

It's a hard, winding road with a happy ending out there somewhere, but it's too steep for him to walk every day without resting. He's been sleeping a lot, almost every time he sits down, and he won't leave my side.

He told me countless times that he's glad the videos leaked, but I catch him so often just staring at the floor or out the window, arms wrapped protectively around himself. He keeps his back to the wall and jumps at sudden noises. In bed at night, or when we fuck, it's like he's trying to climb inside me and never come back out.

Sometimes, when you open the door of a cage after so many years, the wild thing inside is more afraid to be free than it was to be caged. All I can do is sit next to the door and wait.

"Come on." I stand up, groaning, and nudge Victor with my toe. "You can sleep at the apartment while I cook you dinner."

"Can we bring Rio?" he asks for the millionth time without opening his eyes.

"We talked about this. He probably has fleas and all kinds of shit we don't want in our bed."

"Then I'm gonna stay here and eat chicken scraps with my boy."

Despite his words, he lets me pull him to his feet. The sun filters pale green through the trees, sending flecks of gold over his skin as he looks around with that constant, nervous reflex, like Coach might be standing right behind us.

"Shh." I pull his head into my shoulder. "I'm watching your back." Our fingers tangle together as we head home through the quiet, late-afternoon streets.

When we found out we would be staying in Naples for a couple more weeks to deal with the aftermath of the leaks and help Gray arrange his legal plan, he put us up in a short-term apartment rental in the heart of the city. He had to pay from his own pocket, since he parted ways with Werner, who has already flown back to the States to find another lawyer.

Back at the tiny apartment, I try to channel my mother's skills into making chicken parmesan. Victor sits on the counter next to the stove and watches me, stealing essential ingredients at the exact moment I need them. He *perches* everywhere he goes—on counters, chairs, stools, tables, even the floor, and I'm constantly tripping over him or leaning around him to get something I need. I wouldn't have it any other way, because when I turn around and meet his wide, curious eyes, they're tinted the warm, earthy color of home.

I stand between his legs at the counter and he circles his arms around my neck and kisses me sloppy and deep, arching his back under my hands, until I smell the chicken burning to the bottom of the pan.

The dinner turns out passable at best, and we eat on the couch with paper plates and plastic utensils.

He tips his head, a fork hanging out of his mouth. "I'd rate it the two-hundred and sixty-sixth best meal I've ever had."

"Wow. I'd like to see you do better."

"I've never so much as boiled water in my life."

"It's honestly disturbing. The power imbalance in this relationship is—"

He glances up at me as I trail off. We've talked about a lot of things in the last two weeks. His past, the nightmares, the upcoming legal battle, Rio, anything and everything except *this*—and for the first time, the kind of talking that involves my dick up his ass hasn't helped us find the words.

His nostrils flare, and he looks down at his lap, fidgeting with the tie on his board shorts.

"We're going back to Seattle in a couple of days," I say, setting my plate on the coffee table and scooting toward him. "Last time we talked, we said this couldn't work in the real world. But I want to ask again." I hunt for the right words, my heart clenching. "We can find a new name for it, if you want. Our own thing that no one else has."

His eyes find mine; he's chewing on his lip, his eyebrows pulled together. His voice sounds soft, hungry in a way that drives me crazy. "Hey, listen. You can have me any way you want, every way we've tried, any name in the world. I don't give a fuck anymore because I just need you. That's it. I can't live any other way." He smiles, but behind the light in his eyes I can see a primal fear, the story of a man who taught him that love means nothing but torture.

I slide onto my knees on the floor and prop my elbows in his lap, looking up at him. "I just want you to know, I don't hate you."

His smile brightens. "And I don't love you."

He does the dishes, throwing water everywhere, while I lay on the couch and zone out to an incomprehensible Italian game show. My phone buzzes on my stomach, and I flip it over to see a video chat request from Mom. This is the first time we've tried out the webcam Peyton bought her. I spit in my hand and run it through my messy hair, then turn the video on.

"Mom!" I've never needed anything as much as I need to hug her.

"Honey, how is your trip going?" She knows we're involved in some kind of legal issue, but not the details; she doesn't need someone else's nightmares mixed in with her own. "How's the boy with the pretty eyes?" Embarrassed, I tip my phone away from Victor and turn down the volume.

"He's fine."

"Peyton told me you were together." She beams at me, every inch the proud, meddling mom.

"Well, that might be a little prematu—"

I jump when Victor rests his chin on my head and wraps his arms around my neck. "Yep."

Mom's face lights up. "Hi! Your name is Victor, right?"

"Yes, ma'am." I frown up at him, wondering where my brat went and where this gentleman game from, and he gives me an angelic smile.

"Did you two enjoy the cookies I made you?"

Victor doesn't miss a beat. "They were a flying success."

I choke and double up, coughing. He grabs the camera away and sits on the back of the couch, squinting at my mom's pixelated face. "Wow, you really do look just like him. Your face looks better on you than his does, though."

When I grab for the camera, he holds it out of my reach but tilts it so she can see both of us. Her face is about to split in half with smiling. Then she sniffles and big tears start running down her cheeks. *"Mom."* I'm mortified. "Don't cry. It's ok."

"I was scared I'd be gone before I got to see you find your soulmate. I'm just so happy."

Victor's cheeks flush, and he gives me the camera back. *"Soulmate?"* he mouths incredulously.

"Victor," my mom enthuses, drawing him back into frame. I swear I'm just a bystander in this conversation now. "When you two come back, will you come over and stay with us for a while? We can go to the zoo and a ball game and a hike, and we could go thrifting, and I can teach you how to make the cookies Ethan likes, and...do you like puzzles?"

He blinks, face going blank the way it does when he's overwhelmed. "Um, yeah," he says faintly. "Ok."

Seeing that he needs a moment, I turn the phone away and distract my mom with talking about her new flower garden until it's time for her to go. When I hang up, Victor's lying on his back on the couch, staring at the ceiling. "Are you ok, babe?" I sit on the floor next to him and rest my hand on his chest, letting him feel the pressure as he breathes.

His hand moves on top of mine, his thumb exploring the bones of my wrist as he turns and looks at me. This close, his eyes hold every color in the universe and none at all, strange and wild and pure.

"Is this what it's like to be normal?" he whispers unsteadily.

Something throbs bright and painful in my chest. "Yeah. I think so."

"Do you think—" He hesitates. "Do you think I could be normal someday?"

I can feel the tension in his body, the need to find a confined space and hide from a world that feels too big. He closes his eyes as I climb onto the couch and wrap him in a ball underneath me, pressing him into the worn leather cushions until it's hard for him to breathe, the way he needs it. "Yeah, baby, you will. I promise."

Chapter 45

VICTOR

I don't pay attention to anything, especially when Ethan is around to do it for me, so it's not until thirty minutes into our flight that I realize we're flying west instead of east. We've barely gotten to altitude and the plane is already descending with a low thrumming of engines. Even after two weeks of safety, I feel myself getting scared.

He looks up from his book with a slow, warm smile when I grip his arm. "Did you finally notice?"

"Where are we going?"

"It's a surprise." When he sees my expression, he rests his forehead against my temple. "I promise it's good."

I huff and slump in my seat, crossing my arms. Not that there's much room to slump. I've never flown coach class on a public plane and it's not an experience my long legs and wide shoulders are enjoying. Especially not smooshed in next to Ethan's bulk. "I don't like surprises and I don't like you."

He just laughs. Since his bags all got lost at the airport, he had to buy a whole new wardrobe of Italian clothes. The summery linen shirts I picked out look good on him.

"Welcome to Athens," the flight attendant announces as we land.

I wrinkle my nose at him. "What the hell?"

Pursing his lips, he shrugs and ignores my eye roll.

It's eight-thirty in the evening when we make it out of the airport, into the mystical purple glow of sunset against the pale stone buildings. I try to hear where Ethan tells our cab driver to go, but he's too quiet.

When we pull up to a low, white building with a sweeping roof, my stomach turns itself inside out. "Ethan." I wrap my fingers around the headrest in front of me, like no one can pry me out of the car. "Ethan, no."

His hand steadies my back. "It's ok. Just hold on to me."

I watch him pay the cab fare and we walk across the sun-browned grass toward the front door of the Olympic Aquatics Center, home of the pool from the Athens Olympics. I recognize the architecture from when I was just a little kid gawking at the big swimmers on TV.

Relief floods me when I see the dark front doors. "They're closed. Let's go." But he tightens his hand on mine and leads me to a side door. When he knocks, a woman with a lanyard on her neck sticks her head out and looks at his ID. She nods and opens the door for us to come inside. "Take your time."

He must have used my clout to get us in here after hours, because she doesn't look surprised to see me.

Our footsteps echo down the hall until the building opens up into a hushed, towering room with banks of seats leading up the wall on either side of the Olympic-sized pool. Flags hang from the ceiling, swaying in the air conditioning, reflecting their colors in the water below.

"Jesus Christ, Ethan." I pull my arm away and back up against the wall, sitting down and pulling my knees up. "I can't."

He doesn't push me, just sits down next to me and waits in silence. I watch the pool, the way the pristine lane dividers bob and snake gently through the bright blue water. I've never seen anything so beautiful.

ETHAN

Finally, his shoulders relax a little. I hand him the swimsuit and goggles I pulled out of his luggage. "You ready?"

He shakes his head, but he pulls down his shorts and tugs on the suit. Swinging his arms, he walks toward the pool and stands there with his toes on the edge, staring across at the huge windows at the end of the room and the dusk sky beyond. He looks back at me imploringly. "What the fuck am I supposed to do?"

I smile, quoting something he once told me. "Your body knows."

Pulling on the goggles so I can't see his eyes anymore, he steps onto the starting block above the center lane. I come and stand next to him, put a hand on his thigh. "I'm gonna be right here waiting for you."

He makes a small groan in his throat.

"Show 'em how it's done, baby."

I don't know anything about dives, but I know his is perfection, art in motion. Everything he does in the water is a revelation. He could have been the greatest swimmer of all time. To me, he always will be.

He tears through the water with his explosive butterfly stroke, racing his heart out like he's surrounded by the best competitors in the world. My chest aches to see him, his body a deep ripple below the surface on every turn, an explosion of droplets every time his shoulders break the surface.

At the end of his last length, as he grabs the wall and pulls off his goggles, I hear the sound of clapping from the doorway. The woman who let us in offers one last burst of applause, smiling shyly, then disappears back to her office. Victor stares after her, then looks over his shoulder at the row after row of empty seats.

"I couldn't get us to Rio," I say, "but I hope this counts."

He rests his forehead against the tile edge of the pool and goes still for a long moment. Then I hear a wrenching sound in his throat, a helpless, depleted wail, and his shoulders start shaking with sobs. Without even thinking about the water, I slide into the pool and pull him against me. He buries his face in my neck and wraps his legs around my waist and *cries* so hard I can feel it tearing through his body. Something tells me he hasn't cried since before the first day his coach took him home and all his dreams turned into nightmares. "That's right," I say against his wet hair. "You made it. You don't have to fight any more. You're so fucking brave."

He moans, breath shuddering, his tears and snot leaking down my shoulder.

"I'm never going to let you go, ok?" I nuzzle the back of his neck. "I want you to stop listening for a second. Ready?"

He nods.

"Promise you won't listen?"

He nods again, and I can feel his body starting to calm. "I love you so fucking much. It doesn't matter if you want me to or not because I can't help it. It's my secret, and I'll never tell you."

He lifts his face, swipes at his eyes roughly. "Were you saying something? 'Cause I couldn't make it out over all the applause."

"Nope. Nothing at all."

Chapter 46

ETHAN

Balancing an extra-large mug of chai tea in one hand, I flop onto the couch and dive into one of my favorite activities—organizing. I attack my notebook with highlighters and sticky tabs and savor the joy of taking excessive notes as I work out a variety of possible class schedules from a glossy course catalog. I'm being way over-the-top for a vet tech program, but I think I've earned the right to make a big deal out of it.

I sit back and study the living room that is just starting to feel like home after three weeks in our new south Seattle apartment. I savor the peace and quiet, how clean everything is—if you ignore the swimsuits hanging over every fucking piece of furniture.

Until keys rattle in the front door.

A fluffy white missile rockets through the hall and takes a flying leap into my chest. Rio mercilessly tramples my lap, my stomach, my balls in his mission to lick every inch of my face as quickly as possible. I thought it might take him a few months to get used to a new continent, but the little fucker immediately seized his place at the top of the apartment's chain of command, pushing me to the bottom. He pretends not to hear me when I tell him to get down, because Victor doesn't make him do *anything*.

A moment later, Mom appears in the doorway and waves, her smile glowing. I throw Rio off and wrap her in a rib-crushing hug that makes her squirm and giggle. I never realized how much she worried about me, how hard she pushed herself to be independent so as not to burden me. Now that the weight has been lifted off her, she looks hopeful and calm. Happy.

The first three nights after she moved into her facility, I couldn't sleep. I couldn't even close my eyes. Victor sat on the couch with my head in his lap, streaming episode after episode of *The Bachelorette* and coaxing me into arguments about which of the guys were secretly gay. Every time he felt me tense up, he'd pause the show and rub my back, whisper in my ear that she was going to be ok.

On the third night, he told me she was so fucking proud of me and I started crying, hot tears running down my cheek and onto his legs. He curled around me, put his forehead to mine, called me his soft boy. Next thing I knew, I woke up five hours later and he hadn't moved at all, just watched me sleep. He could barely walk when he got up.

"Do tamales sound good for dinner?" Mom hefts a grocery bag with corn husks sticking out of the top.

"Of course they do. He'll eat anything." Victor squirms past us and starts shoveling all my tidy papers off the coffee table in messy armloads. He flourishes the puzzle I bought Mom in Italy, then dumps it out. Settling cross-legged on the floor, he starts probing through pieces with one finger. "Edges first, right, June?"

I love the way she smiles at him, how he grins back. They're completely obsessed with each other, and I think they're helping each other in ways I never could.

Mom heads into the kitchen with Rio bouncing on his hind feet behind her. Losing interest after three pieces, Victor jumps up and climbs on the couch, standing balanced on the cushions. He stares at me with those gorgeous eyes, dressed in one of my biggest t-shirts and a pair of tight running shorts, my Raiders hat crooked on his head, his bare feet sporting a flip-flop tan. His head cocks slightly, the corner of his mouth twitching into a smile as he watches me admiring him.

He holds out his arms. When I come to the back of the couch, he grabs my head and pulls it against his warm stomach. I nuzzle him and hug his ass, cup it in my hands because it's what he's setting me up to do and I'll never turn down an opportunity. "Did you smoke today?" I ask, muffled.

In answer, he smacks his gum loudly. "If I had, I wouldn't be bouncing off the walls, would I?"

He takes my face in his hands and tips it up to look at him, running his thumb over my lips. "I looked at everything," he says quietly. "Talked to the staff. They're really nice. They said she hasn't panicked, and her new meds are looking good." I'm really struggling with going to her facility, so he's been taking care of things, picking her up and bringing her here almost every day until I'm ready.

I run my hands up his warm sides, under his shirt. "Thank you."

"And to think," he murmurs, bending down until our noses are almost touching, "you once told me I was the high maintenance one."

He parts my lips gently with that dirty, bratty mouth that can somehow push back the darkness and erase all the ways I don't feel like I'm good enough. Stepping over the back of the couch until I'm holding him in my arms, he wraps his legs tight around my hips. Even though we're supposed to be helping Mom, neither of us can stop as he tips his head sideways and pulls my tongue into his mouth, tastes it, drinks it down, plays with it.

Eventually, he relaxes his legs and I let him slide to the floor. He hates when his face gets flushed, but I'm obsessed with it. "Come on. June's gonna teach us to wrap these corn things."

He weaves his fingers through mine and tows me into the kitchen, stumbling over Rio.

There are shadows in his eyes. I catch them when he's not paying attention. Sometimes I find him just standing there, looking at nothing. Some nights he nudges me awake and I roll on top of him, letting him feel my weight until his breathing slows.

But every single time life gets to be too much for me, I turn around and he's already there, waiting to hold me or fuck with me until I laugh or drag me to bed. When I'm the one waking him up at night, he sits against the headboard and spreads his legs so I can cuddle with my back to his chest. He rests his face in my hair and whispers all kinds of things, nonsense and truths too deep for words.

Sometimes I remember them the next morning, sometimes I don't, and sometimes the pieces come to me in dreams.

He's all the things that drive me crazy and all the things that lead me home.

Victor

I have a home. A real one, with no hiding places. It's just a two-bedroom apartment, but it's mine.

I have a home. I have a dog I love more than life itself. And I have a man who's pretty good too. He's everywhere, surrounding me all the time, even when he's gone to his vet classes. Everything smells like him, the air warm like his skin, and I can get any of his shirts out of the laundry whenever I want, not just the one I picked out.

He doesn't mind that I still spend a lot of time sleeping and eat him out of house and home. He says I have a lot of catching up to do. I try to make up for it by cooking him all the recipes June is teaching me.

I know I did good when he eats his whole plate and gets seconds or even thirds. When it's burned to hell and has too much salt, we just shrug it off and order takeout. Because here, even when I fuck up, it's not a big deal. No one's waiting to hurt me.

I don't always know what to do with myself, besides swim in the apartment pool and visit June. Now that Alek and I testified, Coach is going to prison. My dad is deep in a fucking legal nightmare without Gray to help him. The ghosts are gone, but I have a hard time remembering not to look for them.

Ethan says there are people I can talk to who are trained to help me piece together who I was and what I am and what I could be, but he understands I'm scared. He tells me it's not weak to talk to someone, that it doesn't make him pity me, that we can take it slow, try as many as it takes to find someone I trust.

I don't know what's left of me now that all the pain is taken out. For the first time in my life, I want to do *something*, help Ethan pay for our house and our food with money that isn't from my future legal settlement. We've talked about it a lot, and the other day he drove me to the local rec pool and asked if they were looking for swimming teachers. The guy behind the counter about shit himself when he looked up from handing me the application. He said I didn't need to fill anything out, and I can have any class I want.

I'm nervous; I've never hung out with kids before, and I don't know what to say to them. But it feels warm and right to sit at the big dining table in the sun, thinking of lesson ideas and trying to remember what it was like to swim for the first time.

And whenever I get tired and lost in my head, Rio or Ethan or both of them come nuzzling and nipping at me until I'm laughing so hard my ribs hurt.

I never thought.

I never thought I'd be here.

I never thought I'd know what it means to be happy.

And sometimes we say I love you, and sometimes we say I hate you, and sometimes we just exist together without a name, two stars in the universe, and it doesn't matter because they're all different names for the same thing, something that will never belong to anyone but us.

Thank you so much for reading *Hold Me Under*! If you enjoyed the book, please consider leaving a review!

Check out the next book in the series, *Make Me Fall*, if you want to read Gray's story!

Subscribe to my newsletter at www.rileynashbooks.com to receive a free, steamy short featuring Ethan and Victor, set after the events of *Hold Me Under*.

Join my Facebook reader group, Riley Nash's Underdogs, or follow @rileynashbooks on Instagram for the most up-to-date teasers, updates, and news on my future books.

MY BOOKS

Water, Air, Earth, Fire Series

Hold Me Under – Victor and Ethan
Make Me Fall – Gray and Jonah
And All Their Stars – Gray and Jonah novella
Show Me Wonders – Oliver and Jackson

Standalones

Christmas Special – Damien and Connor

ABOUT THE AUTHOR

Riley Nash, based in the rainy PNW, writes emotional M/M romances about boys who fall hard, face the darkness, and never give up on each other.

Fueled by cute dogs, those weird Coke With Coffee drinks, and projecting my personal issues onto handsome men and making them fall in love.

Visit www.rileynashbooks.com to subscribe to their newsletter, join Riley Nash's Underdogs on Facebook, and follow @rileynashbooks on Instagram.

Made in the USA
Columbia, SC
19 August 2024